ALEX WISE
vs
THE END OF THE WORLD

ALEX WISE

VS

THE END OF THE WORLD

TERRY J. BENTON-WALKER

LABYRINTH ROAD | NEW YORK

Text copyright © 2023 by Terry J. Benton-Walker
Jacket art copyright © 2023 by Raymond Sebastien

Visit us on the Web! rhcbooks.com

Educators and librarians, for a variety of teaching tools,
visit us at RHTeachersLibrarians.com

Library of Congress Cataloging-in-Publication Data
Names: Benton-Walker Terry J., author.
Title: Alex Wise vs. the end of the world / Terry J. Benton-Walker.
Other titles: Alex Wise versus the end of the world
Description: First edition. | New York: Labyrinth Road, [2023] |
Series: Alex Wise; book 1 | Audience: Ages 8–12. |
Summary: Twelve-year-old Alex leads the charge against the forces of
evil as he tries to stop the Four Horsemen from taking over the world.
Identifiers: LCCN 2023012462 (print) | LCCN 2023012463 (ebook) |
ISBN 978-0-593-56429-5 (trade) | ISBN 978-0-593-56430-1 (lib. bdg.) |
ISBN 978-0-593-56432-5 (ebook)
Subjects: CYAC: Four Horsemen of the Apocalypse—Fiction. |
Good and evil—Fiction. | Fantasy. | LCGFT: Fantasy fiction. | Novels.
Classification: LCC PZ7.1.B45535 Al 2023 (print) |
LCC PZ7.1.B45535 (ebook) | DDC [Fic]—dc23

The text of this book is set in 12-point Adobe Jenson Pro.
Interior design by Jen Valero

Printed in the United States of America
10 9 8 7 6 5 4 3 2 1
First Edition

For Aiden (Doodie):

You were always—and always will be—more than enough.

Love, Daddy

A NOTE FROM THE AUTHOR

My parents divorced when I was thirteen, and I witnessed my mom's constant fight to care for our family all on her own. In my father's absence, I had to grow up quickly to help our family survive—much like Alex Wise. During that difficult time, I was also trying desperately to understand who I was and how I fit into the world—a world that often made me feel powerless and like I didn't belong. And when I needed to escape, books were there for me—even though I had to do so by way of characters who were nothing like me.

Alex Wise vs. the End of the World is an epic story filled with plenty of wonder, excitement, and humor; alongside Alex and his friends, readers will battle homicidal sea monsters, fight back hordes of skeletal zombies with cool magical weapons, and step through portals to other worlds. But at its core, this is Alex's quest to learn to love himself and to fight for the people he loves—no matter what.

Black queer kids across the globe are struggling to understand themselves and their place in a world that often makes them feel they don't deserve love. I created the world of Alex Wise for them, to show them that not only do they matter—but they can be superheroes too.

Happy reading!
Terry J. Benton-Walker

APOCALYPSE COUNTDOWN

4 YEARS · 37 DAYS

10 HOURS · 01 MINUTES

PART I

A Santa Monica mom snagged a movie deal when her indie podcast about her middle school twins' experience with a paranormal entity they named Mr. Shadow was optioned for film by DewDee Productions.

—JOELLE MARSHALL FOR *MOVIE REPORTER WEEKLY*
MAY 31, 2020, 2:33 PM

1

THE BEGINNING
OF THE END

I can't believe I survived sixth grade.

This entire year almost blew the gauge on the Suckage Meter. But I made it out in one piece (barely), and now I'm going to use summer break to set my world back in order—or I'm at least going to try my best.

Kids pour down the sidewalks outside Palm Vista Middle, flooding the air with shouts and laughter, energy renewed by the official start of summer vacation. My best friend and I stroll alongside each other at a slower pace than usual, drinking in the drastic shift in atmosphere. No mountains of homework, no waking up early to get to school on time—summer break has finally arrived in Palm Vista, California.

I don't remember ever liking this place. The last truly exciting thing to happen here was when the highway strip mall got a GameStop and a Cold Stone in the same month. Last summer, I emailed Guinness World Records to nominate Palm Vista as Most Boring Town in US History. They never wrote me back.

There's not much to do here unless you'd enjoy an arcade with prehistoric machines that eat quarters like popcorn or a movie theater with musty, creaky seats and stale candy. My hometown sits smack-dab between San Diego and Los Angeles. Two places I'd rather be any day—but my preference would *not* be San Diego. I have zero desire to be near Dad or his "new family."

I slide my backpack around and peek inside the front pocket. The small white envelope is still safe and sound. I know, I *know*: carrying these tickets around is pointless. The concert's a week away, and I still haven't mustered the courage to ask Sky to go with me. But keeping the tickets close helps me hold on to the hope that he and I might become friends again.

"I think I'll commit to full-on rebellion and loc my hair," Loren Blakewell announces as she loops both thumbs through the straps of her camo backpack, the front of which she's suffocated with colorful enamel pins. She's wearing cuffed olive-green overalls, and her hair is pulled back into a giant pouf, held in place by a black-and-green ribbon that, of course, matches her sneakers. "It's *my* hair. I should be able to do what I want with it."

"You're absolutely right." I zip closed the pocket of my backpack and swing it around to my back. "But if you upset your mom, she'll lock you in solitary for the rest of summer."

Loren groans and kicks a rock, sending it skittering down the cracked sidewalk. She must be angry to risk scuffing her Jordans. I think she'd look great with locs, but her mom told her that hairstyle wasn't "appropriate for a young lady"—and

Loren got her phone taken away for a week for calling her mom a troglodyte. That week also rated pretty high on the Suckage Meter, because I'd grown accustomed to having Loren's usual upbeat mood to distract me from what'd happened between me and Sky.

"Soooo . . ." Loren drags out the word, making my gut flinch preemptively. "Speaking of summer break, there's something I have to tell you."

"What's up?" I try to sound unconcerned despite my stomach revving up to full-on Cirque du Soleil.

"I'm going to LA for break." She winces as if she's the one hurt by the reveal. I still smile. "I finally convinced Mom to let me go to Muay Thai camp."

Loren became obsessed with Muay Thai three years ago, when she started taking lessons at the YMCA. At first, her mom refused to let her take the class, but Loren went on a hunger strike and Mrs. Blakewell caved by day two. Muay Thai camp means a lot to Loren, so I'm def happy she's getting to go. But my heart also sinks into a pit of sludge, because I realize my best friend's going to be gone our *entire* summer break. And that means the only other "friend" I'll have to hang out with is Sky.

Except he and I aren't exactly friends right now.

I swallow the lump of anxiety in my throat as I elbow my bestie playfully. "That's great, Lo."

"You aren't mad?" she asks.

Mad? Nah! Decimated? Only a little.

"I'm going to miss you terribly," I say with an exaggerated sigh, "but I suppose I'll find a way to survive."

Now my mission to fix things with Sky has just become dire; otherwise I'm doomed to spend the entire summer with only the company of my irritating human barnacle of a little sister—who had *better* be waiting at her school's pickup zone like she's supposed to be. The last time she wandered off (yeah, she's a repeat offender), mesmerized by her tablet, it took twenty whole minutes of frantic searching before Loren and I found her curled up on a bench near the playground, reading. The *last* thing I need right now is Mom grounding me on the first day of summer break because Mags got lost on my watch.

Loren and I pass a strip of shops where some of our classmates hang out; then we turn the corner toward the elementary school, leaving the ruckus of the main road behind for the deserted side street. This part of the neighborhood is silent except for the soft shuffle of our sneakers on the pavement.

The back of my neck prickles . . . like someone's watching me.

I look over my shoulder, but we're alone. Weird.

I shrug the feeling off, but something snaps across the street, like a twig breaking underfoot. Either Loren doesn't hear, or she ignores it as she ambles beside me, deep in thought, likely planning how to kick off hair-pocalypse with her mom this summer.

Across the street is a row of paneled cottages with plain, reasonable front lawns, drenched in the shadows of the mature trees lording over the sidewalk. The windows of every house are dark, as if the entire neighborhood's already left for vacation. Creepy.

I start to turn away, but something catches my eye. It looks like someone's shadow disappearing behind the trunk of one of the wide, slanted trees whose roots have broken up the surrounding sidewalk. I stop and crane my neck to see if anyone's hiding behind the tree.

No one's there. But I could've sworn—

"Umm . . . did you forget how to walk, goober?" Loren, a few strides ahead of me, doubles back, looking confused.

"I thought I saw something," I mutter.

"What?" she asks, concerned now.

Before I can answer, the sound of Sky's laugh snatches my attention. He's a block behind us, walking alongside his new bestie. Sky's shoulder-length sandy-brown hair is up in a ponytail, and the sun has flushed the freckly strip of skin beneath his forest-green eyes and across the bridge of his nose. He's wearing a faded San Diego Padres tee—the baseball team his dad, the famous Judas Hollowell, pitched for before he retired last year.

"Nothing," I tell Loren. "Let's go."

She shrugs, and we continue toward the elementary school.

I glance back at Sky, who's so engrossed in his friend that he hasn't noticed me walking ahead of him. It wouldn't bother me so much if his new bestie were literally anyone other than Larry Adams, one of the evil villains in the story of my life. The sight of them together tightens my chest like someone's twisting it with a rusty crank.

I met Sky at the library at the start of summer break last year. His family had just moved to Palm Vista from San Diego, and his parents had forced him and Blu, his ten-year-old brother, to sign up for the summer reading club. While Loren's mom dragged their family around the country on an educational agony—uh, I mean vacation—Sky and I hung out *a lot*. Played video games. Listened to music. Watched TV. Talked for *hours*. And on the last day of summer break, I told him my deepest, darkest, scariest secret—the one Loren doesn't even know. Then the next morning at school, Sky met Larry, and our friendship was obliterated before the homeroom bell rang.

I've wondered all year if telling Sky my secret was a mistake, if doing it right before Larry accosted him that morning was what made Sky change his mind about being friends with someone like me, someone I thought he was too. I need to know the truth.

I look back again. This time, Sky meets my gaze—but Loren jabs me with her elbow, stealing back my attention.

"Are you listening to me?" she asks. "Why are you being so weird all of a sudden?"

"I'm not," I say, fighting the urge to look again.

"Speaking of weird," she says before I can snap back, "there was this creepy influencer dude from LA on TV this morning raving about horsemen and the end of the world. Dad made me turn it off while we were eating breakfast. Have you heard anything about it?"

I shake my head, though I'd welcome the end of the world if it would get me far, far away from Palm Vista *and* Larry Adams.

"Well," I say as we walk through the gates of Palm Vista Elementary, "I highly doubt it, but if these horsemen *are* real, I think it's super rude of them to end the world now, *after* we've suffered through a whole school year."

We both laugh, and I call out to my sister, who's waiting at the edge of the carpool crowd, head down in her tablet with one of her classmates. A sparkly clip pins back one side of her curly mane of hair. She pushes her purple-framed glasses back up on her nose, and the sunlight brightens the warm undertones of the same chestnut-bronze skin as mine.

Thank goodness Mags is where she's supposed to be today. The sandy-haired boy next to her leans close, and they giggle at something on the screen. I yell again to get her attention, and she and her friend look up. It's Blu, Sky's brother, who Mags has forged a close friendship with, because of course she has. What would my life be without my little sister to make it as weird as possible?

"Def not surprised to find those two together." Sky's voice startles me. He stops next to me and motions for his brother to come over.

"Oh, hey," I mutter.

Larry's untethered from Sky and now strolls past the school into the dense neighborhood of shaded cottages down the street. A cool gust of relief kicks up in my chest.

Loren side-eyes Sky before pursing her lips and huffing quietly, but we both ignore her.

"I usually get here before you and have to pry them apart," he says.

Now's the perfect time to ask him to go to the concert with me. Once, I could talk to him forever about anything. Now my mouth turns all cottony and I can't get a single word out.

But the concert's next week. I'm running out of time.

"What do you have planned for summer?" he asks, jerking me out of my thoughts.

This is the most we've communicated all year, aside from awkward eye contact while passing in the hallways. I didn't dare try to break through the impenetrable Larry Adams Forcefield™ around Sky, and he never attempted to talk to me either. Our texts even went dry. But maybe this concert can fix all that . . . I hope.

"Oh, uh, not much." I shrug one shoulder. "I'll be around. You?"

"Nah." Panic electrifies my gut. "Dad's starting a new project in LA that's supposed to last most of the summer. He got a condo near Santa Monica Pier so our whole family can go." He rolls his eyes as if that's such a terrible thing to have happen to him. "We'll be staying in a penthouse at the Zion Condominiums. I'm sick of moving around so much."

I stammer for a moment before getting out, "Oh, so when are you leaving?"

"Week after next. I'll be around till then."

I let out a deep breath of relief, which makes Sky raise a brow.

"You okay?" he asks.

"Not really," Loren mumbles from beside me, concentrating on the Instagram feed zipping by on her phone and ignoring the scowl I throw at her.

Mags and Blu finally stroll over and say hello. Blu looks like a smaller version of Sky, with the same freckles, brown hair (though his is short), and green eyes. Blu hugs his older brother, but Sky nudges him off, complaining about it being too hot for hugs. Blu's eyes meet mine while I'm mid-hug with Mags. We hug every day when I pick her up from school. I'm not sure what the temperature has to do with anything.

Sky nudges Blu's shoulder, and they start to walk away.

"How was school?" I ask Mags as we follow close behind.

"Fine," she mutters into her screen, already sucked back into her book.

"Still on Percy Jackson?"

"No," she says curtly, as if I'm bugging her. "We're on *Hide and Seeker* now."

"But I thought you and Blu just started *The Insiders* two days ago?" Loren interjects.

Mags glares at her, and Loren holds up her hands in surrender. Most people find Mags's large brown eyes far more adorable than intimidating—that is, until they make the mistake of coming between her and a book she likes.

Loren's phone vibrates, and she grumbles before answering. It must be her mom. She signals that she's going to walk ahead, and I wave bye. Her mom wastes no time, dragging Loren immediately into a heated debate, which I unsubscribe from once I notice Sky and his brother drawing ahead too. They're headed in the same direction as us, since they live around the corner. We don't usually walk home together, because I avoid him when he's with Larry.

I rush to catch up with Sky and Blu. Mags follows, though lagging, sucked into the world of fantasy again. I call back for her to keep up, and she nods absentmindedly. On the other side of Sky, Blu begs to join Sky and Larry's Friday Night *Fortnite* session.

Just do it. Blurt it out and get it over with.

"Um, so, Sky, did you hear there's a Gustavo Santaolalla concert in LA next week?" The words tumble over my lips clumsily, and my face heats.

We all stop at the four-way intersection beside the elementary school. Mags slams into my back, stabbing my spine with the rigid edge of her tablet. I glare back at her, and she mumbles "sorry" and returns to reading.

Sky's eyes brighten. "That's the guy who did the music for *The Last of Us*, right?"

I nod, unable to hide my grin. The crossing guard tweets his whistle, and we head across the street, Blu sulking in front of me and Sky, Mags right behind us.

There's no way Sky would turn down an opportunity to see Santaolalla. He was mesmerized the moment I introduced him to the world of soundtracks. Loren thinks it's weird I listen to them like the Hot 100, but I don't care. Muay Thai's her thing, and soundtracks are mine. I'm joining beginner's band next year so I can learn to play the alto saxophone. And one day I want to be a composer like Abels or Djawadi or Santaolalla. Oh, and also move as far away from Palm Vista, California, as I can get.

Sky smiles back at me.

All I have to do is ask.

I have the tickets. . . .

He seems excited. . . .

He'll be around. . . .

There's no logical reason for him to say no. . . .

"That sounds cool," he says.

Okay, I'm going to do it—and whatever happens, happens.

"Yeah, I—"

"HEY!" shouts the crossing guard. "SLOW DOWN!"

I step onto the sidewalk and turn back to see what the commotion is, and my heart seizes.

Mags stands alone, frozen in the middle of the crosswalk. She stares open-mouthed at the empty porch of a home across the street. She doesn't notice the bubble-gum-pink Jeep barreling through the intersection—heading straight for her—until it's too late.

SKKKRRRRTTTT!

The air fills with the choking, pungent scent of burnt rubber.

Mags shrieks and shields her face with her tablet. She dives to one side, her shoulder connecting with the pavement. The Jeep swerves, missing her by only a few feet.

I gasp, shock turning my legs to stone.

The Jeep slows to a crawl, and a girl with rosy cheeks and long dirty-blond hair pokes her head out the window and yells, "Sorry!" over the loud rattle of the speakers blaring music from inside. The crossing guard runs for her, but the Jeep's tires squeal as she zooms off.

"MAGS!" I sprint to my sister and sweep her into my arms. She clings to my shoulder, her nails digging hard into my skin, until I set her down on the sidewalk. I kneel in front of her and stare into her terrified eyes. "Are you okay?"

Her right elbow's scraped and dotted with pearls of bright red blood. She stands teary-eyed and trembling, her tablet clutched against her chest, and nods tentatively.

"Why were you just standing in the street like that?" I ask.

"MAGDALENA!" shouts a familiar voice.

Everyone freezes, and I glance up as Mr. Dexter Levi races toward us like a terrified parent. Loren, Larry, and I were all in his fourth-grade class; he also taught Mags and Blu this year. Mr. Dexter was more than just a teacher to both me and Mags. After Mom and Dad divorced, I got really sad. No one seemed to notice but Mr. Dexter. He cared about me in a way I always wished Dad would. I felt comfortable talking to him about mostly everything, even the embarrassing stuff. After I found out Mags would be in his class too, I told her she was lucky to have the best teacher in fourth grade.

Mr. Dexter's an older man (maybe not old enough to be a grandpa, but older than my dad) with fair brown skin and deep-set lines around his mouth and forehead. Wisps of curly gray hair peek from beneath his plaid newsboy cap. Even though it's a thousand degrees out, he's wearing a button-up, slacks, and a blazer.

He kneels beside me and looks Mags over. "Are you okay?"

She nods and lowers her gaze. Her small frame quivers, and she wraps her fingers tighter around her tablet. My gut feels full of molten lava.

This is my fault. If I'd been watching her, she wouldn't have been alone in the street. And I feel doubly embarrassed that this happened in front of Mr. Dexter.

"I saw what happened from the teachers' parking lot and

I rushed over straightaway." He stands up, still panting from the frantic sprint, and nods at my sister's bloody elbow. "Our poor Mags is a bit banged up, I'm afraid. Let's go inside and see if the nurse is still around. I'll call your mom to come pick you up."

"No," I say, "I don't think that's really nec—"

"Mr. Wise, I won't hear a word to the contrary." Mr. Dexter flicks aside the front of his tweed blazer to rest one hand on his hip, which means he's not budging from this spot or from his point. He gestures back toward the school. "Get a move on."

Sky and Blu both wave, expressions of secondhand humiliation on their faces as they turn and head home. Great. Now even Blu thinks I'm a mess.

Way to go, Alex Wise.

And I still haven't asked Sky to the concert. All I want is one evening with him like we used to have before he abandoned me for Larry so we can talk—and maybe he'll tell me why he stopped being my friend.

I take Mags's hand, and we follow Mr. Dexter back toward the school, where he'll call Mom at work to tell her all about Mags's near-death experience, which I'm hoping won't bring about the end of my summer before it even begins.

Today hit an all-time high on the Suckage Meter, but I'm glad Mags is okay.

When we pass through the main gate into her school, she turns back with a nervous twitch, as if trying to catch someone following us. I'm not sure why, but it sets a chill blistering over the back of my neck.

I give her hand a gentle tug, drawing her attention from the street. "What's wrong?"

She looks up at me, her eyes wide behind her glasses. "Did you see him, Alex?" she whispers, a frightened tremor hanging on every syllable. "Did you see the shadowy man too?"

2

THE COST OF FRIENDSHIP IS APPARENTLY $100

The entire drive home, Mom subjects me and Mags to her gospel oldies streaming station, which she listens to for only one of two reasons: it's Sunday morning, or she's so mad only the Lord can calm her down. And it's clearly not Sunday.

When we pull up to the house, she orders me to my room before she turns the car off. She also promises we'll talk about what happened later, which sets my stomach to a fresh boil.

But no matter how deep in self-pity I wallow, I can't snuff out the creepy memory of Mags claiming to have seen a man made of shadow standing on the porch of the house across the street from her school. And then I remember something else that sends a shock of cold dread through me.

I thought I saw the shadow of a person on the way to pick up Mags. But that's just a coincidence . . . right? I'd be lying if I said I'm not slightly spooked, but when I questioned her,

17

she shut down and refused to talk about it anymore. Either way, my situation with Sky ranks a bit higher on my priority list than unmasking what may or may not have been a creepy ghost dude.

I'm not sure how long I lie on my bed with my tickets, in their envelope, resting over my heart. I wonder if I should just text Sky about the concert, but I can't bring myself to do it. I wanted to ask him face to face because I thought that would mean more than a text.

Someone knocks on the door, and I swallow hard in the thick quiet. This is it. The executioner has come to deliver my sentence, which will surely mean the death of my summer—along with any chance of mending my friendship with Sky.

I slide the envelope underneath my pillow and croak for whoever's at the door to come in. It swings open, and I want to scream when I realize it's only Mags. She's already in her pajamas, and her hair's wrapped in a satin scarf tied way too neat to have been done on her own.

I fall back onto my bed with a sigh. "What do you want?"

"I didn't mean to get you in trouble," she murmurs. "I'm sorry."

"Don't sweat it." I give an apathetic thumbs-up and let my arm flop back to the bed.

Her slippered feet scuffle against the carpet as she eases closer. "I wasn't lying."

I sit up and meet her determined eyes. "About what?"

"The shadowy man," she says confidently, sitting on the edge of my bed. "I saw him on the porch at that blue house across the street when I was crossing. I stopped because he . . . pointed at me. And then I couldn't move. It was like I was . . . stuck."

"Maybe it was a real person trying to warn you to get out the street before some high school girl turned you into a road pancake."

She glowers at me. "I know what I saw, Alex!"

"Okay, okay! I'm not saying I don't believe you; I just don't want you to get worked up over nothing."

"It's not *nothing*." Mags pinches the skin of my thigh—hard.

"Ouch!" I swat her hand away.

I'm about to tell her to get out of my room when I notice that she seems two seconds away from a meltdown.

"How about this," I tell her. "We'll both keep an eye out for Shadow Man. If you see him again, you let me know straight-away, and we'll figure out what to do about him together."

She nods cautiously, considering whether she can trust me. I'm banking on this all being a fluke and us never having to discuss evil shadow people again.

She slides off my bed and heads for the door.

"Where are you going?" I ask.

"To set a trap in my room," she says. "No way I'm leaving myself unprotected tonight. You should probably do the same."

"How do you catch a shadow?"

She shrugs. "I'll figure something out."

I roll my eyes, but she's gone before I can say more.

I fish the envelope from under my pillow and remove the tickets: seats AA21 and AA22 at the Crypto.com arena. I imagine Sky and me sitting beside each other in the dark concert hall, laughing together like this school year never happened.

It's not too late. I can still fix this.

Mom's really angry, but maybe I can persuade her to give me a lighter sentence or even to let me off with a warning. I scrape together what courage I can and go find her.

Mom's room is at the end of the dark hallway, across from our single cramped bathroom. Her door is open a crack, spilling what sounds like an intense conversation she's having with whoever's on the phone.

She's using a voice I haven't heard since that time some random white lady stuck her hand in Mags's hair at Starbucks. If anyone can elicit that tone from her, it's Dad. This reminds me of the whispered shouting matches they used to have. I don't miss those, but I do miss Dad—the one who used to love us.

He left on a Saturday morning. He spent the night before packing up his life and shoving it into the back of his SUV. He barged into my room at seven a.m. to say goodbye. He'd never woken up that early on a Saturday. I'd already embarrassed myself begging him not to leave the day before, so I lay in bed, stone-faced, refusing to hug him or say bye. I'm not sure how long I stayed there, stewing in the soup of emotions Dad had flung me into.

Mom huffs. "Oh, your little cruise can't be that important if you can't even remember signing up for the contest that won you the tickets. And I already said I'll pay for them, so what's really the issue?" She pauses a few moments and sighs loudly.

"I just need the summer, Malcolm. You know how important this is to me. It's been almost two years since the divorce, and you haven't spent any time with your kids. It'll be good for them."

I feel like someone just shoved me off a skyscraper. Mom's shipping us off to Dad's. And he's arguing because he doesn't want us.

I lose track of how long I'm captive in front of Mom's bedroom door, until she yanks it open and I jump back with a start.

"Alex!" She gasps, resting a hand on her chest. She's changed out of her scrubs and into some yoga pants and a tank. "You scared me. What are you—"

"I'm sorry about today. I know you're mad, but please don't make us go to Dad's." Tears sting my eyes. "I can watch Mags while you work, I swear. Give me one more chance, please."

"It's too late, Alex." She leans her shoulder on the doorframe. "This isn't only about today. I've been putting too much responsibility on you. Sometimes I forget you're only twelve. I've been considering this for a while. It's truly what's best for everyone."

"It's only best for *you*." I cross my arms. "Dad doesn't want us."

Mom looks surprised. "Where would you get that idea?"

"I heard you arguing with him."

She straightens up and glares at me. "I know good and well you weren't eavesdropping on my phone conversation, little boy."

"Why would you send us somewhere we're not wanted?"

"Don't say that." Mom massages her temple. "Your dad loves you and your sister. Things are just complicated for him right now."

"His life doesn't seem too complicated online." I blocked Dad everywhere we're linked once I got sick of the avalanche of his smiling photos and happy videos with his upgraded family, complete with one perfect All-American son.

"I honestly thought you'd be excited about getting to do something for the summer besides playing video games and watching television for eight weeks straight," Mom says. "Y'all aren't leaving until next week, but then you get to cruise to Hawai'i! That's exciting, huh? I wish I could kick back on a luxe cruise ship for a few days."

"Then *you* go."

"Sorry, kiddo. I'm pulling rank."

"But what about my concert in LA next week? I was supposed to go with Sky, remember? And you already paid for the tickets, so you have to let me go!"

She sucks a deep breath in and blows it out through her nose. "I did, but I'll make you a deal: I'll give you the hundred dollars I spent on those concert tickets as a little extra spending money to take on your trip. How's that sound?"

Like a hundred claws dragging across a chalkboard.

All my plans to repair my friendship with Sky were just doused in gasoline and set ablaze. But even worse, now I have to endure an entire summer with Dad and his replacement family, which scores higher on the Suckage Meter than being alone in Palm Vista ever could.

Frustrated tears roll down my cheeks. I swipe them away

angrily. "You must hate us, because if you cared even a tiny bit, you wouldn't dump us with *him*."

"Alex, please don't make this more diff—"

"I hate you too." I bolt for my room, half expecting her to snatch me from behind.

But she's still standing in the hallway—silent and shrouded in shadow—when I slam my bedroom door.

3

THE FORGETTING

I rush to my window, fling the curtains back, and raise the blinds. Loren passes by her bedroom window, which is across from mine at the bottom of a small hill between our houses. I flip my light switch on and off until she flashes hers in return. I know I could just text her, but we've been doing this forever.

She opens her window and climbs out. She's changed into some shorts, a white tee, and yellow slides. It's late in the evening, but there's still enough sunlight to render the glow of the streetlights useless for at least another hour or so.

Loren clears the hill in a few strides. I raise my window and extend my hand to help her in, but she laughs and pushes it aside.

"I got it, Prince Charming." She hoists herself up and through my window, then kicks off her sandals and sits cross-legged on the foot of my bed. "What's up?"

"I just found out Mom's shipping me and Mags off to Dad for the whole break!" I announce. "And we're kicking the torture off with a cruise to Hawai'i."

Loren raises an eyebrow. "Not you living a colonizer fantasy this summer—"

"Lo!" I slap both hands hard on my thighs, which startles her off her invisible soapbox. "I never wanted to go to Hawai'i in the *first* place. I mean, I'm sure it's amazing, and I'd like to see it one day, *respectfully,* but that's beside the point right now because I've *clearly* lost control of my *whole* life—and you are def *not* helping!"

"Okay, *okay,*" she says, pumping her hands. "Tell me what happened."

I calm down and spill the entire dreadful story to my best friend.

"I'm sorry, Alex," she offers, but it doesn't make me feel any better.

"I hate her so much for doing this to me."

She winces. "Maybe that's a bit harsh?"

"Dad doesn't wanna be stuck with me for the entire summer, and I don't wanna be with him either. I'd rather hand-wash all Larry Adams's filthy gym socks. And Mom doesn't care."

"I just don't want you to feel like no one cares about you, because that's not true."

"Sure feels true." I sit on the floor with my back against the side of the bed. I wish I knew why everyone keeps throwing me away. Dad. Sky. Mom.

"I care about you," Loren says. "Don't I count?"

"Well, duh, but you know what I mean."

"Oh, I see. It's just that Sky counts more than your best friend."

My heart skips a beat, and I turn to face her. "What are you talking about?"

She cuts her eyes at me. "Seriously, Alex? You think I don't know about those concert tickets you've been carrying around with you everywhere? I only caught you looking at them about a dozen times this week. I was dreading you asking me to go, because you know how I feel about music without words—oh, don't look at me like that! I just think it's boring!"

"Whatever," I mumble.

"Anyway, when you started acting all weird around Sky today, I put it together. I honestly don't know why you care about him so much."

"It's complicated," I say. She rolls her eyes, and I add, "I just thought if he and I hung out again, he might—"

"Stop being a brainless booger and think about someone other than him for once?" When I glare at her, she climbs down to sit beside me and presses her shoulder lovingly against mine—the same way she's done more times than I can remember. "All I'm saying is you deserve better friends than Sky."

I pull my knees up to my chest and hug them tight. "You don't understand."

"I can."

A part of me wants to tell her my secret *sooo* bad. But I'm terrified after what happened with Sky.

We were sitting on the floor of my bedroom—just like Loren and I are now—when I told Sky Hollowell the scariest thing I'd ever spoken aloud before.

"SometimesIthinkImightlikeboys," I blurted out without looking up from my comic.

You see, I had to spit it out, because it was something I *never* thought I'd say, something I never *wanted* to say out loud. Not after Larry Adams thought it'd be funny to call me gay in front of our entire fourth-grade class. I'll never forget that day. I froze, just like Mags did when she saw her "shadowy man." Mr. Dexter punished Larry, but the damage was already done. After school, Mr. Dexter tried to comfort me. He said it was okay if what Larry said was true and that he was bisexual, which meant he might understand how I feel. But I'd been humiliated enough and didn't want to talk about it. I hated even thinking about it.

Then, two years later, I met Sky, and something about him made me feel safe, like he would understand, because he might be like me. Maybe it was the way he never acted weird about stuff, like when we'd watch horror movies and he'd hold my hand during all the scary parts or how we'd sometimes lie on opposite ends of the couch to play video games and nestle our bare feet together in the middle. Moments I don't imagine he shares with Larry now.

After I bared my soul to Sky, he immediately looked at me and let out a long, deep breath. It sounded like he'd been holding it in for a really long time. "Me too," he said. "I've never told anyone, though." In that instant, we suddenly developed this super-special bond that I thought was unbreakable.

It didn't even last twenty-four hours.

Over the summer, when it was just me and Sky, our friendship was fluid, easy. But I knew that could easily change once Sky had more and better friends to choose from than me. That's why I was so anxious about summer ending and sixth grade beginning.

And on the morning of the first day of school, Larry Adams saw Sky and me talking by my locker, strutted up to us with a cheesy grin, and asked Sky point-blank if he was "gay too." Sky was confused until Larry explained that (to him) Sky would have to be gay to be friends with me. I was about to tell Larry off when Sky laughed and said, "Heck no, that's gross!"

I still don't know what exactly was "gross" to Sky—being gay or being my friend. I guess it doesn't matter, though. They both hurt the same.

I wanted to cry, but I also didn't want to give Larry more ammunition, so I just walked away. Sky didn't ask me to come back. And just like that, he flipped the switch on our friendship to OFF. I learned to steer clear of the two of them because it hurt too much to see Sky smile when Larry made an off-color joke about me, whether his amusement was genuine or fake. Sky's betrayal still hurts as if it happened only yesterday. Looking back at the entire situation, I probably should've kept my big mouth shut that night in my bedroom.

I shake my head at Loren. "I just can't talk about it right now."

She sighs and stands up. "Well, when you can, I'm here. But for now, I need to finish cleaning my room. My mom's on a rant and looking for any excuse to sabotage my camp."

"It's cool," I tell her, getting up as well. "Thanks for coming over."

She pulls me into a hug and takes a deep breath, squeezing me tight.

"It's going to be okay, goober." She elbows me playfully.

"I've gotta get back, though—before the 'waaatchful eyeee' realizes I'm gone." She makes a claw with one hand and grabs for me, but I laugh and swat it away.

She leaves through the window, runs back to her house, and climbs into her room. I close the window and wander over to the bed to retrieve the envelope from under my pillow. It's time to begin the Forgetting.

I take the tickets out, rip them in half, and toss them and the envelope into the wastebasket beside my desk. All I have to do now is convince myself to let Sky go too—for good. Perhaps leaving Palm Vista this summer will make the Forgetting easier. If only I could find a way to make it hurt less, I'd be golden.

Once my "Einaudi Favorites" playlist lulls me to sleep, my dream starts beautifully—then quickly descends into a nightmare.

Sky and I are walking into the main entrance of the concert hall, but when we step through the doors, the lights go out. I reach for Sky, but he's gone. Everyone's gone.

I call out for him, but only my voice echoes back in this new dark and empty world.

Then the floor disappears from beneath me, and I plummet into darkness. A white sand beach rushes up from below and slams into me. I pop up, sand creeping into places a person should never have to clean sand from. The sky's become a bruised-blue starlit canvas stretched across a strange world of endless beach and sea.

My sister's voice startles me. "Alex."

But who—or what—appears in front of me is *not* my sister.

A few paces away, black smoke wavers above the ground and forms a human silhouette.

I stumble backward. "Wh-who are you?"

"I am the end. And I am also the beginning." A misty tendril in the shape of a hand unfurls and beckons me closer. "Come and see."

I don't move, and a deep, rumbling voice that is not my sister's roars inside my head—**COME AND SEE!**

I jolt awake with a raspy gasp. Once I realize I'm safe in bed, I groan and fall back onto my pillow. And great—now my shirt's soaked with nightmare sweat. I change and crawl back in bed with my *Walking Dead* compendium. Zombies are way less scary than whatever the heck that dream was.

A floorboard creaks across the room. My head snaps up, and my heart races. But nothing's there. I go back to reading, running my shaky finger over the panels, trying to will my mind to pay attention to the story and not search for monsters.

CRRREEEAAAKKKK.

I nearly leap out of my clothes. The sound came from the corner by the closet. My heart hammers as I turn my head slowly. And my breath leaves me . . . alone with the thing in my bedroom.

The shadow of a man presses itself into the corner across the room, arms outstretched, palms pressed against the walls on either side. Its eerily long fingers splay and drum soundlessly in the stifling quiet. A terrifying black paper doll draped across the wall, and though it's faceless, I know it's staring at me. It reminds me of what I saw in my nightmare just now—except it's not smoke but shadow, and I'm not dreaming.

I try to scream, but I can't open my mouth. I should run to Mom's room, but my legs feel like sandbags. I'm trapped.

The Shadow Man peels one arm off the wall, followed by the other, then starts a soundless, staggered gait toward my bed. A shudder ripples through me. Please, please, *please* let this be a nightmare. A whimper dies in my throat as he draws closer.

He winks out of view and reappears at the foot of my bed. In a quick flash of shadowy arms, he snatches the covers off me and flings them across the room, knocking over a bunch of stuff on my desk that clatters to the floor. Fear freezes me in place. I can't take my eyes off him. I barely blink. My breaths quicken as he climbs onto my bed and crouches on his hands and feet. The mattress doesn't sink under his weight. He doesn't make a sound. He doesn't have a smell. He's a living, breathing shadow.

And I'm definitely *not* dreaming.

I squeeze my eyes shut. I don't want to see my end. I just hope it's quick.

"Hmm . . . Are we sure?" hisses a barely audible, rumbling voice, very different from the bold one that scared me out of that bad dream. A throaty cackle follows, phlegm crackling in the background like Pop Rocks.

Everything goes quiet. Slowly, I crack open my eyes.

Shadow Man stands against the wall by the door now, watching. Silent.

Warm blood floods my limbs again. I bolt out of bed, knocking over the lamp on my bedside table, which hits the floor with a startling *CRASH!*

I grab the lamp and point the cone of light at Shadow Man at the same time Mom throws open the door and flips the light switch on.

"What's going on in here?" she asks.

"Behind the door!" I shout.

She jumps back and slams the door. When she sees the blank wall, sans Shadow Man, she turns a confused frown to me. "There's nothing there, Alex."

I stand back and take a deep breath. He's gone now, but I *know* he was there. I still have the goose bumps to prove it.

"Sorry," I tell her. "Bad dream."

It might be wrong to lie, but trying to convince my mom who doesn't believe in ghosts that I just had a paranormal visitor is a colossal waste of time.

She sighs, and her shoulders sag with relief. "Are you sure you're okay?"

I nod while gathering my blankets. I climb back into bed.

She points at the *Walking Dead* comic on my pillow. "Maybe try reading less scary things late at night." She pauses for a moment, like she wants to talk, but presses her lips together, turns out the light, and leaves.

I pull the covers up to my chin. Still, I shiver.

I can't deny it anymore.

Mags was right. Shadow Man is real.

But what does he want from us?

4

A MERPERSONAL
ENCOUNTER

In the days leading up to the cruise, I don't see Shadow Man again. Nor do I mention a word of the encounter to Mags, because I don't want to upset her. She also doesn't bring him up, which I guess means she hasn't seen him again either. And the more peaceful nights that pass, the more I believe he's gone for good. Maybe we didn't have whatever he was looking for, which doesn't surprise me. I never do.

And while I loathe even the idea of this cruise with every molecule of my being, I'm ecstatic that Mags and I are getting far, *far* away from Shadow Man.

On the morning of our departure, I emerge from my bedroom with a clumsily packed suitcase that I toss next to Mags's yellow one by the front door. I'm exhausted, thanks to dread-induced insomnia, and currently stuck on "over it" mode. The smell of sizzling bacon lures me to the dining room, where I take a seat across the table from Mags.

Mom got Mags's hair twisted last weekend, because she

doesn't trust Dad or his new wife to take proper care of Mags's hair. Today Mags's twists are up in a bun.

She looks up from her tablet with a wide grin. "I'm so excited about Hawai'i. I've been reading all about merpeople, and last night I had a dream that I saw one from the ship. What if I get to see a real, live merperson on the cruise?"

"Mermaids aren't real," I grumble.

Mom emerges from the kitchen with a plate of steaming pancakes and another piled high with crispy strips of bacon.

"It's mer*people*," Mags corrects me. "And that's not what Mom says."

"Then she lied," I say under my breath.

"Alexander Jamal Wise!" Mom slams both plates down in the center of the table, startling me and Mags. "I've ignored your bad attitude lately, but I will *not* tolerate disrespect."

"Sorry," I mumble.

I'm quiet during breakfast while Mags rattles off all the random facts about Hawai'i she's learned over the past two weeks. After we finish, I help Mom load the car, and we all set off for Los Angeles. The moment I sit down in the back seat, anxiety curls around my neck and shoulders like a fat cat hunkering down for a midday nap. The only thing that could make this summer worse is finding out Shadow Man's bunking in the stateroom next door. The thought makes me shudder. *Too soon, Alex.*

Mom calls Dad when we pull into the parking lot at the cruise port, and he meets us at our car. My dad is tall and light-skinned with dark hair that looks sprinkled with salt, and his light brown eyes are naturally narrow and skeptical.

I have his thin nose, but that's about all he's ever given me. Mom, Mags, and I all have the same dark brown eyes, chestnut skin, and full lips.

Dad hugs Mags, then me, but stops to examine my hair. After he left, Mom started wearing hers cut low, sorta like me, except she lets our barber cut designs in mine sometimes. This week I have a string of music notes twisting in an arc above my left ear. Dad never let me get cool haircuts, but I guess that's one of the hidden benefits of being a Divorce Kid™.

I brace for the scolding, but he grins and says, "Cool haircut." He hugs me again, squeezing like he really missed me; but it feels weird, because I know he didn't.

When I was nine years old, Dad signed me up for Little League without asking if I even wanted to play sports, much less baseball. But I went along with it because I thought it would make him proud of me—finally. After I humiliated myself in our first game, I overheard him telling Coach Daniels that I'd embarrassed him. The next day, I told Dad I wanted to quit baseball. Soon after, he quit our family.

I highly doubt he missed someone who embarrasses him.

Now Mags and I only speak to him on our birthdays, when Mom makes us call to thank him for the cards stuffed with bribes, er, I mean cash. He didn't even tell us he'd remarried last year until after the wedding. Not that I would've wanted to go anyway.

Dad and Mom say a dry hello. It's weird seeing them act like they can barely stand the sight of each other when I can still remember a time when Mags and I couldn't walk into a room without catching them sneaking kisses and giggling. Back then we thought it was gross. Now it's a sour reminder that our family will never be the same. Sometimes I wish I could be as blissfully naive as Mags with her merpeople.

Dad starts unloading our bags from the trunk while Mom hugs Mags and says her goodbyes. When she gets to me, I give her a reluctant hug, but she holds me tight anyway.

"I love you," she whispers into the top of my head.

I push away and ignore the sad look on her face.

"I know you'll be with Dad, but do me a solid and keep an eye on your sister, please," she says. "She looks up to you."

I gesture at Dad, who slams the trunk closed. "Why can't he?"

He grimaces at me over the roof of the car. "Excuse me, young man?"

"I got it, Malcolm." Mom's expression turns serious. "Be mad at me, Alex, that's fine, but don't take it out on your sister. Caring for someone who loves you is not a burden." She sighs and smiles down at me. "If you want to talk about why you're really mad, I'll drive up as soon as you're back from Hawai'i. We'll go for ice cream, just you and me, and you can lay it all out. That work for you?"

I shrug and stare at my favorite sneakers. I'm mad because I'm tired of feeling like I don't matter and being powerless to do anything about it.

"Try to have fun," she says. "Don't waste the whole trip sulking."

I wave goodbye and pick up my suitcase at the back of the car. Mom shouts bye and tells us to have fun for the thousandth time before getting in the car and driving away. Once she's out of sight, I feel like I've been plunked into the middle of the Arctic Ocean.

Dad takes Mags's suitcase, and she walks alongside him. "When did you start wearing glasses?" he asks her while we all head through the parking lot toward the port entrance.

"I got my first pair the day before you left," Mags says, frowning up at him. "I was seven. You don't remember?"

"Heh, um, yeah, of course, baby," he says. "Those purple frames are just so cute on you they made my brain go all fuzzy."

She giggles and says, "Thanks," beaming again.

I'm jealous of how forgiving my sister can be with Dad after he deserted us.

He turns to me now. "You're getting so tall, Alex. You made the basketball team yet?"

"I don't like sports," I remind him.

"Oh . . ." He lets out a long, deep breath. "Well, what do you do for fun?"

I wish we could skip past this painful, awkward conversation. It's like Dad and I are meeting for the first time. I stare across the parking lot at a cheery family pouring out of their car to unload an avalanche of bags. Must be nice.

I shrug. "I dunno. Stuff."

Dad chuckles. "Stuff, huh? What kind of *stuff*?"

"Soundtracks, video games, comics, math . . . nerd stuff, I guess."

"Hmm . . . I can dig it." He squeezes my shoulder with his large Lurch hands.

Dad played basketball in high school and college. He

dreamed of going pro until he tore his ACL (a very important ligament in your knee, so Mom says) and had to settle for selling houses to basketball players instead of being one. I doubt he "digs" having an athletically challenged nerd for a son, especially since he traded for a better model the first chance he got.

When we heard about the wedding, I did a little social media sleuthing into Dad's new wife, Angela, and her thirteen-year-old son, Nick Houston—the star point guard of his middle school's basketball team. After they got back from their honeymoon/family vacay to South Africa, Angela posted that she was taking an extended break from real estate law (although I don't know why the heck houses need lawyers in the first place) to focus on family and renovating the new home she and Dad had just bought in the San Diego suburbs.

Mom and Dad used to fight a lot about Mom's school and work. It bothered him that she was gone so much. It wasn't fun for me either, but I never got why it made him *so* angry; especially because Mom's work made her *so* happy. I'm not sure I'll ever understand adults.

Angela and Nick are waiting for us on the curb near the baggage check. They both stand beside a rickety metal luggage cart that's almost full of suitcases, big and small. Angela's wearing a jean romper and sandals, and her gigantic sunglasses hide her eyes (and about half of her squat face). Her hair is cornrowed into long brass-streaked braids that dangle down her back. Nick's about six inches taller than me, and has the same dull, cardboard complexion as his mom. His hair's shaved on the sides with short twists on the top that flop to one side like limp spaghetti. I stare at them both as we approach, wondering what about them is so much better than us.

"Oh! There they are!" Angela cries in a singsong voice that prickles my skin. She rushes to the edge of the sidewalk and gives us each a hug as we step up, but it's one of those fake hugs Mom calls the "church pat."

Dad introduces everyone, and Nick, because he's too cool for us, half waves and mutters a tepid "What's up?"

"'Sup?" I avert my gaze.

"I'm so excited y'all are joining us," Angela says. "Now Nick will have someone to hang out with besides us old folks." Only she and Dad laugh. If they'd really wanted us to crash their trip, Mom wouldn't have had to fight with Dad for him to agree to it.

"Thank you for inviting us!" Mags says, holding Dad's hand now.

I'm about to tell her we weren't invited, but the phantom jab of Loren's elbow warns me against making unnecessary trouble right now.

Dad looks down at his watch. "We need to get moving. Toss the bags on the cart, son."

"Okay," Nick and I both say at the same time.

We freeze.

Nick's eyes meet mine and narrow slightly.

We turn to Dad, who's staring at us both with a look of abject horror on his face.

Then, as if his brain suddenly sputters back to life, he says, "Never mind, I got it." He chuckles under his breath and shakes his head. "Lazy preteens, eh?"

Nick frowns and sidles closer to his mom. I'm hollowed out all over again. I wish Loren were here.

The port's main entrance opens up into a gargantuan room containing a winding line that looks longer than the one for Space Mountain at Disneyland. The room is so tall I can see the massive cruise ship docked at the rear of the port through the glass wall at the back. Televisions stand on poles like cyberpunk scarecrows in the field of people, all tuned to CNN.

We join the line, and I hang toward the back of our group. Nick stands ahead of me, his head down in his phone, and Dad and Angela are up front with Mags, who's reading on her tablet.

I turn my attention to the closest television, where a guy who looks old enough to be my grandpa is rambling on about the apocalypse. I text Loren.

> Hey!

> Turn to CNN!

> That the guy u were telling me abt?

Hiii! Hang on lemme check.

Omg! Yes! That's him!! He's so creep-tastic!!!!

He does seem pretty weird (not the good kind). He's white and has a slender, pointy face, ice-blue eyes, pale clean-shaven skin, and his dark brown hair is overgrown and curly. He's wearing a plain blue suit and light yellow tie. The digital banner at the bottom of the screen reads "Eustice Barnes, Motivational Speaker and Social Media Influencer from Los Angeles."

Eustice turns his hypnotizing stare to the camera. "Each of us around the world must prepare for what is almost upon us. This world is ending"—he pauses to blow out an exaggerated breath—"and a new one will be born under the Horsemen's rule."

The line inches forward, and I move along robotically with the group, still glued to the television. Something about what he said sounds familiar, but I can't recall from where.

"That's quite a premonition," says the anchorwoman, an older white woman with a ginger bob and a sharp mouth and eyes. "And it would seem the rest of the world shares my sentiment, seeing as how your most recent TikTok videos have garnered several *billion* views in a matter of days. I'm curious—as I'm sure our viewers are—how did you come to know this information? Was it a vision? A dream, perhaps?"

He shakes his head. "The divine servant of the Horsemen, a being of great magical ability and wonder, came to me one night and bade me prepare the world for the coming apocalypse. His message for this world is 'Come and see.'"

My heart cinches as if squeezed by icy fingers. Those were the words I heard in my nightmare—the one I had right before I saw Shadow Man in my room.

The anchorwoman looks confused. "And what does that mean exactly?"

Eustice smirks. "If you want to know, you'll have to tune

into my special pay-per-view information session tonight at eight p.m. Eastern, five p.m. Pacific Time, which will be available through most streaming services."

Gooseflesh prickles on my arms. Could Shadow Man be the divine servant of the Horsemen?

"Tuh!" A gruff voice behind me pulls me away from the broadcast. "Trying to turn a profit at a time like this."

I sneak a quick peek. Mr. Dexter? I blink and take a second look. Bumping into a teacher outside of school is super weird, like catching a fish walking down the street.

I'm debating if I should say hello, when he looks down and squints, then widens his eyes. "Alex Wise? What are *you* doing here?"

"Running away from home," I say. "Think I might give being a pirate a try. . . . Arrgh, and all that."

He laughs so hard that he wheezes. Nick turns around and quickly realizes our conversation doesn't register high enough on his Cool Meter to warrant his attention, so he returns to his phone.

"What cruise are you going on, Mr. Dexter?" I ask.

"Ah, we're not at school, so Dexter will do. And I'm going to Hawai'i on the *Kingships Reign*."

"That's the same ship we're on. How random is that?"

Angela shrieks with excitement out of nowhere, which makes my skin crawl. When I turn around, she's smiling wide and shoving her phone toward Dad.

"Lisa just sent over the final adoption documents," she says. "It's done!"

"Whoa, boy." Dad turns to Nick with tears in his eyes and

pulls him into a bear hug. "You've always been my son, but now it's official."

Nick grins and pats my dad's back. "Thanks, Pop."

The sound of Mags's tablet hitting the floor jars our step-family out of their impromptu celebration. My legs go all wobbly, and I think I'm going to puke.

No wonder Dad didn't want us here. This trip is to celebrate his finally getting the son he's always wanted.

Mags scoops up her tablet and makes a beeline for me.

"Congratulations," I tell them, draping my arms over my sister's shoulders.

Angela smiles, but Nick looks at Dad with concern. Dad steps forward but stops short when Mags and I move back.

"Alex, I'm sorry I didn't tell you," he says. "I'd planned to talk to you about it, but I wasn't expecting those documents to come so—"

"It's okay. Seriously." I nod at Nick. "Congrats, man."

Albeit hesitantly, Nick dips his head in acknowledgment.

Dad kneels in front of Mags. "I know this might be a little hard to understand—"

"I know what adoption is, Daddy," she says. "I'm ten, not five."

He stands up and chuckles. "Well, excuse me, ma'am." His eyes shift between Mags and me. "Nick is part of our family now. He might not be blood, but he's your brother all the same." He tells Nick, "And likewise for you, buddy. A lot of responsibility comes with being the oldest—you up for that?"

Nick groans. "Cut it out, Pop. You're being weird again."

Dad punches Nick playfully on the arm, and Nick laughs.

They hug once more, and Dad keeps his arm across Nick's shoulders until we reach the front of the line.

Mags puts her tablet away and doesn't say another word as we make our way through the queue. I hold her close the entire time.

Just before we step up to the security booth, a strong hand grips my shoulder and gives it a loving squeeze. When I glance back, Dexter nods at me. I half smile and turn around, my entire face hot as a griddle at Denny's.

This trip couldn't possibly get any worse.

As we trek through the ship to our staterooms, I'm on constant guard for my supernatural stalker. I hold my breath around every corner, squint into each dim or dark space, and jump at stray shadows—but Shadow Man is nowhere to be found. Maybe I can finally relax.

I haven't even thought to worry about the rooming situation until Dad stops in front of the first of our two rooms. He tells Mags she'll be on her own with a single bed, which adjoins his and Angela's. That must mean I'm sharing with Nick. I take a deep breath and hold it in to stifle the mighty shriek that I want to let loose. I bet he snores like a fat wildebeest too.

Nick doesn't seem thrilled about rooming with me either. He takes the envelope from Dad and hands me one of the keys without even looking at me. At least Mags is next door. I can hang out in her room and use mine for sleeping and storing my stuff. I can make this be okay.

At least there's no Shadow Man.

Our room is so tiny I can hear Nick's annoying whistling breaths from where he sits on the edge of his bed. I set my suitcase on mine and start unpacking my things.

"I'm sorry about all that," he says. "If it's any consolation, it was super embarrassing for me."

"It's not," I say. "But thanks anyway."

"I'm not trying to take your dad away from you."

I shrug and sit on my bed. "He's actually not that great, so help yourself."

"He's been good to me." Nick swallows hard in the harsh quiet. "My dad died when I was nine. He was rushing from work to one of my games and got in a car accident. I was really depressed for a long time because I thought it was my fault.

"Pop was nice to me. He even linked me with a therapist who helps me with my grief and stuff." He stops and takes a deep, hard breath. "Wow, I can't believe I'm telling you all this. I guess what I'm trying to say is I hope you're cool with sharing him."

"Yeah, sure," I say. "Sorry about your dad. I'm glad mine could be there for you."

I feel like the Supreme Emperor of Jerks because Nick's story isn't endearing. Instead, it makes me feel the lowest I've felt since losing Sky. I see the kind of dad that Dad can be—just not for me. And that makes me angry, which probably also makes me a selfish jerk. I dunno.

Nick hangs his head. "Thanks." Someone knocks hard on our door, and he bolts from our awkward morbid conversation to answer it.

Dad's deep trombone voice bounds into the room ahead of him. "You two in here chitchatting, I see," he says. "You boys know there's a court on deck?" He dribbles an imaginary basketball between his legs and shoots it into an imaginary net across the room, complete with his own *swish* sound effect. "Nick, maybe you can teach Alex some of your moves later?"

Nick looks at me. "Sure, if he wants."

He does not want. I half smile anyway.

"I love it," Dad says. "Let's go up top to watch the ship set sail."

5

THE GREAT CHEESEBURGER ESCAPE

Dad, Angela, and Nick huddle nearby, leaning on the railing on the main deck and snapping group selfies on Angela's phone. Mags hangs close by me, silently watching them.

I lean down and whisper in her ear, "Shh . . . Let's go exploring."

She beams up at me and takes my hand without question.

Mags may be annoying, but she's *my* annoying little sister, and I won't subject her to watching Dad, Angela, and Nick play "perfect family." Even if I leapt overboard to swim to freedom, I wouldn't leave Mags behind—and she wouldn't let me. She'd follow me to Mordor as long as she could bring her tablet.

Mags and I slip away and dip into the cool air-conditioning of the ship's corridors. The atrium is brightly lit by a gaudy candelabra with electric candles. The elaborate architecture is just as ugly, with oversized trim painted gold, and tacky medieval tapestries in bold royal colors like purples, reds, and greens hang throughout the ship. It's like we're walking the halls of a castle. Kingships really took their royal theme seriously. They even gave everyone little cheap plastic crowns the moment we boarded. I threw mine in the first garbage can I saw. I don't want any mementos from this horrific experience.

We wander aimlessly, noting all the important places, like the internet café, the excursion desk, the arcade, and all the buffets and restaurants. When we happen upon a section of small shops, Mags gasps aloud at the Royal Readership bookstore and nearly yanks my arm off.

I unlatch her from me. "Have at it."

She yips with glee and disappears behind a bookshelf like a leprechaun scrambling toward a stash of gold. I make my way to the laughably meager graphic novel section and thumb through a year-old X-Men comic while she happily plunders the shelves. She seemed as bludgeoned by the sudden adoption news as me, so I don't rush her. She needs a moment to forget and be happy.

I hold back the tears I feel surging to the surface. I need to be strong for Mags, but I'm not sure *I'm* okay.

Something shuffles in the next aisle over, which gives me a start. The floor shelves are short enough that even I can see over them, but no one's there. I look around, but aside from the cashier leaning on the counter, enwrapped in a romance novel with a beefy guy on the cover, Mags and I are alone in the store. I check the far end of the aisle and drop the X-Men comic I was holding. It thumps to the floor as a long shadow in the next aisle stretches into view.

No. Shadow Man found us.

I creep backward slowly, my eyes tight on the shadow.

"I'm done!" Mags announces behind me right before I back into her.

I scream and whirl around.

She screams too.

And so does the lady who was sitting on the other side of the shelf before popping up like a meerkat. She'd been so quiet that I hadn't noticed she was over there. Now she clutches her chest, staring wide-eyed at me and Mags.

"Sorry," I tell her.

"Everything okay over there?" calls the cashier, annoyed that we've disturbed her story.

I nod and grab Mags's hand.

"What's wrong with you?" she asks as I lead her from the store.

I consider coming clean about my various Shadow Man sightings, both real and imagined, but she's had enough drama today.

"Lack of ice cream makes me scream spontaneously," I tell her.

She sucks her teeth. "Why are you so weird?"

"Do you want ice cream or no? I feel a scream building. . . ."

She pushes me. "Lead the way."

I can only hope ice cream will help me forget about Shadow Man. I don't want to spend the rest of this godawful trip wondering which shadow's going to murder me.

The King's Court Banquet Hall is a buffet with everything from fresh stir-fry to a make-your-own pizza station. Mags and I pass the hamburger grill on the way to the ice cream bar, and the smell of those juicy patties sizzling on the grate draws my eyes. My mouth waters when I see the golden yellow cheese melting and bubbling atop the burgers.

I snap out of my trance to nudge Mags. "I have a mighty need for one of those cheeseburgers. Wanna come back for dinner?"

She nods vigorously. "They do smell really good."

Whoever built the king's ice cream bar left no topping behind. Sprinkles, diced fresh fruit, chopped candy, every sweet syrup and sauce known to human civilization, and even pieces of real bacon. At the end of the bar are two of those old-timey metal soft-serve machines that only ever have vanilla, chocolate, or vanilla-chocolate swirl. I'm more of a hazelnut chocolate fudge kinda guy, but I'll take whatever I can get right now.

I cover vanilla ice cream in a waffle cone with a chocolate shell and drop sprinkles on it before it hardens, trapping them in a delicious, chocolatey prison. Mags double-fists two swirl cones. I almost tell her she can only have one at a time, but we've both had a tough day, and I don't feel like being the ice cream police.

We decide to lounge on the main deck and soak up some sun with our ice cream, but it seems everyone else had the same idea. The chairs around the massive pool and water slides are packed. We wander the deck until eventually, near the aft, we stumble upon three open seats. Mags and I swarm them immediately.

"We should go swimming before dinner," I suggest.

"Yes, please!" Mags says, excitement sparkling in her eyes.

I look up to see Dexter approaching. He's carrying a bowl of vanilla ice cream drizzled with strawberry syrup and has a paperback book tucked under one arm.

"Hey, Dexter!" I wave to him, and so does Mags.

He grins and strolls over. He's changed into some yellow linen shorts and a white polo. A golden straw hat sits on his thick, silky gray curls.

"Alex! Mags!" he says. "How are you two finding the ship so far?"

Mags smacks her lips. "The ice cream's good, but the bookstore selection sucks."

He chuckles and waves his book—*Julius Caesar*. "Why I always carry a backup."

"Only a teacher would read Shakespeare on vacation," I say with a wry grin.

He glances at the cover as if he forgot what he was reading. "I find historical tales quite fascinating, particularly this one. I can relate to the betrayal of a loved one."

"Heh," I say. "You too, huh?" When he raises a brow at me, I add, "Long story."

He gestures to the open chair beside me. "Do you mind? Everywhere else is taken." He sits after I nod and drops his voice so only I can hear—though Mags is hyperfocused on her fast-melting ice cream cones. "I, uh . . . wasn't trying to eavesdrop earlier, but it was hard not to overhear what happened in the security line."

The thought of my family's drama on display makes the ice cream in my stomach curdle.

"When I was your age," says Dexter, "I would've traded my soul for my father's if it would've made him proud." He stares down at his ice cream, which is well on its way to becoming a soupy mess too. "I lost my mother chasing his approval."

Jinkies. Maybe Dexter and I are even more alike than I thought.

"For what it's worth," he says, "I empathize with your plight, Mr. Wise—"

"Aht!" I smirk at him. "We're not at school, remember?"

He chuckles. "Fair enough."

Mags grins too, her lips and fingers plastered with sticky ice cream.

"You deserve better than what you've been given," he says, standing up and tucking the book back underneath his arm.

"Thanks," I say, a slight warmth radiating in my chest.

Dexter nods at Mags and pats me on the shoulder, then strolls off, tossing his melted ice cream in the garbage before disappearing back inside the ship.

After we finish eating, Mags and I head back to our staterooms to change into our swimsuits. Nick's not in our room, which makes me wonder what they're all up to. I bet they haven't even noticed Mags and I ditched yet.

I throw on some red and white trunks and a white tank. Mags meets me in the hallway in her turquoise bathing suit, her twists tucked into a matching swim cap.

Dad's voice bellows from down the hall. "Hey! We've been looking for you two. Where you headed?" He struts toward us with Angela and Nick in tow.

"To the pool," I say.

"Okay," he says, "but stick together and be back by seven so we can dress for dinner."

The thought of a family dinner smacks my heart down through the hull of the ship.

"We really wanted to get burgers at the grill." I clasp my hands in front of me for dramatic effect. "Can we please eat there just this one night?"

Dad sighs, and Angela puts a hand on his shoulder. "Oh, let the kids have their cheeseburgers, Malcolm. We'll still have plenty of time to spend together as a family."

"Fine," he says. "We could use some 'adults only' time anyway." He turns to Nick, who appears just as disgusted as I am with what he knows is coming. "Nick, cheeseburgers are your favorite. How about you tag along with them?"

Nick looks at me like he'd rather volunteer for extra history homework. "Pop, I—"

"It'll be good for you kids to hang without the 'rentals lurking," Angela says with a shrill laugh that makes my skin crawl. Dad chuckles and agrees, but no one else knows what the heck she's talking about.

"Tomorrow morning, we eat breakfast as a family—understood?" Dad commands.

Nick, Mags, and I nod, but I'd rather jump overboard than suffer through a single family meal.

6

THAT TIME I WASN'T CAREFUL WHAT I WISHED FOR

Nick, Mags, and I ride the waterslides and splash in the pool until our fingers prune and everyone's exhausted—and for the first time this summer, I actually have fun. Even more surprising, I have fun *with Nick*. We're def not best friends, but we've figured out how to coexist, which is a ton easier without our parents trying to ram us into undying brotherhood.

Our stomachs growl in harmony as we climb out of the pool and towel off. Dark storm clouds roll and flash with lightning in the distance. It's kinda cool being able to see a storm clearly from so far away. It looks like a portal to another world.

The three of us change into shorts, tees, and sneakers and meet up in the hall outside our rooms to head to the buffet together.

On the elevator to the main deck, Nick holds his stomach and shuts his eyes. "Mmm . . . I can already taste those burgers."

Mags stares at the corner of the elevator, silent. Her tablet is tucked into the Hello Kitty sling bag she's wearing on her back, which matches her pink tee.

I put an arm around her. "You okay?"

She leans into me but doesn't say anything. I noticed her watching the storm through the window in her room. She's seemed nervous ever since.

"It's okay." I hug her closer. "You're with me and Nick, and we won't let anything happen to you." I feel her small frame relax.

But the relief is short-lived, because what we see when we step out onto the main deck makes even me a little nervous.

Hard rain pelts the deck, pulsing in strong waves and not showing signs of letting up anytime soon. The sky's dark, and storm clouds thick as concrete blot out the moon and stars. Mags sucks in a harsh breath and clings to my arm.

Nick looks from the glass doors to us. "Surely you two aren't going to let a little rain get between you and cheeseburgers?"

Mags grips me harder, and I swallow my anxiety. "Run for it?"

He nods.

"Get ready," I tell Mags, who nods too, but her wide eyes say she'll never be ready.

I take her hand as the automatic doors *swish* open. The

room floods with the roar of fat raindrops slapping the deck. We run.

Rain pours down my face and distorts my vision, but I focus on holding tight to Mags and keeping my eyes on the neon KING'S COURT BANQUET HALL sign, which shines through the storm like a lighthouse beacon. A streak of lightning paints the dark sky with glowing cracks, as if it's going to break apart.

The three of us race inside the buffet hall and pile up in front of the host stand, a soggy, dripping mess. Startled, the host clutches an imaginary set of pearls and says, "Oh, my!"

He fishes a roll of paper towels from his station and hands each of us a giant wad, which we use to dry off as best we can. Once we no longer look like we just went for a swim fully clothed, we thank the host and head over to the grill.

It's not until we're standing at the burger station waiting on ours to finish cooking that I feel the boat rocking. I've noticed a subtle pitch every now and again throughout the day, but the occasional drastic tilts of the room are becoming more frequent—and frightening.

We choose a table away from the windows so we don't have to watch the storm rampaging outside. My stomach starts to sway with the ship, and I'm not feeling so hungry all of a sudden. Even Nick seems a little shaken. I try to eat anyway, and I urge Mags to do the same.

I spot Dexter across the room, enjoying a dinner of pizza and orange soda. I wonder if he wants to join us, but I don't ask. He might not want to spend his vacation babysitting former students.

"What if the ship sinks?" asks Mags.

Nick's eyes widen and shoot to me. Neither of us was paying attention during the safety demonstration.

"I, uh, well . . ." I bite my bottom lip and glance out a window across the room. The curtain of rain against the pane is so thick I can barely see out. "We're going to be okay. Finish your burger. Then we'll go check out the arcade."

"And do you know the best thing about the arcade?" Nick adds. When Mags shakes her head, he says, "No windows."

She smiles and goes back to sticking fries in her mouth one by one and flinching along with me at every rip of thunder that rattles the room. There aren't many people eating in the buffet hall, but those who are talk quietly at their tables.

We finish our burgers and sit in silent dread, no one wanting to suggest venturing outside again.

"So much for the arcade," Mags says in a tiny voice.

I get up, but no one stands with me. "Come on. It's only a little rain, right?"

"Maybe we should wait until the storm lets up," Nick suggests.

I gesture at the window. "I don't think that's happening anytime soon. I don't know about you, but I don't want to be stuck in the King's Court Banquet Hall all night. Let's go have some fun."

He sighs. "I know, but—"

"Oh, don't be a fun snatcher . . . Unless—" I gasp dramatically and dip behind Mags. "Careful, little sis, a fun-snatching spy from the Fun Patrol walks among us."

She giggles.

Nick frowns and bolts up from his seat with a huff. "I'm

not a fun snatcher! Let's go, then. I'm looking forward to kicking your butt in *Mortal Kombat*."

Mags gets up, bright and ready to go, rejuvenated by excitement.

The moment we all step outside, I once again wish I'd kept my big mouth shut.

As if it were possible, the rain seems to be coming down even harder. I can barely see five feet in front of me as we break for the main atrium. Are all storms out on the ocean this intense?

I grab Mags's hand and struggle to hold on to her, my grip slick from the rain. She trips and falls. Nick and I stop to help her up, but the ship takes a gut-lurching dip to one side.

For a moment, it feels like we're floating in space—then we're thrown to the slippery ground. My shoulder smacks into the deck and pain shoots through my arm and neck. Nick hits the deck hard with an *oomph!* And Mags tumbles toward the rail.

I push to my feet and help Nick up. Across the deck, Mags pulls herself up. She's lost her glasses and looks around with wild, frantic eyes. I scream her name and scramble toward her. She reaches for me, but the ship dips severely to one side again.

The force flings Mags backward, slamming her into the railing and throwing me and Nick back to the ground. This feels like losing my footing in a bouncy castle when the other kids won't stop jumping. I need to get to Mags, who's slouched against the railing, looking dazed.

I stagger to my feet. But what I see stops me cold.

Something cloaked in shadow claws its way up the outside

of the ship and perches above the railing, hovering over Mags hungrily.

I want to scream for help, but my throat feels locked up.

"What the heck is that?!" yells Nick.

He can see Shadow Man too.

If I had any lingering doubts that Shadow Man was real, they've just been flung overboard. The confirmation that I haven't lost it isn't as comforting as I imagined, because it also means we're all in very *real* and present danger.

Mags goes rigid, then dares to glance behind her. Shadow Man reaches down, his arm elongating and his hand stretching to the size of a catcher's mitt. He grabs my little sister by the face, muffling her scream. He lifts her high into the air. She kicks wildly and claws at his arm with zero effect.

"LET HER GO!" I scream.

Shadow Man turns Mags so she's facing me, then hugs her close, draping his inky arms across her chest.

Dexter emerges from the banquet hall and runs toward us, shouting something inaudible over the noise of the storm.

I ignore him and run for my sister.

But I'm not fast enough.

Mags's terrified eyes lock on mine just before Shadow Man falls backward, still holding her.

I crash into the rail and peer over the side. Mags hits the water, then disappears into the dark and choppy ocean. I can't see Shadow Man either. I struggle to muster enough air to scream, "MAAAGS!"

Dexter and Nick both reach the railing beside me and shout my sister's name too.

Nick turns to me, soaked and trembling. "What do we do?"

"Go find Dad," I shout over the rain.

Dexter grabs my arm. "What do you think you're about to do?"

I snatch out of his grasp. "I'm going after my sister."

Before either of them can say another word, I leap overboard.

THE FALL OF THE
KINGSHIPS REIGN

The drop from the ship rams my stomach into my throat, which keeps me from screaming.

I plunge into the icy ocean, and everything goes quiet except for the rush of water and the thump of my heartbeat. I kick until I emerge above the surface, my teeth chattering. The ship's lights project a bright glow on the surrounding waters, which I'm grateful for; otherwise it'd be pitch-black out here.

"MAGS!" I shout.

But no one responds. A sudden panic sweeps me. What the heck was I thinking, jumping from a *whole* cruise ship?

The *Kingships Reign* towers over me. It's stopped and now floats haphazardly on the shifting ocean, teetering back and forth and creating high ripples that bob me up and down. The rain still hasn't let up, hitting the water with a sound like hail clacking against pavement.

"ALEEEX!"

I barely hear the frenzied scream over the noise of the

storm. I strain my ears, trying to zero in on where the shouts are coming from.

"ALEEEX!"

A few hundred yards in the distance, Mags waves her small arms and disappears underneath the water, then bobs back to the surface, spluttering and coughing. Thank goodness I taught her how to swim at the YMCA last summer. I'm also thankful she's alone. Shadow Man seems to be gone—for now.

I swim for my sister. By the time Mags sinks again, I'm there to lift her back up and rest her arms on my shoulders. She clamps onto me with both hands, kicking to stay afloat.

"Alex, I'm s-scared!" she cries.

"Me too," I say. "But we're together now."

"Did you j-jump after me?"

"Yep. You're my little sister. What else was I supposed to do?"

She hugs me, pressing her cheek against mine, and lets out a shuddering breath.

The freezing water laps viciously at us. Mags's teeth chatter in my ear, and my fingertips go numb. I'm sick of tasting salty, fishy ocean water, and my sinus cavities are still burning from my dramatic dive. I'm not sure what to do now. There's no way we can shout over the storm to get the attention of anyone aboard the ship. If Nick doesn't get to Dad in time, we might not make it.

I'm wondering why the ship stopped when a creaking groan fills the air. The ship tilts toward us. Someone falls overboard! I squint as they disappear into the depths.

The boat leans closer, adding the screams and shrieks of passengers to the ruckus. Mags and I gasp simultaneously as more than a few people pitch over the side of the ship and vanish in the dark waters, one after another after another.

The ship jerks to the other side and rights itself, and I let go of the breath I've been holding. Mags and I tremble in each other's arms, watching the boat rock, each sway bringing the gigantic metal beast closer to going belly-up.

I didn't really think about a plan for *after* leaping overboard and finding my sister, but at least if we both die tonight, we'll be together.

"HEEELP!" A frantic voice cuts through the noise.

I look around but can't find anyone.

"SOMEONE! PLEASE!"

Halfway between us and the ship, I can just make out a person waving their arms above the water. I have to squint hard to see, but . . .

"It's Dexter!" I shout. "Do you think you can swim with me?"

Mags doesn't look confident but nods anyway.

"Hold tight!" I take her hand, and we set off.

We both fight against the waves, pulling and kicking our way to where Dexter is flailing in the rough water. His eyes are wide and terrified when we reach him.

I take one of his hands and Mags grabs the other. "A-Alex?" he says.

"It's me," I tell him. "You okay?"

He nods. I look around but don't see anyone else. I don't want to think about what happened to all those other people who fell overboard. But it feels slightly less hopeless now that Mags and I are at least in the presence of another adult—even if Dexter can't swim all that well.

The three of us link arms, floating in a circle, staring into each other's frightened faces.

"Your stepbrother went to find your parents," Dexter tells us. "I stayed behind to watch out for you kids."

The *Kingships Reign* is in such a precarious state right now, I start to think we might be safer out here in the water. Long as we don't see any sharks—or Shadow Man.

"Everything's gonna be okay." I try to sound confident despite having already peed my pants. (Hey, don't even—we're in the ocean, so *technically* this time doesn't count.) "With all the safety tech on these ships, I bet the Coast Guard's already on the way."

Behind us, the ship groans again.

KABLOOOM!

Mags screams.

The ship flips ninety degrees to one side, revealing half of its barnacle-ridden rusted underbelly. A furious flaming hole stands out in the ship's bottom, bright orange against the darkness and falling rain. Alarms screech and whoop. Life rafts overflowing with people tumble into the water, some dumping their passengers into the ocean.

I close my eyes and hope as hard as I can that Nick made it to Dad and Angela in time. Please let them all be okay.

Finally, the *Kingships Reign* goes belly-up, muffling the screams of the unlucky people still aboard, and sinks. As if our situation wasn't dire enough, the subdued roars of a chain of underwater explosions from the ship resound from below.

And a gigantic wave builds.

My heart stops.

"HANG ON!" I shout.

But it's pointless. I take a deep breath and shut my eyes.

The force of the wave snatches us under, breaking us apart and rolling everyone underwater like spinning bowling pins. My world turns over and over, and I lose sight of the others. When I finally regain control, all I see is dark water, and I can't tell which way is up and which is down. My lungs burn from holding my breath. I want to open my mouth and scream.

I bet on the direction I think is up and swim. My muscles blaze and my chest feels like it's going to explode if I don't inhale oxygen soon. But I keep going.

Panic pushes back on me as I start to think I might've chosen the wrong direction and could be swimming straight to my death. But I don't let up.

The water finally starts to clear, until I can see a bright light glimmering above the surface. Someone, glowing like a dim star, is walking above the water.

The sight startles me, and I expel all the air I've been holding in. Salt water burns my nose. I scream and choke.

My mind goes fuzzy.

Then something grabs me tight around the arm.

I'm rocketed upward, and my world goes black.

8

LOST

A lurching, drowning cough jerks me awake.

Water shoots from my mouth and splashes back onto my face. I gag and roll onto my side, spewing more salt water. When I'm done, I inhale as much air as my lungs can hold, grasping fistfuls of the soft sand beneath me. Those first few breaths burn so good. For a moment there, I thought I'd never get to feel that again. I push up to my knees and gasp.

Mags and Dexter lie next to me on the cloud-white sand beach, both coughing up water and pulling themselves back together. I scramble to Mags, throw my arms around her, and squeeze until she screams for me to let go. Dexter laughs with relief.

We're on an island, which is weird, because we weren't anywhere close to one before the ship sank. A dense jungle borders the beach, which stretches for miles on either side of us. The water laps at the shore, reaching out to claw us back under. The storm has passed, and the moon and stars now reign over the cloudless night sky. A wall of fog encloses the island, towering straight to the heavens. I've never seen anything like it, not even in a science book. I wonder how far we are from where the ship sank. And how the heck did we get here?

"You're awake. Good." The teenage voice startles me from behind. "I was worried I pulled you out too late."

I spin around and rise slowly. A boy stands a few paces away, ankle-deep in water that reflects the soft light of the moon. He looks half god, half human, one side of him awash in moonbeams that his gorgeous dark brown skin drinks up. He's my height, and his hair is cut low, but I'm willing to bet my comic collection that a barber has never touched his head. He's wearing this tunic thingy that looks handmade. A few long strips of different pale-colored cloth are draped around his neck, and he wears a carved wooden bracelet on his left wrist. I guess being shipwrecked doesn't mean you can't be stylish.

Holstered to a braided hemp belt around his waist is a machete, which I keep my eye on. I don't think he went through the trouble of rescuing us just to chop us to bits, but you never know.

"Who are you?" I ask.

"Liam," he says. "What's your name?"

"I'm Alex." I introduce Mags and Dexter, who wave hello. "Thank you for saving us."

Liam waves stiffly, cautious.

Relief at our miraculous rescue gives way to panic once I realize I've lost my phone. Mags doesn't have her sling bag, which means hers is gone too. And so are her glasses.

"Did you happen to hang on to your phone?" I ask Dexter, who shakes his head.

"Phones won't work here," interjects Liam.

"Where is *here*, exactly?" I ask.

"Nowhere," he says brusquely.

I throw my hands up. "That's not very helpful."

"And what if I told you the exact coordinates of the spot you're standing on right now? What would you do with that information?"

"I . . . uh, well . . ." I clamp my mouth shut and glower at him.

I can't argue. Unless there's a working radio nearby, we're stuck until someone happens to stumble upon this island. I wonder how long Liam's been here.

Then I remember the others, and a dark cloud kicks up in the bottom of my stomach. Dad. Angela. Nick. I wonder if they made it to the rafts or—

"Did you rescue anyone else from the ship?" I ask Liam.

He shakes his head. "There were only you three."

Mags looks at me, her eyes already welling. "Did Daddy . . . die?"

My heart withers. No matter how I feel about Dad, despite everything, he's still Dad.

"No," I tell her. "We gotta believe he's okay—and Angela and Nick."

"Well, *we* made it," Dexter says, "so I bet they did too."

A lot of people got on the life rafts. Maybe they're already somewhere safe. I hope.

Mags winces and grabs the side of her head. "Alex, I— I don't feel so good." When she pulls her hand down, fresh blood glistens on her fingertips in the moonlight.

I dive beside her and gently push her twists aside to

examine her wound. It's a deep gash as wide as my thumb. She must've hit her head when she fell back on the ship. I think she might need stitches, but I doubt there's an emergency room on this island, which looks as deserted as deserted can get.

Liam takes off one of his scarves and folds it into a square compress. He kneels beside Mags and presses it to her wound, which is leaking just enough blood to make me queasy.

"Apply pressure," he tells her, exchanging his hand for hers while he shapes another of his scarves into a headband and ties it tight around her head, holding the compress in place. "I can treat that, but we have to go back to my camp."

I turn to Dexter, who hesitates to answer.

"Or we can leave the kid on the beach to bleed to death," says Liam. "Up to you."

"Fine." I swivel around and pull Mags onto my back. "Lead the way."

The white sand is soft and slippery underfoot, making it hard for me to keep my balance with Mags's extra weight.

"I can walk if I'm too heavy," she says.

"Save your strength," I tell her. "I got you."

She rests her chin on my shoulder, and we follow Liam down the beach and into the jungle. The frogs and insects hanging out in the trees and brush screech a nocturnal tune that sounds to me like a frenzied racket. Tall trees loom overhead. Their leaves rustle in the breeze, which carries the tangy smell of salt water into the bush.

Liam stalks ahead of us along a worn, narrow path bordered by thick foliage. He uses his machete to chop back the occasional unruly branch or bush.

"How far is your camp?" I ask.

"Not far," he grumbles.

"We shouldn't stay long," I say. "It's best we stick close to the beach in case a search party comes. But I'm worried about that fog."

"You don't need to worry about that," he says.

"I'm sorry, but have you *noticed* the fog lately?"

"Your questions are getting annoying."

I don't know why this guy even bothered saving us if we irritate him so much. "So I guess that means it's too late to ask why you're so grumpy?"

Liam stops and rounds on me. "You shouldn't be here."

"Oh, my bad," I tell him. "Next time I'm drowning, I'll make sure to do it in someone else's backyard."

He sucks his teeth. "That's not what I meant. It's—"

Mags's hand jackhammers my shoulder. "Alex! ALEEEX!"

"WHAT?!" I hiss at her.

She points down the heavily shadowed path behind Liam, who turns and raises his machete. "Did you see that?" she asks shakily. "Something moved."

My blood runs ice-cold. Please, not him.

"Can you be certain?" asks Dexter. "Without your glasses?"

Mags grips me tighter but says nothing.

"Did you see *him*?" I whisper. "Did you see Shadow Man again?"

"Who are you talking about?" Liam asks, scowling.

He watches me curiously while I narrate the story of the evil shadow thingy that's been stalking me and Mags since the last day of school. I feel Mags tense on my back at the mention of my encounters with Shadow Man, which I've kept from her until now. If she's mad at me, she doesn't say anything.

When I finish, Liam's frown deepens. "I used to know someone who wielded the magic of Darkness."

"Hold up," I say. "Did I just hear you say you had a friend who could do *magic?*"

"Yes," Liam answers matter-of-factly.

I shake my head. "I don't believe you. That's not possible."

I feel Mags shifting on my back, shaking her head in vehement disagreement. "Then how do you explain Shadow Man?" she asks me.

"I . . ." I don't know. I guess I've never considered whether Shadow Man could be magic. I've been too busy worrying he was going to murder me.

"I *always* had a feeling," she says, the stark conviction in her voice biting. "Magic in stories has to come from somewhere. It can't have all been made up."

I believed wholeheartedly in magic once—when I was a little younger than Mags. No matter what anyone tried to tell me, I insisted magic existed somewhere in the world. The joy that came from clinging to the possibility had been enough to keep believing. But then Dad left and Larry Adams launched a personal campaign to make sure I never knew peace again, and hope got harder to hold on to. Eventually, I just . . . forgot that magic could exist.

Yet Mags found a way to believe in spite of everything.

"I'm from another realm, one where magic exists—or used to," Liam says.

He could very well be lying. But he also could be telling the truth. He *does* have an otherworldly vibe about him. Curiosity bats at the back of my brain like a playful kitten.

"Could the person you mentioned, the one who had the power to control Darkness, be the one who sent Shadow Man to terrorize us?" I ask Liam.

He shakes his head. "They died. I saw it happen."

I feel Dexter flinch behind me. The admission catches me off guard too. I've never seen anyone die—nor do I want to.

"My realm was destroyed four years ago, and everyone I knew is gone." I'm about to offer my sympathy when Liam says, "We need to get moving. We'll be safe at my camp."

He leads the way, and I follow, Dexter bringing up the rear.

Mags shivers against my back. I grab her goosefleshed arms and pull them tighter around my neck.

"I'm not going to let anything happen to you," I tell her. "If you're scared, just close your eyes. I'll let you know when we're at Liam's camp. Shouldn't be much farther now."

She buries her face in my back, and we press forward. I don't know what Shadow Man's endgame is, but he'll have to go through me to get his hands on my little sister again.

No one says anything else until the path spills us into a modest clearing. A fire pit sits near the center, not far from a small hut made of logs. The front door is covered with a leopard skin. At the back of the area is a field of stumps; some are old and moss-ridden, others fresh. A garden bursting with healthy green plants also borders one side of Liam's hut. He must've been living here for a while.

He tells me to put Mags on a log bench beside the fire pit. I set her down and take the spot beside her. Dexter kneels in the grass on the other side of the huge hole with a carpet of ashes at the bottom. Liam throws an armful of wood from a nearby stack into the pit. I'm wondering how he's going to light it when the pit rumbles and coughs up a burst of flames.

"How'd you do that?" I ask after relishing the warmth and security of the fire for a moment, but Liam's already disappearing inside his hut.

The firelight chases the creature symphony farther back into the jungle. My aching, freezing limbs thaw while the dancing flames hypnotize Dexter. I breathe in the woody scent of burning logs and let the heat soak into my skin. Even Mags sighs with satisfaction more than once.

Dexter watches Mags and me through the flames. "I can't be the only one who thinks something weird is up with that kid," he says in a hushed voice. "Not that I'm ungrateful, but I'm curious how he managed to save all three of us by himself."

"If Liam knows magic, maybe this is the best place for us to be if Shadow Man shows up again." My mention of Shadow Man draws a violent shudder from Mags.

Dexter purses his lips and gives his gaze back to the fire as Liam emerges from the hut with a basket in his arms.

He rushes to Mags's side and sets the basket at her feet. Inside are several rolled strips of clean cloths, a canteen, a lidded stone jar, and a stoppered container made from reeds.

As Liam cleans Mags's wound, he calls out the names of everything he uses. "Water to clean. Witch hazel to disinfect."

He places a folded cloth on the wound and lifts her hand to hold it in place. He opens the lidded jar, dips two fingers inside, and scoops out a glossy black glob of something that reminds me of that gel my cousin Domonique used to use to slick her edges down—the stuff that came in the black ten-gallon bucket. Though I'm pretty sure that's not what Liam's using.

"And this is a special salve I made from moon cloves," he says, gesturing for Mags to remove the compress.

Her brows furrow. "Moon cloves?"

He nods and spreads the black goop on her scalp. "About a year ago, I got into a fight with a leopard that gave me a nasty leg wound. I passed out in a patch of these leafy black flowers, and when I woke up, they were glowing wherever they touched my body. They looked magical and I was dying and desperate, so I chewed a handful into a paste and stuck it in my wound, hoping I hadn't just poisoned myself. But the pain stopped at once. I could stand a few moments later and walk a few more after that. And by the time I returned home, my leg had healed completely."

"Cool," coos Mags. "It feels warm. And my head doesn't hurt anymore." Firelight flickers in her round brown eyes, a hint of hope in them.

"That means it's working," he says. "I've improved the recipe since I first discovered it."

I lean in to get a closer look at Mags's head. The salve glows dim blue in the moonlight as the wound draws closed, only a thin line remaining where the gaping gash once was.

I blink and rub my eyes, because I'm not sure I'm *actually* seeing what I'm seeing. This is magic. Real live magic. It exists. Right here in front of my face. Mind *blown.*

"Thank you for healing my sister," I tell Liam once I'm able to collect myself enough to speak. "But can you please tell us what's going on?" Liam dials his scowl to confused mode. "You walking on water, the self-lighting fire pit, magical healing glow-in-the-dark plants," I continue. "It's a lot to grasp all at once, and you haven't exactly been forthcoming with information."

He huffs as if I'm annoying him. "I've explained already, but I'll break it down for you again: this island is magic, I possess magic, I am from a magical realm that no longer exists, all my friends and family are *dead*—and you three do not belong here. Against my better judgment, I rescued you and brought you to this place; however, the longer you're here, the more I start to question that decision."

"You actin' like we're on vacation," I snap back at him. "Do you think I want to be stranded here with you, Gandalf the Grouch?"

He scrunches his nose. "Who?"

"Never mind!" I snap. "If you have magic and want us gone so bad, then why not just, y'know, *magic* us all outta here? And why are *you* stranded here?"

"One, that's not how my magic works, and two, I'm not stranded."

Also, totally on-brand for me to find out that not only does magic exist but it can't help with the thing we need most right now. It's too much to take in at once, like trying to shower in Niagara Falls.

Liam's eyes harden to match his stiff posture. "I'm here for a purpose. And it's not safe for you three, so you need to leave as soon as possible."

"Finally!" I roll my eyes up to the dark sky. "Something we agree on!"

Liam storms off without another word. I want to kick sand after him.

Mags nudges me, interrupting my glaring at Liam's back as he flicks the leopard skin aside and whisks into his hut.

"Alex, I have to pee," she whispers, urgency straining her voice.

I sigh. "Okay, I'll take you."

"Where you two going?" Dexter asks when Mags and I stand up.

"Potty break," I tell him.

"Should I come with you?" he asks.

I shake my head. "I got it. Rest for now. Once she's done, we should head back to the beach."

"Don't stray," he warns.

Mags pulls me away from the fire, past the tree line, and into the bush.

I don't like it here. The clearing felt warm and safe, but the jungle is cold, and dread hangs like overgrown moss from the dark branches of the trees surrounding us. The shadows here are denser and far more intimidating when standing in the thick of them.

Mags drags me about twenty paces in before I jerk her to a stop. "This is far enough."

"Turn around and give me some space," she says. "I can't go with you listening."

I roll my eyes and walk a few steps back toward the clearing. "How's your head?"

"Much better," she says. "I didn't feel it until we woke up on the beach. I don't even remember—"

A quiet second passes.

"Mags?"

She doesn't answer, and I spin around.

My heart drops.

She's gone.

"MAGS!" I scream.

"ALEEEX!"

Several feet away, my sister clings to the trunk of a small tree with both hands. Shadow Man's long, clawed arms clutch her ankles, pulling her toward the deep dark of the jungle.

I lunge for her as another inky arm bursts from his back and covers her face with spindly, crooked fingers. Her terrified eyes peek out at me.

Shadow Man snatches my sister and disappears into the bush.

My breath leaves me, and I crumple to my knees.

9

THE BEGINNING
OF THE END . . .
OF THE WORLD

"MAGS!" I scream, darting back and forth.

Liam and Dexter both run up to where I'm freaking out just inside the jungle, where my sister stood moments ago.

"What happened?" asks Dexter.

"She was *right here*!" I stab my finger at the spot where I last saw her. "And then Shadow Man took her. I don't . . . understand. Why does he want her so bad?"

I bite my fist until I can't stand the pain. This is my fault. I never should've taken my eyes off her. I can't believe we survived a whole shipwreck only for me to lose my sister on a potty break.

"You and Dexter go back to the campsite, where it's safe," Liam orders. "I'll find her."

"No way I'm going to wiggle my toes by the fire while my sister is in danger!" I yell, giving him a start. "Wherever you're going, I am too."

"And I'm certainly not letting you two kids go alone," adds Dexter.

"Fine," Liam says. "We've wasted enough time. I have an idea where she might be."

He takes a deep breath and extends his hand palm-up. He bites his lip and flinches as a small ball of orange fire appears over his hand. The fireball swells to the size of a grapefruit, and the light forces back the surrounding shadows, flickering on all our frightened faces. Liam pushes it gently in front of him, where it hovers in the air, moving in sync with him, as if reading his thoughts. I can't believe what I'm seeing. But it's not an illusion or a dream. Magic is real. And watching Liam wield it is pretty freaking cool—I just wish it could be under different circumstances.

Small creatures chitter from every direction, and somewhere in the distance, something growls, then snarls. The hair on the back of my neck stands up. I hang closer to Liam. He leads us on a winding hike through the heart of the jungle, which is almost suffocating in the dark.

"How do you know where Shadow Man's taking Mags?" I ask him.

"There's only one place on this island that would lure darkness," he says, his voice solemn. "I just hope we can get there before something very bad happens."

Dexter grips my shoulder. "We'll find her."

I nod and bite back the anxious cry I want to let echo into the night. I don't care if Mags bugs me every second of every day for the rest of our lives—I just want her to be okay.

Liam leads us to a wide river with a steady current. Even

more jungle lies on the other side. A wooden raft bumps against the bank on our side, tethered to a nearby tree. Liam undoes the knot and grabs a long pole that was tied to the tree as well.

"Everyone aboard," he says. "Sit down and hold on."

The raft sways while I climb on, then reach back and help Dexter on. Liam ignores my outstretched hand, jumps down beside me, and pushes us away from the bank with the pole. The sudden shift knocks me off-balance, and I almost fall backward into the water. I plop down next to Dexter and glower up at Liam.

He frowns right back. "I did say to sit down and hold on."

I'm too worried about my sister to argue with him, so I keep my rebuttal to myself.

Liam steers us along the river, which has lots of deep and twisty curves, but very few areas where dense trees don't press in on us from all sides. Along the way, a few nocturnal animals splash into the river and disappear. We pass a couple of snakes winding through the water, completely uninterested in our little raft. But I look away because snakes make my skin crawl.

After what feels like ages, we approach a cave cut into the base of a small tree-lined mountain. Liam steers the raft toward one side of the cave's mouth, where an old dust-covered lantern hangs on the wall just inside. Using his pole, he hooks the lantern's handle and draws it to him. After he brushes the dust from the lantern's surface and opens its door, his magical flame shoots inside, as if returning home.

Then the cave swallows us.

The darkness is cold against my skin, making me shudder. The sound of rushing water bounces off the cavern walls. Sharp stalactites cover the ceiling, looking super creepy and ominous in the orange glow of Liam's lantern.

He picks up a small coil of rope at his feet that's attached to the raft and passes it to me and Dexter. "No matter what, do not let go of that rope. It's about to get rough."

"Rough?" My voice cracks, but I'm too terrified to be embarrassed. "What do you—"

Liam drops to his knees and wraps one arm around the rope and clutches the lantern close with the other. The raft nosedives down a steep drop, clamping my mouth shut and pitching me backward. Thank goodness Dexter grabs me, which is all that keeps me from flying overboard. We hold tight to the rope with both hands. I ignore the way the rough fibers gnaw at my palms as the rapids jerk us back and forth and up and down through the cave system. It feels like my insides are being blown around in one of those lottery ball machines.

"We're almost there!" shouts Liam over the roar of the water. "Hang on!"

The raft steadies before picking up even more speed. Liam holds the lantern high at the helm and the flame intensifies to near blinding, illuminating the path ahead. A cauldron of bats screech into the dark farther down the tunnel, their eyes glowing like tiny suns before disappearing. We're fast approaching a fork in the waterway.

"I think I'm going to be sick," grumbles Dexter.

"Just please do it over the side of the raft and not on my back," I yell over my shoulder.

Liam steers us closer to the left side of the tunnel. "Everyone move to the right and hang tight. We're gonna take the right fork." Before we can resettle, he lifts his pole and vaults us off the left wall, which sends our raft careening to the other side. My heart flutters as we approach the fork. Liam throws himself down next to me and orders us to lean harder. We do.

And we barely make it.

One corner of the raft smacks the middle wall, sending us spinning. Dexter lies flat, but I tumble to one side. Why am I the only one of us who is so uncoordinated? Liam grabs my arm and pulls me close to keep me from falling overboard. The raft spins a couple more times, then rights itself, and we slow down enough for me to catch my breath.

A dim light bleeds into the cavern from a bend up ahead. When we turn the corner, the underground river spits us out into a large open-air cavern with a thin crescent-shaped beach.

The craggy walls tower straight to the clear nighttime sky. Long, leafy vines drape over the ledges, hanging into the cavern's mouth like curtains. The moon casts an eerie pale glow on the rippling water—and on four gigantic stone skulls, each the size of a small apartment building. They're side by side and set deep into the wall, so moss and vines have tangled at their crowns and nestled into the spaces between them. The second from the left is the largest of the four. Its mouth gapes open, revealing a passageway into absolute darkness.

"Umm, whose skulls are those?" I ask Liam, almost too terrified to hear the answer.

He shrugs. "I have no clue where they came from, but I think my mom and the others put them here to scare humans away from the cave."

Of course that's where we're headed. Liam poles the raft to the shore, and we disembark and help drag it onto the beach.

He points to the skulls. "Almost there."

We walk up to the cave's entrance and stop just before going inside. I hug myself against a haunting breeze that whips past me from the gaping skull's mouth—as if trekking through a dark cave isn't terrifying enough, it's just my luck that the entrance is the mouth of a giant skull.

Liam holds his magic lantern aloft and leads us inside.

My hands trace the damp, cool wall as we make our way deeper into the tunnel. I can feel Dexter's presence behind me, hear his footsteps and his heavy breaths. I'm really glad he's here.

"Liam, what is this place?" I ask in a quiet voice, lest I wake up any frightening creatures napping in the shadowy nooks and crannies.

"What's hidden in this cave is the reason I'm bound to this island," he says. "I made an oath to protect it."

"What exactly are you protecting?" I ask.

"I hope you never find out," he says.

"Gee, thanks. That makes me feel *so* much better about our chances of rescuing my little sister from the homicidal shadow demon."

He takes a deep breath in and blows it out through his nose but doesn't respond.

"How long have you been here?" Dexter's voice cuts through the tension building between Liam and me.

"I came here the day before my ninth birthday," Liam says. "I'm thirteen now."

"I'm twelve," I say, though he doesn't seem to care. "So you've been alone for four years?"

"Not exactly," he says. "I had my Echoes."

"Your wha—"

He turns and presses a finger to his lips, then gestures for us to listen.

A faint, high-pitched shriek resounds from somewhere far ahead.

"MAGS!" I cry out, but the shadows only throw my voice back as if taunting me.

We pick up speed along the path, guided by Liam's light. I have so many questions, but he insists on traveling the rest of the way in silence and says my shouting is useless—and annoying. I'd be mad, but all I care about is getting my sister back.

Every time we turn a corner, I think we're getting close to the end, but Liam leads us farther into the shadowy depths of wherever the heck we are. And this cave smells musty. I pray nothing slimy or gross drops on my head.

Eventually, we turn the final corner, and the path dead-ends at a cavern alight with the bright glow of five jewels of different colors, each about the size of a cell phone. They float in the air above our heads. A milky-white one hovers alone above a row of four others: violet, red, green, and azure.

Mags stands directly beneath them. Shadow Man wraps dozens of long spidery arms around her, one covering her mouth and muffling her screams. I remember when I saw him for the first time, the way his limbs stretched and splayed across my bedroom walls. Fear electrifies my insides now, just like it did that night.

I run for Mags, but the purple stone turns into a jet of bright colored light that shoots her in the center of her chest like a laser. Her body explodes with an array of blinding light.

The force of the energy blast blows me back onto my butt. Dexter and Liam grab either side of me and haul me back to my feet, my tailbone throbbing. I blink away the stars in time to see my sister slump to the ground. Shadow Man melts into a pool beside her and evaporates into wisps of black smoke that re-join the darkness.

Mags pushes up to her hands and knees and looks at me with tearful eyes. "Alex . . . I feel funny."

I try to go to her again, but Liam holds me back.

"No!" he shouts.

"Let go of me!" I squirm in his strong grip. "She's my *sister*!" I should never have trusted him. "Dexter!" I turn to him, but he stands back, looking confused and terrified. "Please. *Do* something!"

"You can't help her now!" Liam bellows. "You have no idea what's just been unleashed on this world." He shakes me so hard my head pounds after he releases me.

Mags sits back on her heels and stares at her palms. Black smoke curls from the bare skin of her forearms. Before she can scream, whistling black flames spring to life all around her, swallowing her completely. I scream enough for both of us. Dexter and Liam each hold on to one of my arms to keep me from running to my little sister as the cold-burning fire chills the air.

After several agonizing moments, the shadowy flames die down. My breath leaves me, and I stop struggling against Dexter and Liam, who turn me loose.

Mags stands beneath the remaining four jewels. She's not hurt, but she's not okay, either. She's . . . different. She's dressed in a pristine black jumpsuit with black boots and a cloak with an oversized satin-lined hood, and her hair's been pressed, swept up into a high bun, and adorned with ropes of black pearls. She appears older and . . . intimidating as she appraises each of us.

"Mags . . ." I inch forward, but Dexter grabs my arm again.

"Something's not right," he whispers.

Mags takes a measured step closer.

Liam leaps in front of us and throws his arms out protectively. "Don't come any closer, Moritz."

"What are you doing?" I snap at him. "That's Mags! Who the heck is Moritz?"

"She's not your sister anymore," he snaps back.

"He's right, you know," Mags says. "I'm Death now."

I shake my head. None of what they're saying makes sense. I'm *hearing* Mags's voice and *looking* at Mags's body.

"You hit your head pretty hard before you fell off the ship,"

I tell her in a voice way calmer than I'm feeling. "Come back to the beach with us; help will be here soon. Everything will be better once we get you to a doctor."

She laughs so hard she doubles over. The jarring sound rings in the tall cavern, and Dexter and I share nervous glances.

Mags straightens up and shakes her head at me. "You truly are pathetic, Alex. No wonder everyone abandons you."

"What?" I wrinkle my brow at her. "What's going on with you?"

"Don't be dense," Liam growls over his shoulder at me. "She's been possessed by one of the spirits of the Horsemen. You should've been watching her!"

Horsemen? Like *Horsemen of the Apocalypse?* My knees turn to Jell-O. I think to pinch myself, but I know I'm wide awake.

Mags peers around Liam and smirks at me. "See what I mean? Everyone knows what a mess you are. But don't worry, *big bro*. I'm going to put you out of your misery. Though it's a pity you won't get to witness the apocalypse. It's going to be one of legend."

Liam snatches his wooden bracelet from his wrist and whips it into a full-length staff. He twirls it so hard, its swishes echo off the walls. He swings at Mags's head, but she ducks effortlessly. He flips his hold and swipes at her ankles, but she kicks the staff upward with the side of her foot and catches it in her hand.

She shoves the end of Liam's own staff into his stomach, and he folds over with a breathless gasp. She cracks him hard on his right temple. He collapses in a puff of dust. She sucks her teeth and tosses the staff to the ground beside him.

"Mags, please." I clasp my hands in front of me and approach slowly. "This isn't you."

She clears the distance between us in one swoop and grabs both sides of my head. Her fingers squeeze me like tiny vises, and she shoves me to my knees. The pressure builds in my head until I can feel the blood rushing behind my eyes.

"P-please," I sputter.

Dexter charges Mags, but with one glance from her, an invisible force tackles him, knocking him to the other side of the cavern. I slap at her small arms, but they might as well be made of steel. My knees dig into the dirt as I try to stand up, but she keeps me firmly in place.

She squeezes my head harder . . . and harder . . . and harder.

"Ma-ags," I wheeze.

Black spots bubble into the sides of my vision.

One corner of her mouth twists up in a crooked grin.

The white jewel above us pulses with bright light. Mags glances up at the same time white light sails through the air and smacks into my chest, throwing me backward. I hit the ground with an *umpf* near where Dexter is crouching.

I sit up and rub my throbbing head and drink in precious air. A warm, tingly feeling circulates through me. I stare down at my hands and gasp. They're glowing with dim white light. I look like some kind of freaky human night-light.

Wait . . . Did I just get possessed by one of those creepy spirit jewels too? Is someone else's thousands-year-old spirit inside me right now? Oh, yuck! Uggh . . . I get the sudden urge to claw whoever it is out of my chest. I don't want to share my body with anyone!

I look up and lock eyes with Liam, who's sitting up now—and glowering at me like I was the one who knocked him out.

"You?" His bottom lip quivers. "Why *you*?"

I'm about to tell him I have no idea what's going on, but Mags groans loudly from the other side of the space, reclaiming our attention. She gets up and storms over to me, moving with superhuman speed as if floating. I throw up my arm to shield my face, and she grabs hold of it. Her fingers are way too strong for a ten-year-old, and her hands are ice-cold, like she just got done double-fisting two jumbo freeze pops.

Liam rushes her, but she waves her hand once more, throwing him against the wall at the back of the cavern. Dexter stands up, both hands aloft, and approaches cautiously.

Mags narrows her eyes at him but doesn't attack. "What is this?"

"Put the boy down," he says. "There's no need—"

My entire body surges with raging heat out of nowhere. Intense light shoots through my pores, illuminating every square inch of the space. Mags shrieks and releases me. I stumble backward, unsure what just happened but no less grateful for it.

Mags retreats to the other side of the cavern, near the remaining jewels, clutching her smoking hand, and glares at me. "Orin." She scoffs. "No matter. None of you can stop what's coming."

"Mags, *please*," I say. "I promise I'll get you back home safe."

She lifts her hand, and the three remaining jewels—red, green, and azure—shrink and float down to her open palm. She pockets them, flicks the tail of her cloak aside, and meets my eyes.

"Please!" I beg again. "Come back to the beach with me."

She snickers and looks at us, huddled at the back of the cavern, terrified for our lives. "You're all going to die."

Then she melts into her shadow and disappears.

10

HORSEMEN

APOCALYPSE COUNTDOWN

0 YEARS · 0 DAYS · 0 HOURS · 0 MINUTES

July 7, 2024—12:34 A.M.

I dive for the spot where my little sister just disappeared, clawing at the packed-dirt floor. "MAGS!" I scream, pawing tufts of sand in every direction and ignoring the searing burn of my fingertips.

A set of strong hands grips my shoulders and pulls me back, but I jerk away and keep digging. They yank my shirt collar, snatching me back onto my butt.

Dexter kneels beside me. "She's gone, Alex. And we need to get out of this cave."

I take his hand and let him pull me to my feet. Liam asks if we're okay, but I can't respond. I'm not okay. Not in the slightest.

I'm silent the entire walk back through the cave, as we board the raft, and as we shove off. Liam announces there's another waterway that'll take us back to the beach near where we woke up. He stands like a sentry at the raft's head, steering us along the underground river.

Mags can't be gone. Not like that.

Tears pour down my cheeks. My nose runs too. I don't care. Dexter sits beside me and leans against me like Loren does whenever I'm upset, but it's not the same. I scoot away and feel him look at me curiously, but I turn to stare over the side of the raft into the dark water and listen to the soft splashes of Liam's pole.

Nocturnal creatures concealed in the thick brush on either side of the river belt out a symphony of chatter that seems to grow louder the longer we float in silence. More than a few times, I want to lean over and dunk my head in the water so I can get a moment of peace and quiet to think how I'm going to get myself out of this grand mess I'm in—which I have to understand if I'm going to somehow find a way out of it.

"Liam . . . ," I say. "Please, tell me what's happened to my sister."

His shoulders slump with a heavy sigh and he turns. His cold stare hits me square in the face, but I don't flinch. "Those jewels in that cave contained the Horsemen—the divine spirits responsible for the destruction of my world—Paradisum. And now that they've been unleashed, they'll do the same to yours."

My hand flies to my chest, and my fingers scratch until my chest burns. "Am . . . am I going to turn into some kind of creepy supervillain too?"

He gives me a look that's equal parts frustration and

confusion. "Orin is"—he pauses and stares down, doing a poor job of hiding the tiny hitch in his breath—"good. They were a god too, and they sacrificed themselves to give their Sense to someone who could help stop the Horsemen if they were ever unleashed." He grimaces at me like he wants to punch me in the forehead. "Which is why I'm so confused they chose *you*." The way he says *you* with the pronounced wrinkling of his nose invokes a familiar feeling in my gut.

It's the same one I felt after I was my truest self in front of Sky right before he betrayed me. *Heck no! That's gross.* The echo of Sky's laughter rings in the back of my head.

"*I* was supposed to be their vessel." Liam jabs his thumb into his chest. "Before she died, my mother swore *me* to protect this realm. Orin is supposed to be helping *me*."

I hold up my hands peacefully, despite the anger brewing in the basement of my gut. "Look, dude, I'm just as confused as you are. If I run into Orin somewhere in my mind, I'll let them know you want them to move in with you. I'm happy to give them to you. I promise. All I want is to get my sister back."

He shakes his head. "You don't get it. You're *not* getting your sister back. The Horsemen have her now."

"Who are these Horsemen?" asks Dexter.

"My mother, Navia, was High Goddess in Paradisum," Liam replies. "She ruled our realm along with five other divine beings for many millennia—until four of them turned on her and led an uprising that ended in the destruction of our world." He stares down at the gently bobbing raft as we float downriver.

"If your mother was a goddess," I say, "does that make you—"

"Not fully," he interrupts my question. "I am of my mother, but she made me part human."

"A demigod," I whisper.

The thickets of trees on either side of the river thin up ahead, enough that I can make out the wall of fog in the distance. We're almost back to the beach.

"The leader of the insurrection was Moritz," explains Liam. "My mother possessed the magic of Life, but Moritz had power over Death and had become the curator of judgment in Paradisum. Once the revolt began, he started calling himself *Death*." He glances at me. "Now he's possessed your sister and is surely on his way to release the others."

I hug myself against the chill that suddenly bustles inside me.

"Malakai, who had Wisdom magic, became *Pestilence*," Liam says. "Exo and her Affection magic became *War*. And Zara with her Flora and Fauna magic became *Famine*."

"The Four Horsemen," I mutter.

Oh, man. I wish I could text Loren right now.

The river widens and flows into the dark ocean, which ends abruptly at the impenetrable wall of fog. Biting air wafts over from the thing, raising goose bumps on my arms. Liam steers our raft toward the beach, and we all get off and help him pull it from the water.

Liam trudges through the thick sand toward the area of beach where we first met.

I catch up to him. "And what about Orin? You said they were good."

He nods. "Orin was my mother's best friend and most trusted advisor. They possessed the most powerful magic of all—the Sense. The Horsemen rose against my mother to take over Paradisum with plans to conquer Earth and as many realms as they could get their hands on. She and Orin combined their powers and withdrew all the magic from our world, but that was still only enough to destroy the physical forms of the Horsemen and conceal their spirits in those talismans. Orin sacrificed themself to create a talisman as well so they could help fight the Horsemen—if it ever came to that. My job was to make sure it didn't. And I've failed, which is probably why Orin chose you instead of me. Maybe I'm not worthy to wield that power."

"What is the Sense?" I ask.

"Empathic magic," he replies.

"Um, no offense, but as far as superpowers go, empathy feels pretty low on the Magical Domination Meter, especially compared to folks with names like Death, War, Famine, and Pestilence."

Liam rounds on me. His chest bumps me hard, nearly knocking me onto my already bruised butt. "Orin gave their life to protect your world, and you will *not* disrespect them." One side of his mouth inches up like he just got a whiff of week-old sunbaked garbage. "I should've let you all drown."

I shove him. Hard. With both hands and all my weight.

It catches him by surprise, and his eyes widen as he crashes butt-first into the sand. He leaps back to his feet, gritting his teeth, fists clenched and ready to connect with my face.

Dexter jumps between us, his large brown hands braced

against Liam's and my chests, holding us both at bay. I don't really want to fight Liam, but he was out of pocket. He would probably pummel me anyway, but that's not the point.

"If you're so mad that you don't have the god of empathy squatting inside you, be my guest and take them back!" I shout, leaning around Dexter's arm.

"Too bad it doesn't work like that," Liam growls. "Because the Sense is *wasted* on you!"

"Enough!" Dexter yells, giving us each a stern shove that makes us step back and take a breath.

The loud *chop, chop, chop* of helicopters pierces the tense quiet of the beach. Dexter and I share an expression of shocked relief. Rescue choppers! But my stomach swan-dives into the sand when I remember no one can see this island through the wall of fog.

Liam steps to the edge of the water and lifts one hand, palm facing the fog. His legs quiver, and he grunts, as if using his magic . . . hurts? An orb of fiery light rockets from his hand and hits the mist wall, then disappears inside.

Liam closes his hand, and the orb explodes in a dazzling display of golden sparks, bright as sunrise, that birth thousands of tiny fires that dance along the wall, multiplying and spreading for a few glorious seconds before all the fog burns away.

Three helicopters hover in the distant starry sky beneath the moon. Their cones of light sweep back and forth over the dark waters, searching for survivors.

Liam lifts his hand above his head. A bolt of red energy rockets from his fingertips and sails high into the air, where it explodes into a stunning rainbow of fireworks. He turns and aims another magical flare into the sand close to where we stand. The red ball of light fizzles, illuminating a wide swath of beach in a ghastly red glow.

"Does using magic hurt you?" I ask Liam, who's winded and panting now.

He presses his lips together, and his nostrils flare. "Sometimes, but that's none of your concern."

"Could it . . . kill you?" I ask, but what I really mean is, can it kill *me*?

"Pray we never find out," he says.

Yeah, that's reassuring.

Liam glances at the approaching helicopters and back at us. "I swore to my mother that I would protect this realm from the Horsemen. Now I have to figure out a way to stop what you all have set in motion before it's too late."

I take an anxious step forward. "Let me help. Mags is my responsibility. We can save her together."

He shakes his head. "You've done enough." I start to say something else, but he holds up a hand. "The best way for you to help me is to stay out of my way."

He stalks off toward the forest and disappears into the dark beyond the tree line without a single look back. I don't bother calling out to him, because I know he won't come back. He's abandoning me like everyone else. I'd kick-start his Forgetting, but I have a sour feeling in the pit of my stomach that we're going to see each other again real soon.

"You okay?" asks Dexter.

I'm too numb to talk. I shake my head instead.

I'm very, very far from okay.

The helicopters shine their blinding searchlights on us as they approach. They land down the beach from us and the rescue crew spills out. The loud chopping of the blades muffles their shouts and kicks up a storm of sand until the copters power down.

Dexter jogs over to meet the rescuers halfway, but I stay behind, rooted in the sand like one of the many old palms standing outside the tree line.

I look down at my trembling hands and ball them into tight fists.

All right, Orin. You can't live inside me rent-free.

It's time we started manifesting these "powers"—whatever they might be. And quick.

We've gotta save my little sister from Death.

APOCALPYSE COUNTDOWN

3 YEARS · 89 DAYS

13 HOURS · 23 MINUTES

PART II

Multiple Irvine middle schoolers claim online to have seen a supernatural *Shadow Stalker* in their bedrooms at night.

—JAYCE MARSHALL FOR THE *IRVINE GAZETTE*
APRIL 8, 2021, 11:11 AM

11

ANNOUNCING THE APOCALYPSE

Well, here I am, all alone and laid up in a creaky, uncomfortable hospital bed back in LA.

The Coast Guard brought us straight here from the island. Landing on the roof and getting so much attention from all the doctors and nurses was kinda cool at first—but then the probing questions started. I was afraid all the adults parading in and out of my room would think I'd lost it if I told them the truth, so I just gave them my name, age, and parents' information and then pretended to be too exhausted to talk so they'd leave me alone.

I wish Mom were here.

I've only been at the hospital a couple of hours, but everything that happened before feels like a fading fever dream. I think I'm going to wake up any moment now and see Mags sitting crisscross-applesauce at the foot of my bed, consumed in some new fantasy story that's swept her from this world. But I'm not dreaming. And she's not there.

My little sister is gone.

I'm not sure why my possession is so different from hers. Death took complete control of her, yet I haven't even felt the tiniest twinge of Orin's presence. I wonder if I'm possessed at all. Regardless, my "What I Did This Summer" essay is going to be phenomenal.

I sit upright at a soft knock on my door. It opens before I can respond.

Dad wanders in, dressed in a gray tee, jeans, and slides. He rushes over, tosses a brown shopping bag at the foot of my bed, and seizes me in a hug.

I want to push him off. I'm not unhappy to see him. It's just, this moment feels . . . weird. Dad's never hugged me like this—at least, not that I can remember. Cautiously, I hug him back. The bare skin of my arms brushes against his, and I'm bum-rushed with sadness and guilt that feels like a hundred snakes wriggling in the bottom of my stomach. The serpentine pit of emotion is fathomless and so overwhelming that I fear I'm going to lose myself in it. I push away, and the emotional onslaught stops at once.

What the heck was that?

Dad sits on the edge of my bed, looking wounded. "Nick found me and Angela at dinner and told us what happened. I wanted to go back, but it was too late." He hangs his head and sniffs. A single tear splashes onto his jeans.

It's strange seeing Dad like this. I've never seen him cry before, though I've witnessed Mom crying lots, especially right around the divorce. Because of him.

"The boat was sinking," he continues, "and they were

rushing people onto the life rafts. We had no choice but to get on. It was like something out of a movie. So many people didn't make it. . . . Angela almost drowned." I glance up at him, but he lifts a hand and says, "She'll be fine. She's in a room upstairs."

"I'm glad she's okay." I really am. She's not my favorite person, but I don't want anything bad to happen to her—or anyone.

Dad sits silent for several moments, staring tight-lipped at the floor. "Yeah" is all he says, though it feels like he wants to say a lot more.

Someone knocks, and Dad's head pops up. "Come in," he announces. The small uptick in excitement in his voice makes me think he's glad for the interruption.

Me too.

Nick comes in, and his breath hitches when he sees me. He pauses, then approaches my bedside. "Can I hug you?"

I nod. We embrace, and Nick holds me tight. This hug also feels different—but not like Dad's. Different in a good way. I feel his entire body exhale with relief.

And then I feel something else.

Our bare-skinned contact triggers a wave of emotion that feels like a soft spring breeze. And I realize: It's the Sense. Orin's magic.

I'm breathless at first, and I feel the knee-jerk urge to shove Nick away, but I resist. I don't want to hurt his feelings. Instead, I hold on to my stepbrother and blink against the intrusive influx of his emotions and the disbelief that I can do magic.

Is this what it was like when the X-Men first got their powers?

I'm not sure I like this ability. I can barely deal with my own emotions most times; unrestricted access to other people's sounds like a nightmare worse than Shadow Man. Why would Liam want this so badly?

Nick stands back (taking his feelings with him) and wipes his wet eyes with his forearm. "Man, I was so scared when you jumped overboard after your sis—I mean, our . . . um, Mags." He runs a nervous hand through his twists. "That was mad brave—braver than I think I'll ever be." He looks at me with a brightness in his eyes that makes me feel like a superhero, except I'm afraid his admiration might be misplaced. I'm no hero.

If I were, I'd have brought Mags home.

Dad stands and puts his hands on his hips. "Rescue crews are still searching the ocean for survivors. I have hope they'll find Mags."

"She's not there," I tell him.

He narrows his bloodshot eyes. "What do you mean?"

It feels wrong to see Dad obviously hurting and not tell him what I know. Something warns me I shouldn't, but that's my brand: *Alex Wise never knows when to keep his big mouth shut.*

"Mags was on the island with us." I swallow the lump of anxiety at the back of my throat. "I know this might be hard to believe, but I need you to try."

Dad frowns, his brow set with deep wrinkles, and shares a tentative glance with Nick. "Okay," he tells me with a sigh.

I explain all about Shadow Man, Liam, magic, the Horsemen, Death possessing Mags, Orin possessing me, and the coming apocalypse. The deeper I get into the tale without Dad interrupting to tell me I'm foolish, the easier it is for me to open up about what happened—like how absolutely terrified I was and still am.

Is this what having a real dad is like? Is this what Nick has had with Dad for all that time since he left us?

"Whoa," Nick mutters, taking a shocked step backward.

Dad cuts his eyes at him. "I don't know if I should be upset or deeply concerned."

My heart sinks to my stomach. I knew I shouldn't have said anything.

Dad blows out a heavy breath and puts his hands on his hips. "It's just the shock and the PTSD talking. This is my fault. I should never have left you kids alone—"

"I'm telling the *truth*!" I say louder than I intended, which startles Dad. I look at Nick, who's standing comfortably at the edge of the conflict. "You saw Shadow Man too. Tell him!"

Nick's jaw slackens and his eyes dart from me to Dad. "I—I mean, it was raining pretty hard and it was dark, a-and—"

"Are you for real right now?" I throw my hands up.

"I—I can't remember clearly." He shrugs one shoulder and winces. "It all happened so fast . . . but I think maybe something did kinda pull her over the railing. . . ."

Dad huffs a frustrated breath and rubs a hand hard across his forehead. "Nick . . . please. Just stop. You don't have to do that."

I want to scream. I want to scream and not stop until

everyone in the world is gone. I can't trust Dad *or* Nick, and it was childish of me to ever think I could.

Nick was right. I *am* braver than he'll ever be.

He turns to me, and I look him dead in the eyes. I don't ask him to take up for me again, because I know he won't. Too afraid of disappointing *Pop*.

"I'm going to check on my ma." He whisks out of the room so fast, it looks like he's on roller skates.

The door clicks shut behind him, drowning out the people talking in the hallway and pitching Dad and me back into awkward silence.

"I'm sorry," Dad says. "I don't mean to be harsh. I'm just stressed. Making that call to your mom was the hardest thing I've ever had to do." He sighs, and his shoulders sag like he's going to melt into a pool of self-pity. "She's on the way here now."

I fold my arms and stare up at the television, pretending to be captivated by the cheesy daytime soap opera presently playing on mute. I'm tired of caring about other people's feelings when no one seems to care about mine. And considering I've been cursed with the Sense, I'm convinced the universe has made me the butt of a really ugly joke.

Dad taps my shoulder, and when I turn back, he's holding out a brand-new smartphone. Why didn't his touch cause a rush of emotion like before? What was different?

"We all lost ours in the shipwreck," he says. "There's a store across the street, so I picked up replacements for everyone."

I take the phone, and our fingers brush, zapping me with a quick pang of shame that feels like getting pinched on the fatty part of my upper arm. I flinch, and Dad knits his brow at me curiously. So *that's* the trick! The Sense only activates via skin-to-skin contact. I wonder what else it can do.

"I, uh, got one for Mags, too," Dad says. "Soon as she—"

"Thanks." I unlock my phone, biting back the urge to tell Dad that Mags never had a phone to begin with.

"And I got you some clothes and sneakers," he says. "They're in the bag."

"Thanks," I repeat, busy logging in to my music app to re-download my collection from the cloud.

"Your mom wants to talk to you. I programmed her number."

I navigate to my single contact: "Mom." I give Dad a half-hearted thumbs-up.

The only phone numbers I know by heart are Mom's and Loren's. The thought of my best friend makes a bit of happiness flutter inside my chest. I should call her, too.

Mom answers on the first ring. The frenzy in her voice bleeds through the phone. The roar of the road outside is a low rumble in the background. She's probably got her car on two wheels barreling up the highway to get here.

"Alex, is that you, baby?"

"Yes, it's me." I feel the burn of Dad's warning glare before I even look up at him.

Mom sobs and thanks God for sparing me. "I shouldn't have sent you and your sister with your dad," she laments. "I should've kept you here with me and figured something out on my own. Maybe then Mags wouldn't be . . ." Her voice trails into a hiccup.

She's right. She absolutely should never have sent us with Dad. But what happened to Mags isn't her fault. Shadow Man followed us all the way out to the middle of nowhere in the Pacific Ocean. I have a feeling he would've taken her eventually, no matter where we were.

"It's okay, Mom," I say. "I know what happened to Mags—"

Dad snatches the phone and glowers at me, pressing it to his ear. "Hey, Racquel," he says. "Yeah, I know. . . . Yep, uh-huh. . . ." He scowls at me once more, and I narrow my eyes at him. "Give me a few minutes and I'll call you from my phone."

Dad ends the call and holds the phone out to me, but when I reach for it, he yanks it away. "Do not upset your mother with your fairy tales. This is *not* the time."

"I *wasn't*," I grumble, balling the edge of my sheet in my fists to keep from screaming.

He holds his disapproving stare. "If you won't behave, I'm taking this phone back."

I nod, but only so he'll go away. He clenches his jaw and stares at me for a few seconds; then his face softens. He drops the phone on the bed beside me and starts to say something, but I snatch it and turn away. I don't look back until I hear the door click shut.

Someone knocks again, and I groan and throw myself back onto my pillow. I'm never going to know peace.

The door opens slowly, and the long shadow of a person stretches slowly into the space. My breath catches, and I inch back in my bed. No, it can't be. . . .

My best friend (who is def *not* Shadow Man) tiptoes

inside and stands in front of the door after it closes, blinking at me as if she can't believe what she's seeing. And to be quite honest—girl, same. The sight of Loren Blakewell is like taking the first lick of a soft-serve cone on a sweltering summer day. I completely forgot that she's in LA for Muay Thai camp.

Loren and I both squeal at the same time. I want to leap straight into her arms, but she's at my bedside and nearly on my lap before I can fling the sheet aside. Her touch sets off sparkling tingles of happiness and excitement, followed by the soothing warmth of affection. We squeeze each other so hard that we both burst into a fit of giggles.

She leans back and we take each other in. Aside from a few bruises and scrapes and this flimsy hospital gown, I don't think I look different. Loren, on the other hand—

"I love your locs," I tell her. "But your mom is going to murder you."

She snorts and brushes her fingers through her long ponytail, draping it over one shoulder. "Worth it. Besides, these are faux locs. I had to see how it looked before I fully committed."

"Makes sense."

"Okay, so I didn't beg my cousin to drive me all the way up from Long Beach in rush-hour traffic to this bougie hospital just to talk about my hair." She kicks off her sneakers and pulls her feet up onto the bed. "Dude. Your shipwreck has been *all* over the news. I called your mom this morning and she told me you were here. What happened?"

I hesitate, but she cuts her eyes at me, which makes me smile. I tell her everything.

Her eyes well once I get to the part where Shadow Man snatched Mags overboard. She sits stunned for a moment.

"She's really gone?" Loren asks.

"Not gone." I shake my head. "Possessed. But I'm going to bring her back."

She frowns down at the bed. "I can't believe he was right. All this time, I thought he was full of it." When I raise a brow at her, she says, "Eustice Barnes. Creepy influencer dude from the news."

It takes a moment for the realization to dawn. "Ohhh . . . *that* guy. Do you think he's connected to all this?"

Loren lifts her shoulders and an eyebrow. "Maybe? But how?"

It's my turn to shrug. "Well, he certainly knew a heck of a lot about Horsemen before all this went down. And that makes me wonder if he might know where Mags is."

"He could, but you don't know where he is to even ask."

"You're right." I sigh. "But you . . . do believe me?" I brace myself for the impact of yet another rejection today.

"Well, yeah. I've known you since you've been worth knowing—which is forever, so don't give me that look"—I fix my face—"and I know how much you care about Mags. You wouldn't lie about this."

A single tear falls as I exhale, realizing I've been holding my breath. I swipe it away. "Thank you."

"So . . . ," Loren says, waggling her eyebrows, "are you like a superhero now, or—"

"No," I grumble. "I'm nobody's hero."

"Some people might find your modesty endearing, but it's

annoying." I scowl at her, and she adds, "You literally jumped from a cruise ship into the whole ocean to save your little sister—and that was *before* you got possessed by some ancient god that gave you superpowers."

I appreciate Loren trying to be nice, but it doesn't change how I feel.

Loren's hand zips out and latches onto my bare ankle with a crushing grip, sending an intense shock of surprise sparking up my leg.

"Ow!" I cry. "What—"

"Look!" She points at the television. "Turn the volume up!"

I scramble for the remote and unmute the frantic shouts coming from the scene of a local news station. An anchor sits behind her desk, frozen and wide-eyed, staring somewhere off-camera. She's trembling so hard that her blond wig shakes too.

Several shadows cross the screen as people run in front of the camera. My stomach plummets when I notice my sister.

Mags, dressed as before in all black, strolls along in front of the desk, dragging a black-bladed scythe across its surface, which trails smoking scorch marks behind. The anchor's eyes jump back and forth between the scythe and my sister, who turns to grin at the camera before looming behind the anchor. It's strange seeing Mags without her purple glasses. I guess a side effect of her possession must be 20/20 vision.

"Someone get that kid off the s—" A high-pitched yelp cuts off the voice from somewhere off-screen.

Mags inclines her head. "Appreciate the assist." She gestures to whoever she's speaking to. "Please. Join me."

Loren and I exchange terrified glances. "Welp," she says,

"I don't think you're gonna have such a hard time convincing people anymore."

My sister's first live television appearance steals my breath. She looks like Mags. And she even sounds like Mags. But that's *definitely* not my little sister. Not anymore.

Could she still be in there somewhere?

Three people line up to one side of the terrified news anchor, who's gone white as a cloud. I'm surprised she hasn't fainted yet. Not gonna lie, I probably would've.

Loren and I mutter at the same time, "Horsemen."

She says, "Jinx," then takes my hand in hers. I feel a sharp, unsettling crackle of anxiety, but I hold on to her anyway. Her palm is as slippery with sweat as mine.

Mags introduces her accomplices one by one on live television. "Famine," she announces, gesturing toward the husky Korean American girl with lively azure shoulder-length hair and a round, soft face, despite the lethal scowl she wears like makeup.

"War." A Latinx boy with a jawline as sharp as his flawless fade. He stands beside Famine, and his eyes burn a deep red, like the fire of the underworld.

Both War and Famine look about my and Loren's age. But the fourth Horseman is . . . an odd choice.

"And my final Horseman," Mags intones, "Pestilence." A hunched old white man, whose eyes are closed or his face is so wrinkled that they just look that way. Though it seems he's asleep standing up, he appears to be aware of everything around him. That combined with his ridiculously bushy gray eyebrows and mustache that fan out from his face like ashen palm leaves and the ugly green robe he wears (that I think looks more like a muumuu) amps up his Creep Factor to a solid 10 out of 10.

Someone off-camera clears their throat, drawing Mags's attention. She frowns and rolls her eyes. "And you, too. Yes, come."

None other than Eustice Barnes struts on-screen, and his deceitful ice-blue eyes and smug grin sour my stomach.

Mags walks to the front of the desk and folds her hands ceremoniously in front of her. "And I am Death. And the apocalypse has begun."

The anchor tries to make a run for it, but Famine yanks her back into her seat and stands guard to one side; War takes up the other. Ignoring the scuffle, Mags calls for Eustice to join her. He grins and saunters over, as if strolling onstage to give an acceptance speech. *And the award for Most Pathetic Adult in an Apocalyptic Performance goes to Eustice Barnes!*

"Kneel," Mags commands him. He gives her a questioning look, until she frowns and swings her scythe around.

He drops to his knees and mutters something, but she ignores it. All his prior gusto flees the building when she presses the edge of her black scythe to his forehead. He shrieks, but she rakes her hand through the air in front of his throat, and the screams die inside his gaping mouth. The studio falls silent. Someone whimpers off-camera.

Eustice stumbles to his feet and turns to face the camera. The garnet "R" emblazoned in the middle of his forehead still smokes from the power of Mags's magic scythe. She waves her hand again, and Eustice moans like a sick goat before gasping, his voice returned to him.

"Wh-what did you do?" he asks, still breathless, running his fingers across the symbol on his forehead.

Loren turns to me, one eyebrow raised. "So, uh, are they Team Rocket now?"

I shake my head.

Mags addresses the camera again. "As a gift to the viewers of this message, I'm offering you a once-in-a-lifetime opportunity to join the Horsemen as we shape the New World Order. Those of you interested in pledging your allegiance and becoming Riders, under the leadership of my Rider General—Eustice—come to my tower by sundown. You won't be able to miss it."

She walks back behind the desk, and Famine and War clear away from the anchor, who stares straight ahead, still trembling. Mags sets her scythe on the desk, and the anchor exhales but tenses again when Mags drapes her arms over the lady's shoulders and hugs her close. The poor lady just bites her lips and shuts her eyes, tears rolling down her face.

"And to those who refuse my generosity . . ." My sister sighs dramatically. "Well . . ."

I blink and rub my eyes, because I think I'm seeing things at first. Loren claps her hands over her mouth to stifle a yelp. Nope. It's real.

The anchor's eyes roll to the back of her head. Her skin wrinkles and sags as she ages decades in *seconds*. The woman's expression goes slack and her face gaunt. Her hair grays and falls away in thick tufts. While all this happens, Mags clings to her, eyes closed, relishing the hug as if reconnecting with a close relative she hasn't seen in years—until the woman decomposes to nothing but bones.

The girl who stopped talking to me for two days because I stepped on a spider instead of setting it free in the backyard could never do something so heinous to another person. But something rooted deep in my gut tells me all isn't lost. Mags is still in there somewhere. I can still help her. I only pray she holds on long enough for me to figure out how to save her.

Death lets go, and the woman's skeleton slumps over onto the desk.

The other Horsemen and Eustice gather behind Death.

She lifts her hands and says, "See you soon."

The feed goes black, then flashes to the emergency alert screen.

12

ADULT SUPERVISION

Loren's and my feet hit the floor at the same time.

A muted explosion reverberates from somewhere outside. The building quakes, subtle vibrations jostle my feet, and Loren and I share a nervous look.

"What was that?" she asks.

"I don't know. But I can't worry about that right now. I have to catch the Horsemen at the news station." I rip off my hospital gown and grab the bag of clothes Dad brought.

Loren shields her eyes. "Bruh!" She spins around and redirects her attention to her phone.

"I'm wearing underwear, weirdo." I put on the new clothes and sneakers and tell Loren she can look again.

"I googled the address of the news station," she tells me. "We just have to figure out how we're getting there."

"Hang on—"

"Alex, don't even!" Loren narrows her eyes at me. "I know what you're going to say, Prince Charming, but after what we just saw on the news, there's *no way* I'm letting you do this alone. A pack of rabid hellhounds couldn't tear me from your side." She pokes me hard in my sternum, and I flinch. "You need me. Get over it."

"I was actually trying to tell you that we'll figure out how to get to the station once we sneak out of this place. Dad's lurking."

"Riiiight."

"Let's get out of here."

But before I can reach for the handle, the door opens and Dexter steps inside.

He's dressed in slacks and a short-sleeved button-up, as if he is leaving too. His silver curls are brushed straight back, and he holds a plaid newsboy cap in his hands.

"Loren," he says, surprise in his eyes. "It's good to see you."

"Hi, Mr. Dexter," she says, then casts a worried sidelong glance at me.

"Dexter is fine, please." He looks me over. "I take it you two have seen the news."

"Yes," I say. "And now I think I know where to find my sister."

Dexter folds his arms over his chest. "You should let the adults handle this one, kiddo."

"I told my dad what happened and he blew me off. Even if I can get him to believe me, he'll never let me go. We'll all be dead if we just wait for an adult to save us."

"That was actually one of the reasons I stopped by," he says. "I wanted to speak with your dad about what happened. Perhaps I should go find him."

He turns to leave, but I block the door.

"Please . . . ," I say. "You were there. You know what kind

of danger my sister's in and that I'm the *only one* who can help. Don't snitch—for Mags's sake."

Dexter sighs heavily. "Alex—" He glances at Loren, then back to me. "It's too dangerous. You should at least let your dad know where—"

"Maybe you can just come with us," I blurt out—and ignore Loren's death glare.

It's a brilliant idea. We'll need someone to drive us to the news station anyway. And if we *must* have supervision, there are far worse adults to be stuck with. Unlike Dad, Dexter can be trusted.

Dexter's quiet long enough that my pits start sweating. We don't have time to waste. Mags could already be gone. I have exactly zero experience with godly possession, but I'm willing to bet my entire PlayStation library that the longer the evil murder god controls my sister's body, the more danger she's in. I hope I'm not too late.

"I can't believe I'm allowing this"—Dexter blows out a breath that puffs up his cheeks—"but you're right. Orin chose you for a reason, so you owe it to them to find out what that is, yeah? And we all owe it to Mags to do everything we can to bring her home. So what's the plan, kids?"

"We need to get to the news station," I tell him. "Loren's got the addy."

"All right, then," he says. "Just promise me you two won't do anything too wild."

Loren and I both cross our fingers behind our backs and agree. Dexter nods and stands aside for me to lead the way.

We step out into the hallway, and Loren leans close and whispers, "I hope you know what you're doing."

I have absolutely no idea whatsoever what I'm doing. If knowledge of what I'm doing were sunscreen, I wouldn't have enough to cover an ant's nose.

"Of course I know what I'm doing," I huff.

The corridor outside my room and the nurses station are deserted. The whole floor has an eerie vibe now, which makes my heart beat a bit too fast for comfort. As we make our way to the elevator bank, I notice that most of the patients are still in their rooms.

Where'd all the nurses and doctors go?

Dexter, Loren, and I take the elevator in anxious silence. The bell dings at the ground floor and the doors slide open slowly, unveiling a scene of unbridled chaos. None of us move a muscle. We're all stuck, aghast, inside the elevator.

People of all ages and afflictions spill from the emergency wing, flooding most of the first floor. Rows of gurneys have replaced what must've been the main waiting area, pastel-colored guest chairs removed and stacked against a nearby wall. Gray ash and dirt coat many of the people from head to foot. The explosion we heard earlier—this must be the fallout.

It's hard to make sense of much else with all the wailing and shouting. Hospital staff zoom back and forth, trying their best to care for the sudden influx of patients. I count at least a dozen people with their phones in the air, live streaming the disaster to their social media. It's pure madness.

And it all happened so fast. How could things have gotten this bad so quick?

"We should get moving." I wedge my arm between the closing elevator doors and they slide back open.

Loren, Dexter, and I hold hands, and I become the head of a human daisy chain weaving through the crowded ground floor. I focus on the glowing red Exit sign across the room and not on the apocalyptic scene playing out around me.

When we exit, the doors slide closed after us, sealing off the bedlam in the hospital. Fresh air hits me in the face with the shock of a splash of cold water. Until I realize things outside the hospital are much worse.

We walk down to the corner, all of us silently gaping at the cars lining the streets, the majority swerved aside, some with driver's side doors swung wide and engines still running. A few have been turned into raging metal bonfires.

The scene reminds me of one of those natural disaster movies where a city erupts into chaos after a cataclysmic earthquake or something. And then The Rock parachutes from a helicopter to save the day. Hopeful, I look up at the sky.

But something tells me Dwayne ain't coming.

Glass shatters somewhere nearby, startling me out of my head. A group of people jump through the broken display windows of an electronics store and take off down the street, leaving a trail of stolen items that tumble from the comically large piles in their arms. The store employees, all in uniforms, flee next—in the opposite direction. We're still gaping when they sprint past us. Why are people looting all of a sudden?

A brawl breaks out nearby in the middle of the street

between a throng of people who've all been shouting at one another. The fight spreads, drawing nearer to where we stand. Dexter braces both arms in front of Loren and me and steers us back a few paces. One of the brawlers tosses another guy aside like a bald-headed Barbie doll.

The ground rumbles, sending vibrations up through the soles of my feet. And then the bulldozer rounds the corner.

The people fighting in the street scatter. I want to run too, but my feet aren't listening to my brain right now. The sounds of metal crunching, glass breaking, and people screaming grow louder as the dozer's engine growls and the steel beast barrels closer. It trundles down the center of the road, knocking aside all the abandoned cars in its path. RIDERZ is spray-painted in red on the curved bottom of the dozer's bucket. I can't believe what I'm seeing. I think for a moment that we might've accidentally stepped onto the set of a movie.

An explosion rocks the opposite end of the street. We all jump as a ball of orange fire rolls into the air, resembling a blazing hot-air balloon, followed by thick black smoke that rolls over the roofs of neighboring buildings.

We've just landed ourselves smack in the middle of a danger sandwich.

The doom dozer gets close enough that I can see people hanging off the cab like monkeys—one of them holds a Bluetooth speaker in the air, which blasts a wild heavy metal song. They all have the Rider "R" drawn on their forehead. The driver grips the controls, grinning wide like the Joker, wild eyes glowing bright red as if he's possessed—but there were only five spirits in that cave. This must be something different.

I don't know what I expected when Death announced the apocalypse, but I wasn't prepared for *this*. All those hurt people back at the hospital—and the ones who didn't make it to help in time. The people looting and fighting in the streets. The mindless destruction surrounding us on a chaotic and endless loop. All because of what happened to my little sister in that cave. I had no idea how far the Horsemen's reach went.

"Umm . . . can we *please* get the heck outta here?" Loren says, an anxious tremor in her voice.

"Let's cut through there!" I point to an expansive surface parking lot across from us.

We take off. The whoops of the Riders on the doom dozer get louder, as do the crumpling of steel and the threat of our seemingly inevitable deaths. Dexter hoists Loren over the fence and into the lot first, then me, and finally climbs over himself. He's surprisingly nimble for an older guy. I'm not sure how old Dexter is, actually. Mom says it's rude to comment on adults' age (I dunno why, though, because it's okay for them to bring mine up *all the time*).

Dexter lands next to us just as the doom dozer trundles by, knocking a minivan into the fence. We dash for cover behind a pickup truck and peer over the bed. All the people hanging off the dozer's cab have wild bright red eyes. We watch until it reaches the end of the street and disappears around a corner.

"It's like everyone's under a spell," Loren mutters, following close as Dexter leads us through the maze of deserted vehicles to the street exit on the other side.

"They have to be under the Horsemen's influence," I say,

wondering if War is responsible for this pandemonium, since all these people have the same haunting red eyes as him.

"This is so wild," she says. "I keep thinking I'm going to wake up on my aunt's pullout couch back in Long Beach."

"Yeah," I say with a sigh, "the existence of magic is a little hard to grasp on a normal day, much less in the middle of mayhem."

"Right," she says. "So how are we going to get to the news station in all this?"

"Good question." Dexter surveys the crowded road in either direction. "It's going to be difficult maneuvering a car through this mess."

The news station is in Hollywood and we're all the way in Santa Monica. It'll take forever to get there without a ride. Unless . . .

"I have an idea," I announce. "Follow me."

I steer our group through a deserted alley to a street that appears likewise abandoned, though I can still hear the din of chaos echoing from a few streets over.

I climb onto the roof of a sedan and peer up and down the street until I find what I'm searching for. "There." I point midway down the road with a smile and leap down.

I lead them to a silver Mini Cooper whose driver's side door is ajar—and lucky for us—with the keys still inside.

"It'll be easier to travel in one of these babies." I pat the hood affectionately. "It's just like in that old action movie your mom's obsessed with, Lo."

Her face brightens. "Ohhh, yeah. She made me hate that movie."

Dexter squeezes my shoulder. "Smart thinking, Alex."

Thank goodness for my abundance of melanin; otherwise Dexter and Loren would see me totally blushing right now. It's about time *something* went right for me.

Dexter climbs into the driver's seat, I take shotgun, and Loren hops in back. He starts the engine and immediately steers the car up onto the sidewalk to avoid a pair of sedans blocking the road ahead.

"Seat belts," he tells us.

He doesn't have to say it twice.

13

TOWER OF TERROR

Dexter parks the car a few blocks from the station because news vans from other networks already have the street in front of the building on lock. A small crowd has gathered right outside the building, including several reporters, some preparing for their broadcasts, others already waist-deep in their stories.

We're too late. The Horsemen are clearly gone. And I feel silly for rushing everyone over here for nothing.

"Maybe there are clues inside that could tell us where they went?" Loren says.

Dexter shakes his head. "Looks like they're not letting anyone in."

I take a few steps back and pace, surveying the building and the grounds. "There *has* to be another entrance somewhere."

"Not without secure access."

I spin around and stare up at the guy standing behind me. I didn't notice him walk up. He's so pale and thin he reminds me of Jack Skellington.

"Who are you?" I ask as Dexter and Loren join me, eyeing the guy curiously.

"I'm part of the camera crew—*was* part of the crew." He takes a long blink and a shuddering breath. "When they first walked on set, I thought it was a joke, a group of kids playing a stupid prank. But then the one who called herself Death, their leader—she was just a little girl—she . . . she killed Karen just by *touching* her."

I stiffen at his words. Death might have control of my sister's body, but that was Mags's face on the screen. I'm not sure I'll ever be able to rid myself of the memory of my possessed little sister turning a woman into a pile of bones on television. I can only hope Mags isn't conscious while Death's wearing her skin and doing all these horrendous things.

"Most of the people inside the station bolted the moment the Horsemen disappeared," explains Camera Guy. "Some ran to gather families, others joined in the pandemonium outside, and a few just froze. I don't even know why I'm still hanging around." He shrugs one shoulder. "But judging by how fast the world is skating toward its end, none of us are going to have a home to go to pretty soon."

Camera Guy looks down and chuckles under his breath—and Loren and I share the same *Is this guy okay?* look. "When I was a kid," he says, "my grandma used to scare the crap outta me with all this talk about us living in the 'last days.'" He rolls his eyes. "And the irony of it all is the old crone had the nerve to die *last week*." He laughs. Neither of us joins him, but he doesn't seem to care. "Beat the apocalypse by a friggin' week!" he exclaims, shaking his head. "And weird stuff's been going down *all day*. I heard from a colleague at another station that all the animals at the zoo lost it—all at the same time. Attacking anyone in sight. At Fort Cristine, every single person just disappeared. Over a thousand people"—he snaps the fingers of both hands—"gone. And in Santa Monica, people just up and started looting and rioting out of nowhere."

Santa Monica. Where we just were. Fear boils in my stomach, sending muggy steam curling up through my chest. Everything's such a mess already.

"Do you have any idea where the Horsemen went?" I ask Camera Guy.

He shakes his head. "Sorry, little dude. Whole gang just sank into their shadows and disappeared. Poof. Gone."

"I think I found them," announces Loren, frowning at her phone.

Camera Guy narrows his eyes at me. "Why are you *looking* for the Horsemen?"

I steel my gaze at him. "Because Death possessed my little sister."

He stumbles back a few steps, shaking his head. "You know what?" He tosses up his hands and walks away. I'm not offended, because honestly—MOOD.

Dexter and I huddle around Loren's phone. She's found a journalist's Twitter feed with pictures of a gargantuan obelisk that appeared out of nowhere next to the Hollywood sign. The obsidian building stretches so high that it seems to prick the edge of space. That must be where the Horsemen set up their HQ.

A new post appears at the top of the feed. It's a picture of a

boy slumped against the base of the tower. He appears unconscious. Crimson blood crowns a few fresh wounds on the side
of his head and neck.

They have Liam.

Time pauses to zoom in on the wave of anxiety building
inside me. Liam was the world's best chance, but if *he* already
got thoroughly molly-whopped, what hope do *we* have?

Loren scrolls to the next post and gasps.

The journalist is ending the feed and getting to safety.
They just heard on a police scanner that the military's on the
way to the tower. Chills ripple over my skin.

I've gotta get there before they blow my little sister to bits!

Dexter, Loren, and I ditch the station and pile into the
Mini Cooper. The whole drive to the Hollywood sign, I can't
evict Liam from my mind. He's a royal jerk, but he's also
the only one of us who truly understands what's going on.
Please let him be okay.

Loren fidgets in the back seat, though she's otherwise
quiet. I feel Dexter's eyes on me, but I stare straight ahead
under the guise of keeping watch so we don't run into any
(more) chaotic surprises. I'm not in a talkative mood. I can't
even muster a bad joke right now.

My phone vibrates, and my stomach wrenches when I see
who's calling. Dexter cuts his eyes at me.

I answer it. "Hello," I say, bracing myself.

"ALEXANDER JAMAL WISE, WHERE ARE YOU?"
My phone isn't on speaker, but it sounds like it from how
loud Dad's yelling. "Did you leave the hospital? Are you aware
what's going on outside? You better not—"

"Dad!" I cry, embarrassment heating my face like a blast furnace. "Stop yelling!"

"Where—are—you?" he asks in a much calmer tone, though still very angry. "Your mom will be here in half an hour. I cannot and I *will not* tell her that I lost you, too. Get your butt back here right now and I promise you won't be in trouble."

Going home without my sister is worse than being "in trouble." Worse than death, actually. But Dad can't understand that, because leaving people is what he does. I'm not sure he and I are ever going to understand each other—and frankly, I'm tired of trying.

"Sorry, Dad," I tell him. "I can't."

"Alex—"

I end the call and turn my phone to airplane mode. The awkward quiet that follows sits on my skin like a slimy film.

"You okay?" Loren asks from the back.

I nod. "All good."

"Hey," Dexter says in a soft voice. "It's okay to be scared. I am too. It's also okay if you want me to turn this car around and take you both back to your parents."

"No," I say without a second thought. "I'm not giving up on my sister."

"Me neither," Loren replies from the back. "My cousin went to work after dropping me at the hospital. I texted her that I told my parents what'd happened to Alex and they were on their way to the hospital, and that I'd ride back with them. That story should buy me some time."

Dexter purses his lips with disapproval but nods anyway.

Did you hear that, Orin? We're going up that mountain to save Mags. So now would be a good time to manifest some cool evil-vanquishing powers, unless you're okay with us getting totally owned and probably murdered up there.

Silence. Of course. Useless gods.

Dexter turns onto the small dirt road that winds up toward the Hollywood sign and pulls off the path at the bottom of the hill.

"It'll be easier to sneak up on them if we walk," he says.

"Good idea," I say.

We get out, and I take the lead, trying my best to ignore the frantic beating of my heart and the anxious bubbling in my gut, both telling me to turn around and run for my life. But Camera Guy was right. If I don't confront Death, there might not be a home to go back to—for me or anyone.

The packed-dirt path is dusty and surrounded by flowering weeds, which make me sneeze several times in succession. I hope my hay fever doesn't give us away. Having to deal with allergies in the middle of the apocalypse feels like especially heinous and unfair torture.

Loren's footsteps hang close behind me, but when I lose the sound of Dexter's, I turn back to check on him. We've barely made it a quarter of the way up the hill, but he's already lagging, winded and clutching a stitch in his side. He takes off his newsboy cap and fans himself with it, his silver curls now plastered to his head with sweat.

"I'm slowing you down," he says.

I feel bad, but at least he admitted it before I had to say it.

"You should stay with the getaway car." I nod toward the

hilltop. "I don't know what's waiting for us up there, but we might need to escape fast."

"And you can also keep someone from stealing our ride," Loren adds.

Dexter lets out a deep breath. "You're right, but you two can't go up there alone. It's way too dangerous."

"It's the end of the world," I tell him. "Everything's dangerous. But I'm the only person who can help my sister. You can't stop me from doing this."

"Then what's your plan, kid?" he asks.

My stomach rolls over, and I hope neither he nor Loren can see on my face the absolute terror I'm feeling. "I'll figure it out before we get to the top."

I turn and head up the path before Dexter can say another word.

Loren follows and glances over her shoulder. "He's heading back to the car."

"Good," I mutter. "I don't need more witnesses to my brutal death."

She stops and yanks on my T-shirt, nearly sending me toppling down the hill. "I might be riding with you, but I'm not planning on dying with you today. We need to come up with a real plan *now*."

The sun bears down on me as intensely as Loren's glare. "My only experience with this stuff is from movies," I admit, unabashed.

Loren rolls her eyes. "Well, naturally, *same*—"

"*But*—I believe the real Mags is still in there somewhere and maybe I can reach her."

"Hang on a sec." She holds up a finger. "Umm, wasn't this the *exact* plot from that god-awful horror movie you made me watch last year?" Her brow furrows. "The one about the lady who thought her cat was possessed by a demon but still tried to be its friend anyway. Oh, what was the name? It was something *really* ridiculous. . . ."

"*Kittyclism*," I grumble.

She snaps her fingers. "Yeah, that's it. And I distinctly remember Mr. Tum-Tums eating her at the end."

"Ohhh," I say. "So *that's* how it ended."

"Are you kidding me? You made me watch that two-hour train wreck and you didn't even finish it?"

I wince. "Sorry. I fell asleep."

The truth is that contrary to the silly name, that movie was utter nightmare fuel. I chickened out halfway through. But that's not what's important here. Stay focused.

"Aaaanyways," I say, dragging out the word so it's clear we're moving on, "if my plan works, maybe I can help her fight back against Death and regain control, hopefully long enough for us to get her back to Mom and Dad so they can get proper help."

"And who are they going to call?" She raises an eyebrow. "The Avengers? You all are literally possessed by ancient gods from another world."

I blow out a frustrated breath. "I don't know, Lo. Do you have a better idea?"

She shrugs. "Let's go. If I die on this hill today, I'm going to annoy you for the entirety of the afterlife, so you better not screw this up."

"That is a thought more terrifying than the Horsemen. Thanks for the perspective."

"Anytime," she says, shoving me ahead.

We continue our stealth trek up the path toward the black tower looming over Hollywood. We're both drenched with sweat and out of breath by the time we make it to the top. I wish I'd remembered to pack some water. Mom would've. I hope she's okay.

The sun glints off the ebony tower, which resembles an impossibly supersized Washington Monument. It must've taken a great deal of powerful magic to create something so colossal so quickly—a thought that further rattles my already fragile nerves as we crest the hill.

The path brought us up on the tower's right side, behind the Hollywood sign, which now reminds me of an eclectic fence across the tower's front yard. Death and the other Horsemen huddle nearby with their backs to us. Liam's not far off, still half-conscious and leaning against the base of the tower. No one notices us approach.

I pull Loren behind some tall bushes so we can hide for a sec to get a better view. As if things weren't already complicated enough, the loud *chop, chop, chop* of helicopters resounds in the distance. Loren, the Horsemen, and I all turn our attention to the sky at the same time. A squadron of military choppers head toward us from the city.

"Well, this sucks," mutters Loren.

"It might actually be a blessing," I whisper. "This distraction could work in our favor."

The helicopters keep a cautious distance, circling the

airspace above the bottom of the hill below the sign. It's good they came from the opposite direction we did: less chance they'll block our escape route back to the car.

Doors of a few of the aircraft slide back and soldiers rappel down ropes to the ground, where they assemble and organize their ranks. They even brought several tanks, which idle at the foot of the minuscule mountain, barrels angled up to where Death stands to one side of the "H" with her hands on her hips, staring down at them. The other Horsemen gather around her, all calmly observing the military.

Pestilence lowers himself to the ground and sits crisscross-applesauce, eyes shut, as if meditating. Famine stands between two oversized jungle cats—one black panther and one leopard. Their tails, thick as baseball bats, swish back and forth as Famine strokes the back of their necks lovingly. War stands to the right of her, his thin brown arms crossed over his chest.

"I have a plan," I whisper to Loren.

"A revolutionary concept," she whispers back.

"You're gonna sneak over to Liam and get him back down the hill while they're distracted."

"And what about you?"

"Once you two are out of here, I'm going to reveal myself. Death will most likely send the others to handle the Army and deal with me herself."

Loren hugs me tight, and for that teensy stretch of time, I feel invincible. Maybe it has something to do with the extra rush of nervousness brought on by her touch, which intensifies the adrenaline already pumping through me. It'd be nice if I knew how to turn this Sense on and off. I don't want to know what someone's feeling every time their skin touches mine.

"Go now," I tell her. "Before we lose our chance."

She nods and takes off in a silent crouch. She's only halfway when Famine turns around. I bolt upright at the same time Famine's hand whips out and the ground rumbles in response.

Loren freezes and tumbles backward as the earth splits in front of and behind her. A bunch of spiny stalks rocket up from the ground with blazing speed, twirling around her. In seconds, they mature into thick cacti with shiny golden needles, each the size of a pencil. They look sharp enough to pierce stone. Loren's stuck mid-fall, in a crab-walk position, one foot planted, the other poised precariously above razor-sharp needles. My best friend's entrapped in a deadly cacti prison. *Great.*

She looks terrified. "Alex! Help me!"

Famine's jungle cats both growl, baring fangs that send a shock of fear straight through my heart. Death, War, and Pestilence all whip around.

Death's eyes find me first. "Well, *well.*"

She steps forward, and my skin ices.

14

BATTLE ON HOLLYWOOD HILL

War moves to apprehend us, but Death throws out an arm, halting him. Pestilence adjusts so he's sitting with one ear toward the amassing army at the base of the hill, the other turned to us.

"Mags," I beg. "I *know* you're in there. It's not too late to stop this."

Death's mouth curls up into a twisted grin.

It's tough standing here in front of my little sister who isn't my little sister and begging her to stop destroying the world. Mags might be the most annoying person I know, but she's one of the few people I know as well as myself. Death's version of her, the one with the dark eyes, silk-pressed hair, and hostile glower, hurts to watch.

But my sister *has* to be in there somewhere.

One of the helicopters hovers closer, the wind from its propellers kicking up loose sand; harsh grains whip against the bare skin of my legs. The door opens and a soldier in fatigues holds up a megaphone. Before he can speak, Death reaches behind her back and pulls out her smoking scythe—from no-where.

She tosses the weapon up to catch it by the base of the handle, then hurls it. The scythe flips end over end, cleaving the air, the sun's rays reflecting majestically off the dark blade. It slams into the side of the chopper with a *sccchwwwwing!*

One hand on her hip, Death waits patiently.

Alarms blare inside the wobbling aircraft. It struggles for stability in the air, then tilts violently. Parachutes deploy as the soldiers evacuate before the massive thing nose-dives into the hillside. The explosion shakes the ground. A ball of fire roars to life and gives way to thick rolls of black smoke rising from the burning wreckage. I need to stop this.

War turns to Death. "Would you like me to handle the rest?"

Death shakes her head. "I got it." Poised at the top of the hill overlooking the mass of armed forces, she flicks her wrist—and every person, every helicopter, every jeep and tank, all of them, drop into their shadows as if falling through a trapdoor. In an instant, the atmosphere atop the hill quiets enough to hear the wind whipping sand around my feet.

I'm not sure I'll ever get used to existing in the same space as magic. It's like I've stumbled into one of Mags's fantasy books, except . . . this is real life. Death has the power to kill any liv-ing thing with her bare hands or her murder scythe and can make people vanish into their shadows to gods-only-know-where. I'm afraid to find out what the others can do.

I hope all those military people are okay, wherever they are.

"Make sure we don't have any more of these sorts of

interruptions," Death orders War. "And take Famine and Pestilence with you. They deserve to have some fun too."

"You sure?" Famine asks, narrowing her eyes at me and Loren.

Death snickers. "I can handle things here. I'll catch up to you momentarily." She waves a hand and Famine and her oversized cats, War, and Pestilence each disappear into their shadows.

I should be relieved, but my skin feels electrified now that the other Horsemen have left Death alone with us.

Liam groans and shifts his feet, but he's not completely conscious yet.

Loren growls from inside her cacti cage, her teeth bared. "On everything I love—I'm going to murder that girl when I get out of here."

Death lifts an eyebrow at her and scoffs.

"Mags," I plead. "I know you're there. If you can hear me, you have to *fight*."

"Aww," she coos. "That's so sweet. Too bad your sister's gone."

I shake my head and bite my bottom lip until it stings. I don't believe that.

Orin! You have to help me! Do something!

Maybe they just need a little push. I hold one hand out in front of me, my palm facing Death. I close my eyes and grit my teeth, concentrating all my thoughts on pulling my sister back from wherever Moritz or Death has shoved her inside her own mind. I'm not sure what I'm expecting—an energy blast? Telekinesis?

I open my eyes and immediately feel silly when I realize Death still stands in front of me, grimacing, hands on her hips, untouched.

Gee, thanks, Orin!

"This is silly." I storm right up to her, channeling my best impression of Mom's authoritative voice. "You're my ten-year-old sister, and you are *my* responsibility, which means you have to listen to me. And I say you're coming straight home with me *now!*"

I reach for her, but she sidesteps and pivots around me with the grace of a dancer. She grabs a fistful of my shirt collar and slams me onto my back. My view tilts up to the dense blue of the sky before the ground knocks every wisp of air from my lungs. I let out a moan and roll onto my side. Dust swirls around me, and I scramble to my feet, coughing.

"You might have my sister's voice, her body, and even her pronouns," I tell Death once I catch my breath, "but you will *never* have her."

She frowns. "And you'll never speak to her again."

"Maybe not until I evict your crusty butt."

She steps forward, and I stumble back.

She's so focused on me that she doesn't notice the soldier who just crested the hill. I'm not sure how they missed being disappeared or where they were hiding, but I'm not questioning it. They creep toward Death with the red laser eye of what I realize is a Taser (once they're close enough) aimed at her back. Maybe they'll knock her out with that thing and that'll be our ticket to getting her back to safety.

"Umm . . . So, this superhero standoff is real cute and

all," Loren interjects, "BUT CAN YOU PLEASE GET ME OUT OF HERE?! I CAN'T HOLD THIS POSE FOREVER!"

I toss her an *I'm trying my best* look, which she responds to with a *Try harder* grimace.

Death ignores her, still laser-focused on me. "I've probed every inch of your little sister's precious mind. I know all about you and your humiliating existence, Alex Wise. And that's how I know you'll never stop me." She steps closer so we're nearly face to face, angles hers up at mine, and lowers her voice so only I hear. "Because you don't have what it takes."

My sister's eyes were once soft brown, like the coats of the wild bunnies we'd find in the yard every morning before school. But now they're solid black—not dark with the mysteries of space or the peace of night; instead, they invoke feelings of unbridled anguish and agony. They're as haunting as Shadow Man himself.

POP!

The prongs from the soldier's Taser smack so hard into Death's back that she lurches forward. They sizzle and crackle, silhouetting her against arcs of bright gold light, but otherwise appear to have zero effect. She reaches around, yanks the prongs out, and flings them aside.

It didn't work. My heart has retreated to my butt, and my brain has flown out the window. What am I supposed to do now?

She turns to face the soldier as two more tanks arrive at the bottom of the hill. Without hesitation, they fire four missiles, each a deafening blast that rattles my chest, one after another. I throw myself to the ground as the rockets zip over the Hollywood sign. But the tower's surface turns viscous, and its facade ripples in the daylight like the surface of a pool. The missiles sink slowly into the tower and disappear. There are no explosions.

A handful of other soldiers flank the first. They all fire their Tasers, but Death bats every crackling prong aside. With a frustrated grumble, she yanks her scythe from the air behind her back and stalks toward them. The soldiers flee down the hill, but Death doesn't stop. I consider following, but it's no use. I won't be able to reach Mags—not like I planned. Apparently, Liam isn't the only one who flamed out today.

"Uggh . . . Alex," groans Liam. "Over here."

I rush over and kneel beside him. He's pretty banged up. I hope nothing's broken.

"What'd they do to you?" I ask. "How bad is it?"

"I'm fine," he snaps, then grunts as he pushes himself to a seated position.

"Glad to see your attitude's fine too."

He scowls at me and pulls off his wooden bracelet. It extends to a full-sized staff in a split second. "Use this." He pushes it into my hands and points to where Loren's still entrapped.

I hurry over to her, but my mind goes blank when I look back and forth between the cacti and the staff. What am I supposed to do with this?

"Are you just gonna stand there or are you gonna get me the heck out of here?" grumbles Loren.

"I . . . uh . . . okay, um, just hang on, sheesh."

I'm already over all this responsibility. I don't even like being in charge, yet I keep finding myself in these predicaments.

I glance back at Liam, who tries to get to his feet but slumps back to the ground with a painful-sounding *oomph*.

So it's all up to me. No pressure.

I poke the closest cacti with the end of the staff and find it strangely pliant.

"Use it like a lever," Loren says. "They're only plants. They should break at the base."

I stick the end of the staff between two cacti and press all my weight onto it. I'm a bit overzealous, because when the plant snaps, I tumble forward and face-plant in the dirt.

I jump back up and brush myself off. *Okay. You can do this. Get it together.*

I set to work breaking enough cacti for Loren to bust out. After I've made a wide enough space, I sweep the broken remnants aside, then haul her from the plant prison.

Once she's free, we tumble back onto the ground. Her fingers brush my arms, cooling my skin with relief and breezy gratitude. She reaches out and pulls me to my feet.

I gesture to where Liam sits slumped over, his head hanging over his lap. "Help me get him out of here."

The bottom of the hill has gone quiet except for the occasional loud pop or hiss from the countless mounds of burning wreckage littering the landscape. I risk a quick look and find the foot of the mountain completely deserted. I expect to see Death standing in the middle of a field of bodies, marveling at her handiwork, but no one's there—dead or alive.

"Alex," Loren calls, drawing me back to the task at hand. She's already gotten Liam to his feet and pulled one of his arms over her shoulders. His head lolls, and he complains in a soft moan, but he seems just conscious enough to stumble down the hill with our help.

"Right!" I run over and duck under his other arm, helping shoulder his weight.

A shock of fear zips through my gut as our arms brush. For a moment, I almost slide from beneath Liam's touch, but Loren glances at me and I hold steady. Then my heart cinches with a tremendous feeling that's familiar, yet so very different—and intense. It's like my heart is on fire and I'm powerless to put it out.

I bite my lip until it hurts, which distracts from Liam's invasive emotions. I can't imagine one kid having to carry all this alone.

Loren and I make short work of getting Liam back down the hill, though we slip a dozen times each and almost send all three of us barreling down the slope.

Dexter is leaning against the rear of the Mini Cooper with his arms folded, like a worried parent. When he sees us, he jumps with surprise, throws open the back door, and scrambles over to help us load Liam into the car.

"What happened?" he asks.

Loren climbs in and helps us get Liam inside. Once he's lying across the seat with his head in her lap, he releases an exhausted breath and falls unconscious.

"We'll explain on the way," I tell Dexter as I take the front seat.

He gets in too, and the tires kick up a storm of dust as he peels our little car from the dirt path out onto the main road.

I glance to the back seat. Loren's worried eyes meet mine. She holds Liam's head steady as the car jerks and jolts from Dexter steering onto and off of sidewalks and grass to avoid blockages in the road.

The pain Liam felt—*we* felt—goes deeper than his physical wounds. I wonder what it is and if it has anything to do with the amount of fear I Sensed coming from him. If we were friends, I'd tell him I'm just as afraid as he is, but slightly less afraid than I was before we linked back up. Together, we have a better chance at stopping the Horsemen and rescuing my sister.

Liam saved my life on the island, and we just saved his, so we're even now. He's not my favorite person I've ever met, but I don't think either of us can deny any longer that we need each other.

We're facing the literal end of the world.

And I'm honestly not sure we're going to survive it.

15

LOVE IN THE TIME OF APOCALYPSE

"We've gotta find somewhere to hide out until Liam recovers," I announce.

"We could always go back to the hospital—where your parents are," Dexter suggests.

"No!" Loren and I both shout in unison.

He holds up a hand. "Fine, fine."

"I have an idea," Loren says. "The Hollywood Hills are full of rental properties. My parents and I stayed in one once when we came out here for vacation. Maybe we can find an empty one to hang out in for a while."

"But the Hills are so close to the Horsemen's tower," Dexter says. "Wouldn't somewhere a bit farther away be safer?"

I shake my head. "Loren's idea is brilliant. I'll bet they won't be expecting us to hide in their backyard. There are far worse places to ride out the apocalypse than a posh rental house in the Hills." Dexter looks like he's about to say something negative and adultish, so I add, "If you're not okay with any of this, we won't hold it against you if you ditch."

Although I care deeply about Dexter and humbly appreciate his chauffeur services, risking our lives to save the world is hard enough without the added stress of an apocalypse chaperone.

Dexter frowns, deepening the wrinkles in his brown skin. "I'm not planning on abandoning you kids."

"Sorry." I feel like a jerk when I notice the somber expression lingering on his face. "But I have to do this—"

"—for your sister," he finishes. "Look, I understand. I just want you kids to—"

"—be safe." I give him a satisfied smirk when he rolls his eyes. "I get it too. I promise to be safe if you promise to trust us."

He blows out a long, exaggerated breath. Sometimes he reminds me of Mom—which is horrifying.

"Me too," Loren chimes in from the back.

"Well, I suppose we have a deal, then," he says.

My new phone has died already, so Loren navigates us to the residential area of the Hills. Along the way, she passes her phone to me to check out potential vacant homes she finds on vacation rental sites. No less than three minutes in, my mind disengages, and I nod at her suggestions robotically. For all I know, I could be agreeing to setting up base in a haunted asylum. But most of my brain's processing power has been redirected to replaying and analyzing Death's last words to me. *Because you don't have what it takes.* What does that even mean?

Not being good enough has kinda become my signature. To my family. To my friends. Everywhere I go, there's a giant sign above my head flashing USELESS in neon colors. I've gotten used to it. But for whatever reason, what Death said cuts deeper—and I can't figure out why.

The car's engine strains as we climb the nearly vertical streets winding through the Hills. The roads are narrow and twisty, only big enough for one car to navigate at a time. More than once, Dexter has to swerve to one side to avoid being run over by a gargantuan luxury SUV with mounds of designer luggage strapped to the roof. I'm even more grateful for our tiny car, which is fantastic at ducking off into tight driveways or side streets in an instant as others careen downhill.

However, not all the Hills residents are getting the heck out of Dodge. Some are hilariously fortifying their multimillion-dollar homes to weather the impending apocalypse. Like this one guy we pass, who's standing with a hand on his hip, the other clinging to an espresso cup as he orders around the people installing barbed wire along the top of his fence. Farther along, a couple hurries up their driveway, each balancing a teetering tower of toilet paper packages in their arms. Across the street, three kids bolt out of a yard, carrying armfuls of lemons and apples, no doubt taken from a tree on the property. One house even has armed security guards outfitted in black suits complete with mirrored aviators and fancy earpieces standing in front of a heavily chained front gate.

The apocalypse has been underway for barely a few hours and the entire city has gone into a frenzy. I wonder what's going on back in Palm Vista.

I hope Mom's okay. I should charge my phone ASAP once we're settled and call her. She at least deserves an explanation—whether she believes me or not.

My mind wanders to Sky and how he and his family are faring in all this. I wonder if they made it to Santa Monica, if he's somewhere across town right this moment. But I dash those thoughts before they whisk me away. I can't get consumed in Sky's world right now—not while the real one's at stake.

Finally, Loren directs us up the driveway of a large house tucked comfortably behind the lush greenery of a short side street.

"This one's perfect and looks empty," she chirps. "Four bedrooms, four bathrooms, and even has a pool and a barbecue."

"This isn't exactly a family holiday," Dexter says as he parks the car and climbs out.

"I call owner's suite," Loren says, ignoring him.

A long set of concrete steps climb toward the black double front doors of the two-story white stucco home. A short but steep hill leads to a squat iron fence that sections off the sides and backyard from the front. It certainly looks much nicer than any place I've ever lived. I feel a twinge of guilt for taking it over like this, but it's for the greater good and all that.

"I wonder if there's an alarm system?" I ask.

"I'll take care of it," Dexter says.

I wrinkle my brow at him. "How?"

He grins. "Stay put. Be right back."

Loren and I share a curious glance, then we watch Dexter hoist himself up over the fence and disappear on the other side. After about ten long and quiet minutes, the front door of the house opens, and Dexter struts out. He comes around to Loren's side of the car and opens the door. She slides out carefully, minding Liam's head.

Dexter scoops up Liam, who stirs but doesn't wake, and cradles him in his arms. "Let's get him resting in one of the bedrooms."

"How'd you get inside?" I ask.

"The house has one of those old alarm systems that's easy to bypass." When I narrow my eyes, he blushes and looks away. "Eh, some parts of my past are better left there, yeah?"

I shrug. "I guess."

Even though I bonded with Dexter more than other teachers, it wasn't until this moment that I realized how many gaps there still are between us. He knows pretty much everything about me—even some stuff I wish he didn't—but I can't say the same about him. I follow Loren up the steps to the front doors and check off a mental list of what I know about Dexter's past.

He's originally from Santa Monica.

He doesn't have a good relationship with his dad (twinsies!), who he tried hopelessly to please in the past.

He moved to Palm Vista three years ago to take a job as a teacher at the elementary school.

He's never talked about siblings, so I assume he doesn't have any—at least, none living.

He told me once that his mother died when he was a teenager, but he doesn't want to talk about the circumstances surrounding her death, which I understand.

He doesn't have friends—none like Loren is to me—and claims to prefer being alone.

And he likes desserts and old books. That's about it.

It'd be kinda cool if he turned out to be some legendary assassin or jewel thief turned awesome elementary school teacher. No matter who he used to be, I'm thankful Present Dexter thought to switch on the AC, because a cool blast smacks me delightfully in the face as soon as I step inside. A relief after baking in the California sun all afternoon.

Loren shows us to one of the bedrooms, where Dexter deposits Liam on a plush, comfy-looking bed that makes me tired just standing beside it. A trio of tall, curtainless windows face west, where the sun has swollen to a deep orange and casts an enchanting glow the same color across half the room. Liam sinks into the bedding, and a glimmer of what seems to be relief settles onto his face. I slip his shoes off and set them on the floor by the bed.

Loren reappears with a first aid kit she found somewhere in the kitchen, and she and I stand aside and watch quietly as Nurse Dexter tends Liam's wounds. He begins by disinfecting and bandaging a large cut on Liam's forehead; then he cleans and inspects the bruises on one side of Liam's face and shoulder that have turned various shades of purple.

"It looks—and probably feels—much worse than it really is," Dexter tells us. "Nothing seems to be broken. I think he'll recover just fine, but he needs rest for now."

Quietly, we file out of Liam's room and regroup in the kitchen, which is easily five times the size of ours at home. In the center is a large stone island with several uncomfortable-looking stools tucked underneath, and there are matching oversized stainless-steel appliances. Dexter immediately sets to plundering the fridge and cabinets, which are all empty except for dishes, pots and pans, and other essentials.

But most importantly, I spot a helpful bank of chargers to one side of the kitchen counter. I plug my phone in and leave it to charge so I can call Mom later. I'm high-key dreading the conversation, because I'm sure she's going to try to convince me to come back to the hospital—which ain't happening. But the drama will be worth it to know she's okay.

To the right of the kitchen is a narrow dining area with a bare wooden table and six chairs. I run my fingers along the soft cream velvet of one as I wander around the table. On the other side is a set of sliding glass doors that lead to the patio and pool, which has a stellar view of the city below.

I push the door aside and step out onto the patio. The familiar pungent smell of chlorine hits me as I walk by the small rectangular pool and Jacuzzi. It reminds me of going to the pool at the Y with Loren and Mags every summer. I wonder if I'll ever have a normal summer again.

I lean on the glass fence at the edge of the space and peer down the steep drop that ends in the lavish backyard of another house slightly farther downhill. Two cars zoom down the windy roads and vanish between the city buildings below.

"We should make a supply run before it gets dark." Loren's voice comes from behind me, giving me a start. She leans beside me. "There's a small grocery store on the corner of Hollywood Boulevard and the street we took up the hill. There are also a few clothing stores nearby we can hit up. I'm dying to take a shower and change out of these disgusting clothes."

I stare down at my shirt, which was white once upon a

time. Now it's covered in a layer of sweat and grime and—ugh, is that Liam's blood? Yeeeaaah ... A bath and some fresh clothes might not be such a bad idea.

"But we don't have any money," I say.

She snorts. "Dude, we're operating on apocalypse rules now. Money's useless."

"How are you so laid-back all of a sudden?"

"You're not the only one struggling, goober. I'm just trying to forget how utterly terrified I am and how much I miss my family, because that's what my best friend needs right now. My cousins and mom were calling and texting so much that I had to turn my phone off. Whether the world ends or not, my mom is gonna end *me* when I get back home."

Suddenly, I feel like a bucket of fart slime. "I'm sorry."

"It's okay," she says. "It's probably best if Dexter stays behind to keep an eye on Liam. There's a golf cart in the garage we can drive to get supplies. I'll go get it ready."

"'Kay. Meet you out front in five."

"Bet." She goes inside.

I stare out at the city for a little longer, and when I turn back to the house, Dexter's stepping out to join me.

"Loren and I were about to go for supplies," I say, hoping to dissuade him from idle chitchat.

"She told me." He places his hands in his pockets and grimaces at his severely creased loafers. "What's next?"

"When Liam wakes up, we'll come up with a plan together."

Dexter's brow pinches, and he opens and closes his mouth, as if struggling to decide whether to tell me something.

"What is it?" I ask.

"I'm just worried you're putting too much faith in someone who already abandoned you once."

His words are a sour prick in the pit of my stomach. "Trust me—Liam and I are a *long* way away from being friends, but he's the best chance we have at helping my sister, and he's the only one who can help me understand Orin's magic. We need him right now."

"I'm only looking out for you, Alex. Truth is, we don't know much about Liam. I think you and I both know from personal experience that we should be cautious with trust, yeah?"

I'm not gonna lie: this conversation makes me want to leap over the fence and tumble down the hill. Every day of fourth grade, Larry tormented me at school and Dad's absence haunted me at home. But Dexter distracted me from the hurricane of emotions constantly blustering inside me by introducing me to new things, like orchestral music, which spawned my love of soundtracks. I trust and appreciate Dexter, but I just don't have the capacity for any additional problems right now. I haven't dealt with the ones already on my plate.

But I nod anyway and leave him standing alone outside.

My phone's charged enough to use again, and since I'm a glutton for punishment, I call Mom.

She answers right away.

"Alex! You and Loren need to get your butts back to this hospital right now! Her parents are here too, and we are worried *sick!*"

"Well, they're in the right place—"

"ALEXANDER!"

"Sorry."

Her voice cracks. "Please, baby. It's too dangerous for you to be out there alone. I saw Mags on TV too, and I know you're upset about everything that's happened to your sister, but y'all kids come back home and let us handle it. This isn't your burden."

"Caring for someone who loves you is never a burden. Remember?" When she responds with silence, I say, "I promise I'll be safe. I'm going to bring her home, Mom. I just need you to trust me."

"Alex, please listen to reason."

"I'll text when I can to let you know I'm okay. At least once a day. More if I can manage. Bye."

I end the call and turn off my phone before she calls back. Guilt laps at my conscience, but I have to do this.

Loren's pulled the golf cart around and is sitting in the driver's seat glowering at me as soon as I step out the front door. "Took you long enough! I was about to come drag you out. It'll be dark soon."

I trudge to the passenger side and plop down onto the seat with a sigh. "Let's go."

She doesn't move. We both glance up at the front door at the same time to see Dexter part the curtain and peek out at us. Loren switches the cart on and pulls out of the driveway.

"Did something happen after I left?" she asks.

I share Dexter's warning as she carefully drives us downhill.

When I finish, she says, "Don't kill me for this, but I don't think he's wrong." That draws a sideways look of ire from me.

"Liam did leave you hanging right after a god from *his* world possessed you and your little sister."

Loren slams on the brakes to avoid a squirrel dashing across the road in front of us, nearly launching me over the hood.

"Sorry," she mumbles when I frown at her. "*Pay attention and think for yourself* is something my Grandma Sadie told me a lot before she died. Liam *did* leave you on that beach, and we *don't* know a whole lot about him. Dexter's right about that much. But only you get to decide how you feel about another person."

"Ugh," I groan dramatically. "You're right."

She chuckles. "I'm always right."

During our journey, the subtle glow of twilight brings an evening chill to the air, along with pockets of dense shadow. We're almost to the deserted intersection at Hollywood Boulevard, which I can see just up ahead, when something stirs off to the side of the street. I catch a glimpse of what I think might be a person, cloaked in darkness.

They stand behind an iron fence, clinging to the railing with both hands. Their head turns slowly, following us as we pass.

I grab Loren's arm. "Stop!"

The cart lurches to a halt. "What's wrong?"

I squint into the darkness behind the gate, barely making out the silhouette of—

A rush of cold tackles me. Shadow Man. Is he back?

But why? The Horsemen have already been unleashed. He got what he wanted . . . unless . . . I swallow the anxious lump in my throat. Unless he wants me, too.

"Gimme your phone," I tell Loren.

She does, and I switch on the flashlight and shine it onto the gate, but the narrow alley is empty. Did I imagine what I saw?

"Alex, you're scaring me," Loren mutters. "What'd you see?"

I hand her phone back. "Nothing. Sorry."

She grips the steering wheel and whispers, "Was it Shadow Man?"

I sit back with a huff. "I honestly don't know anymore, Lo."

The gooseflesh on her arms already tells me what she's feeling, but I press my fingertips to the soft brown skin of her forearm anyway and am hit with a prickling fear that makes me shudder and pull away.

"You're scared too," I say.

She hugs herself. "I'd be freaking out if I was being stalked by an evil shadow entity."

"I am—just on the inside." I rub my hand hard across my face. I feel like standing on the roof of this cart and shouting at the top of my lungs for Shadow Man and whoever else to come and get me already. Stop tormenting me and let's get this over with.

But a powerful yawn takes over instead, stifling my flash of anger. "Maybe I'm just exhausted."

Loren yawns too. "Me too. We'll be quick down here and then we can get some sleep. Tomorrow's a new day."

"It's . . . not just that."

I feel silly having a deep conversation with my best friend as we sit in a stolen—er, *borrowed*—golf cart in the middle of the road at dusk in a full-on apocalypse. But I'm tired physically *and* emotionally—is that a thing? If not, it should be.

"You can talk to me about anything." Loren puts a hand on my arm and a spark of emotion flares inside me from her touch.

I almost pull away when I remember these are her feelings. At first, it's an intense shock of static electricity; then it dulls and settles into something else—something kinder.

It's warm and cozy, like sitting in front of a fire on a chilly night. Love?

A soothing surge of calmness follows that reminds me of the security and comfort of wrapping up in a warm blanket fresh out of the dryer. Trust?

That's all Loren. My best friend for as long as I've known what it means to have one. Maybe Orin's magic is good for something after all. And maybe if I'm honest with Loren, everything else will feel a little less scary.

"I'm gay." I shove the words from my mouth before I can swallow them again.

Loren sucks her teeth. "That's definitely old news for me. But I'm glad you finally felt comfortable enough to tell me. I was honestly starting to get offended."

I feel my face blanch. "You knew?"

She chuckles. "Alex Jamal Wise. I know that you separate your Skittles by color so you can save the oranges—your favorite—for last, but you don't do that for M&M's, because they're chocolate and all taste the same—to you. I know you've been deathly—and hilariously—terrified of goats ever since one bit you at the petting zoo on a field trip in first grade. I know you binge video games and comics when you're sad, because sometimes story worlds are better than the real one for you. And I know how much it hurt you when Sky stopped hanging out with you to be friends with Larry the Homophobic Hobo." That earns a small smile from me. "I knew you were gay just like I knew you were a cool person *and* a goober. I'm glad you've finally wised up. We've missed out on *so* many juicy conversations!"

I chuckle and stare at my feet, battling the urge to cry. "Sorry. . . . It's . . . just a lot."

Now that I've released the tremendous weight of the secret I've been keeping from my best friend, I feel as if I could float up to the stars. After what happened with Sky, I thought I'd regret telling Loren, but now I only wish I'd confided in her sooner.

"I know," she says. "I don't even believe we should have to 'come out.' We should be allowed to just *be* who we are from the start."

" 'We'?" I turn to her with a raised eyebrow.

"You know I don't do well with societal boundaries. I'll like whoever I please!" I laugh and she adds, "However, I'm going to have to ask that you find better boyfriends than Sky Hollowell—*please!*"

I groan and shake my head, still giggling.

I mean, I can try, but I imagine it'll be hard to find love in the apocalypse.

16

GEOFF WITH A "G"

Loren turns our golf cart onto an eerily deserted section of Hollywood Boulevard that reminds me of a scene from a postapocalyptic movie.

Streetlamps cast sad cones of light on the destruction left behind from the first act of the apocalypse. Up and down the street, windows of the shops that aren't shuttered have been broken, trails of merchandise and trash spilling onto the sidewalks. Abandoned cars, some wrecked, engines still smoking, others pulled aside or onto the curb, fill the blocks in every direction. Loren and I appear to be the only souls outside.

I'm wondering where everyone's gone when angry shouts ring out from somewhere nearby. The aggressive *BOOM* of an explosion gives us both a start. The world goes quiet for a moment after; then the shouting kicks up again.

"We should make this quick," I say.

"Agreed."

Loren parks us in front of Fred's Groceries & More! Metal shutters are drawn over the length of the storefront, but the rightmost one isn't closed all the way. Someone has sloppily spray-painted it with a red "R" that dried mid-drip, making the giant letter look like it's melting.

I get down on my hands and knees and peek underneath the shutter. Inside, the store appears strangely untouched by the events of the apocalypse. The white floors shine like they were waxed recently. At the end of one of the neatly organized shelves is a cardboard display of fireworks for the Fourth of July. Otherwise, the place seems deserted, which feels too good to be true. I turn my ear toward the door and listen for a few moments, but it doesn't sound like anyone's inside.

"We good?" Loren asks as I get up and brush myself off.

"Looks like it." I grip the bottom of the shutter. "Help me with this."

Loren grabs the other side, and we both grunt with the effort of lifting the metal contraption, which is way heavier than it has any right to be.

Thankfully, the door's unlocked. Once we're inside, I see a drinks aisle stocked with plenty of Capri Sun and a meat display case I'm willing to bet still has bacon—both of which, in my personal opinion, are snack essentials.

Loren pulls one of the empty half-carts from the storage lane by the wall and wheels it over to me, then gets one for herself. "You start at one end, I'll take the other, and we meet in the middle?"

"Okay," I say. "I know it's apocalypse rules and all, but can we at least leave the owner a note with our parents' names and phone numbers so they can reimburse them later?"

She grins. "Sure, Alex."

She turns to start shopping, and I call after her, "Oh! Don't forget the bacon!"

She tosses back a thumbs-up before disappearing down the meat aisle.

I take my cart back to the opposite end of the store and scan the shelves for stuff we might need. I grab a few cases of Capri Sun, water, some bags of dill pickle chips, chocolate chip cookies, extra-butter movie theater popcorn, toilet tissue, paper towels, matches, flashlights, random toiletries, and a bunch of stuff for Liam—bandages, ibuprofen, and antiseptic. The fireworks display tempts me, but Loren redirects my efforts when she pulls up and frowns at the contents of my cart, immediately making me feel self-conscious about my selections.

She's been a tad more responsible, with choices like oatmeal, eggs, bacon, milk, a couple loaves of bread, cheese, and a bunch of canned goods. She's even grabbed some fresh fruits and veggies. She picks through my cart and shakes her head.

A sudden *thunk* resounds from behind the closed door labeled OFFICE in fading decals, snatching my breath from my throat.

"What was that?" Loren whispers.

Before I can say "I dunno," the office door creaks open, and out strolls a tall, wiry white guy who I doubt is the owner. He has a crude "R" drawn in the center of his forehead. It's backward, like he did it himself in the mirror. I'd chuckle if I weren't terrified.

Rider Guy has dyed his short hair bubblegum pink, and he's wearing a neon yellow tank with fatigue pants tucked into some worn boots. His thin, tanned arms are covered in black tattoos from shoulders to fingertips. The radio clipped to his shoulder erupts in static, and then someone announces that the pharmacy on Sunset has been cleared and secured.

The Riders must be out looting. We can't let this guy call for backup.

Rider Guy glances at my and Loren's carts, then narrows his light eyes at us. "All that stuff belongs to the Riders now, kids."

Loren tightens her grip on the handle of her cart. "You can't just take the whole store, bruh."

He tilts his head slightly. "Maybe not in the old world, but in this new one, Riders make the rules."

"Are you even really one of them?" I tap the center of my forehead and frown at him. "Your Rider logo looks fake."

He looks up as if he can see his own forehead, and I almost laugh again. Loren actually does. He grimaces and makes a rumbling in the back of his throat.

"Were you too scared to go up to the tower yourself and get the real thing?" Loren asks.

He stomps his feet and snarls, "There was a long line! I-I'll do it later!"

"I'm sure," she says. "Look, don't be a jerk and just look the other way this one time. We have a hurt friend at home who needs this stuff."

He shakes his head. "Sorry. Can't."

I sidle closer to Loren and whisper, "Maybe we should just take this L and try to find another store in the morning."

"No," she hisses back. "Riders are already hoarding supplies. There might not be anything left by morning."

A low sound like a groan comes from behind the slightly ajar office door.

I nod toward the office. "Who's back there?"

Rider Guy peeks over his shoulder at the door but doesn't answer.

"Are they hurt?" I ask.

"That's none of your business," he says.

"Okay, you can have all the stuff," I say, and Loren rolls her neck and glares at me, but I ignore her. "Just let whoever you're holding back there leave with us."

Rider Guy's pinched expression relaxes for a moment. He shifts his awkward stare between us and the office door, considering my offer.

"Alex!" Loren whisper-snarls. "What—the—heck—are—you—doing?"

Loren will be angry, but she'll also get over it. We desperately need these supplies, but someone might need help. Their life is more important than bacon and Capri Sun.

Rider Guy's shoulders slump and he exhales an annoyed-sounding breath. He's about to respond when the front door of the store bangs open and another guy walks in.

At first glance, I think I'm staring at a human version of King K. Rool from *Super Smash Bros.*, only ten times more threatening. This guy's neck is as thick as Rider Guy's head. He has a formidable potbelly, but the rest of him appears to be nothing but muscle. Even his bald scalp looks ripped in the bright white store lighting. An old, scarred baseball bat is slung over one of his beefy shoulders, and a radio is clipped to the other. He's wearing a uniform, which helpfully has his name stitched onto the right breast. Geoff.

Geoff glowers at me and Loren and then at Rider Guy. "What's going on here?"

Rider Guy starts blubbering incoherently until Geoff holds up a hand. Fresh beads of sweat drip from Rider Guy's pink hairline, and his Adam's apple dips as he swallows hard.

"Nothing's going on," I announce. "We were just leaving."

"Shut up," Geoff barks without looking at me.

"You bet."

His head snaps toward me, the great grimace on his face wrinkling his nose, and I mime zipping my mouth shut.

Maybe Loren and I should just make a run for it.

"Like I said before: you don't have what it takes to be one of us," Geoff tells Rider Guy. "Your next mistake will be your last." Rider Guy hangs his head. "Report to the tower immediately to get your official brand or go cower in the sewers with the rest of the weak rats. I'll finish up here."

Rider Guy whisks out the front door, never lifting his eyes from the floor. Geoff locks the door behind him, then lumbers back to stand in front of me and Loren, looking us up and down like we're UFC fighters challenging him.

He leans his rear against the counter and nods at us. "You two joining up?"

"Absolutely not," Loren replies.

He gestures at me. "She speak for you?"

"We don't want any trouble," I say. "Someone might be

hurt back there." I jerk my head in the direction of the office. "Please just let them go, and we'll all leave right now."

Geoff snickers and stands up tall, towering over Loren and me. "Anyone who rejects the power of the Horsemen must kneel before it."

He swings the bat down and taps it against the toe of his boot. I flinch, and Loren grabs hold of my arm, sending a shock of her fear rippling through me, amplifying my own. The moment the bat touches Geoff's boot, it ignites in spectacular flames. The heat blasts my face, and Loren and I stumble back into a produce shelf. An avalanche of navel oranges spills to the floor, but I can't tear my eyes away from Geoff and his flaming bat.

Loren and I exchange worried glances.

Maybe I'm naive, but I didn't think we'd have to fight to the death for groceries.

But thus is the end of the world, I suppose.

17

CADILLAC FREDDIE

Neither Loren nor I are ready for Geoff's attack. I mean, I'm not sure what either of us expected after he lit his bat on fire two seconds ago. But when he lunges for us, we both leap aside—and barely make it.

He crashes into the produce shelf, singeing oranges and apples. The sweet and rancid scent of burning fruit follows. For whatever reason, Geoff targets me, swinging his bat wildly, knocking products from the shelves and flinging flames in every direction.

"Dude!" I cry, vaulting over a display table holding a pyramid of yellow onions. "If you're gonna burn the whole place down, why not just let us have some stuff first?"

"It's the PRINCIPLE!" Geoff screams, banging his fire bat on the onion table. The tantalizing scent of cooked onions makes my stomach growl, reminding me I haven't eaten since the crappy oatmeal breakfast at the hospital.

THUNK!

CRASH!

"Leave him alone, you big lug!" Loren shouts.

On my knees, I peek over the table. Loren flings a bottle of soda at Geoff, but he swings his bat and connects. The bottle explodes, splattering sticky soda and bits of glass everywhere. Geoff charges Loren, who shrieks and takes off down the next aisle.

"ALEX! HELP MEEE!" she screams over Geoff's feral growls.

I leap over the checkout counter and almost crash into the wall where the fire extinguisher hangs. I snatch it down and climb back over just as Loren scrambles up the aisle directly in front of me, Geoff barreling behind her and swinging his bat back and forth, setting random fires and knocking everything off the shelves.

"Lo!" I beckon for her to take cover behind me.

Her face shifts from terrified to determined, and she digs in and launches herself over the checkout counter as I pull the pin and squeeze the handle of my extinguisher.

A flurry of frozen white gas hits Geoff square in the face, stopping him on the spot. I sweep the spray over the length of him, extinguishing his annoying flaming bat. He screams and drops to his knees. The bat clangs to the floor. He coughs and splutters, flailing in the thick cloud that I keep pelting him with until I'm standing right on top of him.

I stop and adjust my grip on the extinguisher. When the cloud settles enough for me to make out Geoff's bulky figure in the haze, I swing with every bit of strength in my body. The extinguisher clocks him hard in the back of the head, and he grunts and topples over, facedown.

My chest heaves, and I struggle to hold the extinguisher in

my trembling hands. I've never hurt someone like that before. But it was him or us . . . right?

. . . Right?

Loren claps a hand on my shoulder, and I scream and almost spray her. "Whoa, goober! It's me!" she cries.

I roll my eyes and drop the extinguisher. It clunks to the floor by my feet. Geoff lies on his stomach, spread-eagled, out cold. Tiny crystals of ice cling to his shirt and the back of his bald head, the spot where I hit him already turning a violent shade of magenta. His back rises and falls with shallow breaths. Thank goodness he's still alive.

Muffled shouts sound from the office. I make a beeline for the door but take a moment before going inside to steel my nerves for what I might see. I feel Loren's presence right behind me, which gives my courage a little boost.

I push the door open and gasp.

The small room's been ransacked. Smashed bits of what was once a desktop computer cover the otherwise bare surface of a desk. A tall shelf has been overturned, adding books, crushed boxes, and other ruined items to the piles of multicolored paper carpeting the floor. Next to a toppled office chair lies an older man, his mouth, hands, and feet all bound tight with rope.

When he sees me and Loren standing in the doorway, his eyes widen, and he starts shouting against the gag again.

I drop to my knees beside him and remove the binding from his mouth. His dark brown skin reminds me of these smoky quartz earrings Mom used to love. They were a gift from Dad that vanished after the divorce. This old guy's beard is short and gray, and his eyebrows are thick and gray too. The whites of his brown eyes have yellowed, but that makes him appear no less warm. I'm not sure why, but it feels like I know him already.

In a gruff, exhausted voice, he says, "Thank you, son," and sighs. "Thank you both."

Loren stands to one side and helps me sit the man upright. Together, we untie his hands and feet, and I try not to brush against his bare skin too much, because each encounter, no matter how brief, gives me slightly disorienting pangs of relief, fear, anxiety, sadness, and a mess of other emotions I can't even sort out. I feel terrible for this guy.

"Are you okay, mister?" I ask.

He coughs, a strong one that lifts his thick shoulders and bounces his round tummy. "Freddie," he says, and coughs into the crook of his elbow again. "Cadillac Freddie, to be more precise. And yes, I'm okay. A bit roughed up, but I've survived worse."

Someone drew a fat "R" on the man's forehead with a red marker. Anger flares inside me again as I imagine Rider Guy torturing Freddie, who could be my grandpa, who probably *is* someone's grandpa.

"I'll get you some water," I tell Freddie.

He nods and mutters "Thanks" as Loren rights the chair and helps him off the floor and into it.

Back out on the sales floor, Geoff still lies unconscious, sprawled in front of the register. I tread across his back to the cooler at the rear of the store and grab a bottle of water. I detour to swipe a package of sanitizing wipes, too. I remember Mom using these to clean Mags up after my sister tattooed herself from forehead to foot with marker. Five-year-old me thought it was hilarious until I got blamed for not watching her.

I don't forget to step on Geoff again on the way back to the office.

Loren's doing her best to straighten the room amid weak protests from Freddie, who sits slumped in his seat. The areas under his eyes are puffy with exhaustion. I open the bottle of water and hand it to him. He takes it and winces, straining to sit back. He takes several long, deep gulps, then lowers the bottle, closes his eyes, and releases a hefty, satisfied breath.

I show him the wipes. "I got these for the, uh—" I point at my forehead and nod at his.

"Oh, yes." He casts his gaze at the floor.

I scrub the marker from his skin, which I struggle to do gently because I'm so darn mad. The Riders are no different from Larry Adams. They're just cowardly adult bullies who enjoy picking on kids and old people. We need to end this apocalypse while the world is still worth saving—if it's not too late already. But what causes a tiny sliver of fear to writhe deep inside me is thinking about how tough it's going to be to go back to "the way things were" after seeing how truly ugly people can be to one another.

"What are you two kids doing here?" he asks when I finish.

"We needed supplies," I tell him. "We're hiding out at a house up in the Hills, and we have a friend who's hurt."

Freddie's eyes widen. "Do they need help?"

I shake my head. "Just rest and food and stuff. It's not serious."

"Then please"—he gestures to the open door leading to the sales floor—"take whatever you need."

"That's very kind of you," Loren says. "We were going to leave our parents' information so they could pay you later."

"Consider it a gift from Cadillac Freddie. I insist."

"Thank you, sir," I tell him. "Lo, you stay with Mr. Freddie, and I'll go pick up all our stuff."

She nods and returns to straightening the office. This time Freddie chooses to finish his water instead of protesting.

"I'll grab you a fresh one of those," I tell him on my way back out to the store.

I pause at the edge of the checkout counter and stare in disbelief at Geoff's carnage. In mere minutes, he nearly destroyed the entire store. A disrespectful amount of Freddie's produce has been burned or smashed, and the floors of several aisles are covered with broken glass, exploded chip bags, and about a dozen puddles of varying colors. I wonder if Freddie has someone to help him clean all this up.

I turn our carts back upright and begin transferring our groceries from the floor to the baskets—everything that hasn't been smashed. *Thanks, Geoff. You ruined ten times more than we wanted to take.*

I stoop to pick up one of the boxes of Capri Sun, all of which survived the onslaught. "You never let me down," I mutter, and kiss the dented box before dropping it into the basket.

A hand grips my neck from behind with such force that it feels as if I've been shoved off a cliff. I choke on my scream as a pair of thick hands spins me around and lifts me off the ground by my throat. Geoff's touch registers a red-hot sensation of rage that cracks inside me like a whip made of fire. I'm powerless to stop him. He's too strong—too angry.

He grits his crooked teeth and squeezes my neck so hard that more beads of sweat push through the gargantuan pores on his bald head. I grab his thick wrists and try to pry his hands from me, but it's useless. This is it. This is how I die.

I let my sister down.

I let the whole world down.

I let *myself* down.

I imagine my tombstone: HERE LIES ALEX WISE, THE FOOL-ISH KID WHO GOT HIMSELF MURDERED BY GEOFF WITH A "G."

Just die already, you meddlesome kid! Geoff snarls.

Don't rush me! I'll croak at my own pace, jerk! I think, but . . . wait . . . Geoff's lips didn't move. Unless he's a ventriloquist, I think I just heard his thoughts.

Spots begin pressing into the sides of my vision. I let my arms fall to my sides. I've lost. I'm going to die here, and the Horsemen are going to ravage our world for the rest of eternity.

I imagine what that world might look like at its worst. A place where the sun rarely shines for long, if at all. Where un-imaginable monsters—the really messed-up kind that rede-fine fear for normal people—roam the streets, free to pillage as they please and devour the souls of any unfortunate beings who cross their paths. A small percentage of the population might carry on, existing in perpetual flight mode, persisting despite outliving happiness, joy, and all things similar, which died so long ago even the memories are fading.

Geoff's eyes widen to a comical size. His grip on my throat slackens, and I gasp, drawing in a rush of fresh, fiery air. This time when I try to pry Geoff's fingers from my throat, he lets go.

My feet hit the floor, and I stagger backward, clutching my aching neck.

Geoff, still wide-eyed, falls to his knees. "No," he murmurs, and grabs both sides of his shaking head, his entire body quivering. I don't need to touch him to know this is fear. "What did you do to me?" Much of the threatening bass in his voice from earlier is gone now. "What are you? What *was* that?"

I screw up my face at him. I didn't do anything, but he deserves a lot worse than a scare.

"Those m-monsters," he stammers. "Those things walking the streets . . . They were *eating* people. . . . I . . ."

Hold up. Did he actually *see* what I was imagining? And then it hits me, simultaneously upending my stomach: Orin. I must've incepted Geoff's mind somehow. I guess my Sense has officially leveled up. Cool.

"Wanna see them again?" I reach for him, and he jumps to his feet. It's hard not to smirk at the sight of the brute-sized man flinching so dramatically from a twelve-year-old kid.

"NO! PLEASE!" He stumbles backward and slips on a pile of squished oranges, landing butt-first in the thick of the mess.

"Those are *my* monsters," I tell him. "So tell your Rider buddies they'd better all leave Mr. Freddie and this place alone or I'll send those same monsters—and worse—to hunt you down in your sleep."

Geoff whimpers, launches himself to his feet, and throws himself at the front door. He slams into it hard, then remembers to unlock it, swings it open, and sprints into the dark.

I chuckle under my breath and turn to find Loren and Mr. Freddie gawking from where they stand side by side behind the checkout counter. My smile vanishes at once.

"What's going on, Alex?" Loren asks, her voice small. "What monsters were you talking about?"

I glance at Freddie. "Oh, I, uh, I'm not sure. I hit him pretty hard with that extinguisher. I think he was hallucinating. He was going on about monsters, so I played along, and it worked."

She narrows her eyes, and I give her my best *Girl, hush, we'll talk about this later* look and she drops it.

Freddie walks up to me and claps a strong hand on my shoulder, making my knees buckle. "I don't care what you did so long as those fools don't come running back up in here," he says. "But I can guarantee you one thing—if they do, Cadillac Freddie will be ready next time."

I can't help but smile. I never got to know any of my grandparents, but I wish I'd had one like Mr. Freddie.

"If you're alone here, you should come back to our place," I tell him. "It's safer there."

He shakes his head. "I appreciate the offer, but I must get home to check on my own family—after I lock this place up tight. I have a feeling the people of my community are going to be in need soon, and I'm going to be here for them.

"Speaking of—you kids feel free to stop by anytime for whatever. If you see the light on out back, I'm here. Just knock three times and call for Cadillac Freddie."

Loren and I thank him again, he helps us bag our items, and we help him lock up. After we load our golf cart, he tells us to keep safe and to remember to come visit him as often as we like.

Loren pulls off, and I glance back.

Freddie stands like a sentinel, watching us drive away.

There are definitely still some parts of this world worth fighting for.

18

THE NIGHT STALKER

It's a good thing fashion isn't top of the Riders' list of priorities, so Loren and I are able to make short work of securing a few changes of clothes for everyone—even Dexter.

We make it back up the hill without (further) incident. Dexter meets us out front and helps unload the cart. He tells us Liam hasn't woken yet but is resting peacefully. While Dexter puts away the groceries, Loren and I recount every cinematic detail of our supply run, including the sudden manifestation of my powers.

When I get to that part, Dexter pauses from stacking cartons of eggs in the refrigerator to turn and lock gazes with me. I feel my heart shrink. It's not a look of admiration or pride. Instead, his lips purse as if I just told him I want to be a career criminal when I grow up. He glances over his shoulder in the direction of Liam's room and then back at me.

"What is it now?" I ask.

"Uh, nothing," he says. "Sorry, I'm just tired. It's been a long day."

"I'm going to shower and get to bed," Loren says. "Can we regroup in the morning?"

"Sure," I say.

Dexter nods.

Before he can say more, I slip outside to the patio. I just need a moment to be alone without the crushing pressure of other people's opinions.

I sit on the side of the pool and stick my feet into the icy water, taking a deep breath in and blowing it out through my mouth.

The sound of Dexter clearing his throat behind me makes me want to scream. I fix my face before turning to look up at him. "Oh, hey," I say.

"I'm sorry, Alex," he says, a timidness in his voice I've never heard before, "for how I reacted to what you said. I didn't mean to offend you, I'm just very worried about you."

I frown up at him. "But we told you what happened. I can handle myself out there."

"I don't disagree with you. That's not my concern."

"Then what is it?" I ask, curious, though simultaneously wishing Dexter would stop finding new things to be anxious about.

"Back on that island, Liam's magic seemed to hurt him whenever he used it. And if your newfound powers are from the same place, using them might harm you too." He sighs heavily, and his shoulders droop. "I care about you, Alex, and I don't want to see anything bad happen to you."

I can't deny that it feels good to have someone like Dexter

genuinely care about me, but it'd be even better if he trusted me more.

"Nothing bad has happened so far." I stand up on the side of the pool and turn in a circle so he can see I'm still in one piece. "I'm fine."

"I'm only asking you to be cautious until you better understand these abilities."

I nod, although I feel full of sludge. I'm really tired and just want to go to bed.

"Don't stay up too late," he says. "And don't worry. We'll sort it all out in the morning, yeah?"

I nod again.

"And, um . . . I should let you know . . . I'll be staying the night, but you won't have to worry about me after tomorrow morning."

"So you're ditching after all?"

"Of course not," he says, which weirdly makes me feel as relieved as it does frustrated. "I hate to leave you kids for even an hour, but my family's also here in the city. I need to check in with them and make sure they're okay. And I trust you three won't get yourselves killed before I return at sunset tomorrow?"

"Dying is never on my agenda."

He chuckles under his breath. "Death doesn't care if you plan for it."

"Good night, Dexter," I say as I step around him and back inside.

When I slide the patio door closed, he's still standing with his back to me, staring into the distance, where fires continue to burn among the twinkling building lights. A heavy cloud of gray smog hangs above the city from all the destruction.

In the shower, I turn the water to the hottest setting I can stand, but it doesn't distract my thoughts from Dexter's warning. The only negative side effect I've felt from Orin's magic is nausea from being overwhelmed by too many emotions attacking my mind at once—like what happened back at the Hollywood sign. But how am I supposed to "be cautious" with something I can't control?

I dress and climb into bed. We didn't think to pick up pajamas, but the shorts and tees we got are comfortable enough to sleep in. No wonder adults are stressed all the time. It takes a lot of planning and forethought just to be alive.

With a tired yet determined sigh, I open the Notes app on my phone. I don't care anymore what anyone thinks about what I'm doing. I'll just have to keep looking out for myself—like I've been doing ever since Dad left. I record everything I know about my abilities.

The first time I felt my new power was in the hospital, when Dad hugged me. Touching someone allows me to feel their emotions—but it appears to work only for skin-to-skin contact.

I can push my thoughts into other people's minds. Geoff saw what I imagined the world would turn into if I failed. But how do I control it?

And I can sometimes hear other people's thoughts, but I have no clue how to turn it on or off.

Once I've emptied and exhausted my brain, I close the app and set my phone on the bedside table. But something—the tiniest poke of anxiety in my chest—won't let me fall asleep. I toss and turn until I'm on my side, staring at the soft glow from the dim nighttime lighting in the hallway that beams underneath my closed door. The light is mesmerizing, and my eyelids grow heavier and heavier, until—

Two feet stop in front of my door, distinct stalks of shadow, parting the dim light—and jar me awake. I blink and rub my eyes. When I look again, they're still there.

I'm not dreaming.

I sit up slowly but don't call out. After a few seconds, the feet outside my door turn and disappear, heading down the hallway toward the other bedrooms. I ease out of bed and tip-toe to the door, my heart beating so loud I'm afraid whoever's outside will hear it.

I put my hand on the doorknob and pause. I'm not sure why I'm freaking out. It's probably just Dexter looking in on everyone. I'm surprised he hasn't barged in and insisted on checking everyone's vitals every couple of hours.

But no . . . something else niggles at my mind. And it won't go away until I know for sure.

I open the door slowly and poke my head outside. I grimace at the empty hallway—in both directions. All the other lights in the house are out. But I *know* I just saw someone.

I creep to the last room at the end of the hallway—Dexter's. I don't need to press my ear to the door, because a sound comes from the other side like someone pulsing rocks in a blender. He should probably see a doctor about that snoring.

I knock softly on Loren's door, but she doesn't answer. I

crack it and peek inside. She's sound asleep, her locs tucked into a bonnet, the comforter snuggled up to her chin.

I check on Liam next, who's still out.

My trembling hands fumble with the knob, but I manage to close the door and dart back to my room. I launch myself into bed and lie facing the closed door. The glow of the hallway light doesn't comfort me anymore. I'm too revved up to sleep. Too focused on the question I can't begin to answer.

Why is Shadow Man still stalking me?

19

RSVP FOR DANGER

I don't know how long I lie awake in bed, staring at the space beneath the door, waiting for Shadow Man to reappear. But he doesn't—at least not before I nod off.

The smell of bacon frying snaps me out of a deep, dreamless sleep. I sit up, my mind congested with fog for a moment. I finally manage to slide out of bed and stumble to the bathroom to wash my face.

Once I've cleared away my eye boogers and unfogged my brain, I wander into the kitchen to find Dexter making breakfast. Strips of bacon sizzle in a pan, and the toaster clicks as four fresh pieces of toast pop up. Loren's assisting, setting the table with some plain white dishes she must have found in the cupboards. Liam must still be out.

My stomach rumbles loudly, announcing my presence. Both Loren and Dexter smile at me and say, "Good morning."

"Morning!" I return the smile, though mine feels forced.

"How'd you sleep?" Dexter asks as he transfers a slice of bacon from the pan to a growing pile atop a napkin-lined plate.

"Fine," I lie.

"I checked on Liam about an hour ago, and he seems to be doing okay," he says. "I was hoping the smell of breakfast would rouse him."

I shrug. "Worked for me."

After Loren finishes the table, she motions for me to join her in the nearby TV room. "We'll check the news to see if they're reporting anything about what the Horsemen are up to."

"Good idea," says Dexter. "The food'll be ready in fifteen."

My stomach growls impatiently. Fifteen minutes feels like forever right now.

"You okay?" Loren asks in a low voice as we sit beside each other on the couch across from the television. The sounds of Dexter banging around in the kitchen continue behind us. "And don't lie to me. I can tell when you're off." She side-eyes me and turns on the TV.

"Have you seen anything strange around the house, particularly last night?" I whisper.

She knits her brows. "Did you see him again? Shadow Man?"

"I don't know. Maybe? I thought I saw someone standing outside my door last night. But when I checked the hallway, no one was there, and you all were asleep."

"Why do you think he's following you?"

I shrug. I wish I knew.

"Well, hello there!" exclaims Dexter.

We turn to see Liam poised timidly in the entrance to the kitchen, as if he's not sure if it's safe. His eyes fall on mine. I smile, and his scowl melts. Seeing him awake and well, though still bruised, makes me genuinely happy.

Loren and I stand up to greet him properly. We say good

morning and skip awkward hugs or handshakes, which is fine with me. I have enough of my own emotions swirling around inside me without adding someone else's to the mix.

"You're safe here," I tell him. "We found this place after we rescued you."

He hugs himself. "Thanks for that."

"No prob—"

"But I didn't need your help." He drops his arms to his sides and resumes his signature scowl. "I told you back on the island to stay out of my way."

"Are you for real right now?" I must be hearing things.

His brow knits as he shoves his hands out in front of him and examines them angrily. "Of course I'm for real. What are you talking about?"

"Would you rather we left you to die on that hill?" I ask.

"I *wasn't* going to die," he barks.

"Lies you tell," I retort. "You looked well on your way when we found you."

He narrows his eyes and clenches his fists. I'd think he'd appreciate us saving his *whole life*. But whatevs.

Dexter watches quietly from where he's planted in front of the stove, his eyes ping-ponging between us.

Liam's about to say something else, but Loren interrupts him.

"Hey!" She's standing back near the couch, pointing the remote at the television. "Stop being annoying and come look at this." She turns up the volume.

I join her on the couch, and Dexter and Liam stand behind us.

"I knew things were bad, but I had no idea they were *this* bad," she mutters.

A woman with a jet-black pixie cut sits behind a desk in a news center, reporting on the state of the world. A ticker crawls along the bottom of the screen, which reads, "People claiming to be the Horsemen of the Apocalypse wreak havoc. . . . Major cities around the world declare states of emergency. . . ."

"This morning, we have updates on the situation from around the globe," the anchor announces. "We want to apologize for the graphic nature of the content you're about to see. If you have small children, now's a good time to remove them from the room."

A window appears in the corner of the screen, playing footage from around the world while the anchor gives a rundown of how everything's unraveled over the last two days.

"After a series of unprecedented events, the United Nations has officially declared a Global State of Emergency," the anchor reports. "People around the world are advised to shelter in place wherever it's safe.

"In the midst of the worldwide chaos, prominent political leaders—not just one or two people, folks, we're talking *entire* governing bodies—have disappeared without a trace in every country around the world. Those leaders who remain are doing their best to continue to serve their communities with what few quickly dwindling resources remain."

The room is quiet. No one says it, but we all know it.

The world is doomed.

"Law enforcement agencies from local police departments all the way to Interpol have gone dark all over the world. Much like the world's political leaders, militaries are nonexistent, as soldiers are all either AWOL or MIA."

As she talks, the video shows countless congressional halls, war rooms, and government buildings, all empty, as if they were abandoned years ago. Death's order to War on the hill yesterday replays in my mind—he must be responsible for this.

The footage changes, showing the bustling and frenzied emergency rooms of hospitals around the world.

"The efforts of the Horsemen have had an immediate and devastating impact, but Los Angeles remains the epicenter of the destruction," she continues. "As a result, an influx of patients has driven all Los Angeles's hospitals far beyond operating capacity."

I recognize the hospital in one of the videos and zip to my feet when I catch a glimpse of my mom amid the bustling nurses and doctors, a stethoscope draped around her neck.

"Mom," I murmur, breathless.

Loren grabs my hand, sending a shock of anxiety sparkling up my wrist and arm. I pull away, and she looks offended.

"I'm sorry." I sit back down next to her. "You just caught me off guard. I'm still trying to figure out how to work Orin's magic."

I feel a powerful hotness boring into the back of my head, and when I glance over my shoulder, I find Liam glowering down at me. Yikes. He's not even trying to hide how much he hates me anymore.

I frown back at him, turn around, and scoot closer to Loren. I lean my shoulder against hers gingerly so our skin doesn't touch. I don't care if Liam hates me. I just need him to help us stop the Horsemen and then he can be on his grumpy way.

"I talked to my parents this morning," Loren says. "They told me they're sheltering at a nearby hotel with your family, Alex. They're all there and safe—your stepfamily, too."

"That's good to know," I say. "I guess I wasn't expecting to see my mom on TV."

I'm glad Mom's keeping busy. I feel slightly less guilty for turning my phone on airplane mode.

We watch the rest of the broadcast in awed silence. The world's farms have all been devastated. Normal, everyday pests have turned into superbugs, resistant to every form of pesticide imaginable. They've depleted global food supplies in a matter of hours. Other farmers' newly planted fields became barren overnight. One teary-eyed farmer told a reporter, "It's as if someone salted the earth while we all slept." Shelves of grocery stores and farmers markets everywhere have been picked clean. I bet that's the handiwork of Famine—the girl with the oversized jungle cats.

How powerful must the Horsemen's magic be for them to affect the entire world from right here in LA? Or maybe they can do that weird shadow teleporting thing to zip across the globe in an instant? I wonder if Orin's magic, my Sense, has a global reach too, and I shudder. The only thing worse than the whole world depending on me would be feeling all their emotions at once. *That was not an invitation, Orin.*

The news report ends abruptly, the emergency alert now filling the screen. Loren turns the television off and the four of us steep in silence. I can't believe all this started with me and my ten-year-old sister in a dirty old cave on an island in the middle of nowhere. And now the whole world's gone wrong.

"Have you checked on your family?" Loren asks Dexter.

He glances down as if ashamed. "I was planning to after you kids had breakfast."

"It's okay," I tell him. "You shouldn't make your family wait. In fact, why don't you bring them back here?"

"Yeah," Loren adds brightly. "We have enough room. How many are there?"

"No, no," Dexter says. "They're all stubborn old fools who'd prefer to ride out the apocalypse in their basements. My primary purpose is keeping you kids safe."

Now I feel like a brat for being so annoyed with him last night. He could've ditched at any point, but he stayed. Which is more than I can say for my own dad, and we weren't even in the middle of an apocalypse when he abandoned us. At least Dexter shows that he cares.

"So, dare I ask?" says Dexter. "Now that Liam's recovered: What's the plan?"

"I'm going back to the tower—*alone*," announces Liam.

"Well, that's a *not very great* idea," Loren says.

"Careful, Lo," I retort. "Common sense triggers him."

Liam folds his arms and turns to me. "Well, what's your plan—seeing as how you and your sister started all this?"

"I . . ." My voice trails off as heat rushes my face.

A thundering knock on the front door startles everyone. My pulse rockets, and we all look at one another with wide eyes.

Dexter holds up a hand and approaches the front door. Curiosity pushes me behind him, despite his warning.

He looks through the peephole and says, "Huh."

"What is it?" I whisper.

He stands back and opens the door, revealing the empty front porch and driveway. I step up beside him and look out. The street is deserted, and everything is deathly silent. It's late morning, but birds aren't even chirping in the branches of nearby trees. It's strange.

I glance down, and a colored card jutting from beneath the doormat catches my eye. I pick it up and head back inside. Everyone huddles around me.

"You've got to be kidding me," I say. "It's a flyer. For a party."

It looks like one of those Instagram ads for adult weekend parties. In the center of the flyer is a headshot of Eustice Barnes, grinning wide, the "R" mark prominent in the center of his forehead. I read the invitation aloud:

"'Join the Riders at the Crypto.com Arena to kick off the official New World Order. The event will be streamed live on multiple social media platforms. Sponsored by Eustice Barnes, with special guest appearances by the Horsemen: Death, War, Pestilence, and Famine.'"

Tiny thumbnail pictures of the Horsemen, each wearing a homicidal expression, are arranged at the bottom of the flyer.

I hand the card to Loren, who frowns down at it, rereading the announcement.

"This is our chance to make our move on the Horsemen," I announce. "And we only have three days to come up with a foolproof plan."

No pressure.

20

8 MINUTES

DAY ONE: STRATEGIZE

After we finish discussing the rally flyer, we scarf down breakfast—Dexter, who I had no idea was so great at cooking, made bacon, eggs, and toast. Then he takes the car and leaves to check in with his family, promising to be back by dark.

In the bright light of the late-morning sun, I sit at the head of the long dining table with Loren to my right and Liam to my left.

We only have three days to figure out how we're going to stop the Horsemen at the old Staples Center. I refuse to call it the Crypto.com Arena, because "Crypto" is too close to "Crypt." I'm not usually superstitious, but today ain't a bad day to be cautious.

Liam pounds his fist on the table, startling me out of my thoughts and making Loren flinch. "I say we confront them head-on at the rally. Challenge them all, right from the start."

Loren presses her lips tightly together. "Is that your thing? Capping until you meet a very painful and bloody end?"

"If only your ideas were as smart as your mouth," Liam retorts.

I put my palms on the table on either side of me. "Yeah, this isn't helping."

Liam leans back and crosses his arms. "I'd like to hear *her* plan." He nods at Loren.

She scoffs. "I'm the least magical person in this room. You two need to find a way to work together. I'm here for support and to stop you from doing something incredibly reckless."

"She's right," I say, overlooking the way one corner of Liam's mouth turns downward. "Maybe we could start with you telling me all about Orin's magic and how we can use it against the Horsemen."

Liam frowns hard, like he wants to spit on the table in front of me. After a moment of strained silence, he folds his arms and glances away. Loren rolls her eyes and sucks in a breath, preparing to lay into him, but I hold up a hand, stopping her.

"Fine." I sigh. "We'll save that for later. Can you at least tell us more about your magic? If we know what everyone can do, we can come up with a plan that uses everyone's strengths to our advantage."

Liam takes a deep breath and unfolds his arms. "My magic is descended from my mother's. She possessed Life magic, and I have Light magic."

"That's cool," says Loren. "How does it work?"

"I can create or manipulate light in any form, even fire, mostly for defense or resources," he says.

Loren sits up straighter. "Can you show us?"

Liam's face falls, and he looks vulnerable, a sight so foreign it's almost terrifying. His magic has a cost, and I'm not sure he can afford to waste any of it.

A crueler version of me would sit back and bask in his unease as payback for how awful he's made me feel so many times before. But the satisfaction fades the moment I realize that by taking pleasure in someone else's pain, I'm no better than Larry Adams.

No matter what Liam has done, he's still a person. A kid. Like me. The only difference is he *really* has no one.

"I've seen it already," I tell Loren. "Which gives me an idea." I turn to Liam. "Could you use your light magic to make a shield?"

He nods. "Easy."

"Hmm . . ." I tap my chin and think. It's a stretch, but it might give us a fighting chance.

"You're so dramatic," whines Loren. "Tell us what you're thinking, goober."

"You know how your shield protects *you* from magical attacks?" When Liam and Loren both nod, I say, "Well, theoretically, that would mean you could create a sort of reverse shield—one that could imprison a magical person."

"You may be onto something. . . ." Liam's voice trails off, and he wilts in his seat as if struggling with an unpleasant thought. "Except . . . my magic has . . . limitations. I can create a shielded cage, but I can't hold it for long, especially not if it's a cage powerful enough to contain all the Horsemen."

"What about just one Horseman?" I ask.

He narrows his eyes at me. "I dunno. What are you getting at?"

"Hear me out," I say. "I think our only target at the rally should be Death. It's too risky to try to take them all on at once. We can separate Death and—"

"You only want to go after Death first because she's your sister." Liam narrows his eyes at me. "And now I'm wondering if I made a mistake trusting you."

I fold my hands in my lap to keep from slamming them onto the tabletop. I've had it with his counterproductive attitude. But then I look at him, and for a moment, I can see past the mask he puts on to hide how scared he must be. And I cling to that familiarity to keep this conversation from going (more) left.

"You know what, Liam?" I say, sounding much calmer than I feel. "I get why you're mad, but I didn't choose to be possessed by Orin, so I'm gonna need you to stop hating me for it."

He looks down but doesn't reply.

"He's right, you know," Loren interjects. "We all need to work together if we wanna survive this. And I promise, you can go back to hating each other after we save the world."

That at least pulls a smile from Liam, which is about as difficult as squeezing water from a stone.

"You're right," he mumbles to the tabletop, then looks up at me. "Sorry."

Well, if we can pull a sincere apology out of Liam, saving the world from four homicidal Horsemen should be a slice of pie.

"Since you can't hold a shielded prison, could you enchant something?" Loren asks him. "Like handcuffs we could use to restrain Death until we figure out what to do with her?"

Liam thinks a moment, then nods. "That might work."

I sit back and huff a relieved sigh. Maybe we're getting somewhere after all.

We change locations several times throughout the day, pausing intermittently for snacks, but the debate keeps going about how best to isolate Death from the other Horsemen so we can restrain her and get her back to our parents. At one point, Liam falls asleep on top of the paper he's been brainstorming on all day and drools like a giant Saint Bernard. After Loren and I finished giggling about it, I realize he's actually kinda cute when he's not scowling. Well, he's kinda cute when he's scowling too—just not when it's directed at me. And I catch myself wondering if he and I will ever be *real* friends one day, maybe like me and Loren. Or like me and Sky used to be. Or even something altogether different.

The planning goes on until Dexter returns and long after the sun disappears beneath the horizon and the moon takes over the sky. By midnight, we're all spent, and we wander to our respective rooms to rest so we can resume first thing in the morning.

I shower and tuck into bed to turn my phone on and text Mom.

> Hi Mom.

Alex! I've been calling and texting all day.

Please keep your phone on.

> Sorry! I don't mean to be disrespectful
>
> I promise I'm being safe though

How are things at the hospital?

They need a lot of help and this is keeping me from storming across town and dragging you back by your ears. I know it's pointless to ask but can you please just come back to the hospital and let me help you???

I wish it were that easy. That I could just run back to my mom and let her handle everything.

But I can't do that.

I'm not coming back without Mags. But I have good news!

We have a plan to bring her home

This will all be over in two days

The three bubbles pop up to inform me she's typing, but I turn my phone back on airplane mode.

I hug myself against the anxiety building in my chest like a snowbank. How do I know if I'm doing the right thing? It mostly feels right, but there are a lot of times (like now) where I feel like I'm willingly (and foolishly) marching myself, Loren, and Liam to our deaths. That's why I turn my phone on airplane mode, no matter how bad it makes me feel to ice Mom out. I don't need the temptation of hitting an "EASY" button right now.

I swear as a gentle wave of sleep overtakes me that I hear a voice inside my head that's not my own whisper softly, *You are enough.*

The voice repeats until I'm fast asleep.

DAY TWO: RECONNAISSANCE

How NOT to conduct a mission to gain intel on the layout of the old Staples Center and the plans for a rally to honor the Horsemen, a posse of magical villains who brought about the End of Days™ and are led by none other than your very own ten-year-old sister, who's possessed by the ancient homicidal spirit of Death from another realm.

Please like and subscribe for more lists on how to survive the apocalypse!—AW

1. **Do NOT** forget that Liam drew the fake "R" on everyone's foreheads with Sharpie (thanks for the idea, Rider Guy) and accidentally smudge it once you start sweating in the Southern California sun. Because then you'll have to ask Liam the Grouch to redo it and listen to him moan about it the whole time before you can go inside.

2. **Do NOT** put the person with zero sense of direction (aka ME) in charge of mapping the arena's layout. Befriend someone like Loren, whose navigation skills rival that of a messenger raven.

3. **Do NOT** nearly forget about the mission because you get so caught up in learning that the person you've been fighting with relentlessly since you first met has a

vulnerable, and quite interesting, side that you first notice when he has moments of artistic brilliance while making quick work drawing the map of the arena.

4. **Do NOT** get sucked into your best friend's drama when she makes pointed eye contact with you after the events of #3 and smirks as if she has *any* idea what's going on in your head.

5. **Do NOT** sneak off to scout the backup generator room and get caught by one of the Riders and have to come up with a life-saving lie on the fly. But if you do, bring someone who's good at making up stories. Me. 😀

6. **Under absolutely NO circumstances at all whatsoever, no matter what,** should you nearly blow your cover on the way out by getting into a loud argument with one of your stubborn, know-it-all teammates whose name rhymes with "leave 'em" (which I almost did).

7. **Do NOT** leave Cadillac Freddie's without one of those one-armed crushing hugs that almost squeeze the wind out of you after you pick up critical supplies for your impossible mission.

8. **Do NOT** go to bed until everyone is confident in the plan you've all come up with together, no matter how many fights you got in along the way.

9. **Do NOT** forget to pray to universe that this works.

10. And lastly, **do NOT** forget to hug your teammates. Caution: If you are so magically inclined, be prepared for an influx of warmth in the form of fondness and security from *both* your teammates.

WARNING! SIDE EFFECTS OF THIS MISSION COULD

DAY THREE: REST

Dexter tells us his family's doing well, though they still refuse to leave home. After he cooks breakfast and leaves to visit with them again, I clear the table and smooth out the map of the arena that we marked up with our plans last night. I suck a deep breath in and exhale slowly.

I'm still nervous, but I feel a lot better than I did sitting here two days ago. What a difference forty-eight hours can make, I guess. And Liam and I haven't so much as scowled at each other since dinner yesterday. Progress.

"Let's go over everything one more time, to make sure we're all good," I say, and Loren and Liam nod their agreement. "Once we initiate our plan, we'll be out of there within eight minutes—if this works.

"Liam and I will take our places at the back of the stage." I circle the part of the map where we've drawn a rectangle representing the stage, which takes up nearly one complete side of the court. "And blend in with the crew."

Liam sets two red markers on the table. "For our disguises."

I give him a thumbs-up. "Loren, you'll hide in the electrical room and wait for my text." I tap the electrical room on the map and glance up at her. "Once the Horsemen arrive onstage and let their guards down, I'll give the cue to cut the lights."

She nods, and I trace the path from the electrical room to the nearby stairwell, up to the next floor, and down the hallway to the main doors opposite the front of the stage.

"You have no more than two minutes to get back to these doors," I tell her, then look at Liam, who stands with his arms crossed, staring down at the map like a hardened soldier. I wonder if he's ever not taking himself so seriously. "In the meantime, Liam and I will get into position next to the stage and wait for your signal."

Loren mimics exploding with her hands and says, "Boom." A chaotic glimmer of excitement in her eyes makes me grin—and simultaneously worries me.

"Right," I say. "You'll light the fireworks right outside the doors, and while the Horsemen are distracted by the commotion, Liam and I will rush the stage and tie Death up with the rope Liam infused with shield magic."

Liam sets the coil of thin rope on the table. The sunlight hits it just right and the enchanted surface of the gray nylon fibers glimmers like a field of fireflies. He stares at it with a deeply contemplative expression, as if he's unsure about something.

"It's gonna work," I say.

His eyes snap up to mine. "But what if it doesn't?"

Loren sucks in a breath and holds it, likely anticipating another argument.

"We gotta believe it will," I tell him. "I trust you and your magic. We're a team now."

Liam's face softens. He looks at me, and his lips part

slightly as if he wants to say something but can't or doesn't know how.

"So," I continue, "we've snuck in. Cut the power. And launched our diversion. After Liam lassos—"

"I already told you I'm not doing the lasso thing!" he grumbles.

I huff. "You could totally do the lasso thing if you wanted to do the lasso thing."

Loren snickers from across the table, and Liam glares at her. She shrugs and says, "Sorry. The lasso thing *would* be really cool."

He stares down at the table and shakes his head, but I don't miss the super-brief upward twitch of the corners of his mouth. Not a full smile, but I'll take it!

I clear my throat loudly. "As I was saying, once Liam ties Death up with the magical rope that renders her powerless, he and I will haul her through the exit doors directly behind the stage—ideally before the emergency generators start and the lights come back on. Once we're a safe distance away, we'll call Dexter with our getaway car to drive us home. Easy-peasy."

Loren raises a brow at me. "Now you're being delusional."

Liam does smile this time.

"Well, that actually *is* the easy part," I say. "We still have to figure out how to exorcise Death from Mags's body."

Anxious tension clamps everyone's mouths shut for a few silent moments. We all got so wrapped up in the excitement of actually having a solid plan for the first time that we forgot about the bigger issue looming in the distance. I feel a bit guilty for being a buzzkill after we finally found harmony in our little ragtag team.

"So . . . what now?" Loren asks on the tail end of a deep sigh.

Surprisingly, Liam looks to me for the answer.

"Well," I tell them, "today, we rest. And tomorrow, we're saving the world."

21

THE RIDER RALLY

The lower the sun sinks, the faster my pulse drums. The sky's already darkening, except for the horizon, which looks like it's on fire, a brilliant strip of oranges and reds that complement the fires still burning all around the city. Loren, Liam, and I huddle together on the sidewalk just outside the arena. We spent the day preparing and scoping the area, but now it's finally go time.

Loren is wearing a backpack (not as nice as her camo one with all the pins) filled with fireworks, and Liam is clinging to the straps of the sling bag hanging over his shoulders that contains the coil of magical rope.

Dexter rounds the corner in our silver Mini Cooper and vanishes from view. My stomach dips once I realize I left my nerve on the seat. He's gone to park and wait for our signal to bring the getaway car around. He returned early from checking on his family today to make sure we got to the arena and back safely. I could tell by the strained faces he made when we shared the details of our plan that he didn't agree, but he's at least going along with it.

"It's almost time." Liam's voice is low and grave as he stares at the setting sun. "This thing starts at sundown, yeah?"

If I didn't know better, I'd think we were waiting for a Lakers game—or a concert. This is where I was supposed to come to the Santaolalla show with Sky. Even in the middle of trying to save the world, I can't stop thinking about him. The Forgetting doesn't seem to be working so well anymore.

I nod. "Let's do this. Eight minutes and it'll all be over."

"Eight minutes," Loren repeats, and exhales a trembling breath.

I turn to the row of doors at the arena entrance, but my feet won't move. The air feels thick, as if I'm drowning. I shut my eyes and try to steady my breathing, but it does nothing to stop the encroaching panic. And then I panic, because I can't stop panicking.

I was so confident in the plan last night. In us. In *me*. But what if I'm wrong? I've never done anything like this before. How do I know I'm not making a huge mistake—that might cost us our lives?

You're enough. The calm but stern voice bombards my thoughts, snapping me back to reality.

It's the same voice I heard the other night, but I was half asleep then and figured I'd been dreaming.

You're enough, it repeats.

"Did you hear that?" I ask Loren, who's been talking with Liam in a hushed voice.

She turns to me, confusion wrinkling her brow. "What?"

Liam falls silent and watches me with curious, dark eyes.

Heat rushes my face. "I, uh . . . Nothing. It was nothing."

"What did you hear?" he asks.

For a minute, I consider telling him, but if he knows what's going on with me, I need to know too. Because between this intrusive voice in my head, magic I can't control, and Shadow Man all coming at me at the same time, I feel like I'm losing my grip on reality.

"It was weird," I say. "I don't know if I imagined it or not, but I was feeling super anxious about going inside just now, and I heard a voice say, 'You're enough.' I've heard it once before—two nights ago when we were neck-deep in coming up with our plan."

"You're not hearing things," Liam says. "That's Orin."

"How do you know?" I ask. "Can you hear it too?"

Liam's nose wrinkles. "No."

Oh, yeah. Poked a sore spot again. Way to go, Alex Wise.

"Sorry, I didn't mean—"

Liam rolls his eyes. "Orin helped create me. They were essentially one of my parents. After my magic manifested, they taught me how to control it. At first, I was scared and overwhelmed, but they'd always put their hands on both sides of my face"—he touches his cheek now, as if he can feel Orin's palm—"and tell me I was enough."

Liam clenches his jaw and stares at me, but I don't look away. His anger makes a little more sense now.

"If it's any consolation, I know what it's like to be abandoned by a parent," I tell him.

"Orin didn't abandon me!" The sharpness in his voice hits me square in the face.

"Then who exactly are you so mad at, Liam?" I ask.

The muscles in his jaw tighten. "I don't want to talk about it. We should get going."

I glance up at the sky, which has darkened more since we've been standing on the sidewalk. The moon glows brightly on one side, while on the other, the last dregs of bloodred sunlight cling to the skyline. I'm ready for all this to be over.

I take Loren's hand in mine as we head inside with the rest of the people. I share her fear through touch—it doesn't feel much different from my own. But this time the additional emotional load is not overwhelming, maybe because I'm holding my best friend's hand. Neither of us talks. I appreciate moments like this when we can find comfort in silence together—our own special way of communicating without speaking.

I didn't imagine there'd be so many people at this thing. I don't know what I expected, actually, which makes sense, I guess, since this is my first apocalypse and all. The crowds make their way through the entrance hall to any one of the several sets of doors that open to the top level of stadium seats.

These folks definitely aren't here for a Lakers game. Most of the people I see look downright terrified. Their heads are on a swivel, and their eyes are either wide or brimming with tears, like a herd of gazelles being led to a hyena's den.

And then there are others who think the apocalypse is one big tailgate party. They lug heavy coolers filled with ice, drinks, and food, and some are even dressed in costumes—I see two grim reapers and a person wearing a horse head (a fake one, but no less weird), and one guy's even dressed like Batman, which makes zero sense to me, but I believe in letting everyone live their best life.

Once we're inside, Loren dips off to the electrical room, and Liam and I head toward the main stage, trekking down the long staircase to the court. People fill most of the seats, and even though I'm focused on the stairs in front of me (and not falling), I can't hide from the waves of fear and anxiety crashing into me from *everyone*. The unease is palpable in the arena, damp like humidity. But . . . I'm not touching anyone. How is this happening? *Why* is this happening?

I press my hands to either side of my head. *Orin! This is too much! I'm not ready for this. AND HOW IS THIS EVEN HELPFUL RIGHT NOW???*

A millennia-old magical deity's been squatting inside me for close to a week now, and I've gotten all the hassle and zero benefits. The constant random invasion of other people's emotions is like being spun around until I'm nauseous and then plunged into a tank of ice-cold water. Negative five stars. Would highly *not* recommend.

My chest tightens, and I stop abruptly, almost causing Liam to run into my back.

"What's wrong?" he asks over my shoulder, not caring to mask the irritation in his voice.

I grab one side of my head and squeeze my eyes shut. I don't know if I can do this. The magic is too overwhelming. I don't want to feel everyone's emotions. It's going to burn through my mind—and burn me, too. Am I supposed to deal with this sickening power for the rest of my life? Will I ever be able to watch a movie in a crowded theater again? Or enjoy a packed theme park? Or be around a group of people at all?

Breathe, whispers the voice in my head. Orin. *Focus inward,* they say.

They repeat the chant inside my head. I shut my eyes and take slow, deep breaths in and out. I concentrate on the rise and fall of my chest, oxygen flowing in through my nose, carbon dioxide out. Soon the rolling waves of anxiety begin to recede. I gasp with relief.

Thanks, Orin.

They don't respond.

I nod to Liam, and we continue down the stairs. Along the way, I update my superpowers note in my Notes app with this new tidbit of helpful information: I can detect when a nearby large group of people feel the same emotion strongly. Side effects: nausea, anxiety, extreme annoyance.

At the bottom of the stairs, a conversation between two guys with authentic Rider symbols on their foreheads grabs my attention.

"We're lucky we still have cell service," the first guy says to the other as he examines the phone with a precariously cracked screen in his hands. "I don't know how we could've pulled all this together without it."

The second guy, who reminds me of a taller, white version of Cadillac Freddie, harrumphs and shakes his head. "See how long that lasts."

Their conversation fades behind me as we approach the right side of the stage. I wipe my clammy hands on the front of my shorts and hope beyond hope that cell service doesn't die before I can text Loren to cut the lights.

Anxiety taunts me from the edge of my mind. I should've

already thought about this potential wrinkle, back when we had time to come up with a solution. Now all I can do is pray my mistakes won't have bloody consequences.

Liam and I climb over the short barrier cutting off back-stage from the audience and find a Rider lady busy organizing dozens of cases of equipment and wires. The whole mess resembles a bunch of bird's nests made from tech I have no idea how to use.

She sees us approaching and narrows her eyes.

"We're volunteers," I announce. "We were sent back here to help out."

She adopts a look of respite. "General Eustice wants all this equipment sorted and ready to be moved by the end of the night."

Liam nods. "Got it."

Rider Lady gives both of us one more up-and-down look and hesitates a moment, like she wants to reconsider her decision to leave her assignment to two kids, but then she just shakes her head and walks away.

"*General* Eustice?" I say to Liam. "Is this guy serious?"

"Sadly, I think so."

His deadpan reply makes me chuckle under my breath. I'm not sure if he was joking, but I like this version of Liam a lot more than the arrogant hothead I can't stop fighting with.

The arena lights dim, tossing a veil of shadow across everywhere but the stage. A chilling shudder ripples down my spine. Darkness reminds me of Shadow Man. Too much of it gives him too many places to hide. I hope he's taken the day off, because I can only handle one crisis at a time.

A rumbling of raucous cheers, whoops, and applause draws us closer to the front of the stage. My heart pounds in my chest as intensely as the thundering stomps coming from the crowd. A machine propped at the edge of the stage beside us whirs to life, startling both me and Liam. It emits thick clouds of fog that roll across the stage. Liam and I raise an eyebrow at each other at the same time.

Eustice—excuse me, *General* Eustice—struts onstage. He's wearing a blue suit (who in the world would choose to wear a suit in the middle of an apocalypse? Eustice Barnes, apparently) and shiny, expensive-looking shoes. His usually untidy curls are slicked straight back, the ones in the rear jutting out defiantly.

A nearby speaker as tall as me rattles my insides as music blares from all directions. But the song choice makes me frown. Vanessa Carlton? "A Thousand Miles"? I choke back a laugh when Eustice turns around and frowns at the Rider who perches behind a curtain at the rear of the stage. The guy's face and the ugly "R" plastered on his forehead are eerily lit from below by the glow of his phone's screen as he frantically swipes.

The guitar riff opening of "Eye of the Tiger" starts and almost makes me laugh again, which settles my nerves a bit. The few faces I can make out of the people in the closest seats are mostly confused, but everyone seems resigned to sitting and suffering.

Eustice waves to the audience on all sides as if he's the president or something; then he grabs the mic off the stand and the music stops abruptly. His voice echoes through the arena.

"Riders! Friends! Allies! We're broadcasting *live* on social media platforms around the world. . . ." He pauses to acknowledge the Riders at the front of the stage, each aiming their phone or tablet at him. "As your Rider General, I want to welcome you to our Apocalypse Rally!" Cheers erupt from the crowd again, and he relishes them a bit before holding up his hand and urging for silence. "Humanity is at a pivotal moment—"

CRACK!

Eustice lets out an amplified, high-pitched yelp. I almost leap out of my shorts, but Liam remains unmoved, arms crossed tightly and fingers pressing harder into his deep brown skin.

The Horsemen are here.

And not a moment too soon. Facing off against the Horsemen of the Apocalypse seems like a far better fate to me than having to listen to the entirety of Eustice's dumb speech.

Gasps roll through the crowd, and the bustling din of all the people gathered in the arena dims to a weak rumble of murmurs. But still—not a single soul leaves.

I asked Mom once why whenever there's an accident on the highway, it messes up traffic going in the opposite direction. She told me it was because of something called rubbernecking, which is a fancy word for not minding your business. I never thought I'd see people rubbernecking during the actual apocalypse, though.

Eustice seems annoyed until he turns and sees the Horsemen—the glower disappears from his face then. Death approaches and he holds out the microphone to her, but she smacks his hand away. Without a word, he retreats to the back of the stage with a group of Riders huddling near the curtain.

Bright stage lights illuminate the Horsemen, standing with their backs straight and heads high, staring into the crowd.

Death is at the forefront in her elegant floor-length satin dress, both hands on her hips, gold and black bangles covering the length of her forearms. Her head is crowned in an explosion of loose curls that drape her back and shoulders. She looks like a queen addressing her loyal subjects—except she's the queen of death.

Moritz has turned my little sister into something unrecognizable.

Famine wears black cargo pants, ankle boots, and a tank top. Since I last saw her, she's cut her azure hair short. Her jaguar and panther circle her legs several times before lying down, head to tail, surrounding her in a protective ring of fur, muscles, and claws.

War keeps his hands in the pockets of his dark jeans. It could be the red shirt he's wearing, but his golden-brown skin gives off a warm red glow like the sun's setting somewhere inside him.

Pestilence is still rocking his white muumuu thingy—and he's barefoot, which I would say was odd, but we blew the gauge on "odd" a *long* time ago. He walks to the edge of the stage and sits down, dangling his legs over the edge like a kid.

When Death speaks, her voice booms through the arena even though she refused Eustice's mic. "I've never favored long speeches," she says, "so I'll make this quick."

"Thank *God*," I whisper, and Liam nudges me with his elbow.

"I am here to end this world," Death proclaims. "And

through the ashes left behind from Famine, War, Pestilence"—she pauses after each of the last three words, gesturing to the three Horsemen behind her—"and Death, a new, better, purer world will emerge.

"The Four Plagues are upon you. One quarter of the world's population has ceased to exist in this realm. War has dissolved your world's governing bodies and military forces. Famine has laid waste to your crops and turned many of the creatures of your world against you." Death grins down at Pestilence. "And Pestilence is next to give his extra-special gift to the world, premiering right here in Downtown Los Angeles—and coming *real* soon to a neighborhood near you!"

The crowd breaks into mumbles, but still, no one leaves or disrupts Death's presentation. Pestilence sits still as a gargoyle statue from his perch on the stage's edge. I'm not looking forward to any surprises that creepy guy has up the sleeves of his muumuu.

"Tonight is your first opportunity to choose your path to Dominion." Death chuckles coldly under her breath. "There are only two roads. They both lead to the same destination, but one's gonna hurt a whole lot more than the other. You can take the easy way—pledge your allegiance to the Horsemen and become a Rider—or face the darkness of the Cosmic Shift and the End of Days without our divine protection. And if you survive long enough, you'll be given one final chance to kneel at our thrones or suffer for the remainder of eternity."

I turn a confused look to Liam. "Dominion? Cosmic Shift? What is she talking about?"

His grimace deepens. "I'm not sure."

This is bad. *Really* bad.

"Do it," Liam insists, jarring me for a second. "Send the signal before it's too late!"

"Yes, right."

I take my phone out and type the text to Loren, but when I hit send, an error message pops up. And my heart drops to my feet.

This can't be happening. Not right now.

Liam peers at my phone impatiently. "Did you send it?"

I . . . don't know what to do now. We *tested* this on our recon mission. Both our phones worked then. Now mine says "No service."

"I—I can't," I murmur. "I lost signal."

"What do you mean?" When I don't answer, he hisses, "Alex—"

"Just let me think!"

Liam leans away, giving me some much-needed breathing room.

But my mind's already too frazzled. Only static. How could I not have prepared for this?

"I'm not waiting anymore." Liam pulls the rope from his bag, loops it over his shoulder, and starts toward the stage.

"No! Wait!" I pull him back before he can haul himself up, and he stumbles back into me, nearly knocking me over.

KER-THUNK!

A sound like a gargantuan steel door slamming shut re-sounds, drowning out Death's voice.

The lights die.

And unbridled chaos roars to life inside the arena.

22

CREEPS

In the first second of darkness, the world completely disappears.

I hear Liam's sharp intake of breath beside me.

Eight minutes. Eight minutes until this is over. Until we're free.

The first person's scream ices my blood. The floodgates open then as screeches and shrieks ring out from every direction. I feel trapped in a coffin, my air supply quickly dwindling—but then the inside begins to fill with the rush of fear and anxiety raining in from everyone like sweat from their pores. It's like I'm drowning again, standing in the dark by the stage, right next to Liam. I put my hand on his back, careful to only touch his T-shirt, to ground myself in reality. He doesn't shrug me off or flinch. He remains strong and sturdy, like an old willow.

Breathe.

Focus inward.

Breathe.

Focus inward.

Dim emergency lighting clicks on, illuminating the walkways to the exits. Cell phone flashlights flick on throughout the crowd, strobing across the frightened faces of all the people stumbling over chairs, stairs, and each other to get to the doors. But none of them open. People snatch and bang and push and shout, but nothing works.

This wasn't part of our plan. And now we're all trapped here.

"Time," barks Liam under his breath.

Oh, no. I got so overwhelmed by the influx of emotion from the crowd that I forgot to start the timer on my phone when the lights went out! I mumble, "Sorry," and start the timer.

Liam presses his lips together, his disapproving face underlit by the glow of my phone's screen, which makes me feel like even more of a royal mess.

You're enough, Orin's voice echoes in my head.

Not sure I believe that right now, but thanks anyway.

"It's okay," Liam whispers gently. "I guess about a minute passed before you started the timer. We'll just assume the timer's behind a minute."

Relief curls through my chest. "Good idea."

But my reprieve is short-lived, because Alex Wise never gets a break.

The timer crosses the two-minute mark, and the fireworks haven't gone off yet. This is bad. The lights have been out for over three minutes now. Loren's late.

My heart drops. I hope nothing's happened to her.

"We can't wait anymore," Liam says. "It's now or die."

I boost him onto the stage, then grab his hand so he can help me clamber up too. His grip on my hand is a jumper cable, sending a tremor of power and adrenaline through me. I'm sensitive enough to notice the wisp of fear that follows the moment we release each other.

"Be ready," Liam whispers, slowly uncoiling the rope. "Things are gonna happen fast."

I swallow my nerves and nod.

He takes off in a fast crouch toward the front of the stage, where I can make out the silhouettes of Death, Famine, and Pestilence (who's on his feet now) in a huddle. But something doesn't feel right. Wait . . . someone's missing.

My eyes dart around the stage, but War is nowhere to be found. I think to warn Liam, but he's already halfway to the others, poised and ready to strike.

And that's when I see him.

War slinks through the shadows, smoothly as Shadow Man, and catches up to Liam, who stops abruptly and stands ramrod straight as War whispers in his ear.

Liam turns slowly to face me and pulls the rope taut in his hands. His dark eyes now blaze a furious shade of red, dousing me in color as if I'm standing in a car's taillights.

I stumble backward and trip over my own feet, smacking hard onto my bottom.

Liam lassos me with the magic rope, which snaps around my torso, pinning my arms to my sides. He yanks me toward him. The nylon digs into my arms, and my butt drags across the stage floor. Once I'm in front of him, Liam stoops and clutches me in a headlock I can't escape. I'm nowhere near as strong as him, even without War's magical influence.

Liam's heavy breaths pant in my ear and his bicep flexes

against my cheek. But all I feel is the tenderness of his skin, taut across wiry muscle. He snarls with feral rage, but not a single drop of that emotion slips through our connection. I'm cut off from Orin—and the Sense.

Welp, I'm about to die, but at least we know the enchanted rope works.

KER-THUNK!

The lights pop back on, an explosion of brightness that forces my eyes shut.

"Enough!" Death commands.

Liam lets me go and retracts the rope, which re-coils around his wrist, freeing me. I fall forward onto my hands and knees, but I'm too weak to catch myself and my face hits the stage.

"Uggh . . ." I groan and roll over onto my back.

When my vision clears, Liam is hovering over me, his eyes back to their normal dark color, War's influence lifted.

"Alex!" He shakes me, my T-shirt bunched in his hands, until I hold up a palm and sit up. "I'm so sorry. I—I couldn't stop myself. I wanted to, I swear, but—"

"It's fine," I interrupt. "You can make up for almost killing me later."

The Horsemen stand together at the front of the stage, watching us with callous expressions. Famine's giant jungle cats sit on their haunches, staring with haunting yellow eyes.

The people in the arena haven't stopped shouting or trying to break down the doors, but none have escaped yet. And no one's paying attention to what's happening onstage.

"Ah, there you are," Death says with a hint of cheerful

surprise, as if I'm a lost kitten that's just wandered back onto her front porch.

Liam's the first on his feet. I'm a bit slow to follow because my head's still ringing.

Death eyes me. "I knew you'd come. You're as stubborn as you are brave, and twice as useless. We'll catch up in a moment, but first, I need to wrap things up here. So stay put for now."

Witnessing Death speak to me with my sister's voice and do all these awful things in my sister's body will never not make my skin crawl. I will never get used to this. I shouldn't have to. And that's why I won't.

I'm about to snap back, but Famine's leopard and panther launch themselves into the air. They clear the stage in a single bound, landing in front of us with a *THUMP* that shakes the stage floor. The leopard stops in front of Liam, the panther in front of me. They both growl, lips peeling back to reveal fangs that could chomp my head like a Tootsie Pop.

Neither Liam nor I move a muscle.

Death massages her temple with one hand and says, "I've had enough of this." She turns and sweeps one hand slowly across the audience, every person opposite her fingertips magically silenced. The last voice is snuffed out, and the arena falls so quiet I could hear a flea humming a lullaby.

"Now, that's better." This time when Death speaks, her voice is amplified throughout the arena. She turns to the throng of Riders huddled at the back of the stage. "Get the stream back up—now." The group scatters, and moments later, they're back in position with tablets and phones aimed at Death.

Everyone still crowding the doors stops and returns their full attention to the stage. The panther's stomach rumbles. Liam and I share a nervous sidelong glance. I get the strangest urge to grab his hand, but I don't dare try lest this panther chomp it off as an appetizer.

"I'm thoroughly annoyed now, so let's cut to the chase," Death says. "Bear the Mark of my Rider Legion or suffer. It's time to choose—even those watching the stream around the world. Kneel to pledge your allegiance or suffer until Dominion."

Sheesh. I guess the people who somehow missed the broadcast are in trouble by default.

I want to scream when the first handful of people from the crowd get down on one knee or both. Others watch as those around them kneel, some clasping their hands before their chests. All around the room, among those who give in and those who stand, eyes are closed and lips move feverishly, properly muttering prayers to whichever god is listening.

I bite down hard on my lip to keep from crying out. This is my fault. Not everyone on their knees wants to submit to the Horsemen's will, judging by the many wet faces and trembling, soundless mouths I see in the room. They're just trying to survive—because I failed.

Angry red light sparkles on the foreheads of the people on their knees. It vanishes as quickly as it appeared, leaving the Mark of the Rider Legion emblazoned front and center on the face of everyone who sold themselves to the Horsemen. I scan the room and choke back a gasp. There are now more Riders than non-Riders. If I had to guess, I'd say less than a quarter of the people in attendance resisted Death's lure. The others bear the ugly "R" on their foreheads—they belong to the Horsemen now.

I wonder how many people around the world gave up the fight today. How many souls did the Horsemen win over to help build their new world? All because I messed up.

A chilling tendril of hopelessness unfurls in my chest, and I reach up to hug myself, but Famine's panther snarls under her breath. I clench my fists in my lap instead.

I don't know how to fix this. *If* I can fix this.

"To my legion," announces Death, "welcome to the New World Order. You've chosen wisely. We have a lot of work to do, and I'll be with you shortly so we can get started."

She snaps her fingers and every Rider in the arena drops into their shadow, leaving only those who rejected the Horsemen standing in the bleachers.

"And you all are quite special," Death says, addressing what's left of the audience.

"Leave them alone!" The words burst from my mouth before I can think better. The panther in front of me bares her teeth, but I look her right in her large yellow eyes.

Death ignores me. "Since you all were bold enough to refuse my gift to my face, I'll make an example out of you for those watching at home."

The remaining people don't even have time to panic before Death snaps her fingers. But instead of falling into their shadows like the Riders, the people are blown across the arena in every direction, their bodies disappearing in thick shadows along the ceiling and walls.

And now it's only me and Liam—and the Horsemen.

I have no idea where Loren is, but I'm thankful she couldn't make it into the arena to be disappeared along with all those other innocent people.

"We're in deep doodie," I whisper to Liam, who tenses even more.

Famine calls her jungle cats, who stand and stretch, as if bored with all this, then pad across the stage to snuggle up against her face and purr.

"What did you do to those people?" I ask Death.

"Don't worry. They're not dead—*yet*." She smiles at me, which turns my stomach. "I've sent them to a purgatorial realm. Think of it like an amusement park except the rides and the characters all want to murder you. Fun times. They'll remain there until Dominion, and their souls will be the first we judge."

I can't help but wonder how these Horsemen are so powerful and Liam and I seem so weak in comparison. Our magic originated from the same realm, yet from what I've seen of just Death's and War's abilities alone, we're hopelessly outmatched. And I still haven't seen what Famine and Pestilence can *really* do in a one-on-one fight, but if they're anything like the others, we have a monumental task ahead of us.

"Why are you wreaking havoc in *our* realm?" I ask. "You destroyed your own world and now you want to do the same to ours. Leave us alone, colonizer!"

Death laughs. "That's cute. But you have bigger problems to worry about." She turns to the empty arena and lifts her hands on either side of her.

The ground quakes stronger than anything we've ever felt before in California. A long section of the stadium floor rips like cheap wrapping paper. The floor crumbles at the edges of the hole and falls away into the dark of nothing.

A skeleton hand reaches up from the dark and latches onto the craggy earth beneath the tear. Another hand shoots up and grips the edge of the stadium floor. A skeleton hauls itself out of the hole into the arena. Red embers glow viciously in the eye sockets of its skull. I couldn't guess how old this thing is, but judging by the rusted pirate's sword sheathed in its rib cage and the clothes that have been reduced to ribbons of faded cloth caught on its bleached bones, I'd say pretty freakin' old.

The skeleton yanks the sword from its chest and turns to me. The embers in its eye sockets glow brighter and brighter until orange flames lick the top of its skull. It points the sword at me and releases a hissing howl that makes both me and Liam stagger backward.

Another pulls itself up from the depths. This one has a double axe hanging between its ribs and shoulder blade. More and more skeletons crawl out of the hole until they resemble ants pouring from an anthill. After the last one climbs out, dozens of skeletal soldiers stand at the opposite end of the stadium floor.

Every one of these Creeps (yeah, I def made that name up on the fly, but we're in mortal peril right now, so let's just go with it) has those spooky burning embers for eyes. And they're all armed—though I question the choices of several. Like the one with the giant water cannon that looks like a plastic Gatling gun or the one wielding neon green and yellow flyswatters.

"What's the deal with all this? If you want us dead, why go through so much trouble? Can't you just snap your fingers and—" I drag my finger across my throat.

Liam glowers at me.

"If it were that easy, I'd have nuked you both a *long* time ago," Death says with a snarl. "But your possession and"— she points at Liam—"*your* lineage make it a bit more complex than the snap of a finger.

"It's so bothersome, in fact, that I can't even shadow-travel Alex like the others, unless I want to risk permanently separating his mind from his body." She pauses to sigh dramatically. "And as nice as that sounds, I promised someone important I wouldn't murder you two today. But that doesn't mean I can't have a little fun." She turns back to her Creep army. "Bring them to the tower and lock them up until we return."

Then she and the other Horsemen fall into their shadows.

And it's just me and Liam and a ton of blood-thirsty Creeps.

"Okay, *now* we're in deep doodie," I say.

Liam groans.

23

WORST.
CARPOOL. *EVER.*

Claiming to be terrified would be a massive understatement right now.

We are at a significant magical disadvantage here. I still don't know how to use my Sense properly, and even if I did, I'm not sure how helpful it would be in this particular situation. And Liam's Light is a limited resource, though he has yet to reveal why. I make a mental note to probe further into this when we're not fighting for our lives.

Magic's failed us, so we're going to have to fight the old-fashioned way tonight.

The first Creep that emerged from the hole steps in front of the others and starts a slow march toward the stage, brandishing its sword. The collective sound of all those bones creaking against one another makes my skin crawl.

I bolt to the front of the stage, rip the mic out of its stand, and toss it aside. I grab the tripod stand and snap the legs up so the whole thing becomes a club.

Liam snatches off his bracelet, and when he throws his

arm to the side, his staff extends to its full length, almost as tall as he is. I forgot how cool that is.

We leap down from the stage together.

The moment our feet hit the arena floor, the Creep in the lead releases another blood-chilling howl and charges. The air echoes with the sharp clicks of the Creeps' bony footfalls. Liam and I both cling to our weapons and exchange a glance of rock-solid determination.

We're going to survive this.

Maybe.

Liam makes the first strike, knocking the heads off two Creeps and immediately snapping me out of my daze. Their skulls fall and roll aside, spilling hot embers that hiss when they hit the floor and quickly turn to ash.

I swing my stand-club as hard as I can at one of the Creeps, which catches it off guard. It smacks into the bit of spine between its ribs and hips, knocking a chunk of spinal cord away and splitting the Creep in half. The skeleton crashes to the floor, its top and bottom halves wriggling. I'm admiring my handiwork when two Creeps rush me.

Imitating Liam, who's kicking major Creep butt next to me, I adjust my grip to the middle of the stand and try to whack both Creeps approaching with either end, but these two were better prepared. They catch the stand and try to wrench it from my hands, but I'm stronger. I guess literally not having muscles is a real disadvantage. I plant my feet and yank hard—a little too hard, because when the Creeps' arms disconnect from the sockets, I fall back onto my bottom.

Without arms, both Creeps fall forward facedown on the

floor. I leap to my feet and swing my stand like a golf club, driving their skulls into the encroaching soldiers one after the other.

I avert my eyes for a second to check on Liam, who's accumulating an impressive pile of still-squirming Creep parts all around him—my first mistake.

The Creep ranks part as the one with the Gatling water gun steps forward. The barrels start spinning, and then I make my second mistake: I laugh. Because what is this—a pool party?

But as it turns out, I'm the joke.

A jet of water with the force of a firehose hits me in the face. My feet slip from beneath me and my back slams into the ground, knocking me breathless. A throng of Creeps rush over and pull me to my feet before I can collect myself. I'm not sure how many of the bony fingers dig into my arms, neck, and legs, but it's enough that I can't break free on my own. The magazines on the Gatling water cannon spin again, and the Creep holding it walks closer, aiming at my face.

"LIAM!" I shout, but he can't spare even a quick look in my direction.

Liam's in trouble too. He tumbles and dodges a pair of Creeps swinging tennis rackets like Serena Williams and another with a wet beach towel that—based on the welts on Liam's face and neck—has been giving him a hard time.

Gatling Creep fires, pelting me from head to toe with water spray that feels like a million tiny fists whaling on me. The jerk steers its aim back toward my face, filling my nose and mouth with water, nearly drowning me.

Liam maneuvers between the two Creeps with tennis rackets, and they swing and miss him but hit each other, sending bone fragments flying. He takes a couple of running steps and hurls his staff like a spear. It slams into the side of Gatling Creep, beheading it and ending the water assault. I gasp for air and try to break free, but the Creeps holding me only grip me tighter.

Liam holds up his hand and his staff zips back to him as if attached by an invisible string. Once he's armed again, he drops to a crouch, barely avoiding the sharp *crack* from the beach towel. He swings his staff, connecting with the Creep's knees, sending it crashing to the floor in a pile of squirming bones.

Liam sprints over to me, and for a moment, I feel the Creeps' grips tighten as they panic, not knowing whether to hang on or let me go and save themselves from Liam's wrath.

"Eight against one is hardly fair," he says.

I flinch as he brings his staff down on the heads of two Creeps on my right. The others let me go, and I stoop quickly to grab my mic stand. Liam and I make short work of reducing the rest of the Creeps in our little corner of the stadium to useless bones.

The others hang back, advancing in small waves while replenishing their numbers as more climb from the hole and join those waiting for their turn at battle.

"If we want to stand a chance, we can't stay on the defensive," I say, my voice trembling slightly because I'm now wet and freezing. "We have to take the fight to them."

"You're right," he says. "Let's do this."

This time, we charge.

Lucky for us, the Creeps aren't very good fighters. Like, at all. But what they lack in skill, they make up for in numbers. Every time we make a bit of headway, more crawl from the hole.

Several minutes later, surrounded by Creeps, Liam and I press our backs together, our chests heaving. The muscles in my arms, legs, and back burn with fatigue.

"We can't keep this up," he says. "We have to come up with something else."

"There has to be another way out," I say. "Maybe a maintenance entrance or something?"

"What is that?" grumbles Liam.

Right. I'm on my own here.

The Creeps press in, preparing to beat us senseless and drag us to the Horsemen's tower. I take a deep breath in and blow it out slowly, preparing for our last stand.

None of us is anticipating the explosion. Not even the Creeps, who all turn their attention to the exit opposite the stage. Smoke rolls into the arena in pillowy tufts from the doors, which have been blown open. I have to squint, but I think I see the silhouette of a girl standing in the smoky doorway . . . Loren!

Rockets wail into the arena, blowing the crowds of Creeps to bits and revealing a path to freedom like the parting of the Red Sea.

"HURRY UP!" Loren screams as she lights more rockets and sends them sailing toward the throngs of Creeps. Each lets out a long, whistling shriek until it explodes in a burst of brilliantly colored sparks and shards of bone that rain back down to the floor.

Liam and I sprint for the exit. I want to throw my arms around my best friend and thank the gods she's alive and apparently unscathed, but we don't have time for tearful reunions. More Creeps are emerging from the hole to replace the ones Loren blasted to smithereens.

"How many of those things are down there?" I ask.

"Let's get out of here, unless you wanna stay and find out," says Loren.

Our sneakers squeak against the tiled floor as we run for the exit. The wails of the Creeps that follow not too far behind help motivate my complaining muscles to keep going.

Once we're outside, Liam ties one end of the magical rope to the handle of the last door, then weaves it through the other handles and knots it to the last door on the opposite side.

The Creeps shuffle into the lobby and press up against the glass doors, clicking their teeth, their eye sockets glowing ferociously. The doors jerk and shift, but the rope holds.

"At least it won't go to waste," Liam says, stepping back slowly.

"The rope buys us some time, but I'm not sure how long that glass is gonna hold," I say.

"I agree," adds Liam. "Where is Dexter?"

Loren turns around and gasps. "Uh, guys . . . I think we have a bigger problem."

Liam and I turn to see what she's talking about. My heart almost stops in that first breathless second I realize our already terrible situation has escalated once again.

Pestilence sits crisscross-applesauce in the middle of the street in front of the arena. His wrinkled face splits with a slobbery, nearly toothless smile that's more frightening than anything I've ever seen in a horror movie.

He's been waiting for us.

24

PESTILENCE

The lights above the front doors of the arena paint a horrific dark red glow over Pestilence. His wrinkled, exaggerated features cast ominous shadows across his face. Even spookier, he sits peacefully still, palms resting on his knees, as if meditating after a long day of work.

"This night just keeps getting better and better," I mumble.

Liam steps protectively in front of me and Loren, his staff at the ready.

The Creeps slam against the door. I'm too nervous to glance back. How much longer before those doors fall and we're swarmed? And where is Dexter? Did he ditch us after all?

Ahhh . . . yesss . . . , an unfamiliar voice echoes in my head.

It catches me by surprise and disorients me so much that I almost lose my balance.

That's not Orin.

When Moritz told me Orin had chosen a weakling as a vessel over Navia's own child, I had to see for myself.

Never mind that it feels like a thousand degrees despite

night having fallen, Pestilence's invasion of my mind makes my entire body shiver. I hug myself tight, but it does little against the sharp coldness deep within me. This feels wrong.

I grit my teeth and yell, "GET OUT OF MY HEAD!"

Pestilence's phlegmy cackle booms between my ears. He remains seated in the middle of the street, eyes closed, face pointed directly at me.

I get the overwhelming urge to claw him from inside my brain, but I settle for covering my ears instead.

Loren's muffled voice comes from somewhere nearby. I feel her gentle touch on my back through the fabric of my T-shirt. But I shut my eyes and concentrate.

I'm sick of gods barging into my mind without my freaking permission!

I'm disappointed, says Pestilence. *I was looking forward to a reunion with Orin, but unfortunately, they're trapped behind a wall, of all things! Ha!*

Well, that explains why we've only been sensing such a pathetic dribble of power coming from you. He chuckles again. *You're magically constipated!*

I grit my teeth and concentrate on my breathing and *not* Pestilence's gross laugh in my head. In. Out.

I imagine the door of my mind: Tall and made of thick, strong wood. Like the door of a mansion—no, *two* doors. But they're swung wide, darkness on one side, light on the other. I stand on the dark side, doorknobs in either hand, staring into the white light.

Pestilence's laugh reverberates from somewhere beyond

the light. The sound makes me want to vomit. I slam the doors of my mind shut, locking him out.

The voice stops.

When I open my eyes, Pestilence—in the flesh—flinches as if someone slapped him. Good. I hope it hurt.

Liam turns back to me, looking angry as usual—except this time not at me. He roars with fury and charges Pestilence.

Pestilence doesn't move a muscle. Liam leaps into the air and swings his staff like we're playing real-life Whac-A-Mole. But at the last possible moment, Pestilence's hand arcs up and snatches Liam's staff out of the air.

Faster than I've ever seen him move before, Pestilence jumps to his feet, takes the staff in both hands, and swings it around (Liam still attached), then lets go, sending Liam soaring.

Liam's back crashes into one of the arena's doors, cracking the glass. He falls to the ground with an *oomph*, and Creeps redirect their efforts, clacking their teeth against the spider-web of fissures in the glass. They press harder and harder until the panes creak and the cracks stretch farther.

Loren and I rush over to him.

"I'm fine," he says tersely, not making eye contact. His arms and legs are scraped from the fall, but he seems okay otherwise.

Pestilence stands in the street. Eyes closed. Silent.

And then our silver Mini Cooper rounds the corner on two wheels, tires squealing against the pavement, assaulting my nose with the pungent scent of burnt rubber. The engine revs, and the car picks up speed. Pestilence turns and cranes his neck as if squinting (if his eyes were open) at the person driving. The car slams into him head-on, sending the old man flying several hundred feet down the street.

Dexter throws open his door and gets out. He takes off his newsboy cap and waves it over the roof of the car at us. "Hey!" he shouts. "Get in!"

We break for the car. Loren takes the front seat, and Liam and I head to either side of the rear. I snatch the door open but don't get in.

Pestilence lies on his back down the street. Then he sits straight up—and turns toward us.

His eyes open slowly.

I shudder, and I'm glad I'm not close enough to look into them. I don't even want to imagine what I'd see.

"ALEX!" Both Loren and Dexter scream from inside the car.

Slowly, Pestilence climbs to his feet. Then he lifts his arms on either side of him, palms facing upward, and floats into the air.

"What's he doing?" I ask.

With the worst possible timing *ever*, a group of rowdy teenagers wander onto the block, enjoying their newfound freedom courtesy of the apocalypse. One of them, a white kid with short blond hair and skinny baseball-bat legs, stops his two friends and directs their attention to Pestilence, now hovering in the air, only a few feet higher than the roof of the arena.

I cup my hands around my mouth and yell, "Hey! Get outta here! It's not safe!"

They laugh and, instead of running away, take out their phones and start recording.

Pestilence's eyes glow a sickly green color and his mouth opens—and keeps opening, his jaw stretching wider than any human mouth could. He turns his glowing eyes on the boy with the blond hair. Tendrils of green vapor waft from the black depths of Pestilence's elongated mouth. He hocks a loogie the size of a soccer ball and made up entirely of thick, swirly green gas. It hits the boy in the center of his face and hangs in the air around his head.

"Gross!" the boy shouts, and swats the gas away, but it doesn't dissipate. It thins and spreads but remains in the air.

"What the heck is that stuff?" Loren asks.

No one answers because no one knows.

The boy's friends laugh at him. He pouts at first and then shouts at them . . . until fear consumes their laughter, and they back away. The boy stares down at his hands and whirls back around, screaming frantically at Pestilence. The sight of him takes my breath away.

His skin wrinkles all over his body, transforming him into a human raisin. He turns a sickly shade of green, the same color as Pestilence's murder gas. His mouth falls open but no sound escapes because he evaporates on the spot, leaving behind only a pile of clothing and shoes. A gust of wind disperses his gaseous remains into the air beyond the street.

His friends flee in the direction they came.

Liam grabs my arm and pulls me into the car. I yank the door shut at the same time Dexter stomps on the gas. Tires squeal against the pavement as Dexter spins the car around, throwing me and Loren against our doors. Liam and I both turn and sit on our knees to peer up at Pestilence through the rear windshield in time to see another gas loogie make impact.

I flinch, but Liam points the palm of his left hand at the back windshield.

"No, don't!" I smack his hand down, which zaps my fingertips with the static of his frustration and a hint of panic.

He gives me a look that hits me worse than a punch to the stomach. "We can't risk that gas seeping into the car."

He lifts his hand again, but I don't try to stop him this time. A bright but satisfyingly warm light erupts from his palm. His arm trembles, but he holds his wrist to steady his aim.

The light bleeds through the glass and forms an umbrella shape. The luminescent shield floats above the rear end of our car as if attached by invisible strings. Pestilence lobs two more gas blobs, but they hit the shield and sizzle like hamburger patties on a grill until the light burns them away.

Liam grits his teeth. He's straining his magic—and himself.

The shield flashes brighter as five gas balls hit in rapid succession. Liam gasps and the shield blips out of existence. He grunts and throws the shield up again just as another wave hits.

"You have to hurry!" I shout over my shoulder to Dexter.

Dexter glances up at me in the rearview as he swerves onto the next street. "I'm going as fast as I can!"

He steers the car onto a curb and off again to detour around some wrecked cars.

Pestilence hits us with gas ball after gas ball until we're several blocks away. For whatever reason, he doesn't chase us.

Liam lets loose a grave sigh and slumps. I catch him and lower his head into my lap, gritting my teeth against the overwhelming exhaustion that I Sense from him. But something else follows, something new . . . and terrifying. I can't identify this emotion, but it's cold, like frostbite.

Loren whips around. "What's going on with him?"

"I . . ." I don't know what to say, because I don't actually know what's happening to Liam. I glance up at the rearview mirror and meet Dexter's eyes. "He just overexerted himself," I say. "He'll be fine."

I have to find out what's wrong with Liam, because if today proved anything, it's that we need all the help we can get. We can't afford to lose him right now.

I can't afford to lose him right now.

25

GREEN NIGHTMARE

As we drive back to our base in the Hills, which we've officially established as our safe house, it's impossible to ignore how drastically the vibe of Downtown Los Angeles has changed *again*. Most of the streets are dark and empty except for the stubborn fires still smoldering in trash cans or destroyed businesses.

The Horsemen amped the apocalypse up a couple notches tonight. The looters and rioters from a few days ago have all vanished—I'm not sure to where; hopefully, not to Death's nightmare realm. However, even the Riders are strangely absent from the streets they were working so hard to control only three days ago.

I imagine most of the world's survivors holed up in their homes, struggling to find space for generations of loved ones along with everyone's suffocating anxiety of what's to come in the New World Order. And all because I failed. I let the entire world down.

Way to go, Alex Wise.

By the time Dexter steers the car into the driveway of the

safe house, Liam's coming around, though not fully awake. Dexter carries him inside and places him in bed. Loren and I tuck him in with a bottle of water by his bedside and a cool washcloth for his head. We leave him to rest, and I close the door softly behind us.

Once we step into the kitchen, Dexter pokes his head in through the sliding doors leading to the patio, startling both me and Loren.

"Hey, can you two come out here for a sec?" he says. "You should probably see this."

Loren and I share a look that's equal parts exhausted and nervous. Like me, she's probably wondering if we can postpone any additional bad news until tomorrow. But with a quiet sigh, I head outside, and she follows.

Dexter waves us over to the fence he's leaning on, the sparse remaining lights of the city below. I stand next to him, and we squint to where he points in the distance. I'm about to ask what's going on until I see it.

Two bright green lights spin like a lighthouse beacon, rising into the air. Pestilence's eyes. They remind me of a UFO or a drone—until fluorescent green gas spirals out from just below them, floating down in a toxic pinwheel and blanketing the city streets.

"Pestilence," Loren mutters, an angry bite to her voice.

Everyone who thought they were safe in their homes could be at risk. What if the gas leaks in through windows or vents? My heart aches at the thought of so many people reduced to piles of ashes and clothes.

"What *is* that stuff?" asks Dexter.

"Green Dream," I murmur, forgetting that he and Loren can hear me until I notice them both watching me curiously. "Uh . . ." I shrug. "I made that up because I like to believe the gas fast-forwards people to the Big Sleep, except maybe it's more like a nap that we might be able to wake them all up from one day."

Loren shakes her head. "More like a green nightmare."

"We should warn our families," I say.

Dexter shakes his head. "Cell service is out, and probably not coming back."

I take out my phone and check anyway, hoping Dexter's wrong, though I know he's not. No service. If not for my music archive, which I thankfully downloaded to my new phone already, I'd toss this useless metal box down the side of the hill.

Loren stares at hers for a long while. I think she's stuck in time at first, until I realize she's looking at text messages—from her family. Her eyes take on an unsettling glisten in the low pool lighting. I want to comfort her, but what do I even say? *Sorry you abandoned everyone you love to help your loser best friend fail horribly at saving the world from the apocalypse.*

I wonder how Mom and the others are doing. I cringe internally, thinking about how she must be losing her mind now that phones are dead and I never showed with Mags like I promised. I wish there were a way I could communicate with her telepathically to let her know I'm okay (*hint, hint, Orin, if you're listening*). Making a nighttime trip to the hospital is too risky with Pestilence gassing the city—not to mention if Mom could actually lay a hand on me, she'd *never* let me leave her side again.

"I don't think there's anything else we can do today," Loren says. "If Pestilence is focused on Downtown LA, we should be relatively safe up here for now. I'm going to wash off the muck of defeat."

"Okay," I say. "We'll regroup in the morning."

Loren dips her head at us before going back inside.

Dexter sighs, frowning at the city, which is covered in bright green fog. "You might not want to hear it," he says, "but I'd be remiss if I didn't say something."

"I don't know what 'remiss' means," I reply flatly.

He turns his frown on me. "Liam is selfish to keep secrets that could impact everyone's well-being. What if you kids are in the middle of a fight and his magic incapacitates him? What will you do when he becomes a liability?"

"That's not—"

"Don't say that's not gonna happen, Alex." The disappointment in his voice is like a swift kick to my shins. "You saw him pass out in the car from holding up that force field after only, what? Three minutes, maybe? If that."

Every question Dexter poses that I can't answer empowers the anxiety building inside me. I shove my trembling hands inside my pockets to hide them from his scrutinizing gaze.

"I'm only sharing my concerns because I care about what happens to you," he says. "Liam's the *only* one on your team right now with magic that's actually useful against the Horsemen—"

"So my magic is trash?" I cross my arms angrily.

But maybe he's right. I mean, I haven't heard a peep from Orin since the arena.

"Alex—"

"I know you care about me, but you're making me feel worse than I already do."

"I'm sorry, I—"

"Please," I say. "I know Liam has secrets, but I can't force them out of him. I'm doing the best I can."

We stand there for an hour-long moment, both of us staring at the city below. Pestilence disappeared from the skyline at some point while Dexter and I were talking, though his "gift" remains in the streets.

Dexter touches the bare skin of my forearm, but I snatch it away, not wanting to share any of his feelings; however, I don't even feel the tiniest blip of emotion from his touch. It frightens me at first. Has something gone wrong?

Pestilence's words crop back up in my mind. *You're magically constipated.* Is that why I can't sense Dexter's emotions? And where has Orin gone since the arena? Could the effects of Liam's enchanted rope still be lingering? All these unanswered questions are starting to make my head hurt.

"I should go lie down," I mutter to Dexter.

I leave him outside alone, staring reticently at what remains of the city lights.

I take the hottest shower I can stand and climb into bed immediately after, but trying to rest is futile. My mind is a complete mess. I can't make sense of anything—most of all, Dexter's suspicions about Liam.

Liam's been through a ton of heavy stuff that I feel we haven't even scratched the surface of understanding. At only nine years old, he lost his mother and his home, and he then lived alone on a deserted island for four years. I'm not sure I could've survived all that. Liam might be a demigod jerk sometimes, but he deserves a break.

And I deserve a Capri Sun.

I get out of bed and open the door to my room, but the memory of chasing what I thought was Shadow Man not long ago stops me on the spot. My heart pounds as I peek into the dimly lit hallway. No one's there, real or shadow. The other bedroom doors are closed. Light spills from beneath Liam's.

I wonder if he's awake.

I dip off to the kitchen and grab an extra juice pouch for him. When I knock softly on his door and announce myself, he tells me to come in.

Liam looks up at me from where he sits in bed with eyes that are just as exhausted and depressed as mine, despite his stone-cold face. Seeing him like this is haunting, because even in the short time I've known him, I've only ever seen him be strong and/or grumpy.

His expression softens, but he doesn't say anything. I imagine I look like I'm about to bolt, standing silent in the doorway of his bedroom, half in, half out.

I step inside and gently push the door closed. I approach his bedside and hand him one of the Capri Suns. "Thought you could use something besides water."

He grins and grabs it greedily, not wasting any time inserting the straw and taking a long sip. He closes his eyes and shakes his head slowly. "These taste like magic."

"At least we still have some nice things in the apocalypse. Is it okay if I sit on your bed?"

He nods, slurping down the last drops of his juice, and sets the empty container aside.

I sit facing him at the foot of the bed and finish mine in one extended gulp.

"Those should come in bigger sizes," he says.

"The problem with that is I'd demolish an entire barrel of this stuff a day."

He lets himself laugh for a second, then frowns down at the white sheets of his bed as if it's illegal for him to be happy, even for a second.

"I'm really sorry," I mutter.

He looks up at me, confused. "For what?"

"Today," I say with a heavy sigh. "I honestly thought my plan was solid, but it came apart at the seams."

"We all sat around the table and came up with that plan together over three days," Liam says, sitting up straight with conviction. "It was *our* plan. No one blames you, Alex."

It's hard not to take the blame by default for everything bad that happens when everyone keeps telling (and showing) you that you're not good enough. Liam wouldn't understand. He's literally a superhero in the making.

"Thanks for saving our butts today," I tell him. "But don't make it a habit if it's going to always leave you looking like death."

But Liam doesn't laugh at my joke, which makes my heart sink. I was only trying to lighten the mood.

His shoulders droop, and his eyes slip from mine. "That's because my magic actually might kill me."

I wonder if that wrinkle in Liam's magic might have anything to do with the cold feeling I Sensed from him in the car earlier.

"Oh . . . I'm sorry," I tell him. "I didn't know, or I never would've—"

"It's okay," he says. "My magic isn't unlimited, like the Horsemen's. Instead, it draws power from my own life force, and I don't know why. It wasn't always like this. Only since the destruction of Paradisum. If I make a mistake and use too much, I'm afraid I might die. That's why I was counting on Orin choosing me as their vessel if the Horsemen were ever released. It was the only way to save this world *and* myself."

No wonder Liam resented Orin choosing me. And the guilt of taking that from him sits in the pit of my stomach like a steaming-hot rock.

"That's a lot of responsibility for one kid," I say. "My mom always tells me not to be ashamed to ask for help because we're not meant to experience all of life on our own."

"Your mom sounds very smart."

"Yeah, she is." I bite my bottom lip to distract myself from how much I miss her right now. I wish I'd hugged her and told her I love her that day at the cruise port. "I feel worse now that I still don't know how to use Orin's magic. And the power of emotion isn't too helpful in a physical fight either."

Liam gives me his signature scowl. "Back in Paradisum, Orin was one of the most powerful deities, second only to my mother."

"Really?" I perk up, but only a tad. I mean, it's not like the Avengers are gonna bust down the doors to recruit me, but it's nice to hope I might be able to do more than hug my enemies and share feelings.

Liam nods. "The well the Horsemen draw their power from might be unlimited, but their magical reach isn't. The cool thing about the Sense is that it can touch every single living thing at every stage of existence at once. *That* is real power—if you know how to use it."

"But I don't," I say, slumping back into hopelessness. "And I might never figure it out."

"Why do you think that?"

"Outside the arena, Pestilence invaded my mind. He told me Orin was trapped and I was 'magically constipated.'"

Liam's brow knits. "That's interesting. I don't know anything about that."

I release an exaggerated sigh. "I figured. I was gonna ask if you'd help me learn how to use Orin's magic, but it's pointless if I can't figure out how to get rid of this 'block.'"

"I'd still like to help."

I'm caught off guard. "You would?"

"You were right before, Alex. We can't stop the Horsemen if we don't learn how to work as a team. I wanted to be Orin's vessel and make them proud, and I was angry that they chose a stranger over me. But being chosen wasn't your fault, and I shouldn't have been so mean to you—I'm sorry."

I smile—inside, too. "Thanks. Like I mentioned before, I know how it feels to be rejected by the parent you only wanted to make proud, and not to understand why."

Liam chuckles under his breath. "Who would've thought we'd have so much in common?"

"Not me," I said. "At least, not while you were being a jerk."

He screws up his face at me. "I, uh, don't know what that is?"

I chuckle. "It doesn't matter, because I like this new, sensitive Liam better."

He glances down, and I'm afraid I've offended him again. "Being alone on an island for four years makes you kinda forget that you should be nice to people. I got to shout at the sand and trees and rocks and ocean all day, but they don't have feelings, so it was okay."

"How did you survive by yourself for that long? Weren't you lonely?"

"Yes," he says. "But I had my mother's Echoes." When he notices my confused look, he says, "Here, I'll show you."

He holds out his hand, closes his eyes, and takes a deep breath in then out. A spark ignites in his palm, a miniature firework fizzling brightly. I tense, and his eyes pop open.

"Don't worry," he says. "Echoes are a remnant of my mother's Life magic. They're safe. She and Orin left them for me so I wouldn't be totally alone."

"What are Echoes?" I lean closer, drawn in by the dazzling bit of magic in Liam's hand. I'm not sure I'll ever stop being enthralled by magic. At least this time, it's not trying to kill me.

"Memories," he tells me.

The light in his hand spins and spreads until it forms the image of a woman with delicate umber skin and enchanting eyes of the same color. A gigantic sun of textured hair crowns her head. It's the biggest 'fro I've ever seen—and it's drop-dead gorgeous. Her lips are full, and her nose is wide, proud features she clearly passed on to Liam. A sparkling gown drapes across Navia's shoulders, leaving her arms bare. A smaller, younger version of Liam sits beside her, snugly cradled beneath one arm.

She smiles, dark eyes beaming, then sings. Her voice is clear as a sunray and as soft as gossamer. I have no idea what language she's speaking, but the way the beautiful tune enchants me, it's as if she's wielding the Sense through her voice, strumming my emotions like the strings of a harp. A warm, tingling sense of calm unfurls in the center of my tummy. When the song ends, Navia kisses her son on the top of his head.

Liam closes his fist and draws his hands into his lap.

"That was incredible," I tell him, still in awe. "Thank you for sharing that with me."

He nods. "In the very first Echo, she told me that we don't normally worry about forgetting the past because we're always making new memories with the people we love. But since I wouldn't have that, she wanted me to hang on to the ones I already had—until it was time for me to make more." He frowns down at his clenched fists. "Except I don't have anyone. They're all gone."

I swallow hard in the blank space following his honest admission. The words sitting on the edge of my tongue feel right, but I'm terrified to let them out.

"Can I hold your hand?"

Liam raises a brow at me until it registers why I want to touch him. "Oh, uh, sure."

He places his hand in mine. His fingertips brush gently against my palm, and for some reason, my heart races. I lift my eyes and meet his. He presses his calloused palm against mine, and a spark of something hot and electric ignites where our skin touches. It starts as a gentle crackle and builds to static shock before I yank my hand away.

What the heck was that? First Orin ghosts me; and now what? My Sense is short-circuiting?

Liam's eyes glisten in the low light of the room. "What's wrong?"

"Nothing," I say, but he looks like he doesn't believe me. "You're not alone anymore. You have us now. We'll think of a cool team name later. But this pact means we'll always try our best to be honest with each other and not jerks."

After I explain how to fist-bump, he taps the knuckles of his fist against mine, giving me a brief, sunny sensation of happiness and the soothing calm of belonging. I'm still not sure what that previous sensation was between us, but I'm simultaneously relieved and disappointed it didn't happen again.

"Maybe we can call our team the Not-Jerks," he says.

I snatch my hand back. "Uh, *no*."

We both laugh.

"When I found out you were hearing Orin's voice, I was jealous," he says. "Aside from Echoes, my mother's gone forever, and I've been holding on to hope that I'd get to be with Orin again someday. But that hope died when they chose you instead of me."

"I wish there was a way I could let you speak with them."

He's silent a moment; then his eyes widen, and he snaps his fingers, startling me. "I have an idea."

"Ooo," I say. "Tell me!"

He shakes his head, and I almost go back on the pledge we just made and strangle him.

"I'll tell everyone in the morning," he says. "Try to get some rest tonight. Because tomorrow, we're going to Paradisum."

APOCALPYSE COUNTDOWN

1 YEAR · 26 DAYS
15 HOURS · 09 MINUTES

PART III

BREAKING NEWS: Middle schooler makes terrifying claims of nighttime visits from alleged *Shadow Spirit.* "He's searching for something . . . or *someone.*"

—CHANNEL 2 ACTION NEWS, PALM VISTA, CA
JUNE 10, 2023, 9:25 AM

26

THE MINI CHUM

Liam and I rouse Loren and Dexter right before dawn to tell them they've won an all-expenses-paid trip to Paradisum.

Except neither of them seems excited. And their discomfort grows, manifesting through small eye twitches or a jackhammering leg while Liam explains.

Dexter and Loren sit on opposite ends of the couch. I perch on the edge of one of the armchairs, and Liam takes the other.

"Last night, Alex and I were talking, and he gave me a really good idea," he says. "Back in Paradisum, we had a lot of lakes and rivers, but there was one my mother was really fond of—the Lake of Logic. They built our home next to it. We spent a lot of time on the shores of that lake." He glances down, as if sorting through his mental catalog of memories. "We'd sit there, side by side, and she'd sing or make up stories on the spot.

"The Lake of Logic has no bottom," he continues, "at least, none that someone has lived long enough to reach. We believed the bottom of the lake led to another realm—one where the reservoir of magic was limitless. Whenever she dove, Mother said she could feel the magic rising from the lake's bottom like a current of warm water cutting through the cold depths.

"But if she went deep enough and stayed long enough, she said she could hear faint whispers of powerful entities. She told me their words helped hone her magic, and whenever she emerged, she'd always feel twice as powerful—spiritually and magically rejuvenated. And that's why we're going to Paradisum."

I know where Liam's headed with this before he says it, and I flinch with excitement.

"I'm hoping if Alex and I can dive into the Lake of Logic, it'll supercharge my magic and help awaken his."

Loren shifts uncomfortably in her seat. "But wasn't Paradisum destroyed?"

"My home world may be dead, but it's still there," Liam says. "And the magic deep within the lake was from another realm, so when my mother and Orin drew all the magic from Paradisum, they weren't able to touch what was down there."

Dexter clears his throat and scoots to the edge of his seat. "So let's say we can get to Paradisum and there is still magic left in this lake you speak of—didn't you say only god-folk could dive deep enough to touch it?"

Liam shuffles his feet and shrugs. "Well, yeah . . . but—"

"I don't mean to murder the mood here," Loren says, "but this 'plan' has a few too many loose ends. We had a solid strategy at the arena, and we saw how *that* turned out—and now we're about to interdimensionally travel with no plan, just vibes? I dunno if I'm okay with that."

I vacate my seat and stand next to Liam. "Like you told

me, Lo, no one's ever done the apocalypse before, so we gotta figure it out as we go. And you're right—the Lake of Logic is a long shot, but if there's even the tiniest chance it could work, we've gotta try—for our families."

She softens with a deep exhale, clinging to the edge of the sofa cushions. Dexter crosses his arms, still unconvinced.

Liam glances at me, and I nod. He steels himself a moment, then says, "I need this too."

Then he explains his situationship with magic, to which Dexter and Loren listen intently.

"Maybe the magic in the lake can give my own enough of a boost that I can help stand against the Horsemen and actually live to tell the story," Liam says. "I'm willing to die to save this realm." He hugs himself and stares at the Converse sneakers I picked out for him on our first supply run, which are now so scuffed and dinged-up they look a couple of years old instead of only a few days. "But I don't want to . . . die."

"Why now?" Dexter frowns. "If going to Paradisum would fix everything, why didn't we do that first?"

Liam keeps looking at the patio doors like he wants to bolt. I'm kinda wondering the same thing as Dexter—though he could def be a little nicer about it.

"I couldn't go back there." The pain in Liam's voice grabs hold of me like the icy hands of a stranger gripping the back of my neck. "I didn't want to see my home destroyed. And empty. Maybe my magic started drawing on my life force because I was all that was left.

"I thought I could stop the Horsemen on my own—make them pay for what happened to my realm. I thought I was enough. But I need help. So to answer your question—why now? Because I'm not alone anymore."

Liam's confidence draws me to him like a moth. I wonder what about our different lives made us who we are. He thought he had to be enough all on his own, something I never had the space to imagine for myself, because everyone always told me I wasn't.

He looks to me and Loren. "We're a team, right?"

"Heck yeah," I say.

Loren sighs dramatically. "Well, of course I'm part of the team—you goobers wouldn't survive a single afternoon without me."

We all turn to Dexter, who stammers incoherently before lifting his hands in surrender. "Fine. And how do you propose we get there?"

"We'll need to go back to my island off the coast of Santa Monica," Liam tells us. "The portal to Paradisum is hidden there."

The mention of Santa Monica dredges Sky up and drops him at the front of my mind. I wonder how he and Blu are doing in all this. I really hope Blu hasn't seen his best friend on television or that ridiculous live stream. I'm not sure he'd understand that that's not really Mags. And same, Blu. I'm still grappling with it myself.

"Maybe we can find a boat at the pier to take us there," I say, thinking out loud.

"I can navigate," Liam says. "I'll be able to feel the pull of my home world."

"Okay," Dexter says. "When do we leave?"

"Now," I answer. "We don't have time to waste."

After everyone separates to prepare for our journey, Dexter pulls me aside to the dining room for a private chat. I'm not too thrilled to talk to him right now and I'm sure it shows on my face, but I honestly don't care. I'm exhausted and burned out and ready for all this to be over.

Dexter stands behind one of the chairs and grips the back, staring at the bare wooden surface of the dining table. "I should've been more careful with my words last night when we were talking. It wasn't my intention to make you feel 'less than.' I'm just stressed and worried about my family. This apocalypse business has taken a heavy mental toll on all of us."

"You don't have to come to Paradisum," I tell him. "After you drop us at the pier, you can go be with your family."

He shakes his head. "I can't just yet. I need to see this through—for my family."

I've lost count of how many times I've tried to push Dexter away since this started. But he's refused every time—more than I can say for my own dad. As frustrating and extra as Dexter can be with his over-adulting, I'm low-key glad he's sticking around.

He smiles and glances through the patio doors at the rising sun, burning away the last remnants of the bleak night-time sky. "You remind me a lot of myself, Alex Wise."

Hold on a little longer, Mags. I'm coming.

We load up the Mini Cooper and drive to the closest pier, which happens to be in Playa del Ray, just south of Santa Monica. The streets are oddly quiet and empty. As each day passes, our world is starting to look more and more like the images of the apocalypse from my comics and video games. Burned-out buildings. Piles of clothing strewn about where Green Dream turned people to ashes. Abandoned cars. The longer it takes us to stop the Horsemen, the worse things are going to get.

When we arrive at the pier, my heart slips into the dark waters. It's deserted. No people. No boats. There aren't even seagulls flying overhead.

"Over there!" Loren points to the far end of the pier, where a midsize fishing boat is docked.

The four of us hurry down the long strip of boardwalk until we reach the rusted boat bobbing up and down in the water. *The Chum Bucket* is painted on the side in fading blue script. This thing looks barely seaworthy, but it appears to be our only option.

A man emerges from belowdecks, and as soon as he sees us, he stops and tenses. My eyes graze his slender frame and stop on the machete he clings to in one hand. I release the breath I've been strangling once I see he doesn't have a Rider mark on his forehead—real or fake. He wears what must be decades of sailing experience on his haggard, tanned face. A crown of stringy gray hair rings his head, only a few wispy flyaways on top.

I step to the front of the group and hold up my hands. Dexter stands behind me like a sentinel.

"Hi!" I shout up to the guy on the boat. "We're not here to start any trouble. I swear."

The man's shoulders relax slightly. "What do you want?"

"I'm Alex," I tell him, and then introduce everyone else.

He nods. "Melvin."

"We need to sail to a nearby island, Melvin," I say. "We, uh, we were sorta hoping you would take us."

He appraises our group carefully. A soft wind blows between us, dragging the salty, fishy smell of the sea across my nose.

"Sorry," Melvin says finally. "Even if I wanted to help, my boat's busted."

"What's wrong with it?" I ask. "Maybe we can fix it."

Melvin shakes his head. "Engine's dead. My son and I live on this boat. We were planning to sail west. Maybe to Australia or New Zealand—anywhere but here. As you can see, every other person with a working ship had a similar idea. And now we're stuck, thanks to our faulty electric engines."

I want to tell him that nowhere in this realm is safe under the Horsemen's reign, but so much feels hopeless right now that it seems especially sinister to squash what little hope he's found.

Liam speaks up, surprising me. "If I repair your ship's engines, will you take us where we need to go and back? Then you and your son can sail wherever you wish."

Melvin lifts his brows curiously. "You a junior class of maritime mechanics in training or something?"

"You don't have anything to lose by letting us try," says Liam. "You're stuck here anyway."

Melvin stabs his machete into the sheath on his hip and strokes his stubbly gray beard. "Fine. Come aboard. But don't hold your breath. We've already tried everything possible."

"Everything *humanly* possible," mutters Liam.

I turn my back to Melvin and meet Liam's determined gaze. "Uh . . . how exactly are you planning to fix those engines?"

"Magic, of course," he says. "My Light is energy and should power these engines even better than electricity. I'm sure it'll work."

"What if reviving them takes all the magic you have left?"

"I don't believe it will."

I'm about to respond when Loren joins the huddle. "Alex. Team members have to trust one another. We need to let him do this."

"Okay, okay." I sigh in surrender. "Please, just be careful."

"I promise," Liam tells us.

Melvin extends the gangway, and we file aboard the *Chum Bucket*. The seawater has rusted large swatches of the hull, which Melvin and his son must've been in the process of repainting, judging by the buckets of paint stacked against the front of the pilothouse. The pea-green interior of the house stands out behind the row of square windows wrapped around it. Melvin even has one of those old-timey wooden wheels with the handle spokes. Cool. Gigantic nets are attached to wooden and metal contraptions that I'm guessing they use for fishing. There are horizontal racks along the wall below the pilothouse windows where five harpoons are stored. Hmm . . . I wonder what they catch with *those*.

Melvin takes us around the stern to a set of stairs that leads belowdecks, then down a short winding metal staircase to the engine room. He flips the light switch, filling the space with a bright yellow glow. Bulky blue machinery takes up most of the floor, with a bunch of pipes and tubes that connect who-knows-what. Liam circles the space once, taking in every piece of the ship's engine.

"Pop, who're these people?"

The hard baritone voice startles me, and I whip around to see a barrel-chested man whose tall, wide frame nearly fills the doorway. His skin is the color of pale gold, and his dark auburn hair is pulled back into a curly ponytail.

"They claim to be able to fix the engines," Melvin tells him, then turns back to us. "This is my son, Jamar."

Jamar turns sideways and ducks into the engine room. His height only leaves an inch or two of clearance between the top of his head and the lights. Melvin is a full foot shorter than his son and slightly stooped, as if he's nursing a back injury from decades of pulling on heavy ropes and all kinds of fisherman stuff.

"What sort of repairman shows up with no tools?" Jamar's thick eyebrows pinch together as he frowns at us.

"Let me show you," Liam says.

He finds a flat surface on the blue metal of one of the engine's parts and places both hands against it. He takes a deep breath in, and when he blows it out, his hands glow the color of a ray of sunshine. Melvin gasps loudly, and Jamar says a word I'm not allowed to repeat.

I move closer to Liam, but I don't interrupt him, although

terror has my stomach in a chokehold. Please, I whisper in my thoughts over and over.

Liam grits his teeth. His hands glow brighter and brighter, until we have to look away, because it feels like staring into the sun. But before I shield my eyes, I see Liam's Light seeping into the engines until they start to glow like his hands.

A loud, mechanical whir fills the room, followed by the churning rattle of the ship's engines.

I open my eyes as Liam's Light fades to a faint shimmer and then nothing. The engines' glow dies similarly. Except now they're fully operational.

"You did it!" I exclaim as he removes his hands.

He staggers back a step, and his legs fold beneath him. I dive to catch him, and I'm able to grab ahold of him and lower him gently to the floor.

Loren rushes over, but Dexter gingerly steers her back a few paces so Liam can have some room to breathe.

Melvin's on his knees, teary eyes bulging, staring at the running engines. Jamar and Dexter get on either side to draw the old man back onto his feet.

Liam reclines against me, completely spent. His eyes close, and he moans softly. I hold him steady, just tight enough to let him know I'm here. Relief washes over me, but I realize it doesn't all belong to me. Some of it is Liam's.

Once Liam and Melvin are good to walk back up the stairs, everyone goes above deck for some air. I never thought I'd be happy to be outside amid the overpowering fragrance of fish. I wonder how long it takes to get used to this smell.

Up on the main deck, Jamar puffs out his chest and stands protectively in front of his father. "Are you one of *them*? The Horsemen?"

Liam shakes his head. "Never," he says, only slightly breathless now. He must already be feeling better.

"We're trying to stop them," I say. "If you'll still help."

Melvin shoves Jamar aside and gives him a powerful stink eye. "Ignore my overprotective son," he tells us. "A deal's a deal. Let's get outta here."

Melvin and Jamar zip back and forth preparing the ship to set sail, and it's not long before the *Chum Bucket* backs away from the dock and chugs out into the Pacific Ocean.

Dexter goes to the pilothouse to chat with Melvin, and Jamar holes up in the engine room, taking readings and measurements to try to explain how Liam fixed the boat.

Liam, Loren, and I hang out on the main deck. The three of us lean against the railing, soaking up the salt spray mixed with the warm wind whipping our faces.

Loren leans around me to look at Liam. When she has his attention, she raises an eyebrow. "I'm truly glad that you two goobers have found a way to peacefully coexist, but tread lightly. This one's *my* best friend."

Liam looks equal parts confused and nervous. His mouth drops open, but he doesn't say anything. He just looks, wide-eyed, between me and Loren.

"Lo!" I nudge her hard with my elbow, careful to avoid touching her bare skin. "Leave him alone." I turn to Liam and say, "She can be territorial, but she's just kidding, I promise."

She leans over again, peering over a pair of imaginary sunglasses. "Am I, though?" She chuckles and stares wistfully out at the endless blue ocean and sky.

Liam scoots closer to me and whispers, "Is she?"

"Yes," I hiss back. "Of course."

He smiles nervously and taps his fingers on the railing.

"Why don't people name cars like they do boats?" Loren asks, but doesn't wait for an answer before adding, "We should name our car."

"The *Mini Chum*." I spit out what immediately pops into my head.

There's a moment of tense silence when the three of us stare at one another but no one says anything. Loren's the first to laugh; then Liam and I erupt together.

"I like it," Loren says.

"Me too," adds Liam.

"The *Mini Chum* it is, then," I say.

Loren glances back toward the stern of the ship and gasps, putting a pin in the moment we were trying to have.

Liam turns and grimaces up at the sky behind us, already reaching for his bracelet.

Famine flies on the back of a vulture the size of an Escalade. And she's close enough that I can see her angry eyes aimed straight at me.

27

KILLER CALAMARI

Famine lifts one hand, palm facing the waters below.

I take a step back, wondering how she managed to find us all the way out here, at the same time something splashes nearby. It shoots up from the ocean, and the sun glints on the slick surface of its skin as it arcs through the air and lands on the deck of the boat with a wet *thwack*.

Several feet in front of us lies a single writhing baby squid no longer than my forearm, its skin marbled white like clouds.

"That the best you've got?" I shout up at Famine.

She stands in her vulture's saddle and bows dramatically.

I turn to Loren and Liam. "Is she serious?"

Loren points at the squid. "Yep."

It grows right before my eyes. Its tentacles flop back and forth with renewed vigor as it swells to five times its original size, changing color from white to a glistening gray. When it's larger than either of us, we retreat inch by inch toward the starboard side of the deck until our backs are pressed against the railing. I realize the boat's stopped, and I peer into the pilothouse, where Melvin clings to the wheel, white-knuckled and wild-eyed. Dexter's leaning close, a hand on Melvin's shoulder, saying something to the terrified man.

Jurassic Squid's tentacles feel their way up to the edge of the boat; then the creature hauls itself overboard and disappears. It hits the water with a thunderous splash that tips the boat to one side, knocking everyone onto their butts.

We slide across the deck, knocking into one another, as the *Chum Bucket* tilts again. Two smoky gray tentacles, wide as hundred-year-old tree trunks, wrap around the boat. Pearl-colored claws sprout from the undersides and crunch into the deck. Its metal parts creak and groan. The squid squeezes harder. A blanket of cold wraps around me, reminding me of diving from the sinking cruise ship into the freezing waters after Mags. The air around me grows heavy, too thick to fill my lungs. I struggle to inhale.

Breathe.

Focus inward.

Orin! I listen to the familiar chant of their soft yet commanding voice in my head and focus on my breathing and the hurried thump of my heart until they slow enough that I feel like I'm okay again. And Orin's back.

I never imagined a day would come when I'd be happy to hear voices in my head.

Famine banks her vulture hard and flies along the side of the ship closest to where we stand. Her azure hair whips around her full, round face. I didn't realize until now that her eyes are richly colored, like the sky on a clear spring afternoon.

She sits up straight and looks at only me. A wide smile

stretches her mouth as she raises an eyebrow, lifts both hands, and flips me off.

My mouth falls open. *Rude!*

Famine holds tight to her vulture's neck. The massive beast draws back its wings and flaps them down hard, spraying water as it zooms into the air, flips back, and dives toward the ocean like a heat-seeking missile. But instead of making a great splash, both Famine and her vulture disappear into their shadows on the water's surface—probably off to report back to Death that we'll be spending the rest of the apocalypse in the belly of a sea monster as opposed to continuing to meddle in their world domination.

Jamar emerges from belowdecks and runs over to where Loren, Liam, and I huddle.

"What the—" he starts, but stops abruptly and slaps his large hands on either side of his head, staring at the freakishly huge squid. "Oh, oh, *ohhh!*"

The Kraken's head presses against the starboard side of the ship at an angle, so only one of its three humongous bulbous black eyes, which are the size of beach balls, watches us. Its claws dig deeper into the deck. The sharp sound of splintering wood cracks the air.

"We've gotta get free before it sinks us!" I shout.

Liam yanks his bracelet from his wrist and charges the twin tentacles clinging to our ship. I break for the harpoon rack and grab one for myself and toss another to Loren.

"Right!" Jamal says on his way into the pilothouse. Dexter pulls the machete from Melvin's holster and hands it to him.

Liam thwacks, clacks, and jabs up and down the tentacles, which are as thick as a fence is tall. But the squid remains unbothered. Loren and I spear the thing over and over with the tips of our harpoons, but it might as well be a gigantic pincushion for all the damage it suffers. Every puncture to its wet skin immediately seals itself shut, as if the monster is healing itself. Jamar's not having much luck either, swiping and slicing at the tentacle, which sprays him with bright blue squid blood before the wounds close. After several minutes of this, the four of us stand back, panting with exhaustion—having accomplished nothing.

Jamar grimaces, covered from head to foot in thick swaths of darkening blue blood. It's an almost frightening sight. "The thing's too big. It's like trying to spear a rhino with a sewing needle."

One of the Kraken's arms rises out of the water and splashes down again, spraying the deck (and us) with water. The wet gray skin of the monster's tentacles shimmers with a kaleidoscope of rainbows in the sunlight—which gives me an idea.

"Jamar's right," I tell everyone. "This squid's too big for us to make a difference with these." I hold out my harpoon and gesture at Loren, who hands me hers. "But maybe we can use them like jumper cables to give it a shock."

"Smart," Loren says, "but where's your power source?"

I bite my bottom lip and hand the harpoons to Liam. He blanches immediately.

"Take one in each hand and stick them in both tentacles." I mime stabbing downward, a harpoon in each hand. "Then you can use both as conduits to give it a solid shock of Light. I know you've used a good bit of magic already, and I wouldn't ask if we weren't in danger, but do you think you could spare enough for this?"

Liam looks down at the harpoons laid across his palms. "Using small amounts of magic sparingly is safe, but I'm honestly not sure I'll have enough to take that thing down."

"Good," I say, which causes him to screw up his face at me. "We don't need a lot, only a jolt strong enough to get it to let the boat go. Your Light is similar to electricity—that's how the *Chum Bucket*'s engines are running—and I'm hoping the salt water will make a good conductor."

Liam clutches the harpoons and fixes me with a determined gaze, the force of which almost knocks me over. "I trust you, Alex," he says.

Loren and I cup our hands, kneel at the base of one tentacle, and hoist Liam onto the top. He slides on the Kraken's slippery skin and almost comes tumbling back down but thankfully regains his footing. He takes a deep breath, lifts the harpoons above his head, and plunges them deep into the tentacles, one in each. They flinch, then dig in deeper, drawing out the already long and deep cracks in the ship's old deck.

One foot wedged against each tentacle, Liam grips a harpoon in each hand and lets out an animalistic roar. His entire body flashes bright white, a single strobe that zips down the length of the harpoon like a bolt of lightning. My vision goes spotty from Liam's Light, but I cross my fingers at my side and hope against hope this works.

All at once, the squid glows as if a miniature sun orbits

somewhere inside it. The creature belts out an otherworldly shriek and unwraps its tentacles from our boat. Liam yelps, slipping between them, and falls to the deck. The monster beams brighter, until we have to shield our eyes—and then it explodes. With a sound like a gigantic water balloon popping, the squid erupts, spraying me, Loren, Liam, and Jamar with hot, sticky blue squid blood and guts.

"*Blech!*" Loren gags. "I think some got in my mouth."

I actually do vomit this time. Not my proudest moment, but hey, I think I'm allowed, considering the circumstances.

Jamar runs to the pilothouse to check on his dad and Dexter. The three of us collapse onto the deck in a blue-blooded and battered heap.

"Maybe I gave it a little *too* much juice." Liam lets out a shuddering exhale and whispers, "This is so gross."

I'm the first to chuckle out loud, and it catches. Soon we're crying blue-streaked tears from laughing so hard.

We did it. We survived.

And we're starting to feel more and more like a real team.

Wearily, I lift both hands and flip off the empty sky over the starboard side, even though Famine's long gone.

"Still kickin'," I mutter.

28

RETURN TO PARADISUM

The *Chum Bucket* now resembles what I imagine a bucket of chum might actually look like. The weathered deck is cracked and splintered, and the frame of the pilothouse is crunched in around the middle, thanks to the massive squid's tentacle corset. But the old boat is still seaworthy.

Jamar produces a hose connected to a seawater pump on the ship, and we take turns spraying one another down, washing away the squid blood and guts as best we can. We really should've packed some spare clothes.

From time to time, Liam stands at the bow, closes his eyes, and leans into the wind. He stays like that a few moments, sometimes turning his head as if straining to hear a faraway sound. Then he hops down and goes to the pilothouse to direct Melvin which way to steer the ship.

Liam says he can sense the island's magic, like a Siren calling to him. He also tells us he's the only one who can ever find it, because every time a human sets foot on the island, it moves to another location. We're lucky that it's still off the coast of

California. If it had moved to the other side of the world, I'd probably just lie down and sob.

When I notice the expansive column of fog in the distance after sailing for hours, my heartbeat quickens. I'm back. Where it all began.

As we approach, the fog dissipates from top to bottom, melting into the ocean like cotton candy to reveal the island. Melvin pulls the boat as close as he can to the narrow beach of white sand separating the ocean from dense jungle.

Liam, Loren, and I stand portside, staring at the island, though no one speaks. Being back here feels strange. Maybe because the worst thing that's ever happened to me occurred in this place. The others join us out on the main deck. Melvin and Jamar both wear murderous expressions that I don't understand until Dexter speaks.

"I've commandeered the boat keys for insurance." He jingles the keys for us to see and pockets them.

"Is that *really* necessary?" Jamar huffs. "After all we've been through, you think we'd leave three kids and an old man stranded on a deserted island?"

"I honestly don't know," Dexter says, "but I'm not keen to find out. Besides, I'm going to stay behind and help you two repair the ship." He turns to me, and before I can ask, he says, "Sorry, kid. I'm a bit too old for interdimensional travel. I'll just slow you all down."

Loren's the first to jump overboard, and Liam and I follow right after. The water's surprisingly warm, a stark contrast to my memory of leaping off the *Kingships Reign* into the icy depths after Shadow Man tossed my little sister overboard.

It's a short swim to the beach, thankfully. Once we're on dry land, I glance back at the boat. Melvin and Jamar move back and forth onboard. I don't know anything about sailing, so I'm not sure what they're repairing or how, but it doesn't take a maritime expert to see that Dexter's probably doing more talking than actual helping.

As we trudge through the thick white sand to the tree line, flashes of memories return to me. Like the first time I met Liam. After rescuing us, he stood on this same beach, his dark brown skin drinking up the moonlight as we looked into each other's eyes for the first time. Back then I never imagined he'd become someone I'd consider a friend.

Wait . . . *are* we friends? Teammates without question, but the "f" word makes me a bit nervous. Whenever my mind skirts close to the topic, I can't help but flinch, remembering how the "friendship" I built with Sky crumbled right in front of me. I'm *still* trying to dig myself out from beneath the rubble.

Loren walks alongside Liam, pelting him with questions about the island and his time here, while I hang behind, lost in my thoughts, trying to get ahold of the tiny thread of panic I feel wriggling inside my chest.

I can't look away from the lush dark greens of the trees and bushes or the darkness woven between every leaf, treacherous shadows that beckon us forward, pleading with us to wander in and lose ourselves. Because that's where I lost Mags. Where Shadow Man stole her from me. Even now, I wonder if he's lurking in there somewhere—waiting for my return. The fear bubbling in my gut almost sends me sprinting back to the *Chum Bucket.*

But I have to do this for Mags. For the whole world.

And maybe even a little bit for me.

I take a deep breath in and blow it out hard, puffing out my cheeks. I slip into the jungle.

Liam guides us along the familiar fading dirt path. Several of the bushes I remember him cutting back with his machete have already healed, capped with bright green new growth. Vines and branches tangle high overhead, blocking the sun, so the shadows grow denser the farther we trek into the jungle. I activate the flashlight on my phone and hand it to Liam to lead the way. The one good thing Dad did do for me was get me one of the new waterproof phones.

Loren and I both jump when Liam swings the light in an arc overhead and startles a group of bats hanging on some branches. They drop over our heads and screech off into the dark. Their cries fade into the din of the other insects and animals hidden among the thick underbrush all around us.

I let out a deep sigh of relief once we reach Liam's deserted campsite. His makeshift hut stands alone to one side of the clearing. Weeds have overtaken the little gardens at the back—what hasn't already been pillaged by animals.

We dip back past the tree line and through more jungle until we arrive at the sunny bank of a river. The sun's heat on my skin is rejuvenating.

Liam returns my phone and kneels at the steep edge of the riverbank and dips his hand into the water. He lets it hang there, the river parting gently between his thin, brown fingers, long enough that I'm about to ask him what he's doing—until I notice the raft floating toward us from somewhere upstream.

It thumps into the side of the bank, and Liam leans over and retrieves the long pole, which is lying in a groove carved into one of the logs. He gets on first and helps Loren in, then me.

When his calloused palm touches mine, I feel a comforting warmth radiating from him. I don't know what it means, but it feels . . . safe? He gives my hand a firm squeeze before letting go, leaving behind lingering remnants of his emotion. This is one of those times I kinda like having the Sense.

"So what's the deal with this place?" asks Loren.

I sit and motion for her to sit too, and she does.

"My mother and the other deities created this island to hide the passageway between Paradisum and Earth," Liam says, standing at the helm of the raft and steering us downstream. "They wove magic into every part of this land when they created it, which is how I can tap into it without draining my own."

"Did y'all often travel between worlds?" I ask.

"I don't think so. I'd never visited another realm until my mother died." He casts his eyes down and turns back sharply, scowling at the dark mouth of a cave we're approaching.

I remember from last time.

I turn on my phone's flashlight again and hand it to him. He mumbles, "Thanks," and focuses on navigating us through the river tunnels along the same path we took before.

When Liam yells over his shoulder for us to brace ourselves, I pull Loren down, remembering how I almost wiped out last time I took this ride.

Liam tosses back the rope, and I catch it and hand the end to Loren.

"Whatever you do—don't let go," I warn her.

She links one arm through mine, clinging to the rope and me, and presses her face into the back of my armpit. I endure the anxious fear that sizzles between us like static electricity, because she's really scared. And my best friend is one of the bravest people I know.

The other is steering our raft.

"I'm gonna kill you, Alex Wise!" My pit muffles her grumbling. "You know I *hate* roller coasters. And you need a shower!"

"It's on my to-do list," I say. "But I'm not owning this collective stench we got going on here—this is truly a group project."

Liam peers back and raises an eyebrow at me. He sniffs one of his own armpits and widens his eyes.

"If you die musty and become a ghost, will your ghost be musty too?" I ask.

"Shut up, Alex!" cries Loren at the same time Liam yells, "Lean to the right!"

I roll to the right, still holding tight to Loren, who buries her face in my chest unabashedly for someone who's just been complaining about my smell.

She screams through every moment of the rapids and until the river spits us out at the tiny beach with the gigantic skulls carved into the cliff's face. I hug her close as Liam steers us to the shore; then we get off and help him drag the raft onto the sand.

"Please don't tell me we have to go back the way we came," Loren says as we march up the short strip of beach.

"Fortunately, for you and my ears, no," says Liam.

We enter the shadowy cave through the skull's gaping mouth. Liam takes the lead and my flashlight. We stick so close to each other that I can hear everyone's breaths in the quiet cave between the shuffling of our feet against the dirt floor. The dust makes me sneeze, and the sound echoes ahead of us and dies in the shadows.

The Horsemen are long gone from this place, but I can still feel their presence. It's in the chill of the air that raises goose bumps along the nape of my neck and the shadows in front of us that wait patiently to devour all three of us whole.

I don't want to be here.

Soon we emerge in the cavern that used to hide the Horsemen's spirits. Liam walks straight to the back of the space and places his hand on a bit of odd-shaped stone that juts from the wall. Dust falls as the sound of rock grinding against rock fills the room. The stones shift and slide aside, revealing a small doorway. A thick blanket of darkness veils the opening. Is this really the way to Paradisum? This opening looks like it leads to the place where nightmares are manufactured.

Liam returns my phone. "Just step through here and keep walking until you emerge on the other side," he tells us. "It only takes a few seconds, and it's one-way, so you can't get lost."

"Got it." I turn to Loren. "You good?"

"This *is* a normal, straight walk, right? No hills or loop-de-loops?"

"Huh?" Liam's brow wrinkles and he blinks his dark eyes a few times. I can't help but notice how cute he looks when he's genuinely confused.

"Ignore her," I tell him. "We're good."

He disappears into the shadows first. Loren takes a deep breath in, holds it, and strides into the passageway.

I'm right behind her.

29

THE LAKE OF LOGIC

At first, I feel like I'm walking through a wall of cold water. A blast of chilled air hits me straight on, then warms until it becomes stifling. I step through another area where the air feels wet, and then we crawl upward at an angle through the mouth of a tight tunnel situated between two large boulders. Loren and Liam pull me through the opening, and I climb to my feet and brush the dust from my hands and knees.

I'm in a new, brighter place—but it's far from how I expected Paradisum to look. We're standing on the crest of a hill overlooking an expansive land that takes my breath away.

Shades of gray cover the entire world. An impressive mountain range sprawls in the distance, with peaks so tall they look as if entire realms might exist inside them. Even from so far away, I have to crane my neck to see where the mountains end and the sky begins.

But something about Paradisum throws me off.

It doesn't smell of anything. The silvery wildflowers dotting the plains and hillsides don't fill the air with fragrance, the trees don't give off their usual woody scents, and I can't even smell the earth I kick loose with my foot. This world is also eerily silent. Birds don't fly and sing overhead, bugs don't chirp in the shadows of the surrounding rocks and bushes—in fact, I don't see any animals at all. This realm feels cold and abandoned. No wonder Liam was hesitant to come back here.

As wrong as this realm feels, it's still beautiful, even in the varying hues of gray that paint the gorgeous view before us. I wonder how this world must've looked once, but I don't believe my imagination could even process the full range of colors that existed in Paradisum. Now the three of us are the only color in this entire world.

Liam's jaw tenses as his eyes crawl over the landscape. "I stood on the other side of that passage so many times over the last four years that I lost count. The whole time, it was all so close. But I couldn't make myself come back here. Not once."

"What was it like?" I ask him. "Before . . ."

"Come." He beckons us down the hill. "I'll tell you on the way."

Loren and I walk on either side of him through the gray-scale plains of his home realm.

"Paradisum was endless and full of plant and animal life once." One side of his mouth twitches, as if the memory makes him want to smile but he won't let himself. "My mother would tell me to pick a direction, and then we'd go on days-long walks across green fields and through majestic forests. Our world was bursting with so many colors and so much life. Even the weather was always nice, the sun always shining. Although, during my time in your realm, I grew to love your rain and your nights."

Once we reach the bottom of the hill, we follow a path through a field of gray grass as the white sun beams down on us. My damp clothes finally dried—just in time to get re-drenched with sweat.

"Did other people live here?" Loren asks.

"Only the six deities, me, Ezra, and Ezra's mom."

"Who's Ezra?" I ask. "You've never mentioned them before."

"He was my friend," Liam says. "They're all dead now. Come on. We're almost there."

We take a path through a short field of wildflowers that leads to the bank of a body of water so massive, calling it a mere lake would seem disrespectful. White sparkles of sunlight reflect off the silvery surface. On the distant side of the lake is the silhouette of a mansion so huge it resembles a small castle.

Liam walks to the edge of the lake, the toes of his sneakers barely kissing the water, and stares down at his reflection. Loren and I join him.

"Ezra and I were the only two kids in Paradisum," he says. "He was Moritz's demigod son. He was born to a woman in your realm five years before my mother and Orin created me. The day before my ninth birthday, Ezra and I were going through our lessons in the study when the lights went out. I thought Ezra was messing around at first, because he had the Darkness—magic he'd inherited from his father. He was always doing all sorts of cool tricks with light and dark and zipping us all around the house, using shadows. But he swore it wasn't him.

"The room kept getting darker and darker until it became

pitch-black. Ezra and I called out to each other, and when we eventually found our way back together, he hugged me close. I asked him to make the darkness go away, but he said he couldn't. Then my head started pounding"—he touches his temple now, wincing as if he can feel the phantom pain—"it felt like something was digging around in my brain. It got worse and worse until I passed out.

"When I started to come back around, Ezra had me in his arms and was running fast. I remember feeling his heart pounding against the side of my face. And then my mother's scream pulled me all the way back to consciousness. On the bank of this lake, Ezra handed me over to his father, Moritz, who sat on a cloud-white horse. From that day on, they called themselves Horsemen—Malakai, Exo, and Zara—and they staged their coup, each riding a horse of their own. My mother and Orin stood right over there." He points toward a humongous old willow tree at the edge of the lake, halfway between us and the mansion in the distance. Then he leads us toward it.

The tree grows at an angle, as if leaning over the lake's edge to admire its reflection, the hanging leaves of its branches draped serenely like locks of hair. Its exposed, gnarled roots curl and twist across the bank and disappear into the water. A big, oval-shaped knot on the trunk reminds me of a sleeping face.

"Mother and Orin had been fighting the Horsemen, but I didn't know why at the time," he continues. "There'd been lots of arguments between them before—but nothing like that. When they saw me, my mother and Orin fell to their knees and shut their eyes. After a long, scary moment, Mother shouted that she'd surrender as long as the Horsemen didn't hurt me. Moritz let me go to her.

"She hugged me so tight. And she whispered in my ear that I needed to listen to her carefully and not interrupt. She told me she'd unsealed the passageway to Earth and that it was up to me to protect the realms from now on. And that Orin had chosen to sacrifice themself to help me in case the Horsemen ever escaped. Back then, I had no idea what she was talking about."

"But you were just a kid," I mutter.

Maybe I should stop complaining about having to be responsible for Mags all the time, because I don't know how I'd react if my mom left me in charge of the entire *world*.

"I didn't have a choice," Liam says.

"You *always* have a choice," Loren replies.

"Not when your heart won't let you do anything other than what's right," he tells her.

It's not fair that "right" should require someone to sacrifice themselves—or someone else. Especially if the people who suffer the most from the sacrifice had nothing to do with creating the problem in the first place. Or maybe I'm just selfish. I dunno.

Liam stops underneath the shade of the willow and cranes his neck to stare into the branches that twist overhead in a canopy of weeping leaves.

"Zara—or Famine, as you know her—used her Flora and Fauna magic to summon a circle of magical vines from the ground that surrounded my mother. They grew into thick brown ropes that wound up her legs. She pushed me away, and the vine that'd been slowly wrapping around my ankle snapped in two. When I saw Famine coming for me, I threw up a light shield with my magic, like Orin taught me, like I'd done a hundred times before—but that time, it *hurt*." He winces again, clutching at his chest.

I take his hand, and his touch ignites white-hot fire inside me that feels like it's burning through more than just my organs. It's searing my soul. I gasp and drop his hand.

He looks at me with his gentle dark eyes. "You felt it too, didn't you?"

I nod and hug myself. I never want to feel that again. "Is that what using magic is like for you?"

"Not anymore," he says. "The first time was the worst, but the more I used magic, the less it hurt. It scared me after a while, because instead of getting that scorching sensation in my chest, I started feeling cold—and hollow. It was slight at first, like touching ice, but now it feels like I'm slowly *becoming* the ice."

I think back to all the times Liam used magic to save our butts and I feel hollow too.

"I don't know what went wrong with my magic," he says. "The shield blinked out, and then Famine snatched me up from the ground and restrained me. Mother and Orin were standing with their hands above their heads. The Horsemen were shouting at one another, but I don't remember a word they said. I noticed the color was evaporating from our world, flaking off every plant, rock, speck of dirt, drop of water—turning everything gray. I stopped fighting Famine's grip on me when I realized what Mother and Orin were doing.

"I could *feel* it. They were draining magic from our realm. There was more screaming and a splash. I turned in time to see Ezra swimming out to the middle of the lake, when something sucked him under." Liam pauses his tale to scowl out over the water. "I lost my best friend twice that day. Once when he betrayed me and again when the Lake of Logic ate him."

"I'm sorry, Liam," I say, and he dips his head in acknowledgment. "I guess betrayals are something else we have in common."

I sit down on the soft grass, crisscross-applesauce. My feet throb with relief, reminding me how long a day it's been already. Liam and Loren plop down on either side of me.

"There was an explosion of bright golden light," Liam continues. "It was everywhere. It was all I could see, and then I woke up. I don't know how long I was out, but I was here, beneath this tree—that used to be my mother. She was gone. So was everyone else. And my home was like this." He gestures at the world of gray all around us. "And the five talismans were lying there." He points at a patch of moss on a particularly twisty root that resembles a small nest. "One for each of the four Horsemen and one for Orin. I took them, but I didn't know where to go," he says, hanging his head.

I start to tell him he doesn't have to keep going with the story if it's triggering to him, but for once, I keep my big mouth shut. My gut (or my heart) tells me he needs to talk about this.

He takes a slow, deep breath in and out before continuing. "I thought about just staying here . . . alone forever. But seeing my home every day like this would be a constant reminder of how I lost everything the day before my birthday. I remember kneeling at the base of my mother's tree and letting out this really loud, deep, ugly cry. I don't know where it came from, but it felt like if I didn't get it out, it was going to burst from my chest.

"I scared a mourning dove from where it must've been perched somewhere in the branches of Mother's tree—the only creature left alive in this world aside from me after my mother and Orin drained the realm of its magic. The sound it made as it flew away was so solemn yet comforting at the same time. It's hard to explain. But something told me to follow the bird, so I let it lead me back to the portal to your realm. I left that day and never came back."

Liam hugs his knees to his chest and sighs—I know that one very well. It's the *I've already cried about this so much that I don't have any tears left* sigh.

I scoot next to him. "Can I hug you?"

His head snaps up. I flinch back, bracing for the whiplike sting of rejection. But his mask has finally and completely fallen away, revealing a gentler, more vulnerable Liam—someone I've only gotten glimpses of before.

He nods, and we snap our arms tight around each other. He smells like sweat and lake water and squid guts, but I don't care. For once, waves of unwelcome emotion don't bum-rush me with his touch. Instead, I Sense balance, security, and peace. This might be one of the best hugs I've ever had—musk and all.

Loren bowls into us, throwing her arms around us both. We tumble over in a tangle of arms and laughter. Now, *this* is the best hug I've ever gotten.

"We shouldn't waste too much time," I say once we're all out of giggles and sitting upright again. "We need to get back to the safe house before sundown unless we wanna drive through a fog of Green Dream."

"No worries," Liam says, standing up. "Time moves slower here, but we *should* get to testing out my theory."

"Hang on one second." Loren, already on her feet, puts up a finger. "Didn't you say your traitor bestie got snatched underwater in this same lake we're about to swim in?"

"Well, yeah," he says. "But a *lot* was going on then. Maybe he just drowned." He shrugs. "The lake is safe. We swam in it all the time before that day."

"I trust him," I say. "If you don't feel comfortable, you can stay on the shore, Lo."

For a moment, she frowns like she wants to argue, but she doesn't. "Okay, okay. I'm going. Maybe I'll get some awesome superpower too."

"I don't know if that's how it works," Liam says.

"You don't know a lot," Loren says over her shoulder, already heading for the water.

"It was a joke," I whisper to him before joining her.

Liam's the first to step into the water, and Loren and I follow. The three of us swim out pretty far, then float together in the chilly lake.

"Dive as deep as you safely can—don't forget you have to come back up," Liam instructs us. "Listen closely. My mother said the voices were always quiet, like a whisper."

I'm trembling all over, but I pretend it's because the water's cold and not because I'm nervous this plan is going to fail too. If it does, I have no clue what to do next.

But for now—we dive.

Water fills my ears, muffling the sound of everything but me kicking and clawing as far as I can into the depths. I keep an eye on Loren, who maintains pace with me, and Liam, who glides through the water like a mermaid, because of course he does.

The view is scary at first. The lake has no bottom. Only endless water and a pit of darkness. An underwater black hole. I'm afraid to get too close.

I swim deeper. I clear my thoughts and strain my ears, waiting to hear a voice other than mine or Orin's.

But I don't hear anything.

I'm not sure how much longer I can hold my breath, so I turn back for the surface. Loren does too. I glance back and see Liam, far below, pivot to swim back as well.

I break the surface and bob there like a chocolate buoy. Loren surfaces next, then Liam several moments later.

"Did you hear anything?" I ask Liam. Maybe the magic of the lake only responds to him, since he's from here and we're not.

He shakes his head. "You two?"

"Negative," says Loren.

I shake my head too.

"Then we try again." He dives before either of us can protest.

We try twice more, but the result is the same each time.

No one hears any voices, nor does anyone feel any different—except tired from swimming so much.

Dripping with lake water and defeat, we trudge to shore and sit underneath Navia's tree.

This is what I feared. We're back at square one.

"Well," Loren says, leaning back on her hands and gazing out at the water, "it's not like we expected saving the world to be easy."

"Yeah," I sigh, "but I had no idea it'd be impossible."

"Maybe not quite as impossible as you might think, little ones."

Loren shrieks, and we all whirl around with a start and get to our feet.

The willow glows all over with soft golden light. It feels warm and powerful, but not overwhelming, and smells of honeysuckle and rain. The smooth bark of the large knot on the tree trunk shifts.

It *was* a sleeping face that I saw before.

But it's wide awake now.

30

GIFTS FROM
THE HIGH GODDESS

"Mother?" Liam's voice trembles.

Navia smiles down on us. "Oh, my darling Liam. Look how much you've grown."

He throws himself against the tree, pressing his face against the bark, his arms as wide as he can get them. Tears flow freely down his cheeks. Loren and I stand back quietly, allowing Liam this moment with his mother.

"I wish I could hug you for real," he says.

Liam expresses emotion so freely. I wonder what that's like. I wish I could be more like him. Strong. Confident. Independent. Fearless. Magical.

When he steps back, Liam introduces us to Navia, and the three of us explain the events that led us here and that we were trying to tap into the lake's magic to help fight the Horsemen, but it didn't work.

"I'm afraid there's no more magic in the Lake of Logic," Navia says. "Zara's tree is gradually siphoning my life force. I tapped the lake's magic through my roots and used that power to survive long enough that I could see my son one last time."

Liam hangs his head and digs the toe of his right foot in the dirt. "I almost didn't come back. I was a coward. I failed you."

"No, no, no," Navia coos. "You are blameless, my sweet boy."

"Why did all this happen?" Liam asks.

Navia sighs. "Sit down, children. I'd like to tell you a story. It's long, but you need to know to understand."

We sit in the glow of the tree and stare up at the knot, which watches us with sad eyes of thick bark.

"Many millennia ago—Earth years, of course," she says, "I rose out of a dark pit of nothing. Soon after, five others were born from that same place. First Orin, then Moritz, Exo, Zara, and last Malakai. Together we, the Divine Six, combined our various magics to create this world around the pit from whence we had come, which now lies at the bottom of the Lake of Logic."

The black hole at the bottom of the lake. I swam in the place where gods were born. The thought makes me shudder.

"For a thousand years," Navia says, "the six of us lived here alone. We were at peace. And we were happy . . . for a time. But I yearned for more. I told my two closest friends, Orin and Moritz, how I felt. Orin advised me to find peace in what we'd already built in Paradisum, but Moritz urged me to go search for my happiness—even if it lay outside this realm. Later, in private, Moritz agreed to help me. I accepted. And we both kept it secret from Orin."

Adults sure do seem to keep a lot of secrets and make a ton

of mistakes that affect a bunch more people than just them, yet they're always telling kids *we're* the ones who aren't responsible and can't be trusted. Make it make sense.

"Moritz and I experimented with our magic until we created a tear between worlds," Navia says. "We stepped into the dark, and when we emerged on the other side, we were in a new realm—one we were both completely enamored by. That was over seven hundred Earth years ago. For a century, we kept it from the others and mimicked humans while venturing throughout their world and learning everything we could about them. I was happy for a time, but whenever we returned, I'd grow sad again. I still wanted more.

"I convinced Moritz to show the others what we'd been up to. Orin was the only one resistant at first, and soon they all became as engrossed in the new world as Moritz and I were. For nearly six hundred years, the Divine Six traveled secretly between Earth and Paradisum. But as time advanced, I grew despondent again, this time from witnessing the greed and lack of empathy of the human ruling classes. This angered the other deities, who all had varying opinions on how the people of Earth should be led. Fourteen years ago, Orin urged me to seal the passageway and let my obsession with humanity go once and for all, lest one or more of the others do something we would all regret. And grudgingly, I agreed.

"But Moritz found me at the portal before I could close it. My friend begged me for one last chance to return to Earth to say goodbye to the human he'd fallen in love with. I waited hours for his return, and when he emerged from the portal, he wasn't alone. He'd brought the woman—and their four-year-old son, Ezra. I was hesitant to let Lilith and Ezra stay, but I knew I couldn't live with myself if I broke up their family.

"After sealing the portal, I slipped into a depression. Despite all the drama that resulted from letting Moritz move his family to Paradisum, Ezra's presence in my life showed me what I was missing, why I'd been so sad for so long. I spoke with Orin about how I felt, and they combined their Sense with my Life magic to create a child. I named him Liam Ambros. I was his mother, he was made in my image, and I loved him more than anything in this realm and the next. And for the first time in many millennia, I was happy."

Liam smiles up at Navia's face in the tree.

Loren raises her hand and immediately asks, "Did any of the other gods have children?"

"Moritz was the only deity among us to father children," she says.

"What happened to Ezra's mom?" asks Loren.

Navia's bulky brow creases. "Lilith became a dear friend of mine. But she met her end by Moritz's hand shortly before he launched his coup."

A dark silence rests on the group until Navia sighs and continues her story.

"Moritz wanted more magical children, but Ezra would be Lilith's only child. Moritz's desperation to get back to Earth began to consume him. And the longer he stayed away, the angrier he became. I thought my friend would eventually cool off and enjoy the family he had instead of pining for what could've been, but I never imagined he'd rally Malakai, Zara, and Exo against me. My naiveté cost me dearly. In the end, only Orin remained true. Moritz knew that even with the others on his side, they were not stronger than Orin and me, and he knew that I would stop at nothing to protect the realm of humanity. And that is why he stole the most important thing in the multiverse to me—my child."

"Yeah," Loren mutters. "We've learned the hard way that the Horsemen don't play fair."

Navia's wooden expression hardens even more. "Orin created an empathic link, pulling my consciousness into a private room where time stood still in the outside worlds. For the span of twelve Paradisian days—about three days on Earth—we debated how to stop the Horsemen. Moritz was not interested in family for love, but instead for conquest. He didn't just want to father additional demigod children with humans; no, he wanted to *rule* them. The desperation that had consumed him when I closed off his access to Earth transfigured one of my oldest companions into someone I barely knew. But friend or no, I could not let him succeed.

"Moritz would not stop at your realm. He too had spoken to the entities at the bottom of the Lake of Logic and had heard about the infinite realms of the multiverse, filled with life, ripe for conquest. He was as restless as I was and would've gone from realm to realm conquering and colonizing for eternity."

The responsibility of saving one world from apocalyptic destruction is bad enough—just the thought of *infinite* worlds in mortal peril makes my head spin.

Following Loren's example, I raise my hand and say, "Excuse

me, but are you saying there are other universes just like Paradisum and the one we're from? Are there other versions of us somewhere in the multiverse too?"

"Only one version of you exists," Navia says. "However, there are multiple universes in which you can exist. Does that make sense?"

I nod so Navia can continue her story, because that absolutely does *not* make sense and I'm not sure it ever will.

"On the eleventh day, we had our plan," she tells us. "I spent the twelfth crafting Echoes of my beautiful but too-short life with my child to help him through the incredibly tough time he would face after I was gone."

"Do you regret ever leaving Paradisum?" asks Liam.

"I've had plenty of time to think about that"—she sighs—"and I do not. If I hadn't discovered the world of humanity, I would never have uncovered what was missing from my life and you would never have been born. I only wish I could've found my way to you without the destruction of so many other lives. I failed you, Liam, and for that, I am so very sorry. All I can do now is try to make up for what I've done."

Liam averts his gaze to the lake. "I understand, but I feel I'm the one failing *you*. Maybe Orin already Sensed my failure, and that's why they chose Alex as their vessel instead of me."

His words feel like a finger digging into a wound I thought had healed. I understand all too well how rejection feels. It lingers, like the scent of fish in the kitchen the morning after Mom would fry catfish nuggets for dinner.

"Orin was my most loyal advisor and friend. Even in death, I trust their judgment." When Liam's shoulders slump, she adds, "Liam Ambros, you are the child of the High Goddess. You already possess all you need to honor me."

He lifts his chin and nods. His biceps flex as he clenches his fists in his lap. I'm glad his mother's reassurance comforts him. Liam doesn't deserve to feel like he's not good enough.

I don't want that for anyone.

"Now, I didn't sap all the magic out of this lake and wait four Earth years to see you again only to assuage my guilt," says Navia. "I want to aid you kids in your fight against the Horsemen."

At once, all three of us are on our feet, ravenous with anticipation. A joyous warmth flickers in the center of my chest. This might all finally be over soon.

One of the thick roots rises from the ground slowly, ripping up patches of moss and grass. A curtain of dirt rains into the space where the root was, clinking against something shiny wedged into the loose earth. Liam approaches gingerly and picks up a stemless chalice made from wound strips of clay and precious metal. He steps back, brushing dirt off its surface.

"The Horsemen are powerful, but Orin and I significantly weakened them by destroying their godly forms," says Navia. "I've had lots of time to commune with the spirits of the lake, which led to this idea." Her eyes fall on Liam. "Bring the chalice to me."

He blows the last grains of dust from it and steps up to the tree, his face even with his mother's in the knot. Loren and I edge a little closer too, eager to see what Navia's doing.

"Do not waste any," she tells him.

Resin pours from her eyes like tears. They pool at the bottom of the knot and combine into a single stream. Liam holds the chalice underneath, and it fills to the brim before the flow stops. Something snaps above our heads, and a twig falls to the ground at Liam's feet. He picks it up and looks to his mother curiously.

"That is a wick," she says. "Stick it straight down in the middle."

Liam places the wick into the resin, which has already thickened to the consistency of peanut butter.

"This candle has powerful magical properties," Navia tells us. "Once the Horsemen are vulnerable, light the wick. The magic in this relic will draw the spirits of the Horsemen from the innocents. When their spirits are entwined with the flame, simply blow it out, snuffing them out once and for all."

Loren asks Liam if she can see it, and when he hands it to her, she looks it over carefully. "How does the magic work?"

"The vessel, the resin, and the wick were all made from some of the last enchanted remnants of Paradisum. When lit, this candle will call to the Horsemen. I used a portion of my remaining magic to enhance that pull to ensure they won't be able to resist. A moth to a flame. A single breath to end a god."

"And you're sure this will work?" Liam asks.

Loren passes the candle to me. It's heavier than I thought it would be. It's only the size of a softball but feels like it weighs at *least* three whole pounds. I run my fingers along the side between the ridges of smooth earthen clay and slick shiny metal. Magic is truly incredible. This is like something from a fantasy book. Mags would've loved to experience this.

I'm coming, little sis. I promise.

"The candle alone will not be enough to vanquish the Horsemen," says Navia. "They will only succumb to it once they've been significantly weakened. You're going to need more help."

Her wooden eyes close and a bright light beams from the other side of her trunk. "These weapons will aid you in your quest."

We wander to the other side of the tree, where a trio of golden weapons sits on a shelf inside a hollow.

A golden whip floats from the shelf toward Loren. The entire thing crackles with white lightning, branching off several times along the way to zip into the ground, charring the grass.

She grabs the handle, and her mouth hangs open. "I can't believe this is happening."

She walks a few paces away and swings the whip once around her head and then forward with an impressive crack that ignites the air with sharp veins of lightning.

She turns back to us, wide-eyed. "I—I don't know how I did that. I've never held a whip before, much less a magical one." The handle lights up in her hand, and she shrieks and drops it. "It shocked me!"

"That is only your weapon bonding to your consciousness, which helps remove the learning curve as well," says Navia. "Something else I learned from the spirits beyond the lake."

"I wish they'd made it pain-free," Loren murmurs. She drapes the whip over her shoulders and the end snaps to the handle like a magnet to metal. It shrinks, transforming into a small golden rope necklace. She holds it up and smiles at it, then tucks it into her shirt.

A golden bangle rises into the air and floats to Liam. His wooden bracelet falls from his wrist. The earth splits like a tiny mouth to consume it, then sews itself shut.

Liam holds out his left hand, and the jewelry slips onto his wrist. He steps aside and pulls off the new bangle, which at once straightens and extends into a golden staff as tall as he is. It glows in his hand, and he bares his teeth and grunts loudly but doesn't let go.

He exhales and twirls his new staff in a mesmerizing display of golden blurs and powerful thrusts. When he snaps to a stop, holding it poised over one shoulder as if launching a spear, the tip of each end melts and reshapes into a blade.

He lowers the spear to his wrist and it zips back to a bangle. He's clearly impressed, which makes his handsome face look even more handsome than usual. (It's not what you think; friends can compliment each other without it being romantic, sheesh.)

"Cool," he mutters.

"Your staff is unbreakable," says Navia, "even by a god."

"Even cooler," he replies.

"And last but certainly never least, Alex Wise." Navia says my name warmly, like a beloved relative I haven't seen in a long time.

All that remains in the center of the shelf is a single golden sword. Somehow, I knew the moment I saw it that it was intended for me, and that made me very nervous. I don't know how to use a *sword*.

It floats from the shelf and turns upright, as if held by an invisible hand. The golden blade glimmers with bursts of white and silver fireworks in the sunlight before exploding into brilliant white flame. It hovers in front of me, waiting for me to claim it. The way my hands quiver warms my cheeks with embarrassment. The heat intensifies when I feel Loren and Liam watching.

I swallow the anxiety rising like acid in my throat and take the hilt of my brand-new magical flaming golden sword. Immediately, it shocks my hand with what feels like a powerful jolt of static electricity. I let out a high-pitched yelp, but I manage to hang on to it.

I hold the sword out and admire it. I can't help but grin. I bet if Sky could see me now, he'd ditch Larry for me on the spot. The muscles of my right arm tingle, from my shoulder down to my fingers wrapped around the leather-and-gold hilt. It's like the zap from the connection to this thing injected me with muscle memory—except it seems to have a mind of its own. An itch in my brain that I can't scratch unless I act.

I swing the sword. It cuts the air with a vicious *whoosh*. I twirl it in one hand, and when it comes back around, a button clicks on somewhere in my mind. The first time this happens, I'm hit by the slightly disorienting sensation of time slowing to a crawl. A series of four symbols I don't recognize appears on the blade of my sword, glowing like a white-hot brand. The symbols erupt with flames, which quickly spread over the rest of the blade. Time speeds back up—giving me mental whiplash that leaves me a little dizzy. The fire on my sword goes out with a soft hiss, and I let out a deep breath.

This is strange. All of a sudden, I know how to use a sword, yet I have no memory of ever learning a thing.

"Your weapon's blade is likewise unbreakable," Navia tells me.

I get the urge to tap it to my wrist, like Liam did with his staff. When I do, the blade feels warm. The hilt snaps from my hand, startling me (and making me bite my tongue), and transforms into a golden bracelet similar to Liam's. I slide it off and read "Alex Wise" engraved on the inside. Wow.

"These gifts can never be lost," Navia tells us as I slide my bracelet back on, "and cannot be used by anyone else—god or no."

Although I feel better equipped for what we have to do, the thought of fighting actual gods gives me the bubble guts.

"You three are going to have to work together and use every tool at your disposal to stop the Horsemen," she says. "Weaken them and use the candle. I believe in you."

Liam blanches, and Navia frowns at him.

"I sense your trepidation, my child," she says. "What is troubling you?"

"I'm afraid to use my magic," he says. "I think it's draining my life force—like what Famine's tree is doing to you."

"But you are my direct descendent." Navia doesn't hide the confusion in her voice. "Magic lives within you, natural and limitless. Hug me again."

Liam obeys his mother, putting his arms around her trunk. Her golden glow enshrouds him completely. After a few moments, Navia's voice cuts through the quiet.

"Okay, son," she says.

Liam steps back and she sighs. The light suffusing her tree has dimmed significantly. When did that happen?

"There is a powerful curse on you," she says. "I don't know who could've done it, but it had to have been cast on the day of the Horsemen's uprising—otherwise, I would've known."

I chew my bottom lip nervously. I want to ask if Navia can check me, too, but it feels selfish to intrude on Liam's moment.

"Pestilence invaded Alex's mind," Liam says. "He said Alex had a block that was limiting Orin's magic." Liam glances back at me, and his mesmerizing dark eyes flicker with concern that I can't overlook, especially since it makes something tingle in my chest. "Can you help him?"

My lips part, but I can't find the right words to say. I've been afraid of growing closer to Liam because of what happened with Sky; but Sky would never speak up for me the way Liam just did. Maybe I don't need to be scared of being Liam's friend.

"Come to me, Alex," Navia says, her soothing voice drawing me forward as if I've fallen under a spell.

But really, I just need a hug.

Up close, I can hear the sound of wood grinding against wood as Navia's face in the knot shifts, watching me with a slight smile. I put my arms around her trunk. Ragged bark pokes the side of my face, but the discomfort fades the moment her warm light and the mingled scents of earth, rain, and honeysuckle consume me. We stay that way for what feels like only a fraction of a second, though I know it was longer.

"I'm afraid I cannot help you," she tells me. "The block you are experiencing is not magical."

"How do I remove it?" I'll do anything. *Almost* anything.

"You must find a way on your own to forge a connection

with Orin if you wish to tap into your true power," she says. "You can never hope to understand the feelings of others until you understand your own."

"What does that mean?" I ask, trying my best (and likely failing) to mask my frustration. I don't have much patience for riddles. My sister's life is at stake.

"Your role in this quest is to figure that out," she says. "I have faith that you will."

I'm not sure how a goddess I just met can have faith in me, but I suppose it's a welcome change from everyone treating me like a walking mess.

Navia's eyes shift back to Liam. "But I can help you." His face brightens. "Though it will require all the magic I have left. After I use it, this tree will be free to consume what remains of my life force, and I will cease to exist."

Liam's bottom lip trembles, and he shakes his head. "I won't let you. I just got you back. I can't lose you again."

"My boy," she says, "you are made from me, which means I am with you always. Do not stray from the light and we will meet again someday. Now," she commands him gently, "you must place your hands on my trunk once more."

Liam hesitates for a charged moment that seems to stretch on forever. A sudden barrage of emotion stirs inside me, a vortex of grief and pain that makes my knees tremble. But I clench my fists at my sides and endure. It's not fair that Liam has had to carry all this by himself for so long.

Liam takes a shuddering breath, then crashes into the tree, which immediately explodes in a powerful burst of light. The force throws him back and knocks Loren and me over. I rub the spots from my vision and push myself to my feet.

Navia's tree no longer glows with golden light, but it is the only thing in the gray world of Paradisum aside from Loren, Liam, and me that has color. And it is the most magnificent thing I've ever seen. I was right before: I don't have the proper vocabulary to describe the dark-to-light earth tones of her trunk or the greens, blues, and yellows of leaves dancing in the blazing white sunlight. My eyes follow the tree's great frame all the way to its topmost branches, but then my heart sinks. Color slowly flakes from the tree like peeling paint, except it floats high above and crumbles into nothing.

Liam sits bolt upright and throws his head back. His arms fly out on either side, and geysers of golden light shoot from his eyes, mouth, and fingertips. Loren and I both flinch, but it's over after only a few seconds. He falls back and rolls onto his chest with a wheezing cough.

We both jet to his side, but he holds up a hand before either of us can help him up.

"I'm okay." He pushes to his feet and flexes his fingers on both hands. "It's been a long time since I felt the full force of my Light magic. It feels like I've been spun around a thousand times."

I wonder what Liam's truly capable of now that his powers are uninhibited. Considering I'm still "magically constipated," as Pestilence so eloquently said, I'm def a little jealous.

"Stay strong, sweet children," Navia says. "Blessings upon you. Farewell."

My breath catches when I realize the gray has spread nearly all the way down her trunk. Navia's face freezes in a gentle smile as the color peels away, leaving behind a lifeless knot. The High Goddess of Paradisum, Liam's mother, is gone.

Loren gasps and claps a hand over her mouth.

Liam drops to his knees and hangs his head.

I'm glad time moves slower in Paradisum.

Liam's going to need more than a minute before we head back to the boat.

31

JUMANJI

Liam, Loren, and I sit on the bank of the Lake of Logic in the shade of the giant willow that once contained the spirit of the High Goddess of Paradisum. We've taken off our shoes and socks and now our bare feet soak in the cool water just below the shallow bank.

Liam cradles the magic candle in his lap, carefully, as if it were a newborn bunny. "Losing my mother again reminds me of that cold, hollow feeling I started getting whenever I used magic—except worse." He wiggles his toes in the water. "Sometimes I worry I might have more sadness than I know what to do with."

I want to offer comforting words, but I haven't quite learned how to deal with emotional pain myself, unless hours upon hours of video games or books or movies as distractions count.

"Before that day four years ago, I'd never known anyone who died," Liam says, "and then I lost everyone I'd ever known all at the same time." He releases a long, shuddering breath. "Have you two ever lost anyone before?"

Loren nods.

I stare at my own feet hanging in the gray water. "My dad didn't die, but he might as well have." I roll my eyes at Loren's sharp intake of breath. She hates it when I talk about my dad like that, but it's the truth. "Not calling a baby ugly doesn't make the baby any less ugly."

Loren shakes her head. "You need to stop watching *Saturday Night Live*."

"That was an Alex Wise original, thank you very much."

"What?" Liam interjects, confused.

"Ignore her," I tell him, side-eying Loren.

"I wish my magic could take it away," he says. "Sadness."

"That'd be great." I muse for a moment about how nice it'd be to burn the memories of rejection from Dad over the years—starting with hearing him call me an embarrassment. I wonder if that's something I'll be able to do with the Sense if my ability keeps developing.

"No, it wouldn't," Loren says with stern conviction. "The sadness of grief is linked to happiness. You can't have one without the other. The only way to get rid of the grief from having loved is to never have loved at all. Who wants that?"

I shrug. "Maybe we're just tired of being sad."

Liam sighs his agreement.

"When my Grandma Sadie died last year," Loren says, "I was depressed for a long time."

I'll never forget. Loren knocked on my window in the middle of the night, her face so wet I thought it'd been raining. I was groggy because she'd scared me out of a deep sleep. She crawled through my window and told me what had happened.

Her grandma was like a second mom to her, one who gave her the space to be herself—and encouraged it, even when it got weird, like when Loren insisted on wearing sports jerseys every day in fifth grade. Grandma Sadie also bankrolled her obsession, to Loren's mom's dismay. I'd never seen Lo cry like she did that night in my bedroom. I didn't know what to say, so I hugged her. And I held her while she wept.

"My dad told me that my sadness wasn't something bad," Loren says. "It meant I loved my grandma deeply and genuinely. He said a better way to honor her was through happiness."

"How do you do that?" asks Liam.

"Think of the happiest memory of you with your mother," she says. "Then think of the next happiest and the next. Eventually, you'll fall into a rhythm of remembering the good instead of focusing on the loss. You'll still get sad from time to time, but that's okay."

Liam smiles. "I like that."

"And what about me, Iyanla?" I ask Loren. "What am I supposed to do?"

She shrugs. "Dude, I dunno. Your dad's just a jerk. No offense."

"None taken," I say. "Ugly baby. Remember?"

We stare at each other for a quiet moment before all three of us simultaneously explode with laughter.

Dexter and the others are surprised to see us back at the *Chum Bucket*. They tell us we've barely been gone for two hours, but we spent close to eight in Paradisum. Melvin and Jamar quickly wrap up repairs while Liam, Loren, and I download Dexter on what happened on our interdimensional excursion.

He listens with keen interest and studies the candle chalice, turning it over and over in his thin brown fingers. He returns the candle to Liam and says we'll talk more tonight at the safe house, then goes to chat with Melvin, who seems annoyed when he sees Dexter coming.

We arrive back in Santa Monica easy-peasy. But we still can't relax. The sun hangs low in the sky when the *Chum Bucket* pulls up to the dock to let us off. I remind everyone that we have to get back to the house before sundown unless we wanna bathe in Green Dream. We say a quick goodbye to Melvin and Jamar and wish them well—wherever they're headed next.

I hope they make it.

We all climb into the *Mini Chum*, and Dexter drives us back toward the safe house in the Hills. We travel only a handful of blocks before he slows and squints over the steering wheel.

"What is that?" he mutters.

Cars are arranged in a barricade before the intersection up ahead, the line stretching to the abandoned retail buildings on either side. Dexter creeps the *Mini Chum* closer.

Blood rushes in my ears. This is deliberate.

"Maybe we should turn around," I suggest.

Liam leans up between the driver and passenger seats, close enough that I can feel heat radiating from him. "I don't think *she's* going to let us."

I don't know how I missed her.

In the center of the blockade, Famine lounges on the hood of an SUV, reclined against the windshield. Her green hair is slicked straight back, and she's wearing a black camo jumpsuit with black combat boots, which are crossed at the ankles like she's relaxing at a resort. Her oversized leopard and panther lie side by side on the roof. Their thick tails are wobbly metronomes, swishing back and forth through the air as they stare at us with lamplike eyes.

"Should we try the candle on her?" Loren asks from the back seat.

Liam shakes his head. "Something feels off. She's been waiting for us."

I get out of the car, ignoring the whispers and hisses of protest from inside.

"What do you want?" I shout as I approach Famine, my friends reluctantly following.

Famine sits up and grins. "Just to talk. I was beginning to think you wouldn't show." She glances at the deep-orange sun sinking closer to the horizon at our backs, which casts her in an otherworldly glow. "It'll be dark soon, and time for Pestilence to make his rounds."

"So you'll understand when I ask you to cut to the chase." I twist the heavy gold bangle on my wrist, which catches her eye.

"That's new," she says.

"It does a cool trick," I say. "Wanna see up close?"

Both big cats lift their heads. Fangs bared, they emit low, rumbling growls.

"I'll pass," Famine says casually. "Admittedly, we're all slightly annoyed with you right now." She scrunches up her round face. "I had plans for that Kraken you killed, you know."

I snicker under my breath. "Would you like to speak to a manager?"

"We don't have time for this," Liam whisper-yells at me.

Famine stands on the hood of the car, her heavy boots crinkling the metal. "I have a message for you, Alex Wise. Death says she misjudged you before when she said you didn't have what it takes. She seems convinced you might be willing to join the right side of legend. Me, on the other hand, I'd rather turn you all into steaks for my fur babies."

"I'm sick of her," Loren snarls beside me.

"I disrespectfully decline," I tell Famine.

"When my spirit first claimed this girl as my vessel, she was hesitant too," says Famine. "She was volunteering at the zoo when it happened, looking after these two babies, which she'd done since they were only a few weeks old." She turns and pets both cats, whose eyes close as they purr. "When my blue light hit her in the chest, she was terrified. But she had no idea what great things were to come. You could be part—"

"We good," I say. "And we're also leaving."

Famine's taunting laugh stops me from walking away. It begins as a chuckle and escalates to a raucous belly roar that has her bent double, cackling at a joke only she finds funny. I turn back and glare up at her.

"You get a few party favors from a dead goddess and suddenly you think you're a superhero," she says, still snickering.

Liam bucks forward, but I throw out an arm, stopping him. We don't have time for a street brawl. It's nearly sunset.

"You can't save your sister," Famine says. "And you can't stop what's coming."

"We'll see," I say, turning on my heel again.

"Mags belongs to Death now," she continues. "Their consciousness is one. Let's say you pull off the impossible feat of saving her—do you honestly think she'll be the same? Face it, Alex. She's *ruined*. The only way you come out on top is by joining us."

I round on her, and she extends her hand, palm facing up, like I'm going to take it and let her lead me off into the sunset.

But none of us expect what happens next—not even Famine.

A flash of gold zips by me. The end of Loren's whip latches onto Famine's wrist. Famine glances down as white streaks of lightning crawl over her body like a million spindly spider legs. Loren steps forward and swings her whip so hard she grunts; still attached to its end, Famine shrieks as she circles overhead and crashes through a jewelry store display window.

Loren, panting, drapes her whip around her neck, returning it to necklace form. "I owed her that."

The leopard and the panther are both up on their haunches, but only the leopard leaps to attack. Liam reaches out to Loren, projecting a shield of light around her. She freezes, eyes wide, looking like she's going to pee herself. The leopard thunks hard into the shield headfirst and falls aside, out cold.

Loren turns around carefully and looks at the black

panther, which yawns and lowers itself back onto its belly on the roof of the SUV. Loren crosses her arms over her chest and mutters, "Wakanda forever."

"Come on, Lo!" I shout. "Let's go!"

We hop into the car, and Dexter busts a U-turn in the street and peels off in the opposite direction. In the side mirror, I watch Famine stumble back through the display window and stagger over to her unconscious kitty.

But getting home won't be as easy as we thought. The ground quakes, rattling the car and everything inside—including us. Dexter doesn't slow down, which makes me queasy, but we're almost out of time. I'm guessing we only have a half hour of daylight left before Pestilence bathes Los Angeles in Green Dream.

At the next intersection, Dexter slams on the brakes, throwing us all forward—thank goodness we're all wearing seat belts! An army of zoo animals crosses in front of us, stampeding down the street like rush hour traffic, but instead of car horns honking, we hear the creatures trumpet, bleat, and shriek in passing.

Zebras and gazelles leap along the rubble and abandoned cars, but the rhinos, giraffes, and elephants rumbling behind them charge or knock every obstruction aside, even a few of the animals who are too slow and too naive to get out of the way in time. Gorillas, orangutans, and monkeys swing from building awnings and traffic lights, jumping in tandem over the wreckage.

We don't wait to see what other animals are in the apocalypse parade. Dexter whips the car around and heads in the opposite direction, cutting down a series of side streets.

I'm gripping the door handle in one hand and the hard leather edge of my seat in the other when something out my window catches my attention. Too late, I notice the lone rhino charging toward our little car.

It hits us with the intensity and sound of a bomb exploding.

32

FAREWELL, DEAR FRIEND

The *Mini Chum* barrel-rolls down the street with us inside.

The world spins around and around until I feel like I'm going to hurl. Finally, the car slams into something solid with a jarring metal crunch and falls still.

The car's engine sputters and hisses. My friends' groans and moans resound all around me. I recognize everyone's voice but Liam's. I shake off my grogginess and whip around.

He's slumped against the back door, a fresh bruise blossoming on one side of his head. His chest rises and falls softly.

Loren unbuckles her seat belt and his, then leans over to examine his injury. "He's breathing okay and nothing feels broken. I think he's just knocked out."

"What about you two?" asks Dexter.

Loren and I nod. We're all a bit banged up, but everyone's fine otherwise. Loren retrieves the candle from the floor and inspects it. I'm not sure how it's not broken, but considering all the trouble we've had lately, I won't question this one lucky happenstance.

Dexter and I get out of the car, and he and Loren set to work trying to get the back doors open so we can lift Liam out.

The *Mini Chum* is pressed against the stairs to the front entrance of an apartment building. I run up and peek into one of the narrow windows beside the entrance. The foyer is empty. I pull on the door beneath the ZION CONDOMINIUMS sign, but it's locked. I bang on it with both fists and shout until my throat burns, but no one comes.

A deserted bus that crashed into the side of the apartment building blocks our path to the left. Dust-covered cars line the space to the right of us amid large chunks of concrete from the building across the street, which looks like a recent explosion ripped off its facade.

We're trapped.

And several blocks back in the direction from which we came, the same rhino that murdered the *Mini Chum* trots into the middle of the street. It stops abruptly and turns its attention on us. My heart skips a beat when it lowers its head and huffs, kicking up clouds of dust.

"Umm . . . we've got more trouble," I announce, descending the stairs and pointing in the direction of the rhino, which very much looks like it's about to attack us again.

Loren squeals and becomes a blur of motion in the back seat as Dexter tries to calm her.

I peer through the broken passenger window and tell them, "You two are going to have to get him out from the front."

"Wait, aren't you going to help?" shrieks Loren.

"I am," I say.

Dexter stands bone straight and glares at me over the hood of the car. "Alex, what in the world do you think—"

I shake my head at him, and he falls quiet.

I back up a few steps, then leap onto the roof of the car and slide off the other side.

Loren and Dexter watch me silently.

"Get Liam out of there," I say, startling myself with how strong and commanding my voice sounds. "I got this."

I absolutely do not have this.

And I'm probably about to die.

The rhino charges and time slows. My heart thumps. I wipe my sweaty palms on my shorts and let out the breath I was holding.

Breathe. Focus inward.

I used my magic before to incept Geoff's mind back in Cadillac Freddie's store. I'm not sure if it'll work the same on animals, but the rhino has a brain, so the logic checks out.

Now if I could only figure out how to access this power.

You're enough, chants Orin's now-familiar voice inside my head. It's warm, like a bonfire on a chilly night.

The rhino tosses aside a small sedan in its way as if it were made of plastic and foam.

Breathe. Focus inward.

I step forward a few paces to meet the rhino. It's two blocks away and closing in quick.

I'm enough. I can do this.

The animal gets near enough that I can see its glowing red eyes, which look otherworldly against the backdrop of the red and purple sky, the horizon ignited by the setting sun.

I plant my feet and lift my hands slightly, concentrating on the charging rhino. Its great muscles flex as it bounds straight for me, now only a block away.

I stare into those raging red eyes and focus only on them, locking out all other distractions, every other sound.

It's just you and me, rhino. Let me in.

I close my eyes and let go. For a fraction of a second, I allow myself to be free, to not worry about the charging rhino or my friends or my sister or the apocalypse. In that quiet, I feel that my mind wanders somewhere else, somewhere new. Like when you walk into a room for the first time and the little hairs on the back of your neck stand up when you realize everyone has stopped to stare at you.

I imagine me and my friends standing behind a wall of fire so tall that it'd rival the fog around Liam's island. Bits of flame lean away from the wall, hungrily licking the air. I can feel heat crashing into me and hear the rippling roar of fire.

I open my eyes.

The rhino skids to a sputtering stop less than five feet from me, then turns on its heels and bolts. I'm not sure where it goes, but I'm in such disbelief of what I just did that my knees turn to peanut butter and jelly. I wobble, but Loren appears at my side to prop me up.

"Thanks," I whisper to her.

"Alex," she mutters. "What . . . How did you do that?"

"Did you see the wall of fire too?" I ask.

She shakes her head. "Dude, you were standing there with your arms out like you were an X-Man or something, and then the rhino . . . just dipped."

Dexter steps up, cradling a groggy, half-conscious Liam in his arms. Liam, cupping the candle against his chest like a football, smiles and gives me a thumbs-up, then tells Dexter he should be good to walk now, and Dexter puts him down.

Loren gasps and grabs hold of my wrist, sending shock waves of fear and anxiety tearing through me. I pull away, but my own terror takes over when I see why she's freaking out.

Like a tsunami, a flood of Green Dream rolls down the street, heading straight for us. My shoulders slump. You've *got* to be kidding right now. When does it end?

We're stuck. My magic is useless against Pestilence's death gas.

The door of the apartment building creaks open behind us, and someone shouts, "Get in here! Quick!"

I turn with a start and freeze. "Sky?"

And then I stare up at the ZION CONDOMINIUMS sign and it comes back to me: this is the building Sky mentioned his parents had gotten a penthouse in for the summer.

Finally some good luck for a change.

Sky's little brother, Blu, pokes his head out the door and cries, "Hurry up!"

We all climb over the trashed *Mini Chum* and rush inside, showering Sky and Blu with thanks. Sky slams the door shut seconds before the wave of neon green gas hits the front of the building and rolls over on itself.

I stare out the window at the crumpled remains of the *Mini Chum*, engulfed in a tomb of Green Dream.

"Farewell, dear friend," I murmur.

33

UN-FRIEND-ZONED

"Whoa, whoa, *whoooa!*" Blu exclaims, clutching his head with both hands. "We were upstairs when we heard the car crash, so we came down to see if anyone was hurt, and then we saw you stand up to that rhino, and that was so freaking cool, how did you do that, are you a superhero now?"

"Chill!" Sky taps Blu's shoulder, but the kid is practically vibrating with excitement and ignores him. "Seriously," he adds. "You're embarrassing." By the way he wrinkles his nose when he says it, he doesn't mean that in a playful, brotherly way. And that word—"embarrass" and its many ugly forms—triggers me whenever I hear it wielded this way.

I side-eye Sky and bump fists with Blu, taking in a brief shock of excitement from him. "Maybe I am."

His eyes light up again. "By the way, I know that wasn't really Mags on Instagram." He shakes his head. "I'm her best friend, so I would know. I mean, you're her brother, so you would too, but I'm just saying I *also* know—"

"You're right," I tell him. "This might sound a bit wild, but an evil spirit from another world kinda stole her body."

Blu gasps, then clenches his fists. "I knew it! It's just like when the Eidolons possessed Percy and Leo in *Mark of Athena*!" He glares at his older brother. "*Told* you!"

Sky rolls his eyes.

"Yeah," I say, dragging out the word, because I have no idea what he's talking about, but I'm with it as long as he understands. "Don't worry, though," I tell him. "I'm going to bring your best friend home. Promise."

Blu nods, beaming even brighter, believe it or not.

I introduce Sky and Blu to Liam. They already know Dexter, who they both glance at curiously, as if noticing him standing off to the side of our group for the first time.

"Why are y'all hanging out with Mr. Dexter?" Sky asks, offering a low "No offense" to Dexter as an afterthought.

"It's a long story," I say with an exhausted sigh.

"You guys can stay here tonight," Sky says.

"Will that be okay with your parents?" asks Dexter.

Sky nods. "I'll tell Mom y'all are friends from school. She won't mind. She probably won't even come out of her bedroom."

"Is she okay?" asks Dexter.

"Yeah." Sky looks toward the elevator like he wants to make a run for it. "She's just worried about Dad. He left this morning to get my grandparents all the way from Orange County. He said they'd be back sometime tomorrow morning."

"We'll be gone at sunrise," I tell him.

He nods and takes us to the elevator. On the way up, I nudge Liam so he leans his weight on my shoulder for the long ride to the penthouse on the thirtieth floor. I absorb gentle ripples of relief, exhaustion, and some lingering sadness from his touch. But I concentrate on the shifting numbers displayed on the screen above the metal doors. Every now and again, I catch Sky out the corner of my eye sneaking sidelong glances at me and Liam.

For a moment, I wonder what Sky's thinking, but then I realize I don't really care. All I'm worried about right now is making sure Liam rests and recovers before the sun comes up and burns away all the Green Dream so we can leave. The toxic gas appears to be very dense, so it hangs low in the air and doesn't travel vertically well, so we should be safe in a high-rise building.

Sky's family's penthouse is swanky and modern, like somewhere a celebrity would live, and suddenly I remember, Sky's dad kinda is a celebrity. Sky leads us past a coat closet and bathroom, which Blu dips into, in a short hallway that opens into a grand kitchen, family room, and dining room. A glass-walled staircase leads up to another level. All the furniture still has that newly manufactured smell. Sterile hues of white and beige cover the place from floor to ceiling. But the glass walls on two sides of the gargantuan family room offer incredible— and haunting—views of the ocean on one side and a dimly lit city drenched in Green Dream on the other, which projects an eerie, dim glow.

Sky points at the ginormous sectional couch that looks more like a bed in the center of the family room, set before a fireplace and large-screen television, which is switched off.

"You three can sleep on the couch," Sky says. "I nap there sometimes. It's very comfortable." He gestures to a low-lit hallway off the kitchen. "You can take the spare room, Mr. Dexter. It's where my grandparents are gonna sleep, but I'll just make the bed after you leave. They'll never know."

"Ah, thank you," Dexter says with an air of discomfort, but he doesn't protest, probably looking forward to lying down in a comfy bed after the day we've had.

"I'll go up and let Mom know you're staying the night," Sky announces. "But don't be offended if she doesn't come down to say hi."

"It's okay," I tell him. "We don't want to disturb her."

Sky and Dexter leave for the guest room. Liam sets the candle gently on the floor beside the couch, and he and Loren crawl onto the sofa and fall on their backs, both muttering about how soft and cushy it is. I sit on the edge and run my hands along the plush fabric, which reminds me of suede.

I'm not sure how long I sit there, staring out at the black nighttime sky dotted with a million stars, but Liam's snores pull me back to the present. Both he and Loren are knocked out.

I get up, slide open the glass door leading to the balcony, and step outside. I close my eyes and gulp down the fresh air, thankful we're up high enough that we don't have to worry about the Green Dream and also that Pestilence's gas has no scent. Because if it did, I'd imagine it'd smell like the worst fart I've ever had the displeasure of being caught in.

This balcony faces east, overlooking West LA. Lights are sparse and fires still burn in the darkest sectors. The street below is hidden beneath a thick blanket of gas. It's weird how quiet it is out here, despite being in the city. I hope everyone's learned to be inside by sundown now.

"Alex?"

I turn to see Blu in the doorway. When I smile, he wanders outside to stand next to me at the balcony wall. The gas below lights his pale skin and hair in a sickly-green glow. He keeps sighing and chewing on his bottom lip while staring blankly into the distance.

"You okay?" I ask him.

"Mags talks about you a lot. It makes me jealous sometimes, and I'm scared that means I'm a bad friend."

I look into his eyes, which appear turquoise out here. "Being jealous doesn't make you a bad friend. That just means you're normal. Everybody gets jealous sometimes, even me. It's not bad until it makes you wish good things didn't happen to people." I pause, and he tenses, his shoulders drawing up slowly. "And then you'd become a supervillain."

Blu giggles and relaxes. "Nope. I definitely want to be a superhero like you."

I'm stuck for a moment, unsure how to respond. I want to tell Blu I'm no superhero, but I understand why he thinks I am. And he believes it so strongly, he's beginning to convince me.

"Can I tell you a secret?" Blu asks just above a whisper.

I nod, happy for a new subject.

He leans against the wall and frowns. "I wish I had a brother like you."

I'm about to say "But you do—" when I stop myself,

remembering all the times I've noticed Sky blow off his little brother any time the kid tried to show him some affection. Younger brothers and sisters are annoying more than they're not, Blu and Mags included, but the way Sky treats Blu is mean—and wrong.

I hug Blu. Tight. I feel a rush of warmth and admiration and love at his touch.

When we part, I ask him, "Now can I tell *you* a secret?"

Blu nods eagerly.

I sidle closer to him and lower my voice conspiratorially. "I think you're the coolest person in this condo right now—even cooler than me."

Blu breaks into a fit of giggles, which is interrupted by Sky's voice from the sliding door.

"Blu, it's time for you to shower and get ready for bed."

Blu groans and falls over dramatically against the wall. "Are you really going to enforce a bedtime in the apocalypse?"

Sky huffs. "I don't care if you go to bed or not, but you've *gotta* shower. This is day three, bro."

Blu's cheeks redden and he ducks inside, pushing hard past his brother. Once he's gone, Sky clears his throat.

"Can we talk?" he asks.

His hair hangs loose, pushed back and swept behind both ears. I can see the rows where he's raked his fingers like he always does when something's up with him.

My pulse quickens. "Sure."

"Come to my room."

My heart flutters at the same time something mucky rolls over in my gut. "Okay."

I follow Sky up the staircase and down a hallway to his room. His bed is a tangled mess of sheets. Clothes and snack wrappers mingle together on the floor like guests at a party. There's a huge flat-screen on the wall and an entertainment stand with a PlayStation. I wonder if he brought that with him from Palm Vista, expecting to play *Fortnite* with Larry all summer.

Sky closes his room door and sits on the bed. He looks up at me and pats the spot next to him. "Come sit with me."

I shake my head, intent on lingering near the doorway.

I'm not sure why Sky's being so warm and inviting, like sixth grade didn't happen, because it absolutely did, and it hurt. Still does.

Not long ago, all I wanted was to be alone with my ex-friend so we could repair our friendship. Now that I'm finally in this moment, I'm not sure I want his friendship back.

I'm thankful he saved our butts from the Green Dream, but that doesn't mean I'm ready to throw myself back into his world again. For some reason, it doesn't seem as magical as it did before. And maybe that has something to do with all the ways I've seen *real* magic over the last couple of weeks—and that I now have some of my own.

Sky's face falls. "What's wrong?"

"What did I do to make you stop being my friend?" I ask.

He looks genuinely confused. "But we are friends."

"That's not what you told Larry."

"Larry didn't ask if we were friends," Sky says, his brow dipping into a frown. "He asked if I was gay."

"That's not exactly what happened. He asked if you were

'gay too' since you were hanging around me, and you said, 'No, that's gross,' and laughed. Is that what you think of me?"

Sky looks off to the side and says, "Larry put me on the spot, and I panicked, okay? It was the first day of school and I was nervous. I didn't want some kid spreading rumors about me before I had a chance to make friends."

I stab my chest with my finger. "*I* was your friend."

Sky huffs and throws his hands up. "What was I supposed to say?"

"I told you that I thought I might like boys and you told me that you did too. So why would you later say 'that's gross'?"

Sky's face turns strawberry red. "Because I was mad at you!"

"What?" I recoil, feeling like someone just slapped me. "Why were you mad at *me*?"

"That night you told me no one knew about you," Sky says. "But then Larry said you were gay, which meant you lied to me. And I didn't want anyone to know that about me."

"Just so we're clear," I say, "I'm not mad about you wanting to keep your secret. No one should have to share theirs until they want. But Larry told my secret before even *I* knew it. And after I told you mine, you called me gross and became Larry's best friend. You could've protected yourself without throwing me under the bus in the process. *That's* why I'm mad."

Sky sighs and tosses his head back. "Why are you being so dramatic, Alex? You stopped talking to me too, bro. If you wanted to be friends, you could've come to me anytime. I don't understand why we can't just *move on*."

"Because we're not friends, Sky," I say with stony conviction. "Friends don't abandon each other."

I hug myself tight in the lengthy space of tense quiet that follows. The urge hits me to just give in and be his friend again. Isn't that what I wanted all this time?

But then I think about my real friends, who're down-stairs asleep on the couch. Loren left her family behind with-out a second thought to help me save my sister. Sky would never—and that's why I don't want him on my team anymore.

"I'm sorry if I hurt you, okay?" Sky says.

I chuckle under my breath and shrug. "I guess, man."

I'm more annoyed than angry, because something in my gut tells me this is the best apology I'm going to get from him—and he could've kept it.

"I appreciate you letting us stay here." I head for the door but turn back. "Oh, and stop being mean to Blu." His brows shoot up, but I don't give him time to cut in. "Your little brother loves you, you jerk." I clench my fists and narrow my eyes at him. "You saw how I scared that rhino today. If I even *think* you're mistreating Blu, I'll use my superpowers to lock you in the Sunken Place forever."

He goes rigid and his face turns ashen. He nods like a ter-rified bobblehead doll.

"We'll be gone at sunrise," I say.

He whimpers, "'Kay," as I leave and close the door of his room.

I go downstairs to find that Loren and Liam have left a perfect Alex-sized spot between them. I snuggle into it, lying on my stomach with my head cradled in my arms.

This feels like where I belong.

It's not hard for me to relax on this posh couch (Loren and

Liam were right), which is splendid, because every muscle in my body aches like I've been wrung out. I close my eyes and let sleep take me as a gentle voice intones *You were always enough* over and over in my head like a lullaby.

The creepy sensation of someone standing over me slings me out of a deep sleep.

My eyelids part, revealing the shadow-covered ceiling of Sky's family room. Someone sniffs hard right next to my ear, as if smelling me.

I sit bolt upright with a gasp. But no one's there.

I look around the room, squinting into each dark corner or crevice, waiting to clock any sort of movement. I even slide off the couch and peek underneath it. Nothing's there.

Loren stirs, but neither she nor Liam wakes up.

Was I dreaming?

A shudder slips down my back. I climb back onto the couch and sit crisscross-applesauce between my friends. I glance over at the digital clock on the microwave in the kitchen, which reads 4:26 a.m. Not long before we have to leave.

I'm wide awake now, so I might as well keep watch until sunrise.

I have a weird feeling Shadow Man might be prowling.

34

MEGA-ULTRA-DEEP DOODIE

Sunrise comes. Shadow Man doesn't. I'm simultaneously relieved and irritated, because of course, now I'm sleepy. Pacing helps keep my brain awake and sputtering, though.

The waking sun floods the room with bright orange rays that rouse Loren and Liam from deep, drooling slumbers. Loren sits up, yawning and fixing her locs, which are wild since she fell asleep with them loose. Liam stretches and reaches to scratch somewhere private but freezes, suddenly remembering he's not alone, and redirects his fingers to his knee instead. I laugh under my breath from where I stand in front of the glass doors to the terrace.

"I'm good to go," he announces. "I really needed that sleep."

Dexter appears from the hallway off the kitchen and heads straight over, greeting us with a smile and the strong fruity scent of shampoo. His hair is wet and extra curly beneath his newsboy cap this morning. Footsteps on the stairs draw everyone's attention. It's Sky and Blu.

They wander down, Blu in the rear, rubbing his eyes.

Loren says a quick good morning and disappears to the bathroom. Liam greets them and swings his legs over one end of the couch, still yawning. Blu homes in on Dexter immediately and drowns him in conversation. Before I can figure out what they're talking about, Sky steps into my line of vision.

The skin beneath his bloodshot eyes is dark and puffy, as if he didn't sleep at all. His hair is pushed back, the trails left by his fingers still there.

"I thought a lot about what you said last night," he says in a voice so low only I can hear. "You were right. I'm sorry."

"Thanks, Sky."

Last summer, his mere presence used to ignite sparklers in my chest. All those little moments with him—hugs, holding hands, late-night conversations—used to feel like wielding some forbidden magic that I somehow knew was always meant for me. Now I don't feel anything from him.

I don't know if Sky and I will ever be friends again. But I'm happy to not have to think about it anymore.

Once the sun's burned away all the Green Dream like morning fog, we say goodbye to Sky and Blu and thank them again for letting us stay. Blu, noticing Liam carrying the large candle, runs upstairs and back down like a bolt of lightning to give us a Pokémon drawstring bag to store the candle in for our trip home. I hug Blu again and side-eye Sky, a silent reminder of my promise to end him if he doesn't stop being mean to his little brother.

Dexter leads the way down the hall to the elevator, Liam behind him.

Loren hangs back to fall in step with me. "You good?"

I nod, my eyes on the floor. "Good on him." I look up and lock eyes with Liam, who looked back for my answer.

"About time," Loren mumbles.

The four of us file into the elevator, and Dexter hits the button for the ground floor. I lean against the back wall, and Loren and Liam take up either side of me.

Liam yawns again and rests his elbow on my shoulder. When I look at him, he smiles. Sparklers light up in my chest.

And so does anxiety.

Liam isn't Sky, but these sparklers still terrify me. They're beautiful and feel good most times, but it hurts too bad whenever they get snuffed out. And I'm not sure what to do with that, so I guess it'll be a problem for Future Alex to figure out.

We borrow some bikes from a nearby shop and ride back to the safe house. I'm worried about Liam at first, until he tells us they had bikes back in Paradisum too and that he used to ride a lot with Ezra before his life changed forever. It's super early, so the streets are empty. I'm not sure where all the escaped zoo animals have gone, but thankfully it's not here. It's tough to find the energy to pedal, but once I get started, adrenaline kicks in and wakes me up.

The sky is clear and cerulean today, and the heat from the sun isn't intense yet. It feels great in combination with the wind on my face. We even line up and race down one block. Liam makes us go again at the next, insisting Loren cheated. She wins the second time too. But that's all the fun we get to have, because we've got a world to save.

We walk the bikes up the steep roads to the safe house,

which seems to take twice as long as the fifteen-mile ride across town—and leaves me twice as winded. No one complains about any of the several rests we take before we arrive.

Walking into air-conditioning feels like I've floated through the gates of heaven. But I don't get to enjoy it long.

Before anyone can break off to shower and put on fresh clothes, Dexter murders the vibe with his favorite apocalyptic question: "So what's the plan?"

Fatigue wears heavy on Liam's and Loren's faces, and I'm sure I look the same. The bike ride really wore them out—and they got more sleep than me. Dexter's the only one who doesn't look exhausted. Odd.

I trudge into the living room and plop down on the couch. I guess Dexter's right. We *should* decide what we're going to do next.

Loren sits next to me, and Liam takes an armchair, resting his elbows on his knees, the candle bag hanging by the drawstring from his clasped hands. I glance at the empty spot beside me on the sofa and back at him, quietly wondering why he chose to sit there.

Panic pricks my gut—a familiar sensation. The polar opposite of the sparklers in my chest. And what I was afraid of. Because now I'm wondering if Liam's going to pull a Sky soon.

Dexter stands on the other side of the coffee table with his hands on his hips—like a teacher. Normally it wouldn't bother me, but today he's bugging me for some reason.

"We've been through a lot over the past day," Liam says. "I think we should rest tonight and take the fight to them tomorrow when we're fresh."

"Now, hold on, Captain America," says Loren. Liam shoots her a confused look. "There are four of them and only three of us—and you two goobs are the only ones with actual magic."

Liam sighs and removes the candle from the bag. He lets the bag drop to the floor and holds the candle in both hands, staring at it with a pensive expression. "Then we need to figure out how to separate Death from the others. Maybe the key to this is taking them out one at a time."

The callous way Liam mentions "taking them out," one of *them* being my little sister, prickles my skin enough that it forces out the question I've been chewing on since our encounter with Famine.

"Will it hurt her?" I nod at the candle in Liam's hands. "Could suddenly ripping Death's spirit out of her kill her?"

I feel the couch cushion shift as Loren tenses next to me.

Liam presses his lips together. "I don't know. I understand how you feel, but we don't really have a choice, Alex. I told my mother I would stop the apocalypse—no matter the cost."

I glower back at him. "So my sister's expendable to you?"

He scoots to the edge of his seat and sets the candle on the corner of the coffee table. "There's a chance that it could hurt your sister when we pull Death's spirit from her. There's also a chance she'll be just fine. But if you're worried about what Famine said, you're going to have to get over it. No matter what happens—your sister's *not* going to be the same. Neither are you. None of us will. You're going to have to deal with that sooner or later, but unfortunately, the world doesn't have time to wait for you."

"She's ten!" I shout, which makes everyone flinch.

Liam's face hardens. "My mother is dead. My only friend is *dead*. And Orin is lost to me forever. I didn't get a choice when I lost my entire life. You're being selfish right now, Alex."

Maybe it's a good thing he didn't sit next to me, because I want to punch him in the mouth. This feels eerily like the universe punishing me for letting my guard down with Liam. Maybe he's more like Sky than I thought.

"My sister is the *only* one in this entire mess who's innocent," I say. "She was kidnapped by Shadow Man and possessed by an evil spirit—*both* from your world!" Liam starts to argue, but I cut him off. "Shadow Man is magic, and magic didn't exist in this realm until your mother opened that portal and stepped through it. This is on her."

Liam withers. Part of me wants to apologize and throw my arms around him, but the rest of me wants to hurt him before he hurts me. He doesn't care about me or my sister. I was naive to think he was my friend. This *is* Sky all over again.

"My mother gave up her life along with our entire realm to stop the Horsemen." Liam stares at the candle. "This is all I have left of her. Questioning her sacrifice is disrespectful."

"Your mother had an entire world at her disposal, but because she was greedy and selfish, she ripped apart time and space to come to *ours*—and brought her colonizing friends with her. I'm not sacrificing *my* sister to fix *your* mother's mess."

Liam stands, eyes narrowed, a stone-faced glower fixed on me. I stare deep into his gaze until he storms off to his room. The vicious slam of his door echoes down the hall.

I'm making even more of a mess of things, but I'm too tired

to care. Every fiber of my being is spent. I usually like roller coasters, but I want off this one. Now.

Dexter picks up the candle, turning it over in his hands. "I'm afraid you don't know Liam as well as you think."

I take a deep, exasperated breath. "Please, not right now, Dexter."

"He's been through an incredibly tough time, and as a result, he's a deeply troubled boy," he continues, refusing to read the room. "You were right, Alex. He'll sacrifice anything for his mother's validation. Even your sister. Even himself. You and Loren certainly aren't an exception. Don't expect me to stand back silently and allow that to happen to you kids."

"Our car's wrecked, so you don't have to drive us around anymore," I say, sounding far calmer than I feel. "Don't feel obligated to stick around. I know you want to get back to your family."

Dexter's brows lift, and he blinks rapidly for a few seconds. He looks down at the candle, still in his hands.

As mad as I am with Liam right now, I don't appreciate Dexter making me feel even worse. I don't like hurting him, but maybe it really is time he left.

Loren rubs her hands on her thighs. "Everyone's super tired and stressed, so—"

Dexter holds up a hand, and she falls silent. He steps over and hands the candle to me. I take it, and my fingers brush against his—but I don't feel anything. Strange.

I *know* Dexter's feeling an emotion right now.

I set the candle on the table and grab Dexter's hand. Nothing. I hold his hand with both of mine. Nothing. Only his soft, clammy palm. When I grab both his hands, he snatches them away, frowning at me.

I turn to Loren and hold out my hand. She gives me a questioning look but still places hers in mine—and immediately ignites a dull crackle of anxious fear muddled with a healthy dose of exhaustion—the apocalypse special.

It's not me. I turn a curious look to Dexter. "Why can't I Sense you?" My brow furrows as I sift through my memories. Have I ever felt anything from him since I've had this power?

Dexter raises his hands, sighs, and slaps them onto his hips. "I don't know, Alex." He lifts up his newsboy cap and scratches beneath his silver curls. "I don't mean to cause trouble. I just care about you all, and I don't want to see any of you hurt, Mags included. But you're right—it's time I go take care of my family now. I'll leave for good in the morning, when you depart to confront the Horsemen."

He waits a moment, but when neither Loren nor I respond, he walks away. His bedroom door clicks shut not long after.

Loren and I sit on the couch in uncomfortable silence for what feels like hours. Every time I open my big mouth, everything gets worse, so right now I just want to sit here.

"So you're in a mood," she says.

I pull my feet up onto the couch and hug my knees to my chest. I turn away from her and rest my head on them. I just want to be alone.

"I understand how you feel." Her words are annoyingly soft and careful. "But don't you think what you said to Liam and Dexter might've been too harsh?"

"You're right." I sigh. "I *am* in a mood. I don't want to be psychoanalyzed right now either."

"That's cool with me," she says, standing up. "Always being the voice of reason is exhausting anyway. Good night, Alex."

Her footsteps fade down the hallway. I listen for the sound of her door closing before I lie facedown onto the couch.

I can't hold back the tears anymore. I grab one of the soft cotton pillows and bury my face in it, trying my best to drown out my heaving sobs so no one hears.

I've made such a grand mess of things.

Since I jumped from that cruise ship, all I've wanted is to bring my little sister home safe. I didn't want magical powers. I could've lived a full life without ever having traveled to another dimension. And I resent that the responsibility of saving the world at any cost has been forced on me.

No matter what happens with the candle, my sister's going to lose, whether that thing kills her or merely leaves her a traumatized shell of her former self. Maybe I'm so angry with Liam because he's right. The old Mags I've been fighting so hard to save is gone. The little sister I didn't appreciate when I had her, the one I used to loathe being responsible for, the one whose love I never had to question. After all this, I've *still* lost her.

I dry my face on the couch and trudge to my room. I fall across my bed and lie there. I'm dirty. I stink. I need to shower, but I don't have the energy or the desire. What's the point? The entire world is in Mega-Ultra-Deep Doodie, thanks to me.

I pull a blanket over myself and fall into a sad sleep.

I'll deal with the apocalypse in the morning.

35

SHADOW MAN RETURNS

A familiar unnerving sensation draws me out of sleep. It's less jarring this time, but no less prickly. I lie still while my eyes adjust to the darkness. Goose bumps tingle on my arms.

I'm not alone.

I know he's here. Somewhere. Watching.

My bedroom door is slightly ajar. The hallway outside is dark and quiet. My pulse quickens. The silence in the room rings in my ears. I close my eyes and pretend to sleep.

Still underneath the blanket, I turn onto my side and slip my phone from my pocket in one fluid motion. I drag the blanket up to my nose and wake my phone beneath it.

It's only a few minutes before sunrise. Everyone else must still be asleep.

A faint hint of movement near the door catches my attention, but I don't flinch. Carefully, I press the flashlight button on my phone's lock screen, the light hidden beneath the blanket. I take a deep breath. And wait.

Several tense seconds pass before a shadow on the wall shifts in the dark. *There* you are.

I kick the blanket off and swing my phone up—behind my hand. In my phone's light, my hand casts a giant shadow on the wall beside the door—right next to Shadow Man.

His faceless silhouette is frozen in a crouch, paralyzed with shock at being exposed. I make the shadow of my hand grab him by the throat.

"Gotcha!" I snarl, lifting him into the air, in slight disbelief that my idea actually worked.

He struggles, punching and kicking at my shadowy fingers, but it's no use. I have him.

"I knew it!" I sit up on my knees. "Why are you stalking me?" He doesn't answer, so I squeeze tighter and shake him.

Shadow Man lets out an inhuman half squeal, half screech that sounds like it's coming from a possessed pig. I want to cover my ears, but I don't dare let him go. He turns feral, every limb flailing.

The door slams open, and Loren rushes in, her loose locs framing her sleepy, confused face. "What's going on in here?"

She turns to where I'm staring and sees Shadow Man for the first time. She shrieks and claps her hands over her mouth. Stumbling back, she falls onto her bottom and scuttles backward until she bumps into the bedside table.

Shadow Man braces his feet against the bottom of my shadow hand and attempts to pry himself free. And it's working.

I let go and snatch his ankle instead. He hangs upside down, swinging his arms and screeching.

"I *caught* him," I hiss, focused on my grip on Shadow Man, who's wriggling like a fish on a hook.

Liam bursts into the room next, and his eyes widen when he sees the most traumatizing shadow-puppet show ever. "Whoa!" The shock knocks him back into the closed door of the nearby closet.

I stand in the middle of my bed and shout above Shadow Man's ruckus. "Did someone send you?" He squeals louder. "I'll hold you here until you talk!" I shake him hard, jerking him back and forth like a doll. "I *know* you can speak. I heard you that night in my bedroom."

I shake him again, but somehow, he slips free. Before I can grab him, he takes off and disappears around the corner.

I leap from the bed and chase him. Liam and Loren scuffle into action behind me.

I might've made a mess of everything else, but I *won't* let Shadow Man terrorize me for the rest of my life. If I have to follow him through every realm in the multiverse, I'm going to find out what the heck he wants from me.

Shadow Man, disoriented from my attack, stumbles down the hallway into the kitchen. He falls into the barstools at the island counter and tips them over behind him. I leap over them and almost bust it when my socks slip on the slick stone floor, but I recover, hardly slowing.

He dives beneath the dining table, pops up on the other side, then passes through the closed glass patio doors. Outside, Dexter whips around.

Shadow Man lunges at him. But not to attack. To hug him. Like a child reuniting with their lost parent.

I stumble to a stop. Liam and Loren run up behind me. I shake my head as I approach the doors and slowly slide them open. This must be a dream.

I step out into a pocket of dry, warm air and a symphony of crickets broadcasting from the bushes on the plunging hillside. The concrete patio is hard and warm beneath my socked feet, and the strong scent of chlorine tickles my nose.

Dexter presses his lips together and looks at the three of us but says nothing. Shadow Man melts back into Dexter's normal shadow, now pale in the first light of sunrise.

None of this makes sense.

I shake my head again, still not believing what I'm seeing. "Dexter?"

My fourth-grade teacher wears a pained expression on his soft brown face. He takes off his newsboy cap and scratches his head of silvery curls with the same hand, the other tightly clutching Blu's Pokémon drawstring bag—with our magic candle inside.

"I knew this day was soon coming," he says in a solemn tone that ignites scalding embers in the pit of my stomach. "But I had no idea it would be this hard."

I shake my head. "No," I mutter, and turn to Liam and Loren for reassurance but only meet their shocked faces. "Shadow Man's possessed him . . . just like the Horsemen—"

"Alex." Dexter's voice is soft. I'm almost glad for the interruption, because even I don't believe what I was saying. My eyes trace the bag holding our last hope to save the world, clutched in his fist. My stomach cinches as if he has hold of that, too.

"*You* were Shadow Man?" I ask. "You were my teacher. You were Mags's teacher. You taught us fractions!" I squint at him, examining the man I thought I knew. "But you have magic. Who *are* you?"

Dexter steers his gaze to Liam. "You don't remember me?"

Liam looks confused, shaking his head slowly.

Dexter waves a hand in front of him, revealing a face about forty years younger—like he might have looked when he was seventeen.

His frame shifts from that of a somewhat weathered older man to that of a sinewy teenager. His silver curls darken and lengthen, hanging in black waves to his shoulders.

"How about now?" he asks.

"Ezra?" Liam gasps and stumbles backward. "But I saw the lake take you."

Some of the puzzle pieces click together in my mind. The realization feels like getting drop-kicked in the stomach. Seeing this *real* version of Dexter makes his massive betrayal only slightly less disorienting. I couldn't stand to look into the gentle eyes of the kind man who took an interest in me when no one else seemed to and ask him why he betrayed me. This new, younger Dexter is easier to be angry with.

"This whole time?!" I roar. "You pretended you cared. . . ." My voice trails off as I try to make sense of everything, of how I've been violated on such a massive level. "I *trusted* you."

"I do care about you, Alex," he says with a heavy sigh. "That's what makes this so hard for me. An unexpected side effect of interdimensional domination."

I wrinkle my nose at him. "You're a *liar*."

Liam bristles beside me, another person duped by Dexter or Ezra or whatever the heck his real name is.

"How'd you survive?" Liam asks him.

The muscles in Ezra's jaws tense, hardening his sharp face further. "That day, after my father figured out what Navia and Orin were up to, he told me to dive into the Lake of Logic. When I did, something grabbed me from below and dragged me into the depths. What happened next is difficult to explain.

"I was drowning, and then I wasn't. I was suddenly floating in darkness. Faceless voices surrounded me. Whispers I couldn't understand—either too quiet or in another language or both. Then images appeared in front of me—of other worlds, other times—changing every second. A million realms flashed in front of me, distant worlds containing levels of grandeur greater than anything you've read in your little fantasy books. And it *haunted* my every molecule. Can you imagine how minuscule it makes you feel to discover there are *millions* of other universes and *innumerable* lives and you are smaller than the tiniest pinprick in all of that?"

I don't care what anyone says. The shadows in the bottom of that lake creeped me out. They didn't feel good or evil—just undeniably *wrong*. And whatever's down there seems to have thoroughly messed Ezra up.

"I don't know how long I was under," he continues. "But the last thing they showed me was what was happening on the shore above—Navia and Orin sucking Paradisum dry to trap the Horsemen's and Orin's spirits in those gaudy talismans.

"I woke to the sound of a mourning dove cooing. I was

floating in the water near the shore. The world had changed into a gray shell. I crawled onto the bank and saw Liam following the dove. I followed too—through the portal into a brand-new world, keeping to the shadows the whole way. An easy feat, thanks to the lake spirits who awakened my true power."

I shudder when I realize he's talking about his Darkness, which gives him the ability to control shadows—like his own. A dark talent fitting for someone with such a dark heart. The lake should never have spit him out.

"I was shocked to see that Navia had entrusted the fate of the multiverse to a nine-year-old, until I realized the brilliance of her plan." He nods at Liam, who scowls even harder. "Small children are easily manipulated. They'll do anything to win the affection of a parent. I should know."

"The father you mentioned you were trying to please all your life," I interject, "all along it was Death. Or was that a lie too?"

"Death, or Moritz, as I knew him," says Ezra, "had many relationships with humans from your realm and many children as a result, but none inherited any of his godly powers. Except me. I was special. That's why he brought me and my mother to Paradisum. But I wasn't enough." He glances down. "Father wanted a divine bloodline of magical demigods who could help him rule the realms, but Navia squashed his plans when she sealed the portal to Earth.

"After what happened on the lakeshore that day four years ago, I knew it was up to me to come to my father's aid, to prove to him why I was superior. But Orin complicated things for me by encasing themselves in a talisman too. If Orin chose Liam as their vessel, their Sense combined with Liam's Light would've posed too great a threat to us, especially if Orin plundered Liam's mind and uncovered the life-force curse I'd placed on him."

"It was *you*!" Liam snarls, and launches himself at Ezra, but I pull him back.

Ezra doesn't flinch. He only tilts his head and looks at us with pity in his eyes.

I want to shove him into the pool.

"Back in Paradisum, we couldn't have you ruin our special day," Ezra says. "Similarly, I wasn't going to let you spoil the apocalypse, either, which is why I had to find an alternative vessel to entice Orin. And knowing them, I suspected they'd attach themselves to the most damaged person in the room as opposed to the strongest. They've never been able to resist the pain of a broken individual—it's like a pheromone to them. So I set up shop around Southern California and searched for four years, until I found Magdalena Wise. You wore your pain like a veil, Alex, whereas Mags buried hers deep inside. And that tiny seed of misery your father planted within her was far more powerful than anything you had to offer." He turns his gaze on me, and my disgusted frown intensifies. "However, I must admit, I almost chose you, Alex."

I'm so angry, I'm trembling. I ball my fists at my sides and bite down hard on my bottom lip to stop myself from punching him in his mouth.

The three of us should jump him.

"Installing Eustice as the mouthpiece of the apocalypse,

Mags's near accident on the last day of school, your dad winning the all-expenses-paid cruise to Hawai'i, the storm, the ship sinking—it was all orchestrated by me," Ezra tells us smugly. "But my plans hit a snag when you leapt from that ship, Alex. I never expected that from you. I admit, I've gotten to know you more over the last few weeks than in our entire school year together, and I'm quite impressed."

Once it would've thrilled me to hear that, but now it makes me sick(er) to my stomach.

"And things went completely off script when Father chose Mags as his vessel instead of me," continues Ezra, "which left Orin with only you. I wasn't pleased with the sudden change in plan. You're older and much harder to manipulate, but it wasn't impossible."

I feel like I'm spinning in the drain of a toilet. I'd really begun to think that maybe, for once, I was special, that I could be a superhero. But I guess that was foolish.

"I wanted to show Father that I was up for the challenge ahead," Ezra continues. "So I hung around and pretended to help so I could find out how Liam and Orin planned to stop the Horsemen's reign and put an end to it before it even got off the ground."

"Your plan makes no sense," I tell him. "You're doing all this and your father's just going to replace you with an army of more powerful demigods."

Ezra bristles. "When you were nine years old, why'd you play on that baseball team, Alex?" He cocks his head, and heat rushes to my face.

The moment I shared that story with Dexter years ago, I

regretted letting it leave my lips, but I wanted so bad to talk to someone about it. I needed to know if it was true. If I was an embarrassment. And Dexter was there for me. No, Ezra was there, pretending, lying, using me. Stockpiling personal information to weaponize against me later.

"You knew you weren't athletic," he says. "You weren't even interested in sports, much less baseball. You'd never even watched a single game before. But like me, you wanted to make your dad proud. You would've done anything. Unlike me, you humiliated yourself and him. Myself, on the other hand—"

He turns to the pool. Something dark wavers in the bottom, like a puddle of black sludge—which is exactly what I feel like.

Then a head pushes through the surface, and shoulders, and a torso, until Death herself rises from the water, completely dry. Not a single drop on her. She's dressed in a black hooded caftan. Her dark hair has been pressed and falls in one loose wave down the middle of her back. In the center of the pool, she stands atop the water like a god. And then I remember, technically, she *is* a god.

Ezra tosses the bag with the candle inside to her.

She snatches it from the air with one hand, grinning. "Well done, my son."

"Why are you doing this?" asks Loren. "Why not go fix your own world instead of trying to take over everyone else's?"

Death casually removes the candle and tosses the bag aside to float on the surface behind her. "It's quite simple," she says, examining the candle carefully, sniffing every crevice and pressing her ear to it as if listening for a voice. "Weaker beings need governance. They're destroying their worlds and each other. By sealing us off from the other realms, Navia doomed the multiverse to certain ruin. So in the nine Earth years that followed her dreadful decision, I convinced the others—Zara, Exo, and Malakai—to become my fellow Horsemen, to be the greatest good and save the multiverse from itself, starting with this realm.

"The next phase of our plan will be to reshape this world to better suit our tastes—a *Cosmic Shift*, if you will. And after we enact *Dominion*, firmly establishing our rule over all of humanity, Earth will become our base of operations. Here I'll raise an army of like-minded demigods and Riders who'll fight to their deaths for my cause—across every realm in the multiverse. But first"—she chuckles under her breath—"I need to get rid of this old thing."

She holds out her hand, the candle in her palm. It erupts into black fire.

"NO!" I scream, reaching out, but I can't reach her in time.

Except the candle doesn't burn. The wick won't even light.

She extinguishes the flames and frowns. "Odd. Shadow Fire can burn nearly anything." She walks to the far end of the pool and slams the candle down on the concrete, making me flinch.

It doesn't break. Thank goodness Navia made it indestructible.

"Very well," sighs Death. "I'll figure out a way to break it soon." She bowls it toward one of the deck chairs beside Ezra, and it disappears into the shadow underneath. "I've played along with your game long enough," she tells him. "Wrap this up."

I'm not sure if what happens next was planned, but Liam and Loren split from me and attack at the same time.

I stumble back, unsure what to do, still paralyzed with shock at everything that's just unfolded. Can I trust anyone?

Liam claps his hands together, and a powerful beam of bright golden light surges toward Death, who counters with a magical beam of her own that resembles gray sludge. I catch sight of the occasional howling skull face rushing by. The two beams smash together in midair halfway between Liam and Death as they push all their power forward, straining to overwhelm each other.

Loren cracks her whip around Ezra's ankles and yanks his feet from beneath him. He topples, banging his head hard on the edge of a deck chair. Loren retracts her whip, leaving Ezra half-conscious and moaning facedown on the patio.

"Ho!" Death taunts. "Someone's removed the training wheels, I see!"

Liam grimaces and bares his teeth, shoving all his magic through his hands, which intensifies the beam of Light pushing against Death's. It's almost frightening to witness. I had no idea he'd be so powerful now that he's uninhibited.

But even so, alone, he's still no match for Death.

Death growls, doubling the size and intensity of her beam, which swallows most of Liam's, stopping only a couple feet from engulfing him.

Loren runs around the pool and cracks the whip around Death's neck. She tries to yank Death off her feet like she did Ezra, but Death doesn't budge. Loren sends waves of white lightning through the whip, long electric fingers breaking away to crawl over Death like an army of daddy longlegs.

The entire patio is lit so brightly, I have to shield my eyes to see what's going on.

Loren's attack seems to be working, because Death cries out, and her posture slumps. Liam sees the opening and amps up his attack, walking closer, until he stands at the edge of the pool. His beam swells and consumes Death's beam completely—and her, too.

Loren pulls her whip back right before the force of Liam's attack blows Death from the pool and up against the glass fence at the top of the steep hillside. Loren rushes forward, flings her whip around Death's throat again, and reignites her shock-wave assault.

Death screams and throws her head from side to side, but Liam won't let up with his magical fire hose.

Her howls sound excruciating. They make my skin crawl and my stomach cinch. I want it to stop, but anxiety has me frozen.

Death turns to me, and I must be losing it—because I think I see my sister again.

Her gentle brown eyes shimmer in the light, tears spilling down both cheeks. "Alex! Please! They're *killing* me! This isn't the way! This *isn't* the waaaaay!"

Oh, no . . . No, no, *no* . . .

I clutch my head in my hands and watch Liam and Loren,

both so entrenched in battle, they haven't realized that my sister has somehow clawed her way back to consciousness.

"STOP!" I scream at them.

Loren, unsure what to do, glances at me quizzically and then to Liam. He shakes his head and pushes harder. She gives me an apologetic look, still clinging to her whip.

I run up to her and stand so close I can hear her heavy breaths despite the chaos surrounding us. "No, Lo. You know this isn't right. You're going to kill Mags along with Death. There's a better way. Trust me, *please*."

Loren grits her teeth and pulls her whip back.

"Nooo!" Liam screams. "What are you doing? This is our chance!"

"He's not gonna stop," Loren mutters.

I sprint around the pool and tackle Liam from behind.

In a tangle of limbs, shouts, and shared red-hot flares of anger, we plunge into the ice-cold water.

The sound of our limbs thrashing underwater fills my ears as Liam and I break apart and kick back to the surface.

I pull myself up on the pool's ledge, gasping for air and coughing. Loren runs over and helps me out, then drags Liam out too. Once he's on the patio, he pulls away from her.

I stand next to Loren, dripping wet and shivering. Liam glowers at both of us like he wants to attack us, too.

I'm not sure when, but at some point during the ruckus, the sun rose and is now a swollen red-orange orb hovering in the sky behind us, casting long, blanket-thick shadows across the space.

On the other side of the patio, Death sits upright, her once flawless hair a wild nest atop her head, the black paint around her eyes smudged into a raccoon's mask. Mags's soft brown eyes are gone, and Death's cold black stare has returned.

She's weakened but doesn't seem to be hurt too badly.

"*Big* mistake," she sneers.

Then both she and Ezra fall into their shadows and vanish.

Liam stomps toward me, and I meet him halfway. Our chests bump, and we stand firm against each other. My wet socks squelch on the cement, which feels gross, but I'm not backing down. Liam narrows his dark eyes at me. His nostrils flare, and I stare right back. Angry energy crackles between us like the magic in Loren's whip.

Loren stands off to one side, her eyes bouncing between us. She gnaws on her thumbnail, an old habit of hers I haven't seen since she was stressed about standardized tests at the end of fifth grade.

"I don't care if I'm wrong," I say through clenched teeth. "I won't let you sacrifice my little sister."

Mags is one of the few people in my life worth fighting for. She's always believed in me, even when I felt so low, I'd have to look up to see a worm's whiskers.

Liam's voice is cool and even, which hurts worse than if he'd yelled. "You called my mother selfish, but she did what she did to save the multiverse. And you did what you did to save *one* person." He scoffs under his breath. "So what does that make you, Alex Wise?"

I shrug. "For the first time in my life, I don't care. You're absolutely right, though. I don't have what it takes to be like people who treat lives like tokens to be gambled with and traded away for one cause or another. Mags is the most genuine person I know, and I won't let anyone take her from me, not even you. And if that makes you not want to be on my team, then by all means—go. I'm done begging people to be in my life."

Liam's steely facade crinkles for a moment, and he looks like he wants to give in. A part of me latches onto the faint hope that we can work through this and stay friends. But he won't. He's too stubborn.

"So be it," he says, hardening again. "Death will likely go back to her home base to recoup her strength, so I'm going to the Horsemen's tower to confront her while she's weak." He storms toward the door, but before going inside, he turns back and says, "You're lucky the entire multiverse is on the line, because I don't see much in this realm worth risking my life to save."

He slams the door so hard, the glass shatters, raining shards down onto the patio and inside the house.

Loren and I stand in the loud silence he leaves behind.

I drop to my knees and hide my face in my hands.

Things couldn't possibly get any worse.

APOCALYPSE COUNTDOWN

0 YEARS · 0 DAYS
12 HOURS · 40 MINUTES

PART IV

Where are they now? A trio of Irvine middle schoolers who claimed to have been haunted by the *Shadow Stalker* say the nightmare is over. "None of us have seen him in almost three years. [We] wonder if he finally got whatever (or whoever) he was searching for."

—HOUSTON BENTON FOR THE *IRVINE GAZETTE*
JULY 6, 2024, 11:54 AM

36

ROCK BOTTOM

I *know* there's another way to stop Death *and* save Mags—and I'm going to figure out what that is, even if I have to find the candle by myself.

Liam left in a huff to go finish his fight with Death, and Loren went to chase him down and try to stop him from doing something foolish.

The urge to play some music pokes me, like it always does when I'm upset—but then I remember that my love for soundtracks grew from my fake friendship with Dexter or Ezra or whatever the heck his real name is. Everything was a lie. It's just as well. Seeing as how the world's ending, I'll never get the chance to learn to play the saxophone or be in a band or become a composer anyway.

I stand up and yank my phone from my pocket. I glower at it, then at the horizon glittering with early morning light. And I lean back and fling my phone as hard as I can. It somersaults through the air and disappears somewhere downhill.

I sit back down at the edge of the pool with my knees hugged to my chest and stare at the crystal-blue water. When

I hear footsteps approaching, I look up as Loren steps through the broken door onto the patio and shakes her head.

Liam's gone.

"I'm sorry, Lo," I tell her. "I was a jerk to you last night. I don't know what I'd do without you. . . ." I draw a deep breath in and hold it to keep from crying again.

"I forgive you, goober," she says gently, and sits across from me, mimicking how I'm sitting. She's pulled her locs into a ponytail since she left. Her deep brown skin glows in the sunlight, but her eyes are tired. "You okay?"

I shake my head. "Ezra was right. I'm damaged goods. My dad realized that a long time ago. That's why he left us and replaced me with Nick."

Loren sighs. "Ezra is a liar. You're not broken, and what you've been through is not your fault, Alex." She shakes her head, some of the brightness returning to her eyes, and grins, though I don't see what's funny.

I shoot her a confused look.

"Dude, you haven't realized yet? Ezra made a *huge* mistake letting Orin choose you for their vessel."

"But you heard what he said," I tell her. "He wanted someone so messed up that they wouldn't be able to use Orin's powers properly." I lift my hands. "Voilà. Mission accomplished."

Loren shakes her head. "You're lucky I love you. Use your brain for a second, goobs. Orin's powers are empathic, yeah? Well, who among us has felt emotion more strongly than you? All the people who hurt you didn't break you. And you're not weak or less than anyone because of what happened to you. Only someone who's survived what you have could understand the full range of Orin's Sense. *That's* why it's funny. Ezra thought he was being smart, but he was unknowingly delivering the most powerful person he could to be Orin's vessel—and his downfall."

I sit up, her words like a bonfire raging in my stomach. "You're right."

She rolls her eyes. "I'm always right."

"Then tell me how to get rid of this 'block' so I can access the full range of Orin's power."

"Aht," she says, holding up a finger, "'Always right' isn't the same as 'knows everything.' Now, are you gonna sit by the pool and feel sorry for yourself all apocalypse, or are we going to catch up with Liam and squash y'all's beef so we can get your sister back?"

I've let so many people get away with hurting me. But not Ezra. I'm going to make him pay for what he did. But first, I'm gonna get my sister back.

Loren and I put on some fresh clothes and shoes, grab a couple of bottles of water for the trip, and ride downhill on our bikes. Liam's is already gone. I imagine us running into him after he's doubled back, having suddenly realized he's made a mistake. But then I remember what he said before he left.

It's just like with Sky. Maybe I misunderstood those sparklers in my chest, and they're actually supposed to alert me to people I need to stay away from.

We're gliding at breakneck speed when I cry out and slam on my brakes, almost flying off but managing to stay upright. Loren slows too, wobbling and almost losing control. We steer off to the side of the street and stop in a patch of grass a block from the intersection at the bottom of the hill—where an army of Creeps wait, their ember eyes staring straight at us.

"Are they waiting for us?" asks Loren.

"Looks that way." I remove my bracelet and it transforms into my golden sword, the hilt heavy in my right hand.

She takes down her whip and glowers at the bustling Creep army downhill. "The only way forward is through them."

There must be thirty or forty down there, but they're without a leader—none of the Horsemen seem to be anywhere around. Most of them are armed—there are plenty of rusty old swords, maces, and spears among the bunch. I even see a broom and a golf club, and one of the Creeps grips an old leather boot in each hand.

"Let's not keep them waiting." I ignite my sword; the gold blade glows white-hot with rippling flames.

Loren cracks her whip on the pavement and lightning sizzles where it hits, leaving a faint blackened scorch mark.

The Creeps meet us halfway down the block.

Three run at me, and I stab the lead one through its nose hole. Its skull catches fire, and the moment I draw my sword back, it turns and crashes into the others, spreading the flames to them. In seconds, half a dozen Creeps are reduced to ash. Those remaining are more cautious about approaching after that. So I take the fight to them, hacking and slashing with my sword, creating piles of singed, wriggling bones.

Six Creeps jump Loren. But they regret that decision when she makes quick work of them, spilling bones and red-hot cinders in the street. She kicks, punches, and roundhouses like a

Muay Thai master, between cracking her golden whip to fling some of the Creeps into the others and electrocuting them until they explode into a scattering of bones.

There are only about a dozen left now.

Desperate, a Creep snatches Loren's ponytail, and she stumbles backward onto her bottom. Cheap move. I set another Creep ablaze, then slice through the arms of the Creep who's dragging Loren by her hair. I swing my sword, quartering the Creep, then smash its skull with my sneaker.

Loren pulls the severed arm bones still clinging to her hair free and launches them over my shoulder at a Creep running up behind me. The bones thwack it in the face, one after another, slowing it down.

"Duck!" she shouts, and I drop to the ground next to her.

She swings her whip, coils the end around the Creep's neck, and pulls its head off. The remaining Creeps surround us, closing in.

Loren spins around, the skull still attached to the end of her whip, and clobbers the Creeps with it. After a few revolutions, we're encircled by a bed of squirming bones.

She helps me up, her chest heaving.

"We did it," I say, breathless as well.

A slow clap echoes in the empty street somewhere behind us, nearly startling me out of my skin.

I turn to find War standing at the bottom of the hill, his vicious red eyes homed in on me. He looks like a James Bond villain, dressed in black and red with red sneakers. Holstered to his back are twin short swords whose hilts—one black and the other red—stick up on either side of his shoulders.

Liam's on his knees beside War, sporting a busted lip and a fresh purpling bruise under one eye. Pieces of familiar golden rope bind his mouth, hands, and ankles.

"Thanks for this." War gestures to the ropes restraining Liam. "It's quite useful. We made some slight improvements, though."

I halve the distance between us, brandishing my sword the entire way. Loren readies her whip and remains at my side. Liam's wet eyes glisten in the sunlight when they meet mine. I'm still very, *very* mad at him, but friends shouldn't abandon each other. No matter what.

I point my sword at War, who doesn't flinch. "Let my friend go. *Now.*"

"No," War says coldly.

He shoves Liam's head hard with two fingers, toppling him over onto the pavement like a bowling pin. Liam hits the ground with a grunt and stares lasers at War (not actual lasers—that would be really cool, though).

War yanks his black-bladed swords from their sheaths and charges. I meet him.

Our blades crash together and cut through the air with whooshing roars, barely missing their targets. Loren, a few paces away, cracks her whip over and over, growing more frustrated with each blow that War effortlessly bats away with his swords.

He moves like a brutal ballerina, leaping aside on one foot and spinning around to avoid my sword or to knock Loren's whip away. Hopping over the whip when she tries again, this time for his ankles, then doing a backbend to avoid an elbow to the throat—or what I thought was a backbend. Didn't realize it was a back*flip* until his red sneaker kicked me in the chin. I stumble backward a few feet to regroup.

His red eyes follow me, and he licks his lips with an intensity that would make my heart flutter if, you know, he wasn't trying to murder me.

I move to one side, War following me, until Loren and Liam are both out of his line of sight. I find Loren's eyes and glance quickly at Liam, then back to her.

She dashes over to Liam. He shakes his head and flips onto his stomach, trying to wriggle away from her like a human-sized worm. She grabs the rope tied around his ankles—and a spark of bright red light erupts at her touch. She cries out and slumps over Liam, the magic booby trap knocking them both out.

"You couldn't seriously have thought it would be that easy," War taunts, smirking at me.

His translucent figure shimmers in the sunlight as he ducks out of sight. He's invisible before I can even take a breath to respond. I squint and glance around, trying to find the faint outline of him or pick out the spot in the air around me where the light seems to waver ever so slight—

Alex.

War's gossamer voice invades my mind. I squeeze my eyes shut.

Ho, ho, Alex Wise. There's so much delectable rage inside you.

I take a slow, deep breath in, then breathe out.

We could use that, you know. We could use you. Isn't that what you want? To be truly wanted?

I keep breathing. In. And out. I relax my eyes and unclench my jaw. As I focus on the gentle rise and fall of my chest, the steady rhythm of my heartbeat, and the heat of the sun pressing warmth into my skin, War's voice fades until I can't hear him at all.

I did it! I've locked War out of my mind.

Maybe I *am* a superhero after all.

Something cracks me hard in the back of the head, and I fall forward. My sword clatters to the ground, and I scrape my palms against the rough pavement. I leap to my feet, rubbing my throbbing head.

War blips into view standing over Liam and Loren, who are still out. He lifts them both by their shirt collars, one in each hand, their heads lolling.

"Death has a proposition for you," War says. "She's waiting for you at our tower on the hill. If you don't show, you'll never see your friends or family again."

"My family?" I ask, anxiety ratcheting my voice up an octave. "What have y'all done?"

War smiles and sinks into his shadow, dragging Loren and Liam with him.

I pick up a stray femur bone from one of the vanquished Creeps and hurl it hard as I can. It clacks against the empty street where War stood a moment ago.

Jerk. He could've at least given me a ride.

I return my sword to bracelet mode and jog back uphill to grab my bike.

It's gonna be a long, lonely ride to the Horsemen's tower.

37

AN OFFER
I CAN'T REFUSE

By the time I arrive at the packed-dirt path leading up the hill, the sun is dead center in the sky and I'm thoroughly marinated and baked in sweat.

I grab my water from the holder attached to the bike's frame, climb off, and let the bike fall to one side in the low grass. The last swallows of the water has warmed on the ride over, but that doesn't make it any less satisfying. I only wish I'd brought more.

The tower stands at the top of the hill, a giant obscurity in our world that does not belong here. I frown at it as I trek up this tiny mountain one final time to save my friends and family—and maybe the world.

No pressure.

Near the top, ten Creeps wait in the long shadow of the onyx obelisk, their ember eyes like angry fireflies. I approach cautiously, one hand on my bracelet. But they don't attack.

The one I assume to be their captain or whatever, because it stands at the front and wears a fitted cap turned backward on its bare skull, clicks its teeth at me and points at the hill's crest, a few feet away, then leads the way. I follow its rickety gait, and the others flank me.

At the hilltop, Death stands off to one side, her back to me, staring at the Hollywood skyline. She seems to have already recovered from this morning's scuffle. She's dressed the same, and her long jet-black hair sways with the gentle wind.

Against the back of the "H" in the Hollywood sign is a giant glass tank that reminds me of one of those dunking booths at the fair, except much larger and filled to the brim with Green Dream instead of water. Arranged on a platform above the pit of neon green gas are eight little wooden stools. Seated on those stools are my friends and family, everyone bound and gagged.

Loren. Liam. Mom. Dad. Angela. Nick. She even kidnapped Loren's mom and dad. They notice me at once and shout against their gags and try to squirm out of their restraints. Everyone but Mom. She stares at me with bloodshot eyes. Both her cheeks are sodden, and the sight of me walking up the path with a troop of Creeps at my back starts up a fresh stream of tears. I look away to keep from losing what little nerve I have left.

"Are you alone?" I shout at Death's back.

She turns and approaches casually. "Yep."

The head Creep bows to Death, then stands behind me and pushes my shoulders with its bony fingers, but I stiffen my legs. The Creep kicks the back of my left leg, attempting to force me to kneel. My knee dips, but I catch my balance and turn fast, uppercutting the Creep. Its skull pops off its spine and flies in one direction, its fitted cap in the other. Its body runs back and forth, arms flailing, unsure which to retrieve first.

The other Creeps lunge for me, but Death waves one hand and a hole opens in the ground with a soft rumble. The black expanse inside the rift sucks the Creeps under like a giant vacuum, then sews itself shut.

I turn to Death, confused. "Why'd you stop them?"

"I didn't ask you here to fight," she says.

It's quiet on the hill. Too quiet. I take a cursory look around, but it seems we are indeed alone up here—except for her hostages. "Where are Ezra and the other Horsemen?"

"Handling more-important business."

"And the Riders? Why haven't we seen them around lately?"

Death grins. "Miss them? Don't worry. They'll be back soon. I've sent most of them to the Nightmare Realm to train with War for the final phase of our plan. I was annoyed to have to pull him away to collect everyone"—she gestures to the deadly dunk tank—"but after this morning, I felt I needed to impress upon you the seriousness of what I've called you here to discuss."

"You've got my attention." I cross my arms. "But this is between us. Leave them out of it."

She ignores me. "You demonstrated earlier that you don't have what it takes to stop us. You are too gentle, and you lack confidence. You could never hope to stand against the full force of the Horsemen. I am a god with millennia-old magic at my fingertips and you are just a sad little boy who needs to stop wasting my time."

I snatch my bracelet off, and it transforms in my hand. Death glances at my sword and then focuses her scary dark eyes on mine. I feel a pang of cold from her stare, but I don't flinch.

"See, that's exactly what I'm trying to avoid." She clasps her hands in front of her. "I'm not heartless, Alex. I do understand how you feel. The apocalypse is understandably a lot to cope with. But your sister is gone, and you cannot help her. What you can do is save the remaining people you care about. And the way to do that is simple.

"Relinquish Orin's spirit, and I'll let you and the others go"—she points her thumb over her shoulder at everyone atop the glass tank—"or we fight, and when you inevitably lose, I'll dunk everyone you love in the tank. And after you watch them die, I'll use your own candle to yank Orin's treacherous spirit from your head and pinch them out of existence."

"What have you done with my candle?" I ask.

She points her thumb at the tower. "It's in a safe place. No more stalling. *Decide.*"

"Even if I wanted to take your terrible deal," I tell her, "I dunno how to *give* Orin's spirit to you."

"All I need is your consent," she says. "I'll do the rest."

"And then what? You going to kill me, too?"

Death laughs. "Of course not! I'll ensure you live every year of life left to you—so you can spend every single day alone, knowing that your failure cost you everyone you've ever cared about." She smiles. "Now, what will it be?"

I don't trust Death, but I can't deny it: the opportunity to cut my losses and save eight people *and* myself is tempting. However, to do that, I'd have to sacrifice Orin and Mags. That's not the way to end this. I'm going to save the world *my* way or die trying.

Still, I'm also deeply terrified. Nothing we've done up until now has been easy, but at least I was never alone. How am I supposed to do this all on my own?

Death huffs with impatience. "I have a full afternoon, so we're going to need to wrap this up. You have five seconds to make a decision. Five . . . four . . ."

I look at the faces watching from their perches atop the tank filled with Pestilence's gas. Their pleading stares amplify my anxiety.

". . . three . . ."

But then I remember the promise I made to Blu to bring his best friend home.

". . . two . . ."

Orin's voice whips across my mind like the wind rustling through the bushes surrounding us. *You are enough. You've always been enough. You've got this.*

I lift my sword, and white flames engulf the golden blade. "Zero," I say. "Let's do this."

38

HUG IT OUT

Death reaches behind her back with one hand and retrieves her scythe from a pocket of nowhere. The ebony blade exhales black smoke like a dragon with severe heartburn, and she glowers at me from behind it.

She touches the tip of the curved blade to a nearby bush, and the leaves turn brown and fall away, crumbling to dust before they can hit the ground. The thin, bare branches then wither and curl in on themselves before disintegrating too.

She cuts her eyes at me. "Careful, now."

Then she rushes me as if gliding on air.

Death swings her scythe, and I bring my sword up, barely blocking her from slicing me in two. Our blades clang together, and the smoke rumbling from the end of hers tries to smother my sword's fire. I plant my feet and grit my teeth, pushing myself and my sword's magical flame. Power surges from my gut to my chest, through my arms, and into my blade. The flames respond instantaneously, raging against the fog of Death.

She stomps on my foot and when I slack off to move away, she kicks me hard in the stomach, sending me reeling. I stumble over my own feet and fall onto my bottom. In a flash, I jump back up, hobbling away to put more space between us so I can regroup.

"Oh, nooo," Death sneers. "How are you going to stop me when you're too afraid to harm your little sister's body?"

She's right. I can't win this fight if I'm too afraid of hurting Mags. The sound of my little sister's cries from this morning echo in my head. *This isn't the way.* God or no, Death must have some weakness—and I need to figure out what it is before she turns me into jerky.

Death won't relent, twirling her scythe in swooping arcs that leave trails of faint black smoke in their wake. I keep on the defensive, blocking and parrying her vicious onslaught, looking for an opening where I can use the flat of my blade or the hilt of my sword to knock her unconscious. But I'm getting tired.

Death grows annoyed with my constant evasion of her advances, which end in her scythe kicking up dust or insta-killing the surrounding foliage. She stops her assault to growl with exasperated rage.

I vanquish the fire on my blade and step away to catch my breath. My mind leaps back to the cave when Death first possessed Mags—right after Orin chose me as their vessel. I emitted a shock of golden light that seemed to weaken her. I wonder . . .

This time I make the first move. And it startles Death. Her eyes widen when I lunge, my blade aimed for her heart. She grimaces and dodges, bringing her scythe up to upper-cut me with it. But I spin around behind her and strike from above. Her black blade clashes against my gold one, and she huffs from the exertion.

No one ever expects me to fight back.

A feral creature awakens inside me. It roars, sending a surge of adrenaline through my limbs like an injection of raw power. I move so swiftly and with such deft precision that my mind seems to lag behind my body. Death struggles to keep pace. She ducks and sidesteps, but in addition to blocking and evading, she's searching my eyes. I hope what she finds in them terrifies her.

I bat the blade of Death's scythe aside and light up my sword. She looks genuinely thrown off, and in that brief moment of panic, I slam the flat of my flaming blade onto her wrist. The shriek that rips from inside her conjures a tsunami of chills within me.

I'm so sorry, Mags. I hope you understand that I had to.

She drops her scythe and stares at her wrist in horror. The skin smolders like red-orange embers puffing curls of white smoke into the air. This is my chance.

I toss my sword aside and grab Death in a bear hug. She squirms and screams, but I shut my eyes and hold her as tight as I can. She feels so cold. Our skin touches, but I feel no emotion. Only darkness. It's so cold that it burns. Like hugging a bonfire. But I can't let go.

See, Mags. I'm doing this for you. I'm going to save you. I promise.

Death writhes and howls until my ears ring. I don't care if my eardrums burst, I'm not letting go.

Growing more desperate, she thrashes, knocking me off

balance. We slam into the dirt, kicking up a cloud of dust that expands the more her feet stir up the ground. I cough and sneeze, and the dust burns my eyes, but I hold on to Death. I don't know if this is going to work. I just hope it doesn't kill me.

The coldness builds until my limbs numb and my teeth chatter. Better that my arms freeze in place, clinging to Death like this. So even if I chicken out at the last minute, I won't be able to let go. In case I'm not as brave or smart as I think I am.

Death and I explode in a brilliant wave of golden energy that swallows us both.

Consciousness leaves me, and my world goes dark.

39

ORIN

I sit up with a start in a candlelit room.

I'm lying on a couch so soft that I have to swivel and plant both my feet firmly on the floor or else I'm in danger of napping for the rest of eternity.

"You can relax, Alex." The familiar voice calms my pounding heart.

Orin sits in an armchair across the room. They were so still after I woke that I didn't notice them. Freckles stand out on the sun-kissed-wheat skin of their bald head and gentle, round face like stars in the bold candlelight. They smile at me with full lips framed by the most magnificent beard I've ever seen. They run the bulky fingers of one freckled hand through the silken auburn lengths and return them to where they were resting on their round belly.

They're wearing a pair of satin shorts and a matching shirt embroidered with ethereal patterns in a thread that looks as if it's made from spun fairy dust. Comfortable, fashionable, *and* godly. I'm liking them more and more. If a warm hug was a person—that person would be Orin.

"Where are we?" I ask. "And where's Death?"

Orin leans forward. "We're in a sector of your mind. I drew you here via our empathic link when you fell unconscious just now. Time in the outside world has stopped while you're here. Breathe easy, my friend. You're safe here for as long as you need."

I fall back into the comfy couch and rub my hand hard across my face. It feels good to just stop and breathe for a second. And it's even better that Orin is so patient, quietly letting me take the time I need.

The entire wall behind Orin's armchair is one gigantic bookshelf, every slot filled with books of all sizes, shapes, colors, and types.

"If this is *my* mind, how are there so many books?" I ask.

They peer over one shoulder at the expansive collection. "Most of these are mine. I've read thousands. These shelves represent only a small subset. The selections change often, but I never fail to find an interesting read to revisit. Everything you've read is here too. I've been enjoying those."

"I don't have near as many as you, though."

Orin's laugh is warm and hearty. "No worries, my boy. I've got quite a few millennia on you."

I glance around the room, taking it all in. It's strange that this place exists inside my mind, because it feels both brand-new and familiar at the same time. Tasseled throws hang across every well-worn chair, comfort never more than an arm's reach away. The couch is an ugly cerulean plaid. One armchair is velvet and the color of dark cherries. The other is also velvet, but navy blue, like the sky right before nightfall.

Houseplants of all types grow in a number of vessels, from pots to vases to a soil-packed old rain boot, home to a sprouting kangaroo fern. Nothing in this place matches, yet it all seems to fit together well. Except the windows.

Behind the couch is a wide bay window, its seat lined with cushions of myriad colors and designs. A pair of thin floral curtains has been drawn, and the window lies open—in front of a solid brick wall. A golden airy light shines through a hole in the wall about the size of a golf ball.

"What's that?" I ask Orin, pointing at the light.

They stand and wander over, then beckon for me to come too. I sit on one side of the window seat and Orin takes the other, the light beaming between us.

"This cottage exists in the sincerest part of your mind, Alex," they tell me. "The part where you are your true, authentic self."

I glance at the rough brick facade on the other side of the window. "What's with the wall? Are all your windows like this?"

Orin nods. "And I think you already know why."

Shame warms my cheeks, and I cast my eyes down to my knee, resting atop an orange cotton pillow. That wall is the block that Pestilence mentioned and Navia confirmed. Her words replay over the loudspeaker in my mind: *You can never hope to understand the feelings of others until you understand your own.*

"By rejecting your true self, you've shut me and my abilities away here."

"I'm sorry," I say meekly.

Orin chuckles, which lifts my spirits from the mud. "You have nothing to apologize for."

For the first time since I met them, Orin's kindness annoys me. No one is genuinely this nice—not to someone who trapped them in a crappy cottagecore prison.

"Ezra tricked you," I say. "He knew you'd choose me as your vessel over Liam because I'm a messed-up closet case."

"I respectfully disagree." There's an edge to Orin's voice that cuts into my earlier skepticism of their kindness. "I chose you because of your incredible potential, Alex Wise. You are most certainly not a mess. Quite the opposite, actually."

I shake my head. "You've only known me for a couple weeks. But I've been me my whole life. You can't know everything."

Orin lifts their hands. "I'm in your head. I know all there is to know about you. You were a hero long before I chose you as my vessel."

"I really appreciate what you're trying to—"

"When Mags was struggling with learning to read and your parents were too busy arguing, who patiently spent night after night reading with her until she was comfortable enough to do it on her own?" asks Orin.

I shake my head. "Well, that was just—"

"And after your parents' divorce, when your mother was so depressed that she couldn't bring herself to clean the house, who taught himself to do laundry from YouTube videos to make sure everyone had clean clothes? And who tidied the house every day after school, along with doing their homework and helping Mags with hers, so their mom wouldn't have to worry about it after her long shifts at work and school?"

"Me," I say, "but what else was I supposed to do?"

"You had a plethora of choices," Orin says. "The reason it sometimes seems as if you don't is because your heart pushes you to act from a place of compassion for others. Magic never made you a superhero. It only enhanced who you already were. I chose you because you are the platinum standard, Alex."

I release a guilty sigh. I want to believe Orin, I *really* do, but the thorn that's been stuck in my mind ever since Dad deserted us won't let me have this.

"If I'm so great, why'd Dad leave us and replace me with Nick? Why'd he say I was an embarrassment?"

"I don't know your dad's motivations," Orin says, "but abandoning you was wrong, as was calling you an embarrassment—which you are most certainly *not*." The auburn whiskers above their lip twitch angrily.

"He left because I'm gay. He knew it before I did. If I'm the platinum standard, people would want me around, wouldn't they?" I admit my painful truth, ripping the thorn from my mind and exposing my deep mental wound, and brace for Orin to poke me in it like everyone else does when I'm vulnerable.

Orin sighs and focuses their soft brown eyes on the brick wall. "The feelings you've been having are part of you, Alex. You can hide them, but that won't change who you are. Being queer doesn't make you less valuable. I'm ace and nonbinary myself. And look at me." They spread their arms wide. "I'm a god!"

It's my turn to laugh, and, sheesh, it feels so good. Orin joins me, throwing their head back and emitting great guffaws.

I feel like I'm hanging out with a close cousin. I wish I could stay here forever.

"Queerness isn't a label we can put on and take off," Orin tells me.

Hearing them say "we" feels nice. It reminds me of the solidarity I felt back when I thought I could confide in Sky because we were the same.

"And that might make some people uncomfortable, even those we love," they continue, "but ultimately, that's their issue, not yours. It's okay to be gay. It's okay to be *you*."

I nod. They're right, though I don't know if I have the courage to stand up to people like Dad and Larry Adams. Although Orin makes me feel like I can—like I *should*.

"And when it comes to heroic feats," Orin says, "I think you've got your dad beat. How many cruise ships has he leapt from to save someone? And how many Kraken has he slain?"

"Heh, I guess you're right," I say. "I never thought about that stuff. I kinda just did it."

"And it's not simply heroic acts that make you a hero, Alex; it's your huge heart and the empathy and compassion that drive you to always put the people you love first. *That* is what makes you special, my boy." They smile and pat my knee, but no emotion flares from their touch, only the warmth of their fingers against my skin. "An embarrassment! Ha!" They tut under their breath. "You're the most impressive young person I've ever met." Then they lean forward conspiratorially and whisper, "Don't tell Liam I said that."

I smile and nod, staring at the strange golden light pouring through the hole in the wall. I try to peer out, but the rays are too bright to see what lies beyond. For the first time, I notice an ice pick that's been lying camouflaged in the mess of pillows on the window seat. The sharp steel end is covered in mortar dust.

"I called out to you through that hole," Orin tells me, "offering encouragement when I could. In your moments of self-doubt, the hole would patch itself, and I'd have to dig it back open. The air flowing in is sunny and warm now, but in your darkest times, it turns into a dark, blistering cold. Nearly lost my lips a couple times." They rub a freckled finger across their mouth as if checking to make sure their lips are still there.

I'm floored that Orin would go to such lengths to help me. Not many people in my life have before. But maybe Orin's right—how other people have treated me isn't my fault.

Nothing's wrong with me.

Orin stands, beaming down at me, their freckled cheeks rosy in the candlelight. They walk over to the green front door and pull it open, revealing more brick wall.

They turn and clasp their hands reverently in front of them. "Are you prepared for the final confrontation, Alex? It's okay to say no. You have all the time in the world."

I want to scream *heck no!* and stay here with Orin and trade stories and drink Capri Sun and read books forever. It's so tempting. But like they said, my heart won't let me be at peace here as long as people on the outside need me.

Superheroes don't hide. They fight.

"Yes," I say, and they step aside.

I place my right hand on the wall. The moment my palm contacts the abrasive, red-tinged surface, the maze of mortar between the bricks burns a molten gold and melts like wax. The bricks clink as they fall, then turn to ash and blow away.

Blinding light beams in through the front door and every window of the cottage. I turn, in search of Orin. They're right behind me, silhouetted against the bright white glow of the room that consumes everything but them.

They cup my cheeks in their hands and smile down at me. "I think you're ready. I am so very proud of you, Alex Wise."

"Thank you . . . for everything."

They nod. "You'll never be alone again—unless you want to. I won't be as intrusive as before, only here when you call."

"Okay," I say. "Once this is all done, are you going to exorcise yourself?"

Orin bites their lips, thinking. "My best friend, Navia, is gone now, and I've found your mind to be quite hospitable. I think I'll hang out—if that's okay with you."

I never thought I'd invite an ancient god to take up semi-permanent residence in my head, but I've grown fond of Orin. We've been through kind of a lot together.

"Stay as long as you like," I say.

"Remain steadfast." Orin nods and steps back, disappearing into the light.

I take a deep breath, shield my eyes against the brightness, and walk through the door.

After a few paces, my sneakers shuffle against something loose, like dirt. I uncover my eyes.

I'm standing in a desert wasteland that sets my heart racing at first, because I have zero idea where I am. Is this still inside my head?

The wasted mesa stretches on forever, Orin's cottage nowhere in sight. Brown cacti and withered bushes litter the landscape. A tumbleweed even trundles by.

The air is dry and blazing hot. Swirls of pearlescent clouds fan up around the sun, which lingers close to the horizon, stretching the shadows of tall pillars of earth jutting from the ground like desert skyscrapers. Between two pillars rests the humongous bleached skeleton of a whale—only this one's about a hundred times the size of the biggest whale on Earth.

I only know so much because Mags was obsessed with whales when she learned about them in third grade and made me watch every nature special about them in existence. That was a time almost as dark as the apocalypse.

I shield my eyes and squint once more at the horizon. More than monster whale remains wait up ahead. Someone's there, a single silhouette on the horizon.

I guess that's where I'm going.

40

HALL OF HORRORS

A strong gust of wind picks up, coating my sneakers and ankles in a healthy layer of orange dust. On the heels of the breeze is a soft voice that whispers, *You're enough. Be brave. And go kick some evil god butt.*

Orin. I've finally bonded with them and removed my block so that maybe now I can tap into my true power, like Liam. Funny, though; I don't *feel* any different. As I walk toward the horizon, I examine my hands, which look normal.

Maybe I should've stayed a little longer and gotten a tutorial on how all this magic stuff is supposed to work. Now that I'm unconstipated.

A man waits for me, standing patiently in front of the giant whale remains. He turns as I approach and glowers, his brow dipping sharply. His skin is pale as an eggshell, and his face is lean and haggard, his head crowned with silver and black hair. He's dressed in a long black robe and sandals. One hand rests on the hilt of the black-bladed longsword sticking into the ground beside him.

Mags sits on the ground against one of the bones, bound,

gagged, and unconscious. She's wearing the same outfit she had on the last day I saw her. That Hello Kitty T-shirt has seen some things.

"It's not too late to end this," Moritz says in a deep rumble. "This fight is hopeless for you. However, you've impressed me—so I'll make you one final offer. I am not too proud to admit I chose the wrong vessel. It's clear you care deeply for your sister, so I will give you what it is you want most: I'll free her—in exchange for *you*."

I wrinkle my nose at him. "You really suck at deal-making. I'd rather kick your butt."

Moritz hefts his heavy sword onto his shoulder with a grunt. "If you die here, your mind will be destroyed, and I will have you anyway. And then I am going to drown your family and friends in Pestilence's gas, including your sister."

I remove my bracelet and flip it into my sword. It ignites at once. "Then I guess I better not die, huh?"

We both attack at the same time. And I'm high-key grateful again for Navia's skill bump. Otherwise, Moritz would've skewered me right out the gate.

Our blades clash as Moritz and I trade attacks and blocks relentlessly. He's so vicious that I have to hold my sword with both hands to keep up. My smaller size doesn't even give me a speed advantage, because Moritz moves as agilely as War did.

I lose my grip when Moritz lights up his own sword with black Shadow Fire. The blade hisses like a snake as it carves toward me time and time again with renewed ferocity. For a second, I regret talking so much junk.

Moritz lifts his sword, and I thrust mine at his exposed torso. I don't notice him reach for my sword hand, because I'm too busy keeping an eye on that shadowy fire and trying not to let that stuff touch me.

I spin out of his grip, but not quickly enough to avoid his blade, which slices across my cheek. The dark fire burns like ice. I feel the wound open, then freeze, sending pain pulsing through the side of my face.

I stumble backward, feeling the open, raised skin, which is icy to the touch. No blood runs down my cheek; instead, it breaks off in tiny frozen crystals on my fingertips.

Remain steadfast, intones Orin in my head.

I shake off my nerves and lift my sword again. This time I'm the first to swing. I fire off attack after attack, which Moritz blocks, though not without effort, flaring the nostrils of his thin nose until it burns bright red.

I strike high, and my blade meets his, but I lose track of his other hand again—until it connects with my already injured cheek.

The force of the smack whirls me around. I don't have time to dive aside before Moritz's blade rips through the skin of my back in a diagonal cut from my shoulder to my hip.

I drop my sword and fall forward into the sand. My back feels like it's on fire, an ice-cold raging inferno that's spreading through my chest. My lungs tighten, and I fight to suck in as many shallow breaths as I can, though each one feels harder than the last.

Moritz kicks me onto my back. The frost and frozen blood

press into my wound, reigniting the pain all over again, and I let out a high-pitched howl. If this is in my head, how does it hurt so freaking much?

He bends down, grabs a fistful of my T-shirt collar, and lifts me into the air so our eyes are level. I'm in too much pain to fight back. Instead, I let my arms fall to my side.

"Do you know why everyone abandons you, boy?" he says in a low voice. "It's because you're *worthless*. Nick is a thousand times better than you at everything. He'd even be a better brother to Mags. *He* would've been able to save her."

"You're a liar," I wheeze. "J-just like your raggedy son."

Moritz glowers, deepening the lines in his forehead. At the same time, something magical stirs inside me. It starts with a rush of euphoria that unfurls in my stomach and then swells to fill my chest. It reminds me of the sparkler feeling, except bigger and more powerful. I feel like I could hold the sun in my hands if I wanted to.

I grin, which earns me a bewildered look from Moritz. I stare into the cool blackness of his dead eyes and tell him, "You can't have me."

I clap my hands onto his temples and press as hard as I can. His body stiffens, and his mouth falls agape. His eyes roll to the back of his head, and I immediately feel his magic pushing back against mine.

But I grit my teeth and focus harder. I can feel the magic flowing through my hands and into him, like letting go of a long, throaty scream that's been building up inside me for years.

And that's what I do. I scream in his face. I release every

ounce of my frustration and all of my anger for what he's done to me and my sister and the whole world. The magic valve somewhere inside me opens, and magic pours out until I emit a golden glow.

Moritz can't fight it anymore.

His eyes slide back down to meet mine again. Their darkness expands until it swallows me whole.

✗ ✗

The world around me is pitch-black. And quiet.

I step gingerly through darkness until I come upon a long hallway set back amid the nothingness. The walls and ceiling are black, and the floors are dark marble, almost purple in the grisly lighting provided by glowing orbs floating in the air near the ceiling. The hall is lined on both sides with solid red doors that seem to go on forever in one direction.

None of the doors have handles. No markings, either. And they're all identical. Strange.

I press my ear to one and hear weeping coming from the other side. I jump back, my heart pumping overtime. I listen at the door directly across from the first. Inside, a low voice wails in despair. The disturbing sound sends an avalanche of chills down my back.

I check another nearby door but don't hear anything. Yet somehow, I can feel a presence in there. Waiting. Seething. Goose bumps prickle my arms.

I search the frame for a hidden latch or something to open the door, but there's nothing. I kick it, but it doesn't even shift in place.

"Open, says me," I command jokingly.

The door dissolves into nothing. I stagger backward, surprised that my command actually worked. I wonder if I can open all these doors.

Keeping my distance, I peer through the doorway. There's only darkness beyond.

I hug myself, and my body shivers. The temperature has dropped significantly in the corridor. My breath hangs in front of me in white puffs. The coldness grips me like a set of desperate hands, urging me forward. Trembling, I stand on the threshold and peer into the dark.

"He murdered me," wails a woman.

She sounds as if she's standing right in front of me, but I don't see her—nor can I see her breath when she speaks.

"Who are you?" I whisper.

"I am Lilith." My stomach turns over when I recall why the ghost woman's name is familiar. "I once loved Moritz—until he killed me. I discovered his plan to betray Navia and intended to warn my friend, but he killed me before I could utter a word to her or Orin. And Ezra, our thirteen-year-old son, saw the whole thing and kept his father's twisted secret."

I gasp, recalling my conversation with Ezra—Dexter, at that time—on the cruise ship. He'd said he lost his mother chasing his father's approval. That was a bit of an understatement.

"Moritz is evil incarnate," hisses Lilith. "And he must face the repercussions for all he's done."

I step back until my heel finds the opposite wall. I stare down the seemingly infinite hallway and wonder how many tormented memories Moritz has locked away in this mental dungeon.

"He must pay," Lilith snarls from the shadows.

And then I get a bold idea.

I stand at the end of the cursed hallway and imagine every door wide open.

And they all dissolve at once.

Ghosts wander from their prisons, residual memories of all the people Moritz hurt over the many millennia of his wretched existence. After only a few moments, the space is teeming with nameless spirits and their vengeful cries.

I lift my fist above my head and shout as loud as I can to be heard over the din: "CLAIM YOUR JUSTICE! TO FREE-DOM!!"

The ghosts roar past in a tsunami of coldness that sweeps me from my feet and into the darkness. They fill every crevice of Moritz's mind with shrieking echoes of his evil deeds.

My butt hits the ground—in the desert again. The impact disorients me for a second. I cough and roll over onto my hands and knees. Moritz's frantic murmuring behind me draws me back onto my feet.

His sword lies extinguished on the ground beside him. He claps his hands to his head, his eyes darting back and forth in a frenzy. "Gods, no! What have you done, you little brat?!"

I pluck my sword from the ground and brandish it in front of me.

Moritz screams and falls to his knees, still holding his head as if he has the worst migraine known to any creature with a brain. Good for him.

His eyes are bloodshot, and drool oozes over his thin lips and into the net of his beard.

"You'll never be able to stop the end of the world," he mutters, spittle flying. "This is only the beginning."

"Maybe so." I shrug. "But it's most definitely *your* end."

I impale Moritz through the heart with my sword. His entire body goes rigid, frozen mid-scream. My sword ignites, and the god also bursts into white flames.

I withdraw my sword, and Moritz burns to ashes, which collect in a sad pile on the desert floor. A strong breeze carries him off to be strewn across the landscape, a sendoff far better than someone like him deserves.

I return my sword to bracelet mode and hobble over to my sister, my back and cheek still throbbing, though not as bad as before.

I undo the knots of the ropes binding her hands, feet, and mouth and cradle her in my arms. The moment feels surreal. I never thought I'd be able to hug my little sister again, but here she is. I did it.

But before her eyes open, the sun sinks below the horizon in the distance, and once again, the darkness takes me.

41

US VS. THE END
OF THE WORLD

I part my eyelids in the shade of someone hovering close to me. Everything's blurry, and a dense haze floats through my mind.

I blink the world into focus and meet my little sister's big brown eyes, sparkling with tears. She sniffs and wipes them away with her hand. It's actually her.

The flat, dusty earth presses into me. Dull pain pulses beneath the skin of my left cheek and across my back. Thank goodness it doesn't feel as bad as it did when Moritz's blade almost quartered me like a chicken.

Mags places a hand on my chest. "You okay?"

I feel the pressure of her touch, the warmth of her body. I feel her breaths slip across my face. She's really here. And we're back on the Hollywood hill.

I did it. This is real. I defeated Death and saved Mags.

I'm beaming inside, as if my heart suddenly exploded into a million rays of bright sunshine. I kept my promise. No matter what, I'm never leaving my sister behind.

"Alex"—Mags shakes my chest gingerly—"are you okay?"

I scream (a happy one, don't worry) and spring up, startling my sister onto her bottom. I throw myself into her, and we clutch each other in a bear hug.

Strange. I don't feel an onslaught of her emotion when the skin of our cheeks touches. But I have enough for the both of us, joy already bubbling over inside me. I wonder how she's feeling, when immediately, I feel a rush of the same happiness I'm already overflowing with, though there's something extra. A core of sadness buried deep within the joy. I take a deep breath, inhaling the scent of my sweat and the earth clinging to my sister, and exhale, focusing inward—like Orin taught me. The influx of Mags's emotions dries up, as I suspected it would. Finally, it seems I have control of my Sense, now that I've properly connected with Orin.

"You're a mess," Mags says.

I grin. "You're one to talk."

We're both covered in dust from head to toe, like two human powdered donuts. Mags doesn't appear to have any wounds or injuries—externally. Her long, tight curls have turned stark white—as have her eyebrows and lashes. Worry settles into the pit of my stomach like a mound of sulfur as I wonder in what other ways my little sister has changed.

My eyes find the bit of raised, discolored skin on her wrist, already looking like an aged scar. I take her hand in mine. Tears well in my eyes, distorting my vision. "I'm so sorry. I never wanted to hurt you."

Gently, she pulls her hand back and bites her lip. "It's okay,

Alex." She massages her scar in her lap. "You did what you had to do. I'm not mad."

Even though she says it's okay, it doesn't feel okay. But we've all been through a lot.

After a short, quiet moment, she catches me staring at her hair and pulls a strand in front of her face. She gasps, frantically examining more by the handful. "My hair," she whimpers. "I look like a ten-year-old granny."

I chuckle. "Nah. This new do is totally giving me strong Storm vibes."

Her face brightens. "I could do that." She frowns at the cut on my cheek, which I'm afraid to see. (Thank goodness there are no mirrors on this hill.) "It's not bad. I think it gives you an air of mystery." I raise an eyebrow at her, and she adds, "You remind me of Cable now."

My back stiffens. "Now, wait one minute. You get *the* Ororo Munroe herself and give me *Cable?*" I shake my head. "I'm good being Alex Wise, thank you very much."

She pinches my forearm, and I yelp.

Rubbing my arm, I look into her eyes and ask the question I've been dreading since I woke up. "How . . . are you? How bad was it?"

Mags withers, pulling her knees to her chest and holding them there, as if hiding in a dark cupboard. She sits like that for a while, not speaking, and I let her.

"Moritz locked me away in a memory," she says finally. "I lived the same couple hours over and over."

"What memory was it?"

"The day Dad moved out." Her brows pinch. "I don't want to talk about it. Not yet."

I remember that day vividly. After Dad said his raggedy goodbye and I managed to peel myself out of bed, I went to the living room and found Mags sitting on the couch, staring blankly at the television. Saturday-morning cartoons had ended several hours earlier, and she was mesmerized by an infomercial with a creepy jingle for some kind of lotion-roller contraption for your back. I didn't know how long she'd been sitting there, but I had to snap my fingers in front of her face to break her out of her trance. She laughed it off, and I got annoyed, thinking she was pranking me, and I wasn't in the mood.

But I've never stopped to consider that day from her perspective, to understand how it affected her. And Moritz forced her to relive that moment on an endless loop for days.

"When you *are* ready," I tell her, "I'll be here."

She nods and offers a pained smile that simultaneously comforts me and breaks my heart. I wish I could do more. I wish I could take the pain away. All of it. Mine, too.

Mags glances at the giant tank in the shade of the Hollywood sign and gasps. "Oh! We forgot about the others!"

My eyes widen. "Oh, crap!"

It doesn't take long to get everyone untied and a safe distance from the gas tank.

Loren's mom sweeps her aside to fuss over her at once, much to Loren's dismay. Her dad nods and thanks me for saving them, then goes to pry Loren's mom off her.

Mom locks her arms around my and Mags's heads, pressing

our faces into her bosom and sobbing openly. We don't complain. My sister and I share a look, both of us in Mom's soggy embrace, and giggle.

Mom stands back with a sniff. "What's so funny?"

I rub my neck and wince. "You kinda had us in a headlock."

She cups Mags's face, then mine, apologizing, until I say, "It's okay. We're happy to see you, too."

Mom kneels in front of me and stares into my eyes. I hate when she looks at me like this, like she's accessing the contents of my soul. "I'm so very proud of you, Alex."

I was so angry at her when we left on the cruise with Dad. Because being sent away made me feel like I'd disappointed her one time too many. And those feelings strayed a bit too close to my memory of Dad calling me an embarrassment in front of my Little League coach. But somehow, the compliment I've wanted for a long time feels—*meh*.

"You're proud of me *now*?" I ask. I don't have the nerve to follow up with *Why did it have to take me saving the world?*

She looks confused for a moment; then her expression softens. "I've always been proud of you."

Dad calls Mags over, and she goes to endure the hug-rush from him, Angela, and Nick—leaving me and Mom alone.

I frown. "Then why'd you send us away after I told you I was sorry and it wouldn't happen again?"

"I'm sorry, Alex. What I did was selfish. I was stressed from work and school and frustrated with your dad for leaving me alone to juggle the pieces of the life we built together. I put my own feelings before yours and Mags's, and I never should've done that. You can forgive me in your own time, but please trust me when I tell you I've always been proud of you, baby.

"I should've told you more." She sighs. "You and your sister are both the best thing to ever happen to me, and I love you both exactly as you are—even when you hate my guts."

"I don't hate you, Mom," I say. "I'm sorry I was so mean."

She smiles. "It's okay, baby. Your heart was in the right place. It always is—even when you disobey me and run off to save the world!"

Mags wanders over with Dad, Angela, and Nick in tow, just in time for Mom to pull me and her into another hug.

Mom combs her fingers through Mags's new snow-white hair. "Okay, Storm," she mutters. "We need a good wash and deep condition, but I see you."

I nudge Mags and whisper, "Told you."

Dad clears his throat behind us, and we break apart.

Nick pushes around him and bumps fists with me. "I know it hasn't been official long, but it's kinda cool that I get to be your stepbrother."

We hug and pat each other hard on the back.

Angela, her braids frazzled and frayed, approaches with a warm smile and kisses me on the top of my dusty head. "You the real deal. Thank you for what you did."

I nod, and Dad's eyes snag me before I can say anything.

He steps up to hug me, but I recoil. "Alex . . . ?"

I shake my head at him. "Am I still an embarrassment?"

Dad pales. His brow knits as if he didn't hear me correctly.

"That's what you told Coach Daniels that day," I say.

"I don't know what you're talking about, Alex," he says. "Why are you bringing this up now?"

"Because it *matters!*" I shout, balling my fists.

Mom puts a hand on my shoulder, but I shrug her off. I'm so mad, I'm shaking.

"Okay," Dad says, gesturing for me to calm down, which only makes me angrier. "I honestly don't remember saying that. Why would I do that?"

Tears well in my eyes, but I blink them away. I will not give them to him. My mouth tastes dry and sour, like I could spit acid. I didn't imagine one of the worst days of my life.

"I heard you," I tell him. "I *saw* you."

Dad sighs and slaps his hands on his thighs. "I don't know where this is coming from, but it seems like I hurt your feelings a long time ago and you never got over it, so I'm sorry."

Mom grips my shoulder and steps up beside me. "That's *not* an apology, Malcolm."

"What are you— Whooaa! Ouch! Hey!"

Angela drags Dad off by his ear until we can't hear them. From the expression on her face and the way she's poking him in the chest, she's not pleased with him.

Nick wanders off, looking likewise offended but also conflicted. Mags goes after him.

I appreciate Mom and Angela both standing up for me, but it doesn't change anything.

Mom appears in front of me and leans down so we're on the same level. "Why didn't you tell me about that?" I look away, but she turns my face back. "I can understand why you wouldn't want to tell that to anyone. But what you overheard should've never happened. Trust and believe, I'll be dealing with him—"

"I don't care," I say. "What's the point? He doesn't want me. He never did."

"Listen to me, baby," she says. "Many people are going to come and go in your life, and frankly, a lot of them aren't going to love you how you deserve. We have to find a way to be okay with that. For now, Dad might be one of those people. Things may change in the future—or they may not. But his behavior is a reflection on him—not *you*."

She places her hand on my chest, over my heart. "I've always believed you and Mags would be better than us. And, baby, you proved that long before the end of the world."

I know she's right. I only wish her words made this hurt less.

She frowns at Dad and Angela and says, "Let me go make sure Angela don't kill your daddy after you just saved his life. I think she's gonna be good for him." Before she goes, she asks, "You good?"

I nod.

Loren's still with her parents. Mom and Angela are now *both* yelling at Dad, who's cowering behind a cactus. And Nick and Mags are chatting over near where the Horsemen's tower used to be. I'm missing someone.

Liam stands in front of the tank of Green Dream, examining it so intensely he doesn't notice me walk up behind him. He places both hands on the glass, and they glow with yellow light that seeps in and dissolves the gas into golden sparkles, which fade like fireworks.

"Hey," I say gently.

He turns with a start. "Oh, Alex." His eyes flit everywhere but to my face. One of his eyes has darkened, and a trail of dried blood leads from his busted and swollen lip down his chin. War really roughed him up.

We stand there several moments, neither of us speaking, I'm guessing because he, like me, doesn't know what to say—until eventually we both blurt out "I'm sorry!" at the same time.

We laugh together too. And it feels good. I've missed that.

And the sparklers reignite in my chest.

"You were right," Liam says. "I should've trusted you all along. It was wrong of me to try to sacrifice your sister to stop Moritz." He hugs himself and casts his gaze away. "I—I haven't had friends in a really long time, so I, um . . . I don't really know how to have them anymore." He pauses and takes a deep breath before adding, "If that makes sense."

"It does, actually," I say. "We can work on teaching you how to be a friend as long as you stop trying to murder my little sister." Liam's eyes glisten and he frowns until I spread my arms and grin. "It was a joke!"

He smirks and shakes his head.

"I shouldn't have said that stuff about your mom," I tell him. "I don't think she's selfish or greedy. I'm sorry."

He shrugs. "Maybe she was. I don't know. I was mad because you might be right. But I'd just lost her again, and I didn't want to hear it."

I hold out a hand. "Friends?"

He frowns and slaps it away. "Best friend or nothing."

I wince. "I kinda already have one of those."

"Who says you can't have two?"

I'm about to rebut his proposal but stop and think. "You're right."

He laughs, and we hug. He presses his cheek against mine and sighs as if he thought we'd never embrace again. I've missed *him*.

"You know, you don't ever have to be alone," I tell him. "After all this apocalypse stuff is done."

His eyes glisten in the sunlight and he beams at me. "I think I'd like that."

Mags wanders over—and thank goodness, because it gives me something to focus on besides the way Liam's gaze makes the fireworks in my chest burn brighter.

"Cool hair," he tells her.

"Yeah, I get that a lot." She stands in front of him and tilts her head from one side to the other, examining his injuries. She holds up her hands and says, "May I?"

He glances over at me, and I shrug.

Mags sucks her teeth. "Just trust me."

Liam nods.

She places her hands on his cheeks, and her palms glow with a brilliant cerulean light. She closes her eyes and hums a solemn melody that I've never heard before but that sounds vaguely familiar. In seconds, Liam's lips and eye heal, leaving him looking as good as usual.

When she's done, she opens her eyes and pulls her hands back. "There. I think we're even now, yeah?"

Liam raises his brows, touching his eye and lips in disbelief. "I guess we are."

"How'd you know you could heal him?" I ask her.

She shrugs. "I just did."

"Was that song you were humming magic?" asks Liam.

"No," she says. "It got stuck in my head when Moritz had me locked away."

The creepy infomercial jingle. *That's* where I remember that tune from. I can't find the appropriate words to say, but it's just as well, because Loren joins us, having escaped her parents, who've gone to save Dad from Mom and Angela.

I pull Liam, Loren, and Mags into a tight huddle.

"Serious question," I ask Mags. "Do you happen to remember where inside the tower Moritz hid the candle?"

She shakes her head. "Sorry. He kept that secret from me."

"Of course," I say. "Not like Moritz to make this easy for us."

"Hey, uh, Alex . . ." Nick hovers just outside our group, his hands stuffed in the pockets of his basketball shorts. "Can I talk to you for a sec?"

I nod and step aside, out of earshot of the others.

"I didn't know Pop—I mean, your dad—did that to you." He shakes his head. "It wasn't cool. I'm sorry. I understand now why you feel the way you do about him."

"Thanks, Nick. I appreciate that."

Dad's still a jerk, but as far as stepbrothers go, this might be the *one* thing he got right.

Nick nods. "There's, uh, something else. . . ." He shifts his weight from one foot to the other, as if struggling with what he wants to say, until I raise an eyebrow at him. "I, uh, don't mean to intrude, but I don't think it's exactly fair you all get to save the world and leave me at home by myself. Can I be on your team?"

I smile at him and turn back to the others. "Yo!" I shout, and Mags, Loren, and Liam all hurry over. "I wanted to introduce you to our newest teammate."

"Welcome," says Loren.

Liam and Mags both smile.

Nick pumps his fist, and we re-form our circle—our team.

"We're the only ones who can stop Ezra and the Horsemen," I tell everyone. "It's us versus the end of the world now."

Mags, Liam, Loren, and Nick all agree.

"Our top priority should be getting our candle back," I say to enthusiastic nods. "But first things first—we've gotta figure out how to ditch our parents."

Epilogue

WILLOW

Despite being born from malice, the willow misses the goddess.

As soon as it siphoned the last drop of her life force's sweet nectar, it felt a sharp pang of remorse, if for no other reason than it'd come to enjoy her company over the four years they shared on that bleak gray bank.

So imagine the willow's surprise when four beings arrive in its forgotten world and gather in the cool shade of its branches to conspire with one another.

Four strangers with four familiar souls.

Their leader, a young brown-skinned boy, tells the others—a slightly younger boy and girl and an old man—to wait for him. He won't be long.

They stand silent beneath the willow and watch him wade into the water, swim to the middle of the lake, and disappear into its depths.

For four hours, the three of them stand like statues—except the old man; he sits. The girl leans against the willow's trunk, and its branches groan, flexing toward her, pining for an embrace.

Then the lake boils, bubbling and burping steam into the atmosphere. And from the center rises an old man with healthy silver curls and a plaid newsboy cap. He floats above the water, hovering in the air, six long-feathered black wings attached to his back. Innumerable eyes blink open all over them, peeking out at this new world through shadowy plumage.

The water churns and recedes, lower and lower, until the black hole at the bottom swallows every drop.

Gaping wide now, the hole is still hungry.

The edges of the bank crumble and fall away into the mouth at the bottom of the lake. The ground quakes and splits, giant chunks tumbling into nothing. The willow's roots shake loose from where they bored deep into the earth years ago.

The winged god and his three disciples disappear through a portal to another realm.

Darkness devours what remains of Paradisum, including the willow.

ACKNOWLEDGMENTS

Alex Wise vs. the End of the World was a very tough story for me to tell, because to write it authentically, I had to reach deep into my trauma archives and relive some troubling experiences from my childhood, all while forging my own path as a new parent and trying to understand what that even means for me—and, by extension, my son. This story gave me an opportunity to explore a lot of the feelings I'd locked away for so long. Dredging up those emotions will have totally been worth it if this story touches even one kid who sees themself and their struggles reflected in these pages. To those kids, especially: I see you, and I love you, too. You deserve to be a superhero, just like Alex.

To my husband, Kevin: Thank you so much for your unwavering love and support and belief in me. It's been amazing to be able to go on this incredible journey with my bestest friend by my side.

To my son, Aiden: Thank you for giving me a reason to work so hard but simultaneously giving me a reason to take breaks often and enjoy life. This one's for you, Doodie. I hope I made you proud.

To my agent, the Olivia Pope of publishing, Patrice Caldwell: I can never thank you enough for your fearless guidance and dedication to me and my career. The small kid inside me, much like Alex, who never felt good enough for anyone, smiles constantly when I remember that you were the first person to give me a chance and then stood behind me with steadfast fierceness. I'm forever grateful to you.

To Trinica Sampson: Thank you so much for everything you do, especially all the laughs and kind words. I'm honored every day that I get the privilege of working with you.

Thank you to the entire team at New Leaf Literary for your support in bringing *Alex Wise* to the world and taking such great care of me.

To Liesa Abrams: It was already an honor to publish a book with you, but over the course of this first project, I learned that the real honor has been getting to know you not only as my editorial sensei but also as a friend. Your light shines so incredibly bright, and I will always and forever be grateful that you shared some of that with me and helped me (and the kids who read my stories) shine even brighter. Looks like we both got a nat 20!! 😃

To Emily Harburg: I genuinely had so much fun making magic with you. It meant the world to me that you wanted to join the editorial team for *Alex Wise*, and I'm extremely grateful to have had the opportunity to work with you on bringing this story, which is so special to me, to life. I'm very much looking forward to continuing this incredible journey. I mean, who else is gonna laugh at all Alex's (read as "my") corny jokes?

To the entire team at Labyrinth Road and Random House Children's: The work that you're doing for kids, especially those from marginalized backgrounds, is truly inspiring and remarkable; it's an honor for me to be part of the Labyrinth Road family and to help more kids navigate the confusing maze that is life. Thank you, not just for what you've done for me and Alex Wise but for *all* the work you do in children's publishing.

To Raymond Sebastien and Jen Valero: I couldn't have asked for a more perfect cover for *Alex Wise vs. the End of the World*. Thank you so much for bringing my characters to life better than even I imagined them.

To my wonderful mentor, Bree Barton: *Before & After* has come a looong way since Author Mentor Match, huh? Turns out you were right: this story actually *was* a better concept as a middle-grade book, ha ha. I love you past the farthest star in the farthest galaxy and back. Thank you for always being you.

To my mom, Shirley: Thank you for practicing baseball with me when I was nine and no one else would. And thank you for loving me when it seemed no one else did.

To Naseem Jamnia: I honestly don't know where I'd be without your endless well of love and support. Thank you for always pouring into me even when I didn't know that I needed nourishing. And thank you for continuing to inspire me every day. I love you.

To Adam Sass: Thank you so much for your grace and help as I went through the emotional storm of drafting this story. I'm honored to have a friend like you and grateful for the light you shine in my life every day.

To Domonique Bouldrick: You inspired Loren's character (and me). I hope you see yourself in her, and I also hope twelve-year-old girls who are just like you were at that age, who exist outside everyone's expectations and don't care what anyone thinks about it, see themselves in her, too—and understand that who they are is perfectly okay. Thank you for being the nerdy, weird you that you've been since the day we first met in the airport and I forced you to be my friend. 😃

To Maria Stout: I cannot thank you enough for your constant support and love over the years. I hope that this story is something that you'll not only be proud of but also be proud to share with your students. Thank you so much for everything you do, for me and for your kids.

To Marquis Dixon: Your friendship and your genuine love and support of me and my work means the world to me. Thank you for the beta reads—and the laughs.

To Jamar Perry: Cameron Battle is like Alex Wise's slightly older, more experienced best friend, so it was truly an honor for your blurb to be the first to come in for this story. I believe that Cameron and Alex would be besties in real life. Keep doing what you do and being authentically who you are; our kids need you.

Thank you, sincerely, to everyone who read early copies of *Alex Wise* and blurbed or left reviews.

To every bookseller, librarian, teacher, and BookTuber/BookToker/influencer who read, reviewed, shared, and put my stories into the hands of the people I wrote them for: This author cannot find the words to express how grateful I am to you and how much I appreciate you, but I hope this will do.

And to my readers: Thank you for sticking with me this long. I hope you continue to hang around. 😃